AUTUMN
AFTERMATH

Also by David Moody from Gollancz:

Hater
Dog Blood
Them or Us

Autumn
Autumn: The City
Autumn: Purification
Autumn: Disintegration
Autumn: Aftermath

AUTUMN
AFTERMATH

DAVID MOODY

The right of David Moody to be identified as the author
of this work has been asserted by him in accordance with
the Copyright, Designs and Patents Act 1988

First published in Great Britain in 2012 by
Gollancz
An imprint of the Orion Publishing Group
Orion House, 5 Upper St Martin's Lane, London WC2H 9EA
An Hachette UK Company

This edition published in Great Britain in 2013 by Gollancz

1 3 5 7 9 10 8 6 4 2

A CIP catalogue record for this book
is available from the British Library

ISBN 978 0 575 09148 1

Typeset at The Spartan Press Ltd, Lymington, Hants

Printed an bound by CPI Group (UK) Ltd,
Croydon CR0 4YY

The Orion Publishing Group's policy is to use papers
that are natural, renewable and recyclable products and
made from wood grown in sustainable forests. The logging
and manufacturing processes are expected to conform to
the environmental regulations of the country of origin.

www.davidmoody.net
www.orionbooks.co.uk
www.gollancz.co.uk

Dedicated to:
The Survivors

PART I

TWENTY-SIX DAYS
SINCE INFECTION

1

Jessica Lindt died three days short of her thirty-second birthday. That was almost a month ago. Since then she'd spent every second of every day wandering aimlessly, often drifting in herds with other corpses, occasionally gravitating towards the few remaining signs of life in this otherwise dead void of a world. Jessica had no idea who or what she was any longer: she simply existed. She responded to movement and noise around her, but didn't know why or how. And yet, somehow, she occasionally *remembered*. In her dull, decaying brain she sometimes saw things – just fleeting recollections, for the briefest of moments, and gone before she'd even realised they were there: split-second memories of who she used to be.

Her body, of course, had changed beyond all recognition, bulging in places where gravity had dragged her putrefying innards down, becoming brittle and dry elsewhere. Still dressed in what was left of the Lycra running gear she'd been wearing when she died, her feet were badly swollen and her lumpy, bruised ankles were now almost elephantine in appearance. Her gut was distended, inflated by the gases produced by decay and a substantial insect infestation. Her mottled skin had split several inches below her drooping right breast, leaking all manner of semi-coagulated yellow and brown gunk.

Jessica's unblinking eyes were dry and unfocused, but they saw enough, and the movement of the lone survivor standing in the house up ahead of her was sufficient to attract her limited attention. Suddenly moving with more speed, and something almost beginning to resemble a purpose, she lumbered towards the small terraced cottage, smacked into the window with force and collapsed backwards, ending up on her backside in the gutter. She'd been down only a second or two before others attacked her, attracted by the noise and wrongly assuming she was somehow different to them. They tore apart what remained of Jessica Lindt, and soon all that was left of her was a dirty imprint on the glass, a few lumps of greasy flesh and a puddle of gore, which the others clumsily staggered through.

The survivor stood on the other side of the window and waited for the brief burst of chaos outside to die down again. His name was Alan Jackson, and his faith in human nature was all but exhausted – not that there was much more than a handful of other humans left alive. He'd been standing in the shadow-filled living room of this otherwise empty house for what felt like hours, staring out at the sprawling crowd of several thousand corpses stretching out in front of him for ever, wondering how the hell he was going to get through them and out the other side. He could see his intended destination in the far distance, though his view of the ancient castle was distorted by the tens of thousands of swarming flies which buzzed through the air above the innumerable rotting heads like a heat-haze. He hoped to God – not that he'd believed in God for as long as he could remember, certainly not since the beginning of September – that this was going to be worth the risk.

In the three and a half weeks since the population of the country – most likely the entire planet – had been slashed to less than one per cent of its original level, Jackson had thought he'd seen it all. From the moment the rest of the world had simply dropped dead all around him to right now his life had been a ceaseless tumult of death and decay. The dead were everywhere, surrounding him constantly, whatever he did and whichever way he turned. Death was inescapable, and he was fucking sick of it.

Another of the bodies staggered past the window, a twitch-ing, dried-up stump where its right arm used to be. Christ, how he hated these damn things. He'd watched them change, virtually day by day, gradually regaining a degree of self-control and transforming from lethargic hulks of impossibly animated flesh and bone into the vicious creatures they were now. He didn't dare think about the future, because he knew that if the pattern continued – and he'd no reason to think it wouldn't – they'd be even more dangerous tomorrow. Instead he tried to remain focused on the fact that if they continued to deteriorate, in another few months they'd have probably rotted down to nothing. Jackson was no fool; he knew things would undoubtedly get much worse before they got any better.

Standing alone in this little house, a fragile oasis of normality buried deep in the midst of the madness, it occurred to Jackson that even though he'd outlasted just about everyone else, his life was still little more than a fleeting moment in the overall scheme of things. Mankind had crashed and burned in a day, and he himself probably wouldn't last that much longer, yet it would be decades, maybe even hundreds of years, before all trace of the human race would be gone for ever. His skin and bones would be dust blown on the wind long before the streets he'd walked along to get here today were fully reclaimed by nature.

It made him feel so fucking insignificant.

All the effort he'd put in to his life before the apocalypse had counted for nothing – and the worst part? It wouldn't have mattered a damn if he'd tried ten times as hard or if he'd not bothered at all. Everything that had happened was completely out of his control. *A man makes his own chances*, his dad used to say when things weren't going well. *Yeah, right: thanks a lot, Dad. No amount of handed-down bullshit is going to help me get past those bodies out there today, is it?*

Jackson was dawdling, and that wasn't like him. His reluctance to move served only to increase his unease. It was because the way ahead was no longer clear. Until recently he'd had a definite plan: to keep walking north until he reached the part of the country where there had been fewer people originally, and where the effects of the disaster might not have been so severe. When the true scale of the chaos had been revealed and it had become apparent that things were far worse than he'd at first thought, he'd been forced to reassess his priorities. His original aim had been too ambitious, and he decided instead just to head for the nearest stretch of coastline. Having the ocean on one side would make his position easier to defend, he thought, and also, when he looked out to sea it would be easier to believe that the rest of the world wasn't in ruins.

Three days ago, Jackson had had another change of heart, after a chance encounter with another survivor. The kid had been the first person he'd found alive in several days. He was your archetypal angry teen, all long hair, leather and denim, piercings and a patchwork of bad tattoos he'd inevitably end up regretting if he lived long enough. Adrenalin, fear and untold levels of pent-up sexual frustration surged through the kid's veins, and a cocktail of drink and drugs had clearly added to his volatility. Jackson had found him in the gymnasium of what he presumed was the school the kid had previously attended, rounding up corpses in an improvised corral. The sick fucker clearly had some deep-rooted issues, and had been trying to settle a vendetta or ten with some old and very dead friends. He'd been flagellating the bodies he'd captured, mutilating them beyond recognition, as if he had a serious point to make. Sick bastard.

After a half-hearted attempt to try and deal with him, Jackson had decided there was nothing to be gained from trying to reason with the clearly unreasonable, and knowing that neither of them would gain anything from being with the other, he left the kid to fester. To him, the unpredictable kid presented an unnecessary risk; to the kid, Jackson was just another authority figure to despise and kick back against. As

8

he'd walked away from the school, Jackson had wondered if useless, broken people like the kid were all that was left. That night, the enormity of what had happened to the rest of the world weighed heavier on his shoulders than ever before, heavier even than the rucksack full of survival equipment he'd been lugging around since the first day.

The encounter with the kid had made him stop and think, and after that he'd begun to realise the futility of just endlessly walking. With the dead becoming increasingly animated, just being out in the open felt like it was becoming more dangerous by the hour, and Jackson knew it was time now to stop and think again. It wasn't as if he had anyone else to worry about but himself – there had been someone who'd mattered, once, but she was long gone and best forgotten. He didn't want anyone else now. He didn't need them in the same way they needed him. He'd come across several groups of survivors before the kid in the gym, and they'd all, without exception, asked *him* to stay with *them*. *We should stick together*, they'd inevitably ended up saying to him; *we could do with having someone like you around.* And that was the problem: they needed him, never the other way around. He'd begun to realise that he didn't actually need anyone; more to the point, having other people around actually appeared to make things *more* dangerous. All it needed was for one person to panic and make a mistake and untold numbers of dead bodies would be swarming around them in seconds.

Another surge of movement outside the unimposing little house made Jackson focus again. Up ahead, on the other side of the road, it looked like one corpse had attempted to fight its way deeper into the vast crowd, and all around it, others were reacting to the unexpected movement. They tore into each other, vicious fingers stripping decaying flesh from bone, creating a sudden firestorm of sickening violence. And as the first few began to fight, so more and more of them followed, until huge numbers of the damn things were scrapping vehemently over nothing. As the bizarre swell of activity gradually petered out, Jackson wondered whether he'd actually been running away from the rest of the world, or at the very least trying to hide from it.

Yesterday morning he'd stopped at a prison. His first instinct had been to avoid it, but common sense said he should stop and investigate. *You have to think about things differently these days*, he told himself as he cut his way in through the no-longer-electrified chain-link fence. *After all, places like this were designed to keep people away from each other, and that's what I want.*

The prison proved to be a damn good place to shelter for a while: the kitchens were well stocked, prepared to feed hundreds of hungry inmates, and the vast majority of the prison's current population remained conveniently incarcerated in their cells. Jackson spent a couple of hours walking along numerous empty landings which all looked the same, swigging from a bottle of wine as dead prisoners threw themselves against the bars on either side of him, straining their arms to try and reach him. It had felt like visiting a zoo and intentionally goading the animals.

He broke out onto a section of flat roof where he sat cross-legged and watched the sun sink, marking the end of another day. Unperturbed by the cold, he lay back and looked up into a dark sky filled with more stars than he could ever remember seeing before, their individual brightness intensified by the lack of any ambient light down at ground level. And yet again his personal insignificance became painfully apparent. He felt like a piece of gum that had been spat out on a pavement. He might have mattered once, but not any more.

Half drunk and completely depressed, Jackson had slept intermittently, but when the sun started to rise on yet another day, he looked up and saw the castle.

It had seemed like a good idea at the time – the castle, Cheetham Castle, according to all the brown signs, looked like an ideal place to spend the next few days while he worked out what the hell he was going to do with what was left of his life – but it was surrounded by vast numbers of the dead, many more than he'd expected to find. He could see the grey stone castle gatehouse through the living room window, towering proudly above the heads of the foul masses, still visible through the smog-like swarms of insects. He'd checked out the full scale of the writhing crowd from an upstairs window earlier, and the size of the gathering both terrified and intrigued him. He'd long since discovered that whenever the dead amassed in these numbers, there was *always* a reason. He hadn't wasted much time trying to work out what that reason was – it was impossible to do anything but guess from this distance.

From upstairs he'd seen that the castle was between half a mile and a mile away from this row of houses. Between here and there was a road, a gravelled car park and several acres of grassland which contained several thousand corpses. Interestingly, they had all stopped short of the building's walls, prevented from getting any closer, he assumed, by the steep slope of the large hill upon which the castle had been built. It was simply too high for their weak legs to climb.

The castle walls themselves looked strong, at least from this distance. It was difficult to gauge their height from the house, but they looked to be reassuringly un-scalable. For a while, though, Jackson had actually given serious consideration to trying to improvise a grappling hook and rope so he could drag himself up and over, up and over like some Errol Flynn character. As it was, his best option would clearly be the gatehouse, on the far right of the castle from where he was currently standing. Judging by the number of signs he'd seen on his way here, this place must have been a popular tourist attraction, so the castle's most recent owners would surely have done everything in their power to make it easy for the public to get inside and part with their hard-earned cash. At the very least, getting to the castle would afford him a much-needed breathing space before he moved on again. He had an obvious advantage over the dead when it came to the steep climb, and the view from the top of the rise would no doubt be spectacular.

Jackson packed up his few belongings, finished eating the last of a packet of cereal bars he'd found in the kitchen, and readied himself to fight.

He stepped out into the open and pressed himself back against the wall of the cottage. The cool air outside stank, and he was acutely aware that every move he made sounded disproportionately loud; every footstep thundered, and every breath echoed endlessly. He stayed frozen to the spot as he assessed his limited options, moving only his eyes as he scanned the wall of dead flesh up ahead of him. Virtually all of the corpses now were standing with their backs to him, so it made sense (as much as any of this made sense) to try and work his way closer to the gatehouse, looking for a place where the crowds were thinner, for his success today boiled down to being able to charge his way through the decay and come out the other side.

He began to shuffle slowly along the lane, mimicking the slothful movements of the dead and trying to blend in with those which, even now, were still dragging themselves closer to the castle. Then one sprang out at him from a hitherto unseen gap between two buildings. Whether it was an intentional attack or an unfortunate coincidence didn't matter; it took him by surprise and he swung it around and slammed it against the wall he'd been following, then clubbed its brains out with the short length of heavy metal tubing he carried with him. He dropped what was left of the bloody corpse in the gutter, then looked up as another one began moving towards him, alerted by the noise of his violent attack. This one had a badly damaged right leg, and its unsteady gait made it look more aggressive than it actually was. Jackson angrily shoved it away, reacting before he'd fully thought things through, and it clattered back against a wheelie-bin, which thudded into several others. The noise echoed through the air.

Shit.

He knew even before he looked around again that he was in trouble. Many of the dead had noticed him now, and their reactions had, by turn, attracted even more. He might as well have fired a starting pistol into the air because, up ahead and behind and all around him, huge numbers of them were now reacting to his presence, peeling away from the edge of the immense crowd like a chain-reaction. Jackson knew he had to move fast. Fortunately for him, several of the pitiful monsters had already lost their footing in the confusion and were being trampled by their desperate brethren. He glanced up at the castle in the distance, visible intermittently through the crisscrossing chaos. Could he still make it? It had been a while since he'd taken a chance like this. *Christ*, he thought, *I hope so.*

Jackson swung his heavy rucksack off his shoulders, using it to smack the nearest corpses out of the way as he did so. He started to run, kicking out as a foul, bald-headed creature with a hole eaten through its face where its nose used to be lashed out at him. He jumped sideways, onto the bonnet of a Vauxhall Astra – his sudden change of direction causing temporary mass confusion – then climbed onto the roof. He took a moment to stash his metal pipe in his rucksack, then opened one of the side pockets and dug deep inside, now and then stamping on the fingers of those trying to grab at him with hands decayed into spiteful claws. Then he pulled out a packet of fireworks wrapped in a clear plastic bag, unwrapped one rocket and started fumbling in his trouser pocket for his lighter. Distracted by trying to light the blue touch-paper, he didn't notice that one of the bodies had managed somehow to grab hold of the bottom of his trousers. The crowd around the car surged as more of the dead arrived, and the body holding onto Jackson's leg was pushed back, tugging at him. He tried to pull away, but over-compensated, the heel of his boot slipped down onto the curved surface of the windscreen and he lost his balance, crashing down onto his backside and leaving a deep dent in the roof. He screamed out in pain – swearing as the noise immediately caused another sudden surge of dead flesh – and almost dropped the rocket he was trying to light. He spat in the face of another wretched carcase (a completely futile gesture, but he didn't have hands free to do anything else), then scrambled back up onto the roof.

The touch-paper caught suddenly. Jackson ignored the intense heat and the shower of sparks spitting out over his hand, and aimed the rocket down into the centre of a pocket of seething corpses a safe distance away. The firework whooshed away before coming to a sudden stop, embedded in the chest of a dead car mechanic, judging by the remains of the overalls he was wearing, who reeled back on his heels and looked down at the jet of flames sticking out of his belly just before the rocket exploded.

The noise and flames had exactly the effect Jackson had hoped. Almost immediately the focus of attention shifted away from him and towards the mechanic, who was still staggering around despite the fact he was burning up. Jackson lit a second rocket and aimed it up into the air. The piercing scream it let out as it raced up towards the grey clouds was enough to distract an enormous number of corpses, and as they lifted their dead heads skywards he jumped down from the car and ran for all he was worth. He crossed the road and the car park, then tripped over what was left of a barbed wire fence lying on the ground, already trampled down flat by the crowds. He lit a third rocket as he picked himself up, and shoved it into the gut of something which looked like the kind of punk kid he'd have done his level best to avoid before this. It looked down at itself, bewildered, as jets of blue and green flame started spitting out through various holes in its chest. The stupid thing still had a wrong-way-round baseball cap on, glued to its head by a month's worth of decay. He bloody hated it when they wore their caps back-to-front like that.

As the corpse exploded behind him, he dropped his shoulder and charged deeper into the heaving throng. Many of them were now trying to move away from the castle, heading towards the flames. He felt like a derailed bullet train, smashing bodies away on either side, not entirely sure where the hell he was going or where he was going to stop. He just kept moving, knowing that every step took him closer to the castle in the distance.

He was deep into the dead hordes now, so close-packed they had no idea he was near until he actually made contact. Some were still trying to fight their way towards the fireworks, but most were looking the other way, facing the castle, and those he simply pushed aside and clambered over them when they fell.

And then, unexpectedly, the ground dropped away in front of him. Within a few steps he found himself wading through a fallen mass of tangled bodies rather than running between and around those still standing. A few steps more and he was knee-deep in churned remains. It took him a moment to realise that he'd stumbled into a wide ditch – the overgrown remnants of an ancient moat, perhaps. It was filled with bodies, trodden down and compacted into a repugnant gloop beneath his boots. Horribly, some of them were still moving, and Jackson ducked as a dripping, virtually fleshless hand swung past his face, sharp, bony fingertips just missing the end of his nose by inches. He was struggling to keep moving against the decay sucking him down, when the reason for its depth became clear: the deep furrow here had acted like a valve. The dead had been able to get in easily enough, but none of them could get out again.

Eventually Jackson found himself on level ground again. The corpses on this side of the ditch were fewer in number, so despite being soaked through with gore and desperately needing to stop and catch his breath, he kept on running, side-stepping one cadaver which came at him, then handing-off the next as if he were a rugby player weaving through the opposition to score a try under the posts.

And then he realised he was finally beginning to climb, and he looked ahead and saw the imposing wall of old stone looming, stretching up into the rapidly darkening sky. His thighs burned with the effort, but he kept on pushing until he had passed the last of the bodies, then slowed as the ground became steeper and exhaustion got the better of him. He moved at walking pace now, struggling to keep climbing, stopping occasionally to look back over his shoulder at the crowds gathered at the bottom of the incline and on the other side of the trench. They looked like they were waiting impatiently to pounce the moment he slipped and fell back into their grasp.

Once he'd reached the castle walls, Jackson followed a three-foot-wide pathway around the edge of the decrepit fortress towards the front entrance, but it was immediately obvious there was no chance of him getting inside that way: as well as the fact that the huge wooden gate was shut, there were more bodies here, all crammed onto a narrow wooden bridge. He pressed himself back against the stonework and looked down towards the house he'd been sheltering in, trying to assess the situation. A gently curving track wound its way up here from the car park below, and its relatively smooth surface and steady incline had enabled a stream of bodies to make the climb until the main gate had become blocked by an impassable, clogged mass of rotting flesh. Jackson shuffled back the other way, only moderately concerned. Despite the inconvenience of still not having found a way into the castle, he realised it was also a good thing. *If I'm having trouble getting in*, he thought, *then the dead have no chance*.

He'd worked his way back around half the perimeter of the immense ruin, looking for another entrance or a place where the wall was lower, when he stopped to look down at an engraved brass tourist map set into stone. This had obviously been a popular view-point, and as well as affording him a clear view for miles around, it also gave him a clear appreciation of the true size of the vast crowd waiting for him at the foot of the hill. An almost incalculable number of blank faces looked in his direction, bodies stretching away to the right and left, wrapping around the base of the hill and sealing the castle off in a sea of rotting death.

The brass map had accumulated a light layer of filth which Jackson wiped away with his sleeve. He tried to make out some of the local features it had been designed to highlight: the port of Chadwick, some fifteen miles east (he was closer to the coast than he'd realised), the smaller town of Halecroft to the south. There was a reservoir, a ruined abbey, and a wealth of other beauty spots and landmarks, none of which were of any obvious use to him. He was on the verge of giving up for the day, and he wondered if he should just finish walking around the castle then find a piece of level ground up here to pitch his tent for the night, when something caught his eye: another entrance – a *secret* entrance? This was the stuff of bullshit or legend – but no, it appeared to be real: a smaller, far less obvious way into the castle, through a passage carved into the hillside. There was a brief explanation on the map – for smugglers getting in and tyrants getting out in times past. He orientated himself, worked out roughly where the hidden entrance was, and headed straight for it.

A padlocked gate, a cage of green-painted iron railings set into the hillside, and an unexpected gaggle of more than a hundred corpses were all that stood between Jackson and the entrance to the tunnel. He stood several yards above the dead and composed himself, watching as several of them tried unsuccessfully to scramble up the wet grass to reach him. Hands shaking with nerves, he lit his last firework and aimed it at the back of the ragged gathering. It shot away from him, and before it had even hit the bodies, he was sprinting directly at them. The rocket exploded and they turned and moved towards the light and noise *en masse*, giving him a few seconds of space to fight his way through to the gate, his bolt-cutters held ready. The padlock clasp was too thick and too strong, but he managed to cut through a link in the chain it secured. The firework had burned out and he had again become the sole focus of attention. With the dead already turning back and beginning to grab at him, he wrapped one end of the chain around his hand several times and began swinging it around wildly like a whip. The effect was remarkable, slicing through rotting flesh like a hot wire through butter whenever it made contact. With the arc of the chain providing him with a large enough space, Jackson pushed the gate open, threw himself through, and then turned and started back to shut the gate – but there were already too many corpses hot on his heels, pouring through after him, reaching for him with their clawing hands. He ran for the tunnel, depending on his speed to get him out of immediate trouble.

The pitch-black close confines of the damp tunnel walls made him feel uncomfortably claustrophobic, but he had no option other than to keep moving. He ran with arms outstretched, climbing upwards and bracing himself, knowing that at any second he might reach a dead end. *Christ*, he realised, far too late to be able to do anything about it, *this bloody tunnel might not even go anywhere*. The passage was several hundred years old at least – it could have collapsed, been shut for safety reasons, been re-routed back outside to the bottom of the hill . . . And all the time he could hear the dead behind him, chasing him down with an almost arrogant slowness, and absolutely no fear whatsoever.

The lighter. He dug his hand into his pocket and felt for the reassuring metal outline of his lighter. He was running low on lighter fluid, but what the hell. He flicked it on and the unsteady yellow light immediately illuminated the roughly hewn sides of the tunnel around him. Moving with increased speed now that he could see, he burst into a large, low-ceilinged chamber. There were displays mounted on the uneven walls – all about smugglers, and gruesome pictures of starving prisoners . . . it looked like this had been some kind of dungeon. That'd be about right, he thought as the lighter began to burn his fingers. He swapped hands – not that it made much difference – and desperately searched for another way out. There was another short sloping passageway, leading away at about ten o'clock from where he'd entered the dungeon, then another large open space beyond. He let the flame go out again, conserving what was left of the lighter fluid and ran across this second space. He slowed down to walking pace again and felt for the wall with outstretched hands, increasingly aware of the sounds of the clumsy dead following close behind, their shuffling, scrambling noises amplified by the close confines. His fingertips made contact with cold stone and he worked his way around to the left until he reached another doorway cut into the rock, leading into yet another tunnel.

Feeling his way forward with his left hand, trying to flick the lighter into life again with the right, the dead sounded closer than ever now. The lighter flame caught, and shone on a wooden door directly ahead. It looked relatively modern, and reassuringly solid, and yet he felt the hairs on the back of his neck begin to prick up and stand on end. *If I can't get through*, he realised, the sounds of the dead continuing to increase in volume, *then I'm fucked*.

He hit the door at speed, slamming his hand down on the latch and pushing it open, and found himself falling into another space. The door shut behind him – and he screamed in fright at the sight of a body, hanging from the wall, its arms shackled, before realising it was a plastic dummy, dressed in rags, strung up there for effect. He stumbled back, tripping over his own feet, hitting the deck hard and dropping his lighter, which went out and skittered across the floor. The sudden pitch-black was suffocating, all-consuming. He crawled slowly forward, his hands feeling the ground, desperate to touch the warm metal of the lighter. He found boxes, and packaging, and what felt like the plastic feet of another executed dummy, and kept crawling until his head hit a wall and he yelped with pain and rocked back on his heels. In the distance he thought he could hear the dead advancing with renewed speed now, almost as if they were feeding off his pain.

His head throbbing, Jackson felt along the wall until he found the edge of a door. Was it the same one he'd come through, or a different one – had he somehow turned himself full circle in the darkness? If he went through this door, would he be running head-first into the oncoming dead? He stood up and tried the handle, but it wouldn't open. He pulled at the handle again, then shoulder-charged the door and as it gave way he flew into the next room, landing on his hands and knees in the middle of a small shop. There were shutters pulled over most of the windows, but enough light was filtering in for him to see. *Exit through the gift shop*, he thought as he picked himself up off the ground. He shut the door behind him and looked around for something to block it. He spent a few minutes pulling display stands in front of it, and once he was satisfied it was secure, he jogged down to the other end of the cluttered room, ignoring the key-rings, plastic swords and armour, mugs, stuffed toys and other equally useless tourist tat, shoved the far door open and burst out into daylight.

He found himself standing on the edge of a large court-yard, inside the castle walls, looking down the business end of a shotgun.

'Nice fireworks,' the man aiming at him said. 'Now who the fuck are you?'

'I'm Alan Jackson,' he answered, breathless, 'and I've had a hell of a day. Mind if I come in?'

2

The castle's walls were virtually impenetrable, and that combined with its proud, elevated position at the top of the natural rise made it ideal. The dead were unable to get anywhere close, save for an unsteady stream of corpses – a bizarre slow-motion parade – dragging themselves tirelessly along the road from the car park up to the bridge and the impassable wooden gate, where they formed an unmoving clot of increasingly decayed flesh. The inconvenience of these few hundred was nothing compared to the constant night-mare of the thousands upon thousands which Jackson had become used to.

Inside, the once-magnificent ancient fortress was far less impressive. The outer wall and the gatehouse were the oldest parts of the site still standing. Some of the inner walls had been reduced to little more than crumbled piles of stone, beaten into submission over the centuries by battle and weather. The eastern side of the outer wall was several hundred years newer, but in no better state. What had once been stables, a bakery, a great hall, living quarters and various other rooms were now all roofless open spaces. Some had been repurposed by the most recent owners, either strengthened, or replaced completely with out-of-character prefabrications to make a series of interconnecting rooms: an L-shaped display area and museum with a small onsite classroom in one corner, a café with a reasonably well-equipped kitchen leading off it, and at the end, the gift shop through which Jackson had made his dramatic entrance.

Jackson spent a lot of time up on the roof of the gatehouse tower, looking out over the battlements like a mediaeval lord of the manor. He felt as if he was under siege as the dead continued to gather all around them, spreading to the horizon like a germ-choked army of old, poised to charge. Except he knew they couldn't – at least for now.

Kieran Cope, the man who'd shoved a shotgun in his face when he'd first arrived, had become his man-at-arms. Kieran had been here since the beginning, and had so far been spared the rigours Jackson had endured out in the field. He was tall and slim, and favoured the jeans-and-jacket look, rather than the rugged, practical garb Jackson always wore. He looked less like one of the few remaining survivors of a global apocalypse and more like a student who'd just wandered in from a night at the pub.

Jackson's arrival had revitalised the handful of people who'd already made Cheetham Castle their home. Before the apocalypse, Melanie Hopper had juggled three jobs, as a cleaner and barmaid, getting paid in cash to keep her below the benefits threshold so she didn't lose her council flat but could still go out drinking most nights. She'd been cleaning the museum when everyone else had died and hadn't noticed a thing until half an hour after the event, when she had switched off the vacuum cleaner and pulled out her earbuds and walked into the courtyard for a break to find Shirley Brinksford, sitting in the middle of the cobbled area, sobbing.

Shirley, in contrast, had been a reluctant sightseer. She and her unbearably dull husband Raymond had just pulled up in the car park for another excruciating day touring local historic sites. She'd been looking for a way out of the relationship for a while, but not like this – though dropping dead at the wheel and driving the car into a ditch had been the most exciting thing Raymond had done in almost thirty years of marriage.

No one said much about Jerry. He'd originally been the fourth person at the castle. He had been spotted trundling along the road outside very early on, steering his electric wheelchair with one hand – which proved to be just about the only part of his body he still had any control over, as he'd got some kind of god-awful muscle-wasting disease. No one dared say it out loud, but they all wished they'd never found him, because it soon became abundantly clear that there was nothing they could do for him. Jerry needed round-the-clock help, not to mention constant physical and medical treatment, and none of the other three had really been in a position to provide for their own requirements, let alone Jerry's. They did everything they could – tried to feed him, tried to keep him clean and safe and warm, tried to communicate – but it was pretty hopeless, and though no one actually said the words, it was a huge relief when he died in his sleep.

And now Jackson had arrived, and somewhat to his surprise, he found himself thriving on the sudden responsibility of trying to coordinate the small group of people and helping them to make their castle hideout as strong, secure and comfortable as possible. In the end the decision whether or not he should stay at the castle had been simple.

Getting out and gathering supplies was a priority. When he first found them, they'd been desperately ill-equipped for survival. They had a little food, what was left from the café, Kieran's flat-bed lorry, the late Raymond Brinksford's slightly dented car, and Melanie's (presumably) dead boyfriend's souped-up Ford Fiesta. Kieran had found his shotgun and half a box of ammo in a house nearby; that was the extent of their defences.

Leaving the safety of the castle was a necessity, so Jackson took Kieran and Mel and headed for the nearest village. They bulldozed their way out through the castle gate and over the bridge in Kieran's lorry, and returned several hours later with a full load and two more vehicles. Being down among the dead was always fraught with danger, and Jackson did all he could to reduce the risks, but he decided whatever noise they made coming and going wasn't an issue, for the strength of their castle hideout was such that only a fraction of the dead could reach them. 'We get out,' Jackson had said, 'we get what we need, then we get back. It's as simple as that.'

And for a time it was.

In spite of the differences in their ages and backgrounds, and bound by their shared desire to survive, Kieran and Jackson worked well together, and their expeditions into the dead world became more audacious. They took diggers from never-to-be-completed roadworks and partly finished building sites and used them to keep the gate and the wooden bridge relatively clear. They spotted a holiday camp from the gatehouse and appropriated six large luxury caravans that were warmer and considerably more comfortable than the castle itself – and the extra accommodation was soon needed, because as well as attracting the attention of every corpse for miles around, their activities in and around the castle also attracted the attention of other survivors who'd been hiding nearby.

Living people began to creep through the shadows to get to Cheetham Castle. Some broke through the lines of the dead like Jackson had; others waited and threw themselves at Jackson's feet (or, more accurately, in front of his vehicle) when he and Kieran were out gathering supplies.

The number of bodies beyond the castle walls didn't matter so much as long as the number within the walls continued to grow too. Five people became ten, then more still. Jackson spent hours watching from the gatehouse battlements, scanning the dead world for signs of life and hoping even more people would arrive. But after a while no more came, and the population of Cheetham Castle settled at seventeen.

3

It had been almost a month since Jackson had first arrived at the castle, and weeks since anyone else had made it through the hordes of bodies gathered outside. Half a dozen people sat on deckchairs around a large bonfire burning in the middle of the courtyard. Behind them, other people busied themselves in their caravans, doing what they could to keep themselves occupied, still struggling to find any semblance of normality within the bizarre surroundings of the castle walls.

'Well, I'm with you, Steve,' said Bob Wilkins, swigging from a bottle of lager. The drink made the cold night feel even colder still, but he was past caring.

'Me too,' said Sue Preston, sitting next to him. She was a short woman, and the extra clothing she had on tonight made her look round, almost double her normal size.

Steve Morecombe, a tax inspector until his job had been added to the endless list of now-completely-redundant occupations last September, looked at each of the others in turn. He zipped up his anorak, as high as it would go, then turned back to face Jackson. 'You're the boss. It's your call.'

'This is bullshit,' Kieran protested.

Jackson silenced him with a glance, then knocked back another slug of whiskey-fortified coffee and winced at the bitter aftertaste. 'Not bullshit, Kieran,' he said, 'common sense.'

'It's got nothing to do with common sense,' Kieran argued. 'It's because this lot are too damn scared to—'

Jackson glared at him again, and he immediately became quiet.

'First things first,' Jackson said, returning his attention to the group. He sniffed and wiped his nose on the back of one of his fingerless gloves. 'I'm not the boss. I don't want any of you turning around and pointing fingers at me if this all goes belly-up. We're all in this together, okay?' There were a few quiet mumbles, but no dissension, not even from Kieran. 'I think Steve and Bob are right.'

'It makes sense,' Bob interrupted, and went on, 'the way I see it, we've done all the hard work we need to for now. We've stockpiled enough to get us through the winter, and no one new has turned up here for weeks. We need to start focusing more on those who are already here and forget about everything that's going on out there, on the other side of the wall, until it's safe. If we think we can batten down the hatches and survive the winter with what we've already got, then I think that's what we should do.'

'Agreed,' said Steve, rubbing his hands in front of the fire.

'I think you're wrong,' Kieran said. 'You're making a mistake: things are going to start getting easier out there, not harder.'

'Maybe in another couple of months,' Bob argued, 'but not yet. I think there's worse to come before things get better, and if we don't have to take risks, then we shouldn't be taking any.'

Jackson looked at Kieran on the other side of the fire, trying to gauge his reaction. The arguments continued, and he dropped his gaze to the flames, concentrating on the glowing embers, trying to shut out the noise by focusing on the crackle and pop of the burning wood.

'The risks are minimal; the potential gains are huge,' Kieran said.

'A risk's a risk,' Bob replied, 'no two ways about it.'

'We should put it to a vote.'

'You know you'd lose – face it, Kieran, you're the only one who wants to keep going out there.'

'Bull. Mel said she'd go if—'

Jackson, tired of the bickering, cut across them all. 'Way I see it is this,' he said. 'What Bob and Steve are saying makes sense, and Kieran, I think you're wrong. But the thing is this: if we do this, then *everyone* has to buy in, and we *all* have to follow the same rules. Food and drink will need to be carefully controlled so we don't run short. Folks have to be free to leave here if they're not happy, but they need to know that if they willingly walk away, we'll not be chasing after them. Agreed?'

He looked around at the people sitting with him.

'Fair enough,' said Sue, sinking deeper into her seat, her face disappearing into her padded jacket.

'Kieran? You know you can't go out on your own.'

At first Kieran didn't react, and Jackson stared at him until he grudgingly mumbled, 'Okay.'

'I'm in,' Steve said. 'I'd rather bloody starve myself for a couple of months than go out there again unnecessarily.'

'Probably do you good, you fat bastard!' Bob joked, relieved that the decision had gone his way.

'So let's do it,' Jackson announced, 'and we'll see how things go. So we keep the gate locked until those fuckers out there have rotted down to nothing, right? And you reckon that's going to be six months maximum, Sue?'

'Give or take,' she replied, 'but don't forget I was on a children's ward, not a mortuary nurse. It was my job to try and keep people alive, not watch them after they'd died.'

'The only exception,' Jackson continued, 'the *only* exception, mind, is if we get wind of other people like us outside. I don't much fancy sticking my arse out there and risking getting bit, but by the same token we can't turn our backs on people we might be able to help. The more of us there are here, the better. That sound fair?'

A few more mumbles, a few more nods; no one answered properly, but no one argued either, not even Kieran, the youngest apart from Aiden Parker, who was just a kid of twelve. No one else at Cheetham Castle had Kieran's boundless energy, or shared his apparent (and as yet untested) fearlessness; over the weeks they were becoming less confident, while his confidence had been steadily increasing.

'Just one more thing,' Jackson said, raising his voice to stop those people who were already halfway out of their seats and heading for their beds. 'This is important, and you all need to remember this: we're safer here than anywhere else any of us has come across, but *nowhere* is completely safe, not any more. If anyone does anything that puts the rest of us at any risk, I'll personally drag them to the top of the gatehouse and throw them over the battlements, do you understand?' He looked around the circle, holding everyone's gaze until they'd each nodded their agreement. 'If we're patient and sensible,' he finished, 'then we'll all get through this mess and come out the other side in one piece.'

FIFTY-EIGHT DAYS
SINCE INFECTION

4

THE BROMWELL HOTEL – TOP FLOOR, EAST WING

Driver had seen this coming long before the rest of them. He'd suspected this place was too good to be true from the first moment he'd driven his beaten-up old bus along the twisting road which led to the front of the hotel. *Way I see it*, he thought at the time (though he didn't waste his energy trying to explain to any of the others), *there's plenty of different ways to survive; you just have to make sure you're all pulling in the same direction.* And that was the problem they'd had here – too many chiefs – and that was why he'd planned to take evasive action long before the shit had actually hit the fan. He'd already seen the cracks starting to appear.

Ask any of the others and they'd all have said Driver was incapable of showing any emotion. What would they have thought now, if they could see him perched on the end of his bed, his head in his hands, sobbing like a frightened child? They thought he left his beard to grow wild because he was lazy; the truth was he grew it to hide behind. But they were silly, foolish people, more concerned with one-upmanship and scoring points over each other than anything else. They'd all been so preoccupied with their bickering that they hadn't questioned him when he'd feigned sickness and hidden himself away in this room, as far from everyone else as he could get. In fact, they'd positively encouraged him to do it, figuring it would be best for all concerned to put maximum distance between him and themselves. And so, armed with little more than the stash of food he'd been steadily siphoning off for himself on the quiet, he sat alone in his room on the top floor of the east wing of the hotel and watched as the rest of the idiots threw away everything they'd worked for.

He'd expected the end to come soon, but not with such speed. Within a couple of days they'd lost everything. It had begun with the usual fights over food, then some chaotic stupidity as some of them had tried to attract the attention of a helicopter they all knew full well was never going to see them, then someone – he wasn't sure who – had cracked under the pressure, and that was that; the floodgates had well and truly been opened.

It was time for him to move.

His gear packed – not that there was much; just his stash of food and water, a few clothes and his well-read newspaper – Driver crept back downstairs and waited outside at the furthest edge of the hotel grounds until he was certain that this really was it. He needed to be sure. There would be no turning back. He watched from a distance as those cracks he'd seen widened to chasms with incredible speed. He cursed the fools he'd wound up with. He'd heard several explosions out on the golf course, and then some idiot had taken his precious bus and managed to crash it, completely blocking their only escape route. They'd written him off long ago, but he was used to it. *Just because I don't talk all the time, or get involved in their pointless bloody arguments, it doesn't mean I don't care,* he thought. They'd always grossly underestimated him, assuming that he wasn't interested in their ongoing fight for survival when nothing could have been further from the truth. They presumed he was a selfish, uncaring bastard – bloody hypocrites!

Driver stood by the boundary fence and watched the unstoppable descent into chaos begin. *When it comes to the crunch*, he'd said to himself, *I'll be the one who gets them out of this mess.* He felt like he knew all of them intimately – their strengths and weaknesses, their likes and dislikes – and yet none of them knew a single damn thing about him other than the fact he used to drive buses for a living. They assumed that was all he was good for, but the reality was that he ended up driving buses because that was what he'd *wanted* to do; he'd spent ten years in the Royal Navy, had a spell working as a tour guide across Europe, got a first class honours degree in Greek history and art – no, they knew *nothing* about him.

Up ahead, a considerable distance away from him but still far too close for comfort, he could see the bodies beginning to surge through the gap in the fence he'd seen Martin Priest use previously. That gap wasn't the only way through, though, contrary to what Martin had said. Taking care not to be seen – there'd only be another bloody argument if they saw him trying to leave, and then no one would get out of here alive – he ran across the wet grass, to a section of fence where he'd found the loose railings two days previous. He lifted a couple of the railings just enough to be able to squeeze through the gap, then replaced them. No one had noticed anything.

He took one final long look at the immense tidal wave of rot rolling this way, a moment's hesitation, both to make sure beyond all doubt that the hotel was lost, and to consider, for the last time, if he really was doing the right thing. And then he was gone.

5

Several hours had passed, but it felt like much longer. Driver was still sitting in the cab of one of the lorries blocking the junction at the end of the road leading up to the hotel. He was still struggling with his conscience. Just a short distance, no more than half a mile from where he was sitting, were the people he'd left behind in the hotel. He wondered how many of them were still alive back there. He sat up straighter in his already elevated seat, but it was no use: he could see nothing beyond the angular outline of the roof of the hotel through the tops of the trees.

He'd had no choice, he kept telling himself; he'd had to do it. Even if he'd shown the rest of them his escape route, it wouldn't have done any of them any good – by the time they'd finished bickering about who was going and who should stay, the unstoppable avalanche of corpses would most likely have settled the matter for them. And even if, somehow, they'd actually managed to get away, he knew exactly what they'd be doing right now; he could picture the lot of them, either standing in the middle of this junction or crammed into the back of one of the lorries, and all arguing about whose fault it was the hotel had been lost. Not one of them would be accepting any responsibility; they'd all be too busy pointing the finger at everyone else to take the blame.

No, as harsh – as *wrong* – as it felt, this was the best option for all concerned. He'd go back for what was left of them when he could.

Driver armed himself with the golf club he'd stashed in the cab and psyched himself up, ready to move out. The disturbance around the hotel and the fires on the golf course would provide him with a brief moment of freedom in which he could make his escape. Short, sharp hops, that was the key to getting away from here in one piece, he'd decided. He would move fast and stay exposed for the briefest periods he could manage. And with so many thousands of corpses in the immediate vicinity the best way to keep quiet was to stay on foot, at least until he was more confident about his surroundings. He peered out through the windscreen, surveying the landscape through the steadily deepening late-evening gloom. About fifty yards ahead was the outline of a lone house, and before the light completely disappeared he'd seen that the front door had been left invitingly open. He could see only two bodies between him and the house, and as far as he could tell, neither of them yet knew he was there.

Driver took a deep breath and carefully eased his bulky body out of the cab and onto the road. He reached back up to grab his duffle bag and the golf club, then ran like hell. In his Navy days he wouldn't even have broken into a sweat covering so short a distance, but he was no longer in good shape, and the rigours of life since the end of the world – including poor diet and next to no exercise – definitely hadn't helped. He was barely halfway there and already panting for breath. He paused for a moment, swung the putter around and hit the first corpse's skull, leaving a neat rectangular indentation which perfectly matched the head of the club. The corpse immediately collapsed at his feet as if he'd flicked an off-switch and Driver half-ducked, half-fell out of the way of the second creature as it made an uncoordinated grab for him. Picking up his speed, he scrambled into the house and kicked the door shut, just in time, for the remaining body was outside almost immediately, banging on the door.

He'd have to move fast, before the noise brought countless others here.

There's something in here with me.

Before he'd even consciously realised it was there, Driver had caught the pint-sized cadaver of a small boy by its blood-crusted jumper as it leapt up at him. He held it at arm's length, its arms and legs thrashing wildly, and shoved it into a cupboard in the corner of the kitchen, then wedged the back of a chair under the handle to stop the damn thing from getting out. Great: two of them filling the house with noise now. Why did there have to be so bloody many of them? As he made a mad thirty-second dash around the kitchen looking for food and any other useful items he realised the noise might actually help, if he could get away without the dead guessing he'd gone. He paused by the back door and looked out. There was another building, about a hundred yards away, maybe a hundred and fifty – it looked like a used car salesroom. If he could get there without any of them noticing, he might still have a chance.

Several more corpses were already stumbling towards the house as Driver slipped out and ran for all he was worth.

He'd done eight or nine of these stop-start sprints now, and he was exhausted. Each mad dash was getting harder, every breath-catching gap between them taking longer. It would be completely dark soon. Time to find somewhere to rest.

By the time he reached a shack-like roadside café, which appeared to be constructed almost entirely from sheets of corrugated metal nailed to a creaking wooden frame, he was doubled-over with effort. The door was shut but not bolted, and as he let himself in he found he was alone, to his immense relief. He didn't have the energy to fight again tonight. He collapsed into a chair, pulled out his last bottle of water and looked out through the filthy window as he swigged from it, just like any normal diner might. After the frantic, frightening events of the last few days this moment of calm was both unexpected and blissful.

And then, in this snatched moment of almost-normality, the enormity of recent events finally caught up with him and Driver found himself weeping openly, for himself, and for those he'd left behind. Once again he struggled with his conscience, feeling a very real need to double back to try and help the others, though he knew he couldn't do them any good – even if he did make it back to the hotel, the huge, seething crowds surrounding the building would make any attempt at rescue nigh on impossible. This was the very worst time to try and get back.

A lone female corpse stumbled in the road outside the café, its awkward movements illuminated by the moonlight. The tatters of the dead woman's shredded blouse rippled in the gentle breeze, and the soft blue light on her ice-white skin gave her an unsettling, almost ghost-like appearance. She must have tripped over something, for she dropped heavily to her knees, before awkwardly picking herself up again. She was nearly naked and decayed almost beyond all recognition, and she must have suffered some more damage in the fall just now because she was suddenly limping badly, barely able to keep walking.

Driver stood up and moved closer to the window, keeping hidden from view by the grimy curtain. The dead woman in the street outside looked so helpless, so alone, and for the very briefest of moments he began to pity her. But then she spotted something he couldn't see, and without warning her lurching pace became predatory and quickened to an ominous speed.

Driver leant back against the wall and screwed his eyes shut. He really was not sure whether it was even worth trying to keep going.

He didn't move again until first light. He felt surprisingly rested and, deciding that if he was going to give up (and he still wasn't sure) there'd be countless better places to do it than here in this dingy little roadside café, he went back outside.

The long, straight road was clear in both directions, and this morning he could see for miles. Today he walked rather than ran, moving slowly and silently, trying to mimic the slow crawl of the dead. Whenever he thought he saw movement he would slow even further, dragging his feet along the ground, drooping his head, even when one particularly hideous monster crossed his path. The completely naked corpse with skin like a badly sewn-together patchwork quilt crossed the road just a few yards ahead of him, and still he forced himself to keep moving forward, not to make any sudden change in direction. Even when it stumbled and then appeared to start coming towards him, he stopped himself from reacting in any way – that would mark him out as *different*, and he didn't know if he could keep fighting these damn things, not today. He watched covertly as it staggered past, but he didn't flinch, not even when his nostrils filled with its foul, decaying stench, nor when it came so close that he could hear its putrefied innards sloshing about inside its barrel-like gut.

He didn't know how much longer he could keep on going like this.

After almost an hour of painfully slow and frustratingly directionless progress he reached the summit of a hill. Before him, on the downward slope of the other side, he could see three corpses, and there, parked neatly at a request stop, was a bus – only a small single-decker bus, which was par for the course in these rural parts, of course, nothing like the big inner-city double-deckers he used to love to drive – but that didn't matter. Provided it had enough fuel and he could get it started, his fortunes had just taken a turn for the better.

One of the three corpses moved to intercept him as he cantered down the hill. It had a gaping hole in the side of its face where insects and rot had eaten away much of its right cheek, and he could see into its mouth, its yellow teeth grinding and its lolling tongue clacking tirelessly. He stepped back out of the way as it lurched at him and thrown off-balance by his sudden movement, it dropped to its knees. Before it could pick itself up, he had smashed in the back of its skull with his golf club, then immediately swung the club around and knocked the second of the dead completely off its feet. He didn't bother wasting any effort on the third but just shoved it out of the way and climbed onto the bus.

Only one of the trapped passengers was still mobile, but as soon as it saw Driver it hurtled down the narrow aisle between the two rows of seats, the lack of space making it look like it was moving faster than it actually was, but it clipped its hip on the back of one of the seats before it could reach him and hit the deck heavily. Driver grabbed it by the scruff of its neck, dragged it along the bus, and manhandled it out of the door.

It was good to be back on a bus again, he thought to himself as he dealt with the rest of the dead (but thankfully immobile) passengers. One old crone was particularly difficult to budge from her seat. She'd been holding onto the handle of her shopping trolley when she'd died and now her gnarled hands were welded to the plastic grip. It took him longer than he'd expected to prise them apart, but at last he managed to get her out.

The bus driver was the last body to leave the bus. The eviscerated remains were much easier to remove, and Driver carefully peeled the dead man off his seat, then used the jacket which had been draped over the back of his chair to wipe it clear. He used the golf club to clear a way through the steadily increasing activity outside, and carefully placed the body in the undergrowth at the side of the road, draping the soiled jacket over it. He felt almost honour-bound to treat his fellow driver with respect. He returned to the bus, pushed the doors shut and then, finally, Driver was alone.

He walked the length of the long vehicle, just as he did at the beginning of every shift, opening the high, vented windows to let the stale air circulate, picking up the odd discarded ticket or bit of litter. He was pleased to see the bus' former driver had kept a clean vehicle too. Then, with an audience of eight corpses now watching him from outside, he took his rightful position behind the wheel. It had been only a few days since he'd last driven, but it felt good to be sitting in a cab again: elevated, protected, untouchable. He took a deep, calming breath, closed his eyes and started the engine. It took its time, rumbling and dying several times, but eventually it caught properly and burst into life.

Driver made himself comfortable. He carefully placed his newspaper in the gap between the windscreen and the back of the dashboard, revelling in the familiarity of routine. For a moment he relaxed and imagined himself driving his old familiar routes around town, picturing himself anywhere but here.

6

Driver felt protected in his new bus, pleasingly isolated from the rest of the dead world through which he travelled. As he drove further away from Bromwell, he had to swallow his guilt and constantly ignore the nagging voice which told him he should be driving in the opposite direction. He kept telling himself there was no point; that he couldn't risk trying to get to the others, not yet – if they managed to survive the hotel being surrounded and made it to safety, he reasoned, then as long as they had enough food to last a while, their situation wouldn't change. It would be better to wait until the dead were less of a threat.

For much of the last thirty years, Driver had either spent his time taking orders or driving from point to point following fixed schedules. He was finding driving aimlessly particularly difficult to handle. A few bad choices of direction, made under pressure from the dead, found him struggling to keep the bus moving forward on narrow country lanes for which this most urban of vehicles had definitely not been designed. With no obvious means of refuelling and in desperate need of something resembling a plan, he decided to park up somewhere remote enough to be safe, yet not so far out as to risk being stranded. Late in the afternoon he shunted the bus through the narrow entrance to a National Trust car park, near a farm and alongside the ruins of an ancient abbey that was nestled deep in a valley between two moderately large hills and parked up overlooking a vast swathe of uninterrupted countryside.

For a while Driver sat and read his newspaper, an instinctive reaction whenever the silence became too loud to stand. He'd held on to that same paper, ever since that morning back in September when the world had gone to hell. He'd driven out of the bus depot as normal on that warm and sunny morning, and had pulled up outside the newsagent's he used every day to buy his regulation paper, cup of coffee, bottle of water and packet of gum. Making those purchases had been the very last thing he'd done before people had started dropping dead all around him, and since then this newspaper – those seventy-four precious, increasingly crumpled pages of smudged print – had taken on huge meaning for him. Apart from the obvious connections with the world which had been wrenched from him – all those stories about once-familiar people and places, lying politicians and vacuous 'celebrities' famous only for being famous, the weather forecasts and sports reports, the photographs of a normal world now gone for ever – the paper even *smelled* like the old world used to. It felt familiar, and sounded strangely reassuring as he rustled the pages and folded them back on themselves. Even the puzzle pages, a section he rarely used to bother with, had helped him while away countless hours during the last two months. Concentrating on the crossword, Sudoku and anagrams had stopped him thinking, just for a while, about the relentless hell life had become.

The paper wasn't having the same effect today. He threw it across the bus with frustration and it hit one of the windows opposite, pages spilling everywhere.

At the end of the car park was a small café and toilet block. When Driver investigated he found the apron-wearing corpse of a young girl trapped behind the counter. She was slumped against a wall and penned in on all sides, but as soon as she saw him she clawed herself upright, brittle bones bursting into life, and threw herself forward, straining to reach him over the chest-height displays. He looked into her pallid face for a moment and tried to picture what she might have looked like before she'd died, but it was impossible. Her badly discoloured skin was aged before its time, covered in dirt and the glistening silver traces of insect infestation. Several of her teeth had fallen out, the dried-up gums no longer capable of holding them in place, and there was something about those big black gaps in her mouth which filled Driver with sadness and disgust in equal measure. He remembered a young girl he'd known, Rachel, the daughter of a friend, who'd lost her front teeth in an accident, and how badly that loss had shattered her confidence. He thought about Rachel as he gazed into the dead girl's milky-white eyes. A large semi-circular flap of skin covered with brittle, straw-like hair had peeled away from the side of her head and now hung down over one of her ears. This had once been a young girl with her whole life ahead of her, he thought, a girl like Rachel, and now look at her. What a cruel bastard of a disease.

He turned away from the corpse, even as it swiped at him again, and used his golf club to smash the outward-facing food display cabinets. He helped himself to everything that was still edible, snatching items between the dead girl's vicious, barely coordinated attacks and piling them into his duffle bag.

After ensuring it was corpse-free, Driver used the toilet around the back of the café. The dank, unwelcome building was a mildly more appealing option than squatting in the bushes, but he hated every second of it. It terrified him – it made him feel as if he were suddenly a child again, afraid of the monster hiding in the corner – and he realised he didn't know which was the worse option: doing what he had to do in utter darkness, or propping open all the doors and sitting on the loo, exposed to the world, with his trousers around his ankles.

Finally done, he went outside and wiped his hands on the dew-soaked grass – where he found the remains of a small dog, tied to a post, as dried-up as the empty water bowl it was lying next to. The dog's body looked as if it had been vacuum-packed in its own skin, its ribs protruding through what was left of its short grey fur, its dry eyes bulging from its head. Its lips were drawn back into a permanent snarl, almost as if it had died trying to ward off whatever it was that had killed its owner, wherever he or she was. Seeing the dog took him by surprise, and for the second time since he'd fled the hotel, Driver was reduced to tears. The thought of this poor little bugger waiting faithfully for its owner to return, and the long, slow, frightening, painful death from starvation it had inevitably endured was heartbreaking.

Driver curled up on the long seat at the back of the bus, eating chocolate and listening to the never-ending silence. Alone for the first time in weeks, with space to breathe, the true extent of what had happened to the world now began to hit him.

Driver thought of the depth of the loss, the extent of the damage, how little remained untouched – and how much everything had changed.

Time slowed down to an almost undetectable crawl. Driver stared at his watch; he would have sworn every second was taking twice as long as usual to tick by. Finally abandoning any idea of sleep, he got up and walked to the front of the bus. He looked out through the windscreen at the huge, empty world outside. The land stretched out ahead of him for ever, and he wondered how far he could actually see – ten miles? Twenty? Further? He knew little about this area, and there were no obvious landmarks he could use to try and get his bearings – not that it really mattered, because one dead place was much the same as the next now; there was nothing of any worth left anywhere.

Apart from one flicker of light.

Driver rubbed his eyes and leaned against the glass, for a moment convinced his mind was playing tricks. Was it just a reflection, a desert-less mirage? Whatever it was, he could still see it; it looked like the glow of a distant fire: a single bright interruption in the midst of the otherwise endless sea of darkness outside.

'Bugger me,' he said out loud, surprising himself with the sound of his own voice.

Desperate not to lose sight of it, though still not entirely convinced there was actually anything there, Driver ferreted around the dashboard, looking for the thick black marker pen he'd picked up on his travels. He used it to circle the position of the light on the windscreen, then drew a number of arrows all the way around it, all pointing inwards to make sure that, when the morning came, he'd be able to locate it again.

Driver sat behind the wheel all night, waiting impatiently for the dawn, when he would be able to tell *what* it was he'd been looking at – and more importantly, *where* it was. As the grey light began to edge reluctantly across the empty land, Driver returned to the café. He'd seen a selection of tourist guides in the wall mounts behind the dead girl yesterday, but he'd paid them little attention at the time. As he approached the dead girl the corpse immediately sprang into action, and this time he grabbed hold of her left shoulder and spun her around. The decayed flesh shifted under the pressure of his grip like wet clay as he pushed the body into the wall, face-first, and held it there. He reached up with his free hand and took as many maps, brochures and leaflets as he could, then ran straight back to the bus.

He unfolded the largest map and spread it out over the steering wheel, looking from the map to the view outside, trying to orientate himself. For a while he was stumped, despite his naval training, distracted by the constant movement of another tireless husk, a dead woman which had just stumbled out of the trees and was now biting at the glass in front of him, moving from side to side and covering the window with greasy stains.

The simple map had few real details, but it suddenly

dawned on Driver that the best landmarks were the hills he was parked between and everything finally began to click into place.

Got it: that's where the fire was last night. And now he was focused on that spot, he could see a faint but steady wisp of smoke still rising up from it: a perilously thin trail of darker grey against the off-white clouds. He looked back down at ground level, and now he could see that the smoke, bizarrely, looked as if it was coming from a ruined castle. He picked up one of the tourist guides and flicked through the pages to find anything that looked even remotely similar.

And then he found it: Cheetham Castle.

7

Driver accelerated towards the castle, obliterating anything foolish enough to get in his way. The closer he'd got, the lighter the smoke trail hanging in the air had become, to the point where he was beginning to doubt he'd seen anything at all. Had he been hallucinating? Was it just a cloud formation he'd willed into being something else? He also knew there was a very real possibility that if there was a fire, it might have started accidentally, and that this place was as dead as everywhere else. But whatever it was, whatever had or hadn't caused the smoke, he was here now.

For the first time he was actually pleased to see bodies around, because the more bodies, he thought, the more likely that there had been other survivors here recently. At best he might have stumbled upon a fully operational base camp; at worst he'd found a damn good place to hide out for a while – that was assuming that he could get in, of course.

He followed a road which roughly matched the curve of the castle wall, albeit at some distance, and between him and the fortress was a vast crowd of cadavers, perhaps even more than he'd seen approaching the hotel back in Bromwell, and close to the mass he'd seen around the flats. The fact there were so many of them, and so tightly packed in such a relatively confined space, was both a help and a hindrance. Those that'd had already noticed him were trapped and were finding it difficult to move, but their numbers were also preventing him from making out much of the immediate area. Even from his elevated position it was difficult to see beyond the dead.

Driver forced himself to concentrate on the road, steering

hard around the back-end of a burned-out car and wiping out several stragglers in the process. He watched one he'd just ploughed down in his rear-view mirror. He'd driven straight over it, crushing its pelvis and spine – he knew that for a fact – he'd felt the crunch – and yet it was *still* coming after him, doggedly, *persistently*. It might only able to move its arms now, but it seemed almost to be trying to *swim* along the tarmac.

As the road climbed, he was afforded a slightly better view of the land around the castle, and he saw with relief that the crowd of bodies didn't stretch all the way to the castle walls – that was clearly because of the steep hill the castle was built on. A little further ahead he spotted a bizarre queue of bodies, stretching away from the bulk of the crowd and up towards the gatehouse entrance. They looked like they were following some kind of track, and lining up to get inside – and that, he decided, would be his best chance of getting in too.

Driver continued moving forward, passing the snaking column of corpses. He could see the wooden gate of the castle up ahead of them, shut fast, and a swollen bottleneck of dead flesh directly outside it. The turn onto the track was too tight an angle for the bus, so he continued further down the road to the large car park. It was only partially filled with corpses, but all of them started dragging themselves towards him at the sound of the powerful diesel engine. As he turned in a big circle some started flinging themselves at the bus, bouncing off the front of his vehicle like flies hitting the windscreen.

As he accelerated back towards the castle, he had a far better view of the approach road. Judging his moment, he wrenched the steering wheel hard around, and for a few seconds the wheels slid through mud, until just as Driver was beginning to fear the bus was becoming mired, the wheels hit the tarmac. As the tyres gripped the road, his speed increased and the bus began to climb. The bodies further up the road were more spread out than they'd looked from below and he realised the road was so steep that it might've been as much about them *having* to keep going as wanting to get to the castle. Hearing the bus, some of them turned and started stumbling down towards him, only to be obliterated on impact, but others seemed to be trying to get out of the way, almost as if they were aware of the danger approaching them at speed.

A flash of movement higher up caught his eye, and he looked up from the road momentarily, then looked back down as he clipped the kerb. He slowed, and looked back, and now he could see there was someone gesturing wildly at him from the top of the gatehouse – not just some*one*; there were two of them now, a man and a woman, and they were gesturing broadly at the wooden gate below.

As Driver continued hurtling towards the gate he noticed the road was lined on either side with piles of dismembered bodies, looking almost as if they'd been shunted out of the way by a snowplough. As he reached the wooden bridge before the gate he started to wonder if he should pull up and wait for the gate to open, but almost before he'd started to worry his question was answered and the two halves of the gate began to slowly part. Driver gripped the steering wheel tight, kept his foot on the accelerator and flew through the narrow gap before skidding to a halt in the middle of a vast courtyard filled with vehicles, caravans, equipment and—

—people! Healthy people – *living* people!

He didn't move for a while – he couldn't. He switched off the engine and slumped forward over the steering wheel, exhausted, his heart thumping so hard he thought it might burst from his chest. Out of the corner of his eye he watched as the handful of corpses which had slipped through the gate with him were rounded up and destroyed. Some of the people were hurriedly putting on hazmat suits; others wore leathers like Jas, Ian Harte, Greg Hollis and the rest of them used to wear. Working like a team he saw some were concentrating on getting the gate shut, leaving others to deal with the disposal and removal of the dead. He was transfixed by this un-expected display of organisation and cooperation.

A sudden knock on the door of the bus startled Driver, who sat up quickly and opened it to allow a tall, clean, and remarkably well-presented man come on board.

'You okay?' the man asked.

'Think so,' Driver mumbled, not entirely sure.

'My name's Jackson,' he said, holding out his hand.

'Anthony Kent,' he replied as they shook. 'Tony – but most folks just call me Driver.'

'Most folks? There's more of you?'

'There were – probably still are.'

'We'll get you some food, get you cleaned up, then you can tell me more,' he said, gesturing for Driver to follow him off the bus.

Driver did as he was told, looking around him in disbelief. 'What is this place?' he murmured.

'Home,' Jackson replied.

8

Several hours later, Bob Wilkins ushered Driver into another part of the castle, once part of the small museum space used as an on-site classroom by visiting schools, now, thanks to its size and relative comfort, appropriated as a communal lounge by the current occupants of the ancient building. Driver waited in the doorway, feeling unexpectedly nervous, until Bob gently pushed him through. There were four other people in the room already, and he felt like a definite outsider.

'Come on in, love,' Sue Preston said to him as she carried in a loaded tray from the adjoining café and kitchen. 'No standing on ceremony here.'

Driver did as she said, but stopped again when he caught sight of his reflection in a window. He had to look twice to be sure it really was him – he'd almost forgotten what he looked like. Jackson had given him the wherewithal to shave, for the first time in weeks, and one of the others – a lady called Shirley – had cut his long hair for him, rather than leaving him to hack at it. He still wore his bus driver's uniform overcoat, as he had almost every day since the beginning; he didn't have anything else to put on.

Jackson was sitting with another man in front of a paraffin heater which glowed a comforting orange. Even from here Driver could feel the heat it was producing. It was warmer than anything he'd felt in weeks. Jackson, seeing him, beckoned him over, pulling another chair up next to him.

Driver sat down, still feeling unexpectedly uncomfortable.

'This is Kieran,' Jackson said, introducing the other man; 'Kieran, this is Tony.'

'I prefer Driver.'

'How're you doing?' Kieran asked as they shook hands.

'Been better, been worse,' he replied, giving little away. He still wasn't sure how he felt.

'Smoke?' Jackson offered.

'No thanks. Bad for you.'

'Coffee?' Sue asked, leaning between them with a tray.

'Now that I won't say no to,' Driver said quickly, taking a mug. He sipped the drink, revelling in its warmth and its bittersweet taste, and stared at the glowing heater, trying to work out how he'd managed to get from yesterday's nightmare to here.

'Something wrong?'

Driver shook his head, then glanced over at Jackson. 'Just doesn't feel right, that's all.'

'What doesn't?'

'Sitting in a place like this, with people like you, enjoying a drink in front of the fire like nothing's happened.'

'If there's somewhere else you'd rather be—?'

'No,' he said quickly, 'of course not.'

He drank again, almost hiding behind the mug, and remembered the people he'd left behind at the hotel. He wondered what state they were in right now – assuming any of them were still alive.

'It takes folks a few days to get used to being here,' Jackson said. 'It's a bit of a culture shock. Thing is, the castle is safer than most other places.'

'I've heard that before.'

'No, seriously, it is: it's too steep, so the dead just can't get up here – well, apart from the few that make it up the road. The only downside of being somewhere as good as this is that it gives you time to think.'

'Tell me about it,' Driver said quietly. 'I've been doing too much of that myself recently.'

'Anything you want to share?'

Driver paused before answering. 'This time yesterday,' he

eventually started, feeling like he was confessing, 'I was sitting in that bus out there, freezing cold, wondering if there was any point going on. I didn't have a bloody clue what I was going to do next. The night before that I spent hiding in a café. The night before that I spent sitting in a lorry. Before that it was a hotel . . . You just get used to running, don't you? You forget how to stop.'

'Well, maybe it's time we all got used to stopping again,' Jackson said, putting a reassuring hand on Driver's shoulder.

'It's been the best part of two months since all this started,' Kieran said, his tone a little harsher than Jackson's, abrasive almost. 'You've told us about the last few days. Where were you before that?'

'I spent most of the time in a block of flats.'

'And why did you leave?'

'Same reason anyone leaves anywhere these days: a few thousand dead folk outside the front door that didn't want to leave us alone.'

'*Us?*'

'That's right.'

'So what happened to the others?' Kieran was sounding almost accusatory now, and Jackson reeled him in quickly.

'Take it easy, mate. Driver's had a tough day.'

'They're all tough days now,' Kieran said, unimpressed. 'So what happened? Where are they?'

'We left the flats when the bodies got too close.'

'How many of you?'

Driver paused, trying to remember, picturing the faces of each of the people who'd been at the flats with him. At last he said, 'Eight.'

'And you're all that's left?'

'So where did you go?' Jackson asked quickly, taking control of the questioning. 'You said something about a hotel?'

'That's right, over in Bromwell – we found more people there.'

'How many more?'

Another endless pause.

Jackson rocked back in his chair as he waited for Driver to answer. He was obviously having trouble remembering. *Christ*, Jackson thought, *we've all been through a lot, but this is like getting blood out of a stone.*

'Five,' he answered, finally. 'And a dog.'

'So that's thirteen of you all together.'

'And a dog,' Kieran added sarcastically.

Jackson shot him a withering glance. 'So where are they all?'

'Don't know for sure about all of them,' Driver replied. 'Things were getting bad, same as they always do, and I knew the situation was most likely about to go shit-shaped so I shut myself away in one of the rooms, kept my distance from the rest of them.'

'You hid?'

'You could say that if you like. Thing is, sometimes it's better just to keep yourself to yourself, don't you think?'

That comment caught Jackson off-guard momentarily. He happened to agree, but he wanted to get to the bottom of this. 'Okay, so cut to the chase,' he said, 'and tell us what happened to all the others?'

'I'm not entirely sure,' Driver admitted. 'They'd been keeping the bodies out of the way for a while, distracting them with music.'

'Smart move.'

'But you know what's been happening: the bloody things started to get smarter; they were working out what was what, and someone lost their nerve and screwed up and properly let the cat out of the bag, and before we knew it the whole place was surrounded.'

'So you just did a runner?' Kieran interrupted. He couldn't help himself.

'What else was I supposed to do? It didn't take a genius to work out what was going to happen next. All the escape routes were blocked – if I hadn't gone, no one would have got away.'

'So you were just looking out for yourself,' Kieran sneered, 'and fuck the rest of them.'

'No, it wasn't like that – I was planning to go back. I still am.' Driver tried to defend his actions.

'Like hell—'

'Easy,' Jackson warned. 'Give the guy a break.'

'You'd have done the same,' Driver continued, sounding close to tears. 'If I'd have stopped there with them, we'd have all been buggered – I thought I'd leave it a few days, maybe a couple of weeks, then try and get back and get them out. I know how it looks, but I swear I was going back.'

The awkward conversation faltered, and although neither Kieran nor Jackson said as much, they both remained unsure about this strange man.

'So let me see if I've got this straight,' Jackson said after a moment. 'Back at this hotel, there are potentially as many as twelve people stranded?'

'That's right.'

'And this is in Bromwell.'

'Yep.'

'I know the place. It's not too far from here.'

The other people in the room had been eavesdropping and now Bob Wilkins walked over. 'Come on, Jackson,' he protested, 'we *agreed*. Surely you're not suggesting we should leave here and—?'

'That's *exactly* what I'm suggesting,' Jackson said, cutting across him. 'We said we'd help other folk if we came across them. I'm not saying we should go today or tomorrow or even next week, but as soon as possible we should do all we can to try and reach those people. We can't afford not to. You know as well as I do that numbers are important now.'

'I think it's a risk too far,' Bob grumbled.

'Bob Wilkins,' Sue Preston sighed, 'sometimes getting out of bed in the morning is a risk too far for you.'

A few laughs punctuated the silence and Driver found he was enjoying the banter. It had been a long time since he'd seen people getting on with each other like this. He watched Sue as she leaned against the window and sipped her drink.

'For what it's worth,' she said to him, 'I think Jackson's right. We should try and help your friends. You'll not find a better place than this, lover. We've got food, we're safe, there's room for everyone . . .'

'Well, I'm sold,' Driver said, 'but I do want to go back. I meant what I said, I didn't want to walk out on them like that. I just didn't have any choice.'

'We understand,' Jackson told him, 'and like I said, the more people we have here, the better. I think we need to head on over to Bromwell to see what we can find.'

'When?'

'I don't think we should rush, or do anything hasty we might end up regretting. Sounds like your friends aren't going anywhere fast.'

'They're not going anywhere at all.'

'Then we sit tight for now. We'll know when the time's right.'

SEVENTY-SIX DAYS
SINCE INFECTION

river had settled quickly into the routine – what little routine there was – of life within the crumbling walls of Cheetham Castle, and in comparison to everywhere else he'd been recently, this was bliss. Okay, so he was finding it increasingly difficult to skive, meaning he was having to work harder than he was used to, and sometimes Jackson's 'all for the common good' ethos got a little hard to stomach, but he was safe and his mind was kept occupied, so it was a small price to pay.

He'd been tasked with keeping the group's vehicles in good working order, but as no one had ventured beyond the castle walls in all the time he'd been there, that didn't require a huge amount of effort. He did all he could to make a little work last as long as possible, managing to make himself look busy when, in fact, none of them actually had very much to do at all.

He'd made the decision to live on his bus. It was as good a place as any, and being windproof and relatively warm it was better than most parts of the castle itself. It was as spacious as most of the caravans, and less crowded, too. It suited him just fine.

This morning, however, it was particularly cold, and Driver opened one eye, then quickly closed it. It was still dark, and he was nowhere near ready to start another day just yet. He snuggled down deeper into his sleeping bag and wrapped his arms around himself, trying to retain as much precious heat as possible. He was on the verge of drifting off again when something slammed against the back end of the bus, close to where he was lying, and he sat bolt-upright in an instant, his heart pounding, expecting to see bodies surrounding him.

He relaxed a little when he saw that it was just Jackson, wrapped up like an Arctic explorer, and when he gestured for Driver to let him in, he grudgingly shuffled down the aisle, still wrapped in his sleeping bag, to open the door.

'Bloody hell,' he said, 'do you know what time it is?'

'Do I look like I care what time it is?' Jackson replied, irritated. 'Get yourself ready, Driver, we're going out.'

'Out? Where?'

'Bromwell.'

Within the hour, Driver found himself standing inside the prefabricated museum with a small team of volunteers. He looked around at them. Most people (himself included) did as little as they could get away with, content to leave much of the work to the minority who were prepared to put in the extra effort. And here they were: the usual suspects – the same faces which always appeared whenever anything important needed doing: Bob Wilkins, despite his frequent and vocal protestations about staying inside the castle walls and not taking risks, and next to him, wearing a grubby hazmat suit, was Steve Morecombe, someone else who talked a lot but said very little worth listening to.

Leaning against the nearest wall was Zoe, a tall, athletic-looking student. Driver liked Zoe, though he'd had very little to do with her so far. She was different to the others, and liked to keep herself to herself. He could identify with that. She was what his ex-wife Sandra would have called 'an individual'. Much to the bemusement of the rest of the group, Zoe always referred to herself as a student because technically that was what she still was. She could often be found in the corner of the classroom or the caravan where she lived, poring over her university textbooks. *What good's all that going to do you now?* people asked her with infuriating regularity. They didn't see the point in her studying a now-defunct subject like criminal law – or studying anything else, for that matter, but Driver understood. They were missing the point entirely. He didn't need to ask Zoe why she studied because he already knew. Like the newspaper he had read over and over, Zoe's studies were her coping mechanism, both distraction and occupation; a link to the past she wasn't yet ready to lose completely. 'Just because you've all forgotten who you used to be,' she'd sometimes tell them when she was feeling particularly frustrated, 'doesn't mean I have to.'

Kieran and Jackson marched across the courtyard towards the classroom, feet crunching through the frosty gravel. They'd barely got through the door before Bob was at them.

'Well?'

'Well what?' Jackson asked.

'Is it safe?'

'No way of knowing that for sure until we get out there, is there, Bob?'

'That's reassuring,' Steve grumbled. Driver said nothing, but he shared their concern. This seemed like the most tenuous of plans.

'All I can tell you,' Jackson said, 'is that thanks to last night's frost, which was severe, they're all pretty much frozen solid right now. I tried digging a hole just now, and I could barely get the spade to break the surface of the soil, so those things outside shouldn't be much more than chunks of ice. As long as we're back before they start to thaw out, we should be fine.'

'*Should* be fine?' Bob said.

'*Will* be fine. Now, are we set?'

There was a muted response, except for Zoe, who clapped her hands together and announced, 'I'm ready.' She was happy to give the others a bit of a kick up the backside.

'Good stuff,' Jackson continued. 'I know you all know what we're doing, but just so we're all completely clear, I'll go through it one last time, okay?'

Nothing.

Jackson ignored the silence and said bracingly, 'Right, so Kieran's going out there first in the digger to clear those iced bastards off the road. Driver follows with the rest of us. He'll get us to the hotel, then it's in and out and back again as quick as we can. No messing around. Got it?'

'You make it sound so easy,' Steve said.

'It *will* be easy,' Jackson replied, 'trust me.'

'Oh, we trust *you* all right,' Bob said with a half-laugh, following Zoe as she walked out of the classroom. 'It's what's left of the rest of the world we have a problem with.'

Driver was the last to leave. His stomach was knotted with nerves. He didn't know what scared him more – the prospect of leaving the safety of the castle walls, or what he might find back at the hotel.

10

Mark Ainsworth's fifteen minutes of fame had ended shortly before the rest of the world had died. He'd worked in a call centre selling car insurance for eight years until just before last summer, when a chance encounter on a busy high street had resulted in him appearing on a couple of episodes of a poorly rated fashion-based reality TV show. Most people's professions had been rendered redundant by the apocalypse, none more so than Mark's, but with the blissful ignorance of someone who truly believed that a brief appearance on television had suddenly promoted him from a nobody to a *somebody*, he refused to shut up about it. He still put gel in his hair every morning and used copious amounts of deodorant, still checked his appearance in the mirror whenever he left the caravan. But there were no televisions now, no fashion, no advertisers – none of it mattered any more, not that any of it ever had to most people.

Melanie was sick and tired of hearing about Mark's moment of glory. 'Just give it a rest, Mark,' she said, teeth chattering in the cold. 'You've already told me.'

'I know. Pretty cool though, eh?'

'If you say so.'

'They were talking about getting me to do a few PAs at Oceania in town – now that would have been awesome. Did you ever go to that club?'

'Yeah. It was shit.'

'You're kidding me – Oceania? That place was the dog's bollocks.'

'Well, it was bollocks,' she said, 'I'll give you that.'

'You're a total dick, Mark,' Will Bayliss said. 'Shut up

about your fucking TV and all that – you're doing my fucking head in, you are.'

Mark finally shut up. Will, several years his junior but with the offensive swagger of a wannabe bad boy, intimidated him.

Will tutted and looked Ainsworth up and down dismissively, and Paul Field, standing just behind him and as usual doing all he could to stay on the right side of him, shook his head and mumbled something that no one else could make out.

For the first time she could remember, Melanie was actually pleased to see Jackson walking towards her.

'You lot ready with the gate?' he asked.

'We're ready,' she said.

'Get it shut again as soon as Kieran gets the digger back inside, okay?'

'Okay,' she said.

Neither Mark nor Will made any comment, but he was used to their disrespect. He nodded his approval at Melanie, then walked back towards the digger and gave Kieran a thumbs-up. Kieran started the engine, filling the air with noise. Jackson looked around at the others – Sue Preston, Charlie Moorehouse, Shirley Brinksford, Phil Kent – all armed with clubs and axes, standing ready to mop up any corpses which managed to avoid being crushed by the digger and squirmed through while the gate was open.

Shirley's mouth was dry with nerves, and her legs felt heavy. She didn't know if she could do this. She glanced over her shoulder and saw Aiden's young face, pressed up against the caravan window. *He shouldn't be watching this*, she thought. *He's too young. I should go back inside and look after him, leave all this violence to the boys.*

'Okay,' Jackson shouted, 'open up!'

Mark and Will pulled their respective ropes, and the two sides of the gate slowly opened. The nearest dead were immediately visible. *Here comes the flood*, thought Kieran, watching nervously from his elevated position, but they didn't move. A vast number of them had crowded up against the gate, but the gore-soaked mass was completely frozen, stuck in position like someone had hit the pause button. The gate was fully open now and still there was no movement other than a slight twitch here, a barely visible shudder there – but that was all. The relief was palpable. Shirley beckoned Kieran forward, and he lowered the digger's heavy scoop and accelerated.

Kieran had a clear and uninterrupted view of the frozen dead and the world beyond the castle walls. It was a truly bizarre sight, one of the strangest things he'd ever seen – and that was saying something, given everything he'd witnessed since September. He couldn't begin to estimate just how many bodies had crowded onto the road leading up to the castle gate, for they were completely unrecognisable. Packed together like this they'd long since lost all semblance of individual form. First decay had deformed and distorted them, grossly altering their once-standard shapes in random ways, then the constant crowding had caused more damage, and now the bitter frost had welded them together. Limbs and torsos were largely obscured within the general mass, but countless heads remained poking up out of the frozen bulk, the features given a strange, glassy sheen by a thick layer of ice.

Kieran stopped before the first impact. It was both terrifying and pitiful: terrifying, because even though they were motionless and unable to attack, the dead were still here in almost incalculable numbers. And it was pitiful, because these damn things which had caused them so much pain had been rendered completely harmless by a sudden change in the weather. It was almost as if they'd been cut off mid-sentence. He found it strangely reassuring, although he knew that some of them would just as quickly regain their freedom with a sudden thaw. He almost laughed out loud at one of them: it had an arm raised and its head held high as if it were an athlete, caught in a freeze-frame photo sprinting for the finishing line. Then he thought he saw it tremble slightly. It could have been vibrations from the digger, a slight increase in temperature, gravity, intent, or something else entirely, but whatever it was, he shoved his foot down on the accelerator pedal and drove straight into it.

Jackson got on the bus and stood next to Driver and together they watched as Kieran carved a remarkably clean groove through the motionless ranks. He imagined the noise of the bodies crunching and snapping, and he stared as random limbs were broken off like the dried-out branches of dead trees. He glanced across at Driver, whose eyes were fixed on the path left by the digger. His face was expression-less. *He's either completely focused or completely fucking terrified*, Jackson thought, *and I can't tell which*.

When the curve of the road took Kieran out of sight, Jackson decided it was time to move. He nudged Driver, who pulled away smoothly and followed the channel through the dead left by the digger. Even as Jackson watched, he was sure he could see movement in the steep banks of decay on either side. It was slight, but it was definitely there. He guessed some of the bodies buried deepest had been protected from the worst of the frost, and now they were starting to slowly inch back towards the area which had been cleared. If they just sat there and waited long enough the track would completely disappear, so they had to get out and get back again before the corpses thawed out. The sun was beginning to show in the grey sky. They didn't have long.

11

Driver's nervousness reached almost unbearable levels as they approached the hotel. His initial trepidation at being out in the open again had quickly faded and had been replaced with an even more uncomfortable feeling of apprehension. What were they going to find at the hotel? Whichever way he looked at it, it was going to be tough. Contrary to what the people he'd left behind might have thought, he felt genuine affection for them, and he really hoped he'd find them all safe. If they were dead, he knew he'd be riddled with guilt. And yet, the prospect of finding them alive made him feel equally nervous: how much would they all hate him for running out on them? Even though he'd eventually returned for them – albeit a fortnight later – would any of them ever be able to trust him again?

There was no time to think about that now. They were here. He could see the hotel up ahead.

'So does anyone actually have a plan for getting them out?' Zoe asked. She was sitting just behind Jackson.

'Sort of,' Jackson replied, 'but it's difficult to plan much when you don't know what you're going to find.'

'Great.' She knew Jackson was right, though; her sarcasm was just her nerves talking. Of course making detailed preparations had been impossible from a distance. Driver had explained the basic geography of the area, describing the road between the hotel and the golf course, the fences and gates, the blocked road junction and the crashed vehicles (those he knew about, anyway).

Driver had deliberately chosen a route which looped around the site so they could come from the direction of

Bromwell itself. This way, he'd explained, they'd be able to get access to the hotel through the field below the golf course – that was where he thought Jas and the others had blown up their cars, and it seemed to be the most direct way to get into to the building without having to waste time moving lorries or scrambling over the wreck of his poor old bus.

Driver stopped at the entrance to the field. The steep slope ahead was covered in the remains of the dead, some still standing upright, most decayed down to an almost unrecognisable mulch. Like the hordes of bodies camped around the castle, the crowds here had been vast in number, and as a consequence it looked like many of the dead had literally been trampled into the dirt. Much to the survivors' collective relief, the area was almost entirely motionless. The bodies here were still frozen.

'I'll never get this bus up there,' Driver said, looking at the gore-covered hill.

'Let us out,' Jackson said, barely acknowledging him. Driver opened the doors, and the four disembarked.

Zoe, keen to get this done and get back, marched ahead, her steel-capped boots crunching through the ice and sliding on the fleshy muck below. Vile-smelling liquids splashed up her over-trousers. Bob followed close behind, carrying a long-shafted screwdriver as a weapon. They walked along the bottom edge of the field, then began to climb when they reached the hedgerow nearest to the hotel building. A body lying on its back beneath the hedge must have been shielded from the worst of the frost, for it reached out for Bob and grabbed hold of his foot. Barely pausing, Bob kicked its hand away, trod down on its neck, and plunged the screwdriver deep into one of its temples. He shook the screwdriver clean, then looked over at Zoe, who was standing a short distance away, looking up into the sky.

'Problem?' he asked.

'Possibly,' she replied. The skies overhead had cleared and were now relentlessly blue. Although it was still cold, the sun was bright, and the bodies were beginning to defrost, steam snaking away from them, carried on the gentlest of breezes. Listening closely, they could hear the steady *drip, drip, drip* marking the beginning of the thaw.

Steve and Jackson caught up. They were carrying two long ladders between them.

'We need to get on with this and get it done fast,' Steve said, voicing everyone's fears. 'I don't fancy being stuck out here when those fuckers start moving around again.'

Jackson didn't bother saying anything more, but started up the hill, and Steve followed, carrying the other end of the ladders. Each step forward became increasingly difficult, a combination of the slope and the slush underfoot making it hard to keep their balance. The further they climbed, the more statue-like corpses they had to negotiate. Jackson watched them intently as he weaved around their frozen shapes. Maybe it was the way its face caught the light, but he could have sworn the one he was approaching now had just moved its eyes. Was it looking at him? For no other reason than spite he kicked out at it, and it fell back into the icy mire like a felled tree.

'Gate,' Zoe said, taking the lead again. She hauled open the metal gate in the top right-hand corner of the field where the land levelled out slightly, scraping away an arc of once-human remains. 'Here's the road Driver was on about,' she added, looking up and down the curving track which wound around the perimeter of the hotel grounds. Jackson caught up and Steve and Bob took the weight of one ladder while he set the other up against the impenetrable hedge in front of them and held it steady for Zoe to climb.

She lifted her hands to shield her eyes from the brilliant winter sun and after a moment, said quietly, 'Bloody hell,' to no one in particular.

'Trouble?' Steve asked anxiously.

'You could say that.'

The other ladder appeared next to her and Bob climbed up. 'Fuck me,' he said.

'My sentiments exactly.'

From this high vantage point, the hotel and much of the surrounding area were clearly visible, and for as far as they could see in every direction, the ground was covered in bodies. Many of the dead had been crushed, but many, many more remained standing: a frozen forest of corpses. Zoe looked back towards the bus, waiting on the road at the bottom of the hill. The sunlight reflected off the windscreen, making it impossible to see Driver. Though she'd never said anything to him, she, like everyone else, had questioned his actions in abandoning his colleagues and getting away from this place by himself. Now, standing at the top of this ladder and looking at the sheer scale of what had happened here, his actions seemed eminently sensible. Even frozen, crushed and wedged together as they were now, the immeasurable mass of dead flesh up ahead was large enough to make Zoe question what the hell *they* were doing here. She couldn't even begin to imagine what terror the people who'd been here must have felt, seeing this foul, germ-ridden, unstoppable tidal wave of rot rolling towards them. Given the option, she had to admit, she'd probably have done exactly what Driver did.

'See anything?' Steve yelled, casually kicking at a single hand which jutted up from the decay covering the road and which had begun to twitch, as if trying to form a fist. Both Zoe and Bob had been so overcome by the scale of horror in front of them that neither replied. 'Oi!' Steve repeated, 'what's happening?'

Zoe had to force herself to turn away from the slowly defrosting mass of corpses and start looking at the hotel instead. She scanned the building from right to left, catching her breath when she thought she saw people at a ground-floor window – but it was just more damn corpses, their faces shoved up hard against the glass by the force of the countless others which had crowded into the same rooms behind them and were pushing them forward.

'This is hopeless,' she shouted down. 'No one could possibly have survived this.'

'It's full of bodies,' Bob added redundantly.

'What, the grounds or the hotel itself?' Jackson asked.

'Both,' Bob replied. 'The ground floor is, definitely.'

'Well, keep looking. It might be like when you capsize a boat.'

'What are you on about?' Bob scowled, looking down at Jackson.

'You know, the air gets trapped, so you can survive as long as you keep your head up at the top.'

'Yeah,' Bob said, 'but you haven't seen this place. There's no air here, only death—'

'Wait!' Zoe yelled. 'Look!'

She pointed at the hotel, and Bob squinted against the sun, trying to see what she'd seen. 'What is it?'

She paused, momentarily unsure herself, but then she saw it again: movement on the first floor, definite, *controlled* movement. There were faces at the windows, in two adjacent rooms.

'Bloody hell,' she gasped, looking at Bob then down at Steve and Jackson. 'We've found them!'

The sudden euphoria at finding the survivors was quickly replaced by now familiar feelings of unease. With every extra minute that passed, so the dead around the building became increasingly animated.

Jackson climbed the ladder after Bob and pulled a rope from around his waist and tied it onto the top rung, then he and Bob pulled themselves over onto Zoe's ladder. Together they hauled Bob's ladder over the hedge and dropped it down the other side, keeping hold of the rope, and once it was securely positioned, used the rope to tie them together. With a little careful negotiation, first Zoe then Jackson, then Bob and Steve got over and climbed down to the other side and started wading through the semi-human mire, grimacing in disgust as every footstep through the knee-deep gore crunched ice and bone into the ground. The upright corpses looked like dead stumps of trees after a forest fire, but many more had collapsed in various stages of deterioration. Withered hands were constantly reaching up at them from the foetid sea, fingers dripping with putrescence, and as they thawed out in the brilliant winter sunshine, so the appalling stench steadily worsened. Both Zoe and Bob started gagging and dry-heaving; it was only the desperate faces gesturing at them from the first-floor windows which kept them moving forward. Zoe counted at least five people; how many more were there?

At first Jackson and Bob tried to find a way to get inside the overrun building, but they quickly realised that that was impossible – not only was the entire ground floor full to overflowing with rotting bodies, but the comparative warmth inside had kept them animated, unlike those exposed to the elements outside. One of the trapped women opened a window and shouted to them that they'd also blocked the staircases to prevent the corpses from getting any closer – but as well as stopping the dead from getting up, they could not get down.

Zoe struggled to stay focused. Whenever she stood still for any length of time, those dead able to move began to gravitate towards her, and though their speed was barely noticeable at first, as soon as she realised what was happening, it became hard to concentrate on anything else. They were like giant slugs, glistening with slime and moving almost undetectably slowly, but if you became distracted for any length of time, when you turned back they'd be right at you, poised to attack. It reminded Zoe of playing in the school playground; she could almost hear the dead shouting at her, 'What's the time, Mr Wolf?'

Finally they devised an escape plan: those inside threw

down mattresses, and while Jackson kept off the slowly animating corpses, Zoe, Bob and Steve piled the mattresses on top of each other until they had a thick-enough landing mat – though it soon became clear to the rescue party that the drop was of little concern to the survivors in comparison to the prospect of remaining trapped in the morgue-like hotel for even a minute longer. Their desperation to get away was painfully clear.

Once they were set, three men and two women jumped down without hesitation, then there was a momentary delay as the last man tried to get a dog to jump down. Bob, beginning to get irritated, yelled, 'Just leave the fucking mutt!' as he wrestled with a dripping corpse which had completely shaken off its icy bonds and was trying to attack. It was only when the man gave up and jumped from the window first that the hound almost immediately followed.

Questions and explanations were initially the furthest thing from anyone's mind. For a blissful few minutes, all that mattered to those who had escaped the hotel was that somehow they were finally free. It felt unreal – maybe it was? Their interminable incarceration had seemed set to continue until they'd each breathed their last – but now it was over.

The rescuers lost no time in shepherding the survivors back the way they'd come. The dog's owner had to have help to get the animal get up the ladder and over the hedge, but at last they were all clear. Together they walked down the steep slope to the road, moving quickly to avoid the dead which staggered and crawled towards them from every direction.

Driver couldn't see anything from inside the bus, but he'd left the door open, and now, at last, he could hear voices approaching.

'There's one thing I don't get,' he heard a woman's voice say. *Was that Caron?* 'How did you find us? This place is so isolated . . .'

'Got a mate of yours with us,' he heard Jackson explain. 'Go easy on him, though. The delay's not his fault – we couldn't risk coming back out to look for you until now.'

Driver got off the bus, but he didn't go any further. He was too nervous. Instead he waited for the others to come into view. The relentlessly bright sun made it difficult to see who was who. He tried to count heads, then stopped when he saw Ian Harte. Their eyes met, and he felt his legs weaken with fear. There was a brief, unexpected delay – was it disbelief? Or maybe it was because they didn't recognise him – none of them had ever seen Driver clean-shaven before.

'Driver?' Harte said uncertainly. His voice was impossible to read. 'Driver, you sly old bastard, is that you?'

'I'm sorry, Harte,' Driver began, not knowing whether he should move forward or turn and run the other way. 'I thought it was for the best. If I'd stuck with you lot, we'd have all been buggered . . .'

He braced himself as Harte moved closer, but the man unexpectedly threw his arms around him and squeezed.

'Thanks, man,' Harte said, almost in tears.

Driver looked over Harte's shoulder at the others approaching. There were more of them – more of his friends, Greg Hollis, and Lorna, and Caron. And there was Howard Reece, and that bloody dog of his. And there was Jas . . . Christ, he looked traumatised; he was barely interacting with the others.

A corpse managed to raise itself by Jackson's feet and he booted it in what was left of its face. 'We need to get out of here,' he said, and ushered the survivors onto the bus. Howard brought up the rear, carrying the dog.

'What about . . . ?' Driver started to ask, but Howard shook his head, pre-empting his question.

'This is it, mate,' he said. 'This is all of us.'

'But what about Webb and Gordon? Martin? The others—'

'We lost Amir and Sean out here,' Howard said, 'and Webb and Martin bought it when the bodies got in.' His voice was a low monotone, almost like it was an effort to remember. 'Gordon and Ginnie just didn't want to keep going any more – we found them in their room a couple of weeks back, dead in bed together. They'd nicked a load of drugs from Caron. I'd been starting to think they might have been the sensible ones.'

'I'm sorry—'

'Sorry? Bloody hell, what have you got to be sorry about? Believe me, you've got no need to be sorry, mate. This time yesterday I was close to giving up. You've done us all a favour.'

12

Lorna led Hollis up the spiral stairs of the gatehouse to where she'd left Harte and Jas earlier. Neither of them had moved. Both men were standing at the top of the tower, their backs to each other, looking out over the battlements. It was getting dark, but she could see that Harte was looking down into the courtyard directly below. Jas' focus was clearly elsewhere.

'Hollis!' Harte said finally as the sound of their footsteps registered. 'How are you, mate?'

'Good, thanks,' he said quietly, his voice barely audible. 'Really good.'

'You had something to eat?'

'I didn't think he was ever going to stop eating,' Lorna answered for him, tenderly squeezing his arm. 'Howard's still down there, feeding his face.'

'Where's Caron?'

'Asleep in one of the caravans, curled up with an empty bottle of wine. Did you really need to ask?'

'And Driver?'

'On his bus, I presume.'

'The gang's all here, eh?' He grinned.

'Well, those of us who are left alive,' she said quietly.

Hollis slowly sat down, moving like a man twice his age, and she sat next to him. They'd all suffered during their imprisonment at the hotel, but Hollis had been affected more than most. When he'd lost the hearing in one ear, he'd really lost confidence, at first becoming aggressive and unpredictable, then, over the last couple of weeks, becoming increasingly withdrawn. Now he barely said anything to anyone, and he rarely moved, unless Lorna was there to help him up and drag him around. He was half the man he used to be.

The silence was getting too loud. 'You okay, Jas?' Lorna asked, but he didn't even bother to turn around – he hadn't even acknowledged her presence. 'Much going on out there?' she asked, unperturbed by his behaviour.

'Nothing much,' he said at last. 'Nothing much going on anywhere any more.'

'Bloody hell,' Harte sighed, 'cheer up, will you?'

'Why should I?'

'Because this time yesterday we all thought our number was up. We were completely fucked.'

'And this place is different because . . . ?'

Harte couldn't believe what he was hearing. 'This place couldn't be more different.'

'And you're sure about that?'

'Yes, of course I am—'

'Well, I'm not – not yet, anyway. Way I see it, it's just out of the frying pan, into the fire.'

'You think?' Lorna said, disagreeing strongly. 'It's way better than that. Way I see it, we're safely away from the dead. This is somewhere we can live and breathe and walk outside and . . .'

'As long as we stay inside the castle walls.'

'Yes, but—'

'Look, I'm not saying this place isn't better, I just don't think it's as good as you're making out.'

'It's as good as it gets for now, I think,' Hollis mumbled, but Jas still disagreed.

'They only came out for us today because the dead had frozen,' he said, talking to the others more than Hollis. 'It was a particularly harsh frost – that's not going to happen every day, is it? So they're still trapped, just like we were.'

'Yes, but we only have to worry about the dead for a few more months,' Harte said. 'Six months, that's what we've always said – we're almost halfway there now. It'll get easier.'

'I've been hearing that kind of bullshit since day one,' Jas interrupted, sounding increasingly angry. 'I talked to that guy Kieran when we got here. He said he cleared that road down there when Driver and Jackson went out looking for us.'

'So?'

'So by the time we got back it was blocked again, wasn't it? They had to get the digger back out and clear it before we could even get close to this place. And that's on a day when the conditions are in *our* favour.'

'Oh, just have a drink,' Harte said, offering him a bottle of whisky. 'Calm the fuck down.'

Jas took a swig, winced, then passed the bottle back. Lorna watched him, concerned. Harte came over and sat down next to her. The stone was cold under his backside, but the strong walls shielded them from the icy wind. As uncomfortable as it was outside, they'd all had enough of being trapped indoors. Jas remained standing on the opposite side to the rest of them, staring out into space.

'What are you thinking?' Lorna asked him.

'I'm thinking how fucked-up everything still is,' he replied, his voice wavering, 'and how little of it I still understand. I'm asking myself why I'm stuck here in a bloody castle with you lot when this time last year I'd have been at home with Harj and the kids and . . .' His voice broke and he didn't finish his sentence, but it didn't matter; he'd made his point. Being here tonight was a hollow victory. It depressed him to think this might be as good as his life was going to get. It still hurt too much to think about his life before the apocalypse in any great detail, but now, strangely, thinking about more recent times was becoming equally painful. Standing out here tonight reminded him of the endless hours he'd spent out on the balcony back at the flats, drinking beer while looking out over the dead crowds and discussing the practicalities of daily survival with Hollis, Stokes and the others. He'd felt like the king of the world back then, like he and the rest of them were in almost total control. Christ, how things had changed. The flats were lost now, and the hotel too, and Stokes and Webb and all those others were dead. Hollis was just a shell of a man . . . and as for the dead? Well, those fuckers continued to fight for all they were worth. Their decaying flesh might have been weak, but their intent was still clear.

'I was just thinking,' he said, 'how it feels like we've been here before.'

'I've never been here before,' Hollis said, mishearing him.

Jas ignored him and continued speaking. 'Look down there,' he said, gesturing out over the castle wall, 'and what do you see? I'll tell you: a fucking huge crowd of dead bodies. Same as we saw when we looked out of the hotel windows every bloody morning. Same as we saw when we were back at the flats.'

'But this is different,' Lorna sighed. 'Can't you see? Look at the condition they're in, Jas. Look at the state of them.'

'Look at the state of *us*,' he countered. 'For fuck's sake, there's barely any of us left. Most of us are dead – Gordon, Ginnie, Martin, Webb, Ellie, Anita, Stokes . . . They're all gone.'

'But we're still here,' she protested. '*We've* survived.'

'So far, yes.'

'And what about all the other people Driver found here?'

'What, all fifteen of them? Out of a population of something like sixty million people, there's only just over twenty of us left?'

'We don't know that – there could be hundreds more scattered all over the country.'

'*Hundreds* more? Doesn't change the fact that *millions* have died.'

'But this place is incredible,' Harte said. 'It's safe and it's strong. They've got a decent level of supplies and—'

'Spare me the bullshit,' Jas interrupted.

'It's not bullshit.'

'It is! We've heard it all before, again and again. Remember the early days back at the flats? You were walking around the place like the bloody cock of the roost, telling me how perfect it was, how we were going to build this barrier to keep the bodies back, how we'd do up the flats and make them inhabitable, and—'

'And that's exactly what we did,' Lorna said.

'Up to a point,' Jas continued. 'I believed it, though – we *all* believed it – but it didn't last, did it? And when we got to that fucking hotel, it was the same again. Remember the first couple of days there? How we were swanning around playing football, checking out the gym equipment, talking about draining the swimming pool and all that?'

'I know what you're saying, Jas, but nothing that happened there was because we did anything to—'

'What happened was *avoidable*,' he yelled, the sudden raw emotion in his voice taking everyone by surprise. He held his hand out for the whisky bottle and knocked back a mouthful.

Lorna wondered whether this was just the drink talking – maybe a combination of alcohol and relief that they'd finally escaped the hotel. 'This place *is* different,' she said, risking his ire. He glared at her, but when he didn't immediately start shouting her down, she continued, 'This place is different, and the bodies are much weaker now. Give it a few more months and there won't be anything left of them but bones.'

'A few months? I don't know if I can *take* a few more months of this. I don't know if I can take another day.' He drank the last of the liquor and hurled the bottle over the battlements. It was a few seconds before he heard it smash.

Lorna, Harte and Hollis watched him cautiously. Lorna suddenly felt the cold, and wanted to go down. She stood up, and helped Hollis to his feet. She was about to disappear down the spiral staircase when Jas turned and spoke to her again.

'You're right, Lorna,' he said, 'this place *is* going to be different, and we *will* be okay here. And I'll tell you why: it's

83

EIGHTY-SEVEN DAYS
SINCE INFECTION

13

Within the castle walls there was now a community of twenty-one, fifteen men and six women, and one dog. Jackson, maintaining his position of unelected leader by virtue of the fact that no one complained and no one else seemed to want the role, was keen to try and keep everyone occupied. Boredom was an enemy: it gave people time to think about how much they'd lost and how little they'd still got. Whether it was to keep them occupied, distracted or out of trouble . . . the reasons were unimportant. Most people willingly took on the duties assigned to them, and completed them to the best of their abilities, despite the fact that it was blatantly obvious that much of the work didn't actually need to be done.

Caron was an intelligent woman, and she knew when to keep her mouth shut. This was definitely one of those times. She was less than pleased with the duties she'd been allocated, but she carried them out without complaint. Since arriving at Cheetham Castle, she'd done more cleaning than she had in the previous ten years combined. At least it was relatively warm and dry indoors – winter had barely begun, but it felt like it had been like this for ever.

Working in the museum was particularly sad. They were using part of it as a storeroom now, and all the exhibits had been shoved down to one end of the large, L-shaped space. She'd spent some time this morning hidden around the corner, looking at all these valuable antiques, which were now worth nothing: beautifully restored and preserved artefacts now less important than food and water supplies, spare clothes, and pretty much everything else. A number of wall-mounted displays had been taken down and stacked against the back wall and she'd flicked through them, avoiding doing any work for a little longer. There were paintings of the castle hundreds of years ago, newly built and full of people, then there were pictures of the 'second stage' buildings within the perimeter wall – a great hall, an armoury, stables, living quarters, kitchens, all fallen to ruins, all those different ages, the lords of the manor, the kings and the generals, all gone now. She couldn't help but think she was living through the last chapter of this once-great place. If she'd had any artistic talent – and she was under no illusions, because she certainly *didn't* – then she'd have seriously considered painting a final frieze and hanging it on the museum wall. Twenty-one thin and frightened people, a handful of caravans, some basic supplies, and an invading army of corpses waiting on the other side of the outer wall – hardly a grand finalé to the castle's hundreds of years of history.

This kind of physical work didn't come naturally to Caron any more, but she bit her tongue and smiled when she needed to so as not to offend anyone; after all, there were worse jobs to be had around here. As she left the museum/storeroom she looked out across the courtyard. Jackson had a group of people gathered around him, and they were trying to assemble something, some kind of bizarre construction out of wood and ropes. According to the plans she'd been looking at, that's where the kitchens had been. Elsewhere, people were chopping up wooden pallets for firewood, making an industry out of something which probably didn't require such large amounts of effort. They were grading the wood into large, medium and small pieces before storing them in a dry shelter. Others were cleaning the caravans. Someone else was burning rubbish . . .

Too busy watching what was happening elsewhere, she literally walked into Hollis, who jumped back in surprise.

'Sorry, Greg.'

'My fault,' he mumbled apologetically, 'I wasn't looking. You okay?'

'Fine.'

'Been working hard?' he asked with a grin. He knew she hadn't.

'To all intents and purposes.' She glanced around before putting down her bucketful of cleaning equipment, then moved a pair of unused yellow rubber gloves to one side to reveal a well-thumbed paperback, half a bottle of wine and some empty chocolate wrappers. 'Between you and me,' she whispered, 'I've been taking it easy.'

'I'm surprised at you,' Hollis said, shaking his head with mock disappointment. 'What would our Mr Jackson say if he found out?'

'You're not going to rat on me, are you?' she asked, knowing full well that he wasn't. 'Honestly, Greg, I know we didn't know each other before all this madness, but you know me well enough by now. Dirty, hard, physical work . . . it's just not my style.'

'Caron,' he said, grinning, 'I know you well enough to understand that you're probably the person least suited to dirty, physical work I've ever met. Just keep your head down and get it done though, eh? A few more months and we'll be able to stop hiding away like this and you can go wherever you want then – let your new house get as dirty as you damn well please. You could live like a pig in shit if it'd make you happy.'

'Quite,' she said, not sure how she was supposed to respond to that.

'Anyway,' Hollis said, excusing himself, 'speaking of shit, I'd best get to work myself.'

'Oh, Greg, you're not?'

'And you thought you'd got it bad, eh?'

Caron laughed and picked up her stuff and walked on, leaving Hollis to head in the opposite direction. He'd have gladly swapped duties with Caron, but he knew she'd have baulked at the very idea of slopping out. Someone had to do it, though, and at least working around the chemical toilets kept him away from everyone else. Right now, that was how he liked it.

14

Jackson was standing at the edge of the courtyard, looking at the ground. The walls that had once stood here were just crumbled ruins now, like so much else, but there was one feature remaining which interested him: a well. They'd not yet managed to ascertain whether there was still a water source there, or if it was accessible, but he intended finding out. They had enough bottled water to see them through for a while longer, but having a steady supply would make things immeasurably easier for everyone. Bob Wilkins had some engineering experience, and Charlie Moorehouse had been a Scout leader; between them they thought they'd be able to improvise a basic rope-and-pulley system to lower a bucket far enough down to find out whether or not the well was dry.

He'd conscripted a number of other people to help: Lorna, Mark, Paul and Harte were busy digging a series of four holes around the well. Bob and Charlie were constructing two A-frames from the working model of a catapult they'd taken from the museum. They'd sink the feet into the four holes, then connect the two frames to make something that would hopefully resemble a child's swing. That was the plan, anyway.

'Want a hand?' Mark asked Lorna.

'You've got your own hole to dig,' she said.

'I'm almost done. You've barely started.'

'I'm fine, thanks.'

'We could swap sides if the ground's too hard over there. I don't mind.'

'Did you not hear her?' Paul sighed. 'Fucking moron.'

'I said I'm fine,' Lorna snapped, panting with the effort of the dig.

'Just trying to help, that's all,' Mark said.

'Well I don't need any help. Jesus Christ, this isn't the 1970s: women are able to dig holes, you know.'

'Bloody hell, you're touchy today, aren't you?'

'Leave her alone, Mark,' Harte said.

'And what are you, her boyfriend?' he sneered.

'Get a grip,' Harte said, carrying on digging, then as Lorna dropped her shovel, asked, 'You okay?'

'Going to get a drink,' she said. 'Back in a minute.'

The three men watched her disappear. Mark caught Harte's eye and grinned at him. 'She's great, isn't she? Cracking pair of tits.'

'Damn right,' Paul sniggered.

'For fuck's sake,' Harte sighed, 'is that all you've got to say about her? Lorna's got me out of more scrapes than I can remember. She's a fucking diamond. Bloody hell, the whole world's fallen apart and all you can say about her is she's got nice tits – there are better ways of assessing a person's worth, you know.'

Jackson was watching Harte and Mark, feeling unexpectedly uneasy. Their conversation sounded alien and out of place: Mark was talking the way people *used* to talk, back in the days when trivialities seemed to be all that mattered. The stakes were much higher now; there was no room here for petty arguments or superficial romances. Maybe in the future things would be different, but not yet. Not for a long time yet.

'Hold it steady,' Charlie grumbled.

'Sorry.'

Jackson went back to supporting the top of one of the A-frames, trying to keep it steady as Charlie attempted to drill through a wooden post with a hand-drill which looked so old it could have come from the museum. They'd lashed the sections together with tow-ropes they'd found in the back of a lorry.

Charlie grunted with effort, changed his grip and his stance, then began drilling again. His round, almost child-like face was red and uncharacteristically flustered, and sweat poured from him. But he was almost through, and after another few minutes' effort the tip of the drill bit finally poked through the other side.

'Bloody hell,' he said, wiping his brow. 'Half an hour, that took.'

'I know,' said Jackson.

'Used to be able to cut a hole like that in seconds.'

'I know,' he said again. 'We need to source some generators when we next get out of here, try and get a decent power supply going.'

Jas walked past, heading in the direction of the kitchen. He stopped and looked at the digging and the frame-building, shook his head and walked on.

'You're not going to help then?' Jackson shouted after him.

'Nope,' he replied, stopping again.

'But you'll be happy enough to use the water if we get this working.'

'You won't get water out of there.'

'We might.'

'Come on, Jackson,' he said, 'get over yourself. You know as well as I do you're only doing this to keep yourself busy. It's the same as all your bloody cleaning rotas.'

'We have to start somewhere, Jas.'

'Do we?'

'Of course we do.'

'Well I think you're overcomplicating things, and I think you're doing it intentionally. Water flows down, not up. It's easier to collect rainwater than to try dragging it up from the ground. We need to build rain-catchers, not climbing frames.'

'Okay, okay,' he said, walking up to Jas so their conversation couldn't easily be overheard, 'so I'm trying to keep people busy. Nothing wrong with that.'

'Except it looks like you're the one doing all the work.' He looked at Harte, Paul and Mark, who were now leaning up against their shovels, watching Lorna coming back towards them.

'Maybe I am. Anyway, it's not just me – I just want to keep everyone sharp, make sure we're ready so we can clear out of here after the winter and make a fresh start.'

'What's there to be ready for? What do you think's going to happen? I'm guessing we'll all just wander off in different directions and forget about all of this. That's what I'm planning: as soon as the bodies are gone I'm going to find myself a decent-sized house, get plenty of supplies in, then do as little as possible for as long as I can.'

'And you'll be happy with that?'

'I reckon I will.'

'There's got to be more to life than that, though.'

'Has there? Sounds pretty idyllic to me.'

'But we don't all have that freedom, do we? What about Aiden? He's only twelve. We can't leave him to fend for himself.'

'He'll be okay – he won't have much choice, will he? He'll grow up fast enough. Anyway, there's a few mother hens here who'll be more than willing to take him under their wings.'

'There might be other kids out there.'

'You think?'

'I don't know, and that's the point: we can't just split up and look after ourselves at the expense of everyone else. If we want the human race to survive then we—'

'Who said anything about that?'

'What?'

'All this "human race" bullshit – it's not my concern, mate. I've tried all that and it doesn't work. It's over – we're too far gone. You should stop stressing and get used to relaxing. We don't need to dig for water, 'cause there's millions of bottles of the stuff in the supermarkets up and down the country just waiting to be taken. And there's plenty more besides – lakes, rivers, reservoirs . . .'

'So what about food?'

'Same: just keep looting.'

'But it'll all run out eventually, and then—'

'—and then it won't be my problem because I'll be long gone. Dead and buried.'

'Well, not buried, not if you're alone. You'll die in your armchair, feet up in front of your telly that doesn't work.'

'So just dead then – so what? I won't care. Point is, Jackson, I've already lost everything that mattered. I worked my bollocks off for my family, and I did everything I could for them. They meant more to me than anything else in the world, you know. But none of that meant anything because in the end there was fuck-all I could do to help them. I couldn't save them; I couldn't ease their pain – bloody hell, I wasn't even there for them when they died. I was on my own – I was a security guard, looking after a new-built shopping centre that wasn't even going to open for another month, and I should have been at home. Seems to me, the harder I've tried since then, the more fucked-up things have got. So I've made a decision and I've stopped. I'm not even going to try any more. And if you want to waste your time doing stuff like this, then you go for it. Just don't expect me to help.'

15

The small classroom had begun to resemble a sixth-form common-room. Someone could be found in there most of the time, but the only person who used the room for its originally intended purpose now was Zoe, and the only reason she chose to work there was because it was the warmest place in the entire castle. It was nigh on impossible to concentrate in her caravan, even if she shut herself in the small bathroom and sat on the disconnected pan. As well as the sub-zero temperature, she was also having to contend with sharing the confined space with Caron and Lorna, and with Melanie too now, who'd moved out of the caravan next door a few days earlier after an argument with Sue about something so trivial that neither of them could even remember what it was. And sharing with Melanie inevitably meant having to put up with either late-night visits from a stream of men (which drove Lorna crazy) or her coming in and out at all hours, usually having had more than a few drinks. Will Bayliss, Phil Kent, Paul Field . . . Zoe had almost lost track of all the different blokes Melanie had had through the door.

Zoe was beginning to loathe this place. With six caravans all lined up in a row outside, it was starting to resemble the holiday park from hell. She had to keep reminding herself that this wasn't going to last for ever, and that no matter how bad things were here, they were infinitely worse on the other side of the castle walls.

Mark, Will, Paul and Jas were sitting around the paraffin heater, blocking most of the heat and making a hell of a lot of noise. The light was beginning to fade, but Zoe was determined to finish the section she'd been working on all afternoon. It was a particularly heavy-going section on the intricacies of one particularly complex aspect of international commercial law, and it was quite possibly the most redundant topic she could have chosen to study. Much of it hadn't even made sense to her when there'd been a corporate world left to apply it to.

'Zoe, love,' Sue called from the kitchen next door, 'give us a hand, would you?'

Zoe looked over her shoulder through the connecting doors between the classroom, café and kitchen. Sue had left them propped open with chairs. As usual, she'd been preparing an evening meal for anyone who could be bothered to drag themselves over to the café to eat.

'I'm busy,' Zoe shouted back. 'Ask someone else. There's four blokes in here all sat on their arses doing nothing. Ask one of them.'

Sue walked over to the door. 'I can't do that.'

'Why not?'

She stumbled for an answer, then said, 'Because they've been working all day, that's why.'

'So have I.'

'Yes, but what you're doing is just for you. They've been doing stuff outside.'

'So have I,' Zoe said again, 'and I've been doing this since I came in while they've been doing sod-all. I'll ask them to help if you won't.'

'No, don't. I'll just—'

It was too late. 'Oi, Will,' Zoe shouted, 'Sue needs a hand.'

Mark began a sarcastic slow clap.

'Why don't you help her, then?' Will shouted back.

'Because I'm busy.'

'So am I.'

'Doing what?'

'Planning.'

'Planning what?'

'Can't tell you.'

'Doesn't matter,' Sue said, sounding uncomfortable, 'I'll do it myself.'

The men turned their backs on Zoe and Sue and continued their plotting and laughing. Frustrated, Zoe stood up and shoved her chair back. It scraped across the floor, filling the classroom with ugly noise as she grudgingly went to help.

Fifteen minutes later, Sue was standing outside the café, repeatedly hitting an empty saucepan with a wooden spoon, her makeshift dinner gong. It felt good to stand out in the open and make such noise, liberating almost. After weeks of silence, being able to scream was a blessed relief.

It took less than five minutes for virtually all of the people living within the castle walls to descend upon the café next door. Sue's food might not have been anything particularly special, but it was warm and filling, and it was genuinely appreciated. She served up with a certain amount of pride.

With most people eating, the crowded room became relatively quiet, and Jackson seized on the opportunity to speak. 'I've been thinking,' he said, standing up, 'does anyone know anything about planting vegetables?'

'You dig a hole, chuck a seed in and it grows,' Mark joked.

'Well, I had an allotment,' Bob began to say before he was interrupted by Jas, groaning.

'Bloody hell, Jackson, what are you on about now? We'll be out of here by the time you can start planting.'

'You might be, Jas, but some of us might decide to stay. I'm not sure what I'm doing yet. I'm just trying to start planning for the future – looking ahead.'

'Why would anybody want to stay here? And I've already told you, we don't have a future. Not like that, anyway.'

'We'll have to agree to disagree then, Jas,' Jackson continued. 'I just think we need to start thinking about these things sooner rather than later because if we don't we could end up missing planting dates and then—'

'—and then we'd just have to keep looting from the

supermarkets for another year. No big deal. We'll be doing that anyway.'

'But we need to think about our health. We'll need fresh fruit and vegetables.'

'We can get by with tins for now. Bloody hell, how many times do we have to have this conversation?'

'Until we've found some answers. I don't think things are as black and white as you see them. The fact remains, at some point soon we're going to have to start fending for ourselves. You can put it off, but all you'll be doing is delaying the inevitable.'

'Whatever,' Jas grumbled, returning his attention to his food. 'Depends on your definition of "soon".'

Jackson looked around the room, hopeful of catching someone's eye and finding a little support somewhere, but there was nothing. Bob had shut up and was concentrating on his dinner to avoid being drawn in to the argument. Even Hollis and Howard, both more mature men who'd got stuck in, been involved, since they'd arrived here, kept their heads bowed; Howard, as usual, was more interested in his dog than anything else. Jackson wondered if he really was the only one bothered about their survival. Surely that couldn't be the case? Why would any of them have bothered fighting to get through to today if none of them cared? Or was it just some pointless survival instinct forcing them to keep plodding on, even when there was no longer any hope? He refused to believe that . . .

'For what it's worth,' Lorna said quietly, almost as if she didn't want to be heard, 'I think you're probably right. Thing is, though, this lot are going to need time before they start thinking about farming and stuff like that. Jas has got a point: there's enough on the shelves to last us for now.'

Jackson sat down next to her, dejected. 'But we've already had months.'

'No, we haven't,' she said, patting his arm. 'We've spent months just trying to cope with all the shit that's constantly been thrown at us. Now the pressure seems to be easing off, and those dead fuckers outside are rotting away to nothing, so it's inevitable that people are going to start asking themselves big questions.'

'Such as?'

'Such as: why did I lose everybody I gave a damn about? Is it worth going on? Do I want to live if all I have to look forward to is people like these and places like this?'

Jackson knew she was right. Since the very first day everything he'd done had been focused on surviving at all costs, without ever stopping to question why. And now, as Lorna had so succinctly pointed out, things were beginning to change. Instead of just trying instinctively to cope and adapt, people now had the opportunity to see if they actually *wanted* to cope and adapt first. Now Lorna had said it, he could see that asking stupid fucking questions about planting seeds of a group of people who clearly couldn't give a flying shit wasn't helping. It might be his way of dealing with the pressure, but all it was doing was pissing everybody else off. Jas clearly had a different strategy. Right now he could see there was no common ground between them. Maybe Jas was right; maybe he was trying too hard?

'We're all going to need time,' Lorna said, seeing his dejection. She leaned closer again and added, 'and this is the first opportunity most of us have had to really think about the future. We need to make sense of what's left – we need to remember how to be human again – before we decide if it's worth trying to carry on. I know I do.'

16

Hollis screwed up his face in disgust as he dragged over the last of the chemical toilets and emptied it into the vast cesspit which had been dug in the furthest corner of the castle grounds. He swilled out each of the four plastic tubs with a little reclaimed water, tipped them into the pit, added an inch or so of an acrid-smelling chemical to each and replaced the lids before lugging them back to the area of the castle which had been designated as the lavatory. These crumbling half-height walls had apparently been a stable block, many hundreds of years ago. *All that progress we made*, Hollis thought, smiling wryly, *all those years and all those technological advances, and now look at us: shitting in buckets behind a wall and pissing into a narrow, foot-deep trench lined with stones for drainage. It's like the last five hundred years never happened.*

As basic as these conditions were, Hollis recognised the importance of maintaining good sanitation – in fact, it had become something of an obsession. After what had happened to Ellie and Anita back at the flats he'd taken it upon himself to take charge of this side of things. Not that anyone else had been vying with him to take on this particular responsibility, but their indifference didn't bother him. It didn't matter what had caused the disease which killed the two girls; they couldn't afford to take any similar risks here. No one was trapped inside the castle, but getting in or out of the place wasn't easy – it was practically impossible on foot while the dead outside still retained even the slightest spark of reanimation – and any such outbreak within these walls would inevitably be catastrophic. He couldn't bear to think about such a disease running rampant through these close confines . . .

Hollis was preoccupied with his dark thoughts when he returned to the cesspit. It had been almost a day since his last visit here, and he decided to spend some time spreading a little soil and lime to try and neutralise the steadily worsening smell. He was too tired to do it by hand – strange, he thought, how the less he did, the more tired he felt these days – so he started up a small digger and drove it over, picked up a scoop of earth from the huge pile left from digging out the pit, then emptied it over the small lake of waste, spreading it as best he could.

After repeating the operation a couple more times, Hollis left the digger running and threw a couple of shovelfuls of the pungent-smelling white powder onto the pit, then returned to the digger to drop another couple of scoops of soil. He swung the arm around, picked up more dirt, then swung back again – and smacked it straight into someone walking the other way.

The force of the impact knocked the person off his feet and he collapsed to the ground, clutching his right arm and screaming in agony.

As Hollis jumped from the digger to help, he realised it was Steve Morecombe, and as he watched, Steve tried to get back up, but his foot slipped off the edge of the pit and sank into the foul-smelling waste. In his haste to get Steve away from the edge of the cesspit Hollis grabbed him under his injured arm, which made him scream twice as loud and thrash out with his good arm.

'Get off me, you fucking idiot!' he railed as Hollis staggered back. People pushed past, there before Hollis had even realised they were close: Jas and Kieran first, closely followed by Howard and Zoe, then Jackson.

'What the hell happened here?' Jackson demanded, pushing his way to the front of the small crowd.

'*He* happened,' Steve yelled at Hollis. He couldn't move

either arm to point. The pain was excruciating. He was drenched with sweat and he felt horribly nauseous, as if he was about to faint. Zoe crouched down next to him and gingerly tried to examine his arm. He was wearing layers of thick winter clothing, but they couldn't disguise the unnatural angle of the limb. She looked into his face, overawed by the obvious seriousness of his injury. This was way past her limited first-aid skills. Steve's eyelids fluttered.

'It's shock, I think,' she said, and as Jackson took Steve's weight and lowered him onto his back he could see Steve was drifting in and out of consciousness. Zoe looked up into the crowd of useless faces staring back at her. 'Well, don't just stand there,' she shouted, 'someone go and get Sue!'

In the melting pot of meagre skills and redundant past-life occupations within the castle community, Sue Preston had unwillingly found herself promoted to chief medical officer. She'd trained as a nurse, though she'd only been working part-time for the last five years, but she still had more medical knowledge than the rest of them put together. Even as Zoe sent people off to find her, Sue arrived at the scene, summoned by the racket.

Hollis was still trying to get back to help Steve. He was distraught, almost crying. Howard tried to pull him away from the others.

'It was an accident,' Hollis said, overcome with guilt. There were tears in his eyes, and his voice was quieter than ever. 'Honest, Howard – I didn't even know he was there. I just turned around and . . .'

'I know,' Howard said, trying to lead him back towards the caravans.

Jas caught Howard's arm as he passed him. 'Probably best to keep him away from the machinery from now on,' he said to Howard. 'Don't want to risk anything like this happening again.'

'Bloody hell, Jas,' Howard said, 'he didn't mean for it to happen, you know!'

'It was an *accident*,' Hollis said, shaking himself free from Howard's grip.

'Well, we can't afford to have accidents any more—'

'I know that! Christ, you make it sound like I did it on purpose—'

'I don't know what happened here,' Jas continued, as if Hollis had never spoken, 'but there are a couple of things I *do* know. First, you can hardly hear anything any more, so we can't risk having you operating machinery and—'

'I *can* hear,' Hollis protested. 'There's nothing wrong with my hearing—'

'Spare me the bullshit,' Jas sighed. 'You're lip-reading. I know it must be hard for you, but it doesn't take an idiot to work it out. Christ, I stood right behind you last night trying to get your attention and you didn't hear me.'

'It's not that bad . . .'

'We all know that's not true.'

'Come on, mate,' Howard said, trying to drag Hollis away, but Hollis again shook him off.

'There's no reason why I can't do anything that—'

'There's a damn good reason why you can't be trusted with anything like this any more,' Jas interrupted, pre-empting Hollis' protest. 'Thing is, if Steve's arm is as badly damaged as it looks, then he's fucked if no one here can fix it – no NHS any more, no hospitals, remember? Even a little slip can become a big problem these days, and that's not a little slip, is it?'

'He's not stupid, Jas,' Howard said, speaking up for Hollis. 'He understands—'

'Thing is, I'm not going to risk *my* neck because your friend here likes playing with diggers.'

'I *wasn't* playing,' Hollis tried to interject, but they both ignored him.

'He was *working* here,' Howard said. 'He was keeping this place in order because no one else ever does. If it wasn't for Hollis slopping out, we'd all be ankle-deep in shit by now.'

'Not interested,' Jas said, making it clear the discussion was over. 'He stays away from machinery, right?'

'Who are you to say who does what? If he—'

Zoe looked up disapprovingly at the raised voices as Sue tried to treat Steve's arm. Harte tried to position himself between Jas and Howard, intending to try to defuse the tension, but Jas simply turned his back on him, blocking him.

'You keep him away from machinery,' he said again, pointing threateningly at Hollis, 'or I will. Understand?'

NINETY-EIGHT DAYS
SINCE INFECTION

17

Almost an entire week of bitter frosts followed, and beyond the walls of Cheetham Castle the dead continued their slow, relentless advance, impeded only by the extreme weather. Most mornings they started frozen solid, slowly defrosted as the temperature climbed until by mid-afternoon some had regained the ability to move, only for them to be halted by the ice a scant few hours later when the sun disappeared below the horizon.

The body of a teenage boy continued to stagger forward. He'd been on the verge of beginning a new chapter in his life when he'd died; he'd just left school, and was about to start his first proper job, working as an office gopher for a firm of solicitors. He'd been eighteen years old. Now he was barely even recognisable as human. He'd lost almost all of his clothing after weeks of dragging himself tirelessly around the dead world. What was left of his innards had putrefied and slowly seeped out through the various holes where his flesh had rotted away. The remaining gunk froze each night, leaving tiny brown icicles of decay. And yet, despite the appalling condition of the dead boy, he still continued to move towards the castle whenever he was able to free himself from the grip of the ice, oblivious to his gradual demise. How much – if anything – he understood of what was happening was impossible to tell, but his ceaseless fascination with the faint light and noise made by the survivors remained undiminished.

The general mood within the castle was unexpectedly lifted one evening when heavy snow began to fall. By next morning the ground was covered in a layer several inches deep, and when the survivors looked outside the castle walls, for the first time in months, everything appeared relatively normal. Where yesterday there had been hordes of partially frozen, partially animated and intermittently incessant cadavers, today there was nothing but white: pure, clean and unspoiled.

From the top of the gatehouse, Lorna felt like she was looking at a Christmas card from long ago, and it made her think about Christmas itself: her head began to fill with carols and seasonal songs, and she could think of nothing else to block them out and shut out the pain. It felt wrong even remembering Christmas, like an unspoken taboo. The end of December was only a couple of weeks away, but there would be no celebrations this year, no presents, no gorging on food and drink, just a hell of a lot of quiet introspection and, no doubt, vastly increased amounts of private hurt for each of them to deal with.

When she went back down, Lorna found almost everyone crammed together into the classroom to escape the cold. Jackson was talking to Jas and several of the others. Over the last week he'd made a conscious effort to lay off the future planning and sermonising, instead concentrating on just getting them all through to a time when such subjects might be discussed freely again.

The arrival of the rescued group from the hotel had started to put an unforeseen strain on the castle group's resources. Jackson, both thinking ahead and also trying to appease Jas, had been planning a supply run for the last few days, and this morning's snow made a run a much more viable proposition. 'Remember how the snow used to slow us down?' he'd said to Lorna earlier that morning; 'it'll be a hundred times worse for the dead.' As long as there was snow on the ground, they had a bigger physical advantage than usual over the corpses outside, and without the benefit of long-range weather forecasts – or *any* weather forecasts, for that matter – it made sense to take advantage of the conditions now, while they lasted.

Lorna couldn't help thinking she'd heard this all before, back at the hotel: *one last massive trip out for supplies to see us through* . . .

Driver was uncharacteristically animated, and he wasn't happy.

'What's up with him?' Lorna asked Caron as she sat down next to her.

'He doesn't want to go out,' she replied.

'But why me?' Driver said, and obviously not for the first time.

Jackson looked to the heavens. 'The clue's in your nickname, mate. You're the most experienced driver we've got. We need someone who knows what they're doing behind the wheel. Do you have any other pointless questions?'

'There must be someone else who can go.'

'No,' Jackson said, remaining unfailingly calm, 'you can. Listen, for all your faults – of which there are more than a few – there's no one else can drive anything as big as a lorry as well as you. And with the snow and everything else out there, I really need your experience.'

'Thanks for the compliment and all that, but I'm not going,' he said defiantly.

'Yes, you are,' Jas interrupted.

'Says who?'

'Says me—'

'Driver,' Jackson said, talking over Jas, trying to defuse some of the unnecessary tension Jas' belligerence was clearly causing, 'I know you better than you think. I know exactly what you do and what you don't do around here. I know you spend most of your time sleeping in the back of your bus when you tell us you're out working on the vehicles. I've seen you wiping grease on your hands and trousers to make it look like you've been grafting for hours.'

'I'm not the only one,' he protested. 'There are plenty of other folks around here who skive. What about—?'

'You're right,' Jackson interrupted, 'I know you're right, but my point is this: right now we need to play to all our strengths, and your strength is driving, so you're going out with us.'

'Bollocks to that,' Driver said, remaining unimpressed.

'Can't you just give the bloke a break?' Harte said from across the room. 'I'll drive the bloody lorry if it's that big a deal.'

'The decision's made,' Jackson said calmly. 'Let's just get it done.'

'Did you not hear me?' Harte protested.

'He heard you okay,' Jas said, 'did you not hear him? We play to our strengths. Driver drives; Jackson, Kieran, you, me, Mark and Will go out to loot.'

Harte slumped back into his seat. There was no point arguing further.

Caron, sitting next to him, leaned across to speak to Lorna. 'Surprised you're not going,' she whispered.

'Don't even go there,' Lorna said, crossing her arms defensively.

'Why?'

'Because as far as Jas is concerned,' she said angrily, ' "playing to your strengths" means keeping us "girls" safely locked away in here to cook and clean up for the blokes. It's a bloody joke.'

'What about Jackson? He seems a more broad-minded kind of chap.'

'You think? I spoke to him too, because bodies or no bodies, I'd actually love to get out of this fucking place for a while.'

'And?'

'And he was as bad as Jas – worse in some ways. He said he doesn't want us girls – me, Zoe and Melanie – taking risks by going out when there're plenty of men who can go.'

'I don't understand,' Caron said, confused.

Lorna sighed. Was Caron being deliberately thick? 'He didn't say as much,' she explained, 'but he's talking about babies. He was on one of his "planning for the future" kicks again.'

'Dirty old bugger.'

'For Christ's sake, Caron, get a grip! He's not interested in any of us in *that* way; he's just trying to protect *the stock*.'

'That's disgusting!'

'Yes – and that's how it is. But I'll tell you something: if he thinks I'm going to sit here, pick a mate or two from this bunch of losers and pop out a kid or five on demand, then he's got another bloody think coming. Fuck that; I'll be over the wall and out of here before any bloke dares lay a bloody finger on me.'

18

The two-vehicle convoy crunched steadily through the ice and snow with an almost arrogant lack of speed. Kieran was up ahead, driving the digger, with Jackson along for the ride, while Driver followed behind, grudgingly steering the group's largest vehicle through the carnage. It was a box lorry, and had enough room for several tonnes of food – if they could find that much. Jackson had acquired it shortly after arriving at the castle. It had originally been used for furniture deliveries, and both sides had advertised a happy family relaxing on their newly delivered sofas before someone – he didn't know who – had painted over them with white emulsion a couple of weeks back.

Jas and Ainsworth sat in the cab with Driver, and Harte and Will were in the back with the roller shutter half-open. They were all watching the world around them, their eyes wide, disbelieving. This was the first trip outside the castle walls for Mark and Will since they'd arrived there, and the difference between what they were seeing now and what they remembered was stark, almost impossible to comprehend.

As they drove further away from the castle they were able to increase their speed slightly, for the hordes of bodies which had gravitated to their base, drawn there by the survivors' disproportionately loud noise, had left the rest of the surrounding area looking reassuringly empty. The blanket of snow helped perpetuate the illusion. They were forced to stop occasionally, when the route of the road ahead was unclear; when that happened Jas ordered Harte and Will out of the back of the lorry to shovel away the ice and the frozen once-human detritus which now seemed to cover the world.

Kieran was the only local, and after consultation Jackson had decided to aim for Chadwick, a medium-sized port town, and the nearest place of any substance in the immediate vicinity. Harte sat in the back of the lorry, holding onto a securing strap fixed to the wall, and as he watched the empty world pass him by he couldn't help comparing their journey with the scavenging trip into Bromwell with Jas, Hollis and the others, just before their incarceration at the besieged hotel had begun. That had been the last time he'd been anywhere even remotely urban. Now, once he looked past the visible devastation, he found himself filled with wholly unexpected optimism at what he was seeing as they approached Chadwick. He tried to explain it to Will, but he just sat there, his face covered with a scarf, staring into space and saying nothing.

They passed bodies on the way into the town – why they were still there, Harte couldn't even begin to hazard a guess, but that didn't matter; like the rest of the dead they'd seen today, these were completely motionless, standing like statues, trapped in bizarre poses. One looked as if it had stopped mid-stride; another was slumped against a wall like a drunk. Some were standing in the middle of open spaces, almost looking like standing stones. A clot of dead passengers were frozen in position inside a bus outside a station. They'd formed a bizarre plug of flesh at the driver's end, as if they'd all been rushing to get off when first death then the ice had caught them.

Kieran led them around the centre of town so they were approaching the port from the south, along the seafront. The snow was thinner here, and those bodies they could see looked substantially more decayed, both due, Harte assumed to the salty air eating through everything. The ocean on his left looked calm and inviting, especially compared with the carnage so prevalent everywhere else. Apart from the beached wreck of a huge passenger ferry, tilted over at an almost impossible angle and showing the first signs of corrosion, it all looked deceptively normal. Sunlight slipped through the gaps between increasingly broken clouds overhead, casting random shadows on the surface of the water.

The lorry stopped, and Harte heard Jas yell for him and Will to help. He grabbed his shovel and jumped down, then jogged up the road to see what the problem was. He was relieved to see it wasn't anything major – just a build-up of ice the truck couldn't quite get through. He and Will started digging, and when progress wasn't fast enough for his liking, Jas jumped down from the cab and pitched in too. The noise of their three shovels scraping along the tarmac filled the air.

'Pretty grim, eh, Jas?' Harte said as they worked, but Jas said nothing, just made momentary eye-contact, then returned his full attention back to digging. He looked apprehensive.

'That'll do,' he said quietly when enough of the street had been cleared, and he climbed back up to his seat. As Harte walked around to the rear of the lorry he looked around at their desolate surroundings. He'd never been to Chadwick before, but he could picture what it must have been like before all of this happened. He imagined it packed with people last summer, and then thought how unreal it still felt that those same people were almost certainly all dead now, struck down a scant few weeks after returning home.

The main seafront was now a desperately sad affair. The numerous cafés and amusement arcades, many with snow-covered children's rides outside, looked abandoned. On the other side of the road was a funfair, with its distinctive outlines of the helter-skelter and carousels, now blanketed in snow but with hints of their brightly painted surfaces peeking out. Once again Harte found the extent of the visible devastation humbling. Nothing had been left untouched. It made him start to question the point of staying at Cheetham Castle – were they actually doing anything positive by being there, or were they just burying their heads in the sand, trying to hide themselves away from the full impact of all this decay?

He jumped back onto the lorry as it pulled away, and was relieved when Driver turned left and drove away from the sea and into the town. Up ahead, the digger rumbled along, its scoop lowered, clearing away the icy remains that filled the main road. The sun disappeared behind a cloud and the sudden low winter light combined with the shadows from the buildings which now surrounded them made the dead world look increasingly frightening and bizarre. More of the random corpses were trapped here like ice-covered statues, caught in a literal freeze-frame.

As the digger churned through the increasingly slushy snow with ease Harte stared down at the mounds on either side of the road. Broken bones were clearly visible in amongst the grey detritus, which made him feel how misguided the whole human race had been about its importance in the overall scheme of things. You had only to look around now to see: when it came down to it, mankind had been discarded, just like the empty bottles and fast food wrapping that normally littered any street in any town. Humankind had been chucked onto the great landfill site along with everything else. In time, he thought, even this will be gone. When the snow's melted and spring comes, there will be green shoots everywhere – the aftermath of man. Weeds will grow through what's left of the bodies, forcing their way between paving slabs and through cracks in walls. Wild animals will roam free, making dens and nests in empty houses. In a couple of years, much of what he could see now would have disappeared. There was a part of him that actually wished he could see that.

The sudden hissing of brakes brought his depressed daydreaming to an abrupt end. He leaned out and peered around the side of the lorry and saw that they'd pulled up outside a small mall, The Minories, according to the signs. It didn't look very inviting, with its bleached-out posters and knocked-about window displays. The icicles hanging from every ledge and sill were all dripping, though some looked big enough to cause real damage to anyone unfortunate enough to be underneath them when they fell. Imagine that, he thought, slipping too easily into daydream mode again: surviving everything they had, only to end up getting speared by a bloody icicle.

Now that both engines had stopped, the silence was overpowering. He shivered.

Jackson called for the others to gather around the digger. 'Right,' he said, 'the plan's simple. Kieran says there's a few useful shops in here, and the more we can get in one place the better. So let's get inside and strip it clean. We don't stop until this lorry is as full as we can get it, okay? Let's make sure this is the last trip out we have to make until winter's over. Got it?'

There were a few mumbles, but little positive reaction. Harte looked around at the faces surrounding him. Strange to think that just an hour or so ago they'd all been full of bravado and bullshit, almost to a man.

'Got it,' Kieran said, feeling obliged to at least say something.

'Our priority is food and water,' Jackson continued unnecessarily.

Christ, Harte thought, *as if we need this spelling out to us*.

'Fuel, medicines, clothing, bedding . . . all that kind of stuff, okay?' He stopped talking momentarily and looked past the others at Jas, who was hanging back. 'Everything all right, Jas?'

Jas didn't answer, but remained staring at the entrance to the mall. Will Bayliss, his scarf now lowered but much of his face still hidden behind an unruly mop of blond hair, suddenly saw what Jas had seen. 'Fuck me,' he said, 'would you look at that—'

'Bloody hell,' Kieran muttered, unable to hide his unease when he saw it too.

Jackson turned around to see what was happening behind him, just in time to see a lone body stumbling up through the interior of the mall, coming steadily into the light as if it was coming into focus. It slammed against the glass with a heavy slap, then staggered back into the shadows before coming at the door again.

'I thought you said they'd all be frozen,' Jas said nervously.

'Well, most of them still are,' Jackson replied quickly, gesturing at the statues down the street. 'But come on, how naïve are you? There was always going to be a few of them active, wasn't there? The ones trapped in buildings as long as they've been dead – it's not going to be tropical in there, but it'll be a damn sight warmer than it is out here.'

The corpse approached the glass again, even slower this time, almost as if it had learned from its initial mistake. Harte walked towards the entrance, studying the creature inside. There were several more of them, emerging from the darkness.

'They've been protected in there,' Harte said. 'There's no wind or rain indoors, and probably fewer insects too.'

'Should we be doing this?' Will asked. 'I mean, is this a good idea? What if they—?'

'This doesn't change anything,' Jackson said quickly, talking over him to silence him. 'It just makes things a little more interesting, that's all. If we're careful and we take our time, we'll be okay.'

'I'm not sure . . .'

'Then fuck off and start walking home,' Kieran said.

Jackson walked around to the back of the lorry. He climbed inside, then re-emerged carrying a sledgehammer. The others watched him. No one moved. An icy gust of wind whipped down the otherwise silent street, but no one even flinched. All eyes were on Jackson as he marched over to the front of the mall, his boots crunching through the snow, and shook the door. When it wouldn't open he swung the hammer around repeatedly, each time smashing a different pane of glass. The nearest corpse was showered with shards, and then took a hammer-blow right to the centre of its chest, sending it flying back into the darkness. Jackson turned his attention to the locks, and began battering the top, bottom and middle of the doorframe, quickly buckling it out of shape. The mangled door scraped along the ground as he shoved it open, then he quickly stepped back and waited. A second corpse walked towards the light, tripping over the torso of the first and landing on all fours at Jackson's feet. Before it had a chance to move he attacked it, slamming the hammer down onto the back of its skull, squashing it almost paper-thin. The force, speed and precision of his attack were so effective that the creature remained exactly where it was, hunched at his feet as if it were praying for mercy.

There were more of them coming. Jackson looked back over his shoulder at Jas and the others, then he turned back and swung the hammer around again, shattering the pelvis of another cadaver. 'Let's move,' he ordered. 'I'm not doing this all by myself.'

The seven men – Driver included, despite his frantic attempts to stay behind the wheel – were standing in the middle of the mall by a dried-up fountain, waiting for orders. The sun had broken through again outside. There was a glass ceiling directly above them, but what was left of the snow prevented anything more than a fraction of the usual morning light from getting inside. There were bodies trapped in some of the shops around them, workers who'd died before trading had begun on the last day of their lives. Now they watched the living, clawing at the glass to be released, some even trying to bite at the windows, all of them desperate to get out and attack.

'We should split into two groups,' Jackson suggested. 'I'll take Kieran, Driver and Harte. Jas, you take the others.'

Jas didn't move. He was staring into a newsagent's, where a dead woman wearing a red and white checked apron tripped around the remains of a trashed window display, falling, then picking herself back up, falling again, then getting up . . . repeating the same actions, again and again.

Mark Ainsworth, as nervous as hell and desperate to get out, made the first move, but as he approached the door of the shop the woman became even more animated. She lurched forward, then took a few unsteady steps back.

'Go on, then,' Will said, egging him on, but he stayed back with Jas. Mark didn't move, and neither did Jas, and at last Will barged past them both. 'For fuck's sake, it can't be that difficult,' he snarled. 'She's *dead*.'

He shoved the door open and grabbed at the woman as she came towards him. She managed to duck away from him at first, more through luck than anything else, but she couldn't match his strength or his speed. He caught her by the arm, then pulled her closer and wrapped his gloved hand tightly around her neck. He spun her around through almost a complete circle, then threw her back up against the window and let her drop. She slid down the dirty glass, leaving behind a thick trail of brown-black gore. Jas stepped over her sprawled legs and began clearing the shelves.

Harte, still standing by the fountain, was watching events unfold in the newsagent's when he realised he was alone. Jackson and the others were breaking into a small supermarket, but as they smashed their way inside, a group of bodies were readying themselves to fight their way out. As they crowded on the other side of the glass it almost looked as if they were squabbling among themselves, baying for blood. He took a deep breath and readied himself for the fight.

19

The two groups of men worked with frantic speed to clear out their allotted stores. Everyone adopted the same simple strategy: break in, deal with any corpses still strong enough to cause problems, then strip the shelves. Once the initial trepidation at being this close to active bodies again had dissipated, the hard work began to feel unexpectedly cathartic. Being properly occupied like this – doing something worthwhile for once – was a welcome break from the norm.

When they stopped and regrouped at the truck almost two hours later, their nervousness immediately returned. Time had passed quickly while they'd been working, and the situation outside had changed.

'That one's moved,' Will said, pointing at a corpse lying in the middle of the street. Harte knew he was right; he couldn't remember having seen it at all before. And as they watched, it slowly moved its legs, digging in with its feet, and half-crawled, half-shuffled a few inches further. It was so badly decayed that it was difficult to make out any real detail. The damn thing looked like it had been dunked in tar.

'So what if it has moved?' Kieran said. 'The temperature's rising and they're thawing out. We knew this would happen.'

Harte stood still and listened. Kieran was right; the bitter cold of early morning had eased and the intermittent dripping he'd heard earlier had now become constant. Water was dribbling down the fronts of buildings and running into the drains. The creaking of thawing ice was no longer occasional. Most ominously, Harte could see slight movements from some of the mannequin-like frozen corpses: the twitch of a finger here, a slight shuffle forward there, the roll of a dead eye . . .

'We should think about getting out of here,' Jackson said, hauling another box of food up onto the back of the lorry.

'Not yet,' Jas said, surprising everyone. He'd been quiet since they'd arrived in Chadwick. His voice was lacking in emotion now, but not intent. He wasn't throwing out a suggestion to the rest of the group for them to think about and discuss; he was giving an order.

'Bollocks,' Will said, 'let's go. The lorry's half-full. We've got enough to last us weeks.'

'The lorry is half-empty, and we need to get more,' Jas said. 'I'm not coming back out here again.'

'I'm with Jas,' Kieran said. 'Another half-hour's not going to kill us. We're here now.'

'We should go,' Driver said, already heading back towards the cab. 'They're thawing out – I do not want to be here when they're fully defrosted.'

As if on cue, one of the cadavers nearest to Kieran managed to break its shoulder free and move an arm up towards its face, swinging it up in an awkward, juddering movement, almost like a puppet, then dropping it down again.

Kieran didn't flinch. He looked directly at Jackson and Driver, then shoved the body over. It fell backwards, clipping a bollard on its way down and snapping its right arm completely off. He picked up Jackson's hammer from where he'd left it leaning against the side of the lorry and thumped it down hard into the dead body's frustratingly expressionless face.

'Is this what you're scared of?' he asked, looking at Driver then Will. 'Get over yourselves, for fuck's sake. Jas is right, we should do this right now we've started.'

'Come on,' Harte said, 'is it really worth it? Seriously? Like Jackson said, we've probably got enough stuff.'

'Probably isn't good enough,' Jas said.

'Bollocks,' Driver said. 'I'm going.' He hauled himself up into his cab.

Kieran walked around and stood in front of the lorry. 'Where're you going to go, then? You'll have to try backing up 'cause you can't go forward, can you?' He dangled the keys to the digger, which was blocking the road.

'There are two more decent-sized stores in there we should clear out before we leave,' Jas said, 'and Iceland, and a camping place. We clear them, *then* we go.'

For a moment no one moved. Driver remained in his seat. Harte took a very definite step out of the way, as did Mark and Will. Jackson felt like volunteers had just been asked to step forward, and everyone else had stepped back, volunteering him by default. His choice – and it suddenly felt like it *was* his choice – was stark: fight with Jas and Kieran, or fight with the dead.

The entire town was silent, save for the ice melting and the trickling of water running down the drains.

'Okay,' he said. 'Two more stores, then we're leaving.'

By the time they'd managed to crowbar their way into the Iceland store they could see several more bodies moving slowly but freely outside, gravitating towards the lorry and the mall entrance. Metal creaked and glass cracked and more of the dead staggered closer as Harte forced the door. He held it open as the unsteady corpse of a store worker lurched forward and fell straight into Jackson's path. He caved its face in with his sledgehammer and it dropped at his feet, slumped against the wall in an untidy sitting position, dark blood slowly seeping down over its uniform.

This particular shop was uncomfortably dark, the darkest place they'd been today. Stores like this always used to be permanently drenched in harsh white light and the shadows felt unnatural, somehow wrong.

'What's the point of coming in here?' Driver asked nervously. The floor was covered in water, and the contents of the freezers that filled the place had long since deteriorated into a mush of soggy cardboard and spoiled food.

'There're cans and packets on the shelves above,' Jas said, 'and there's an aisle of drink back there. Clear that one out first.'

The men began to move with renewed energy, buoyed up by both the prospect of booze and the thought of finally leaving Chadwick and returning to the castle. Harte left the rest of them and made his way to the back of the store, looking for the loading bay and stockrooms, where there was often more food stored in easy-to-shift crates. Another dead shop worker lurched at him from the shadows, taking him by surprise, but he caught it mid-attack, then dragged it out in the open and fuelled by tension, began pounding it with his fist until he'd reduced its face to an almost unrecognisable mess.

It was only when it stopped moving and he dropped it that he even bothered to look at what it was he'd just destroyed. Even through the rot and the damage he'd inflicted, he could tell that the thing at his feet had once been a young girl: what was left of her hair was still tied up in a ponytail and under her overalls she'd been wearing the kind of clothes the girls who'd hung around outside the school where he'd taught used to wear. That unexpected connection with the past took him by surprise for a moment, and made him stop and think about what he'd become. This time last year he was teaching kids like this, trying to help them grow into responsible adults. Now here he was, beating the shit out of one of them as he looted food from a mall.

He shook the thought away and continued walking until he found a back door leading into an outside delivery area shared with several of the neighbouring units. He could hear water dripping all around him, amplified by the sudden closeness of this small area. There was a barrier across the road up ahead, and everything around him felt unexpectedly calm. This was a safe place, he realised: *an inaccessible place.*

If only they'd found it earlier – it would have made looting a lot easier.

'*Get it off me!*'

Harte heard Will screaming and immediately ran back to the others, to find Will had been caught off-guard as he'd gone out through the mall to the lorry. A trio of freshly thawed corpses coming the other way had literally knocked him off his feet, and now they were crowding around him, attacking him in unison. Mark and Kieran managed to get him free, but as they helped him up and collected the supplies he'd dropped, even more of the dead began to approach, slipping and skidding through the slush both inside and outside the mall. Though they were barely able to stay upright, and though their capacity was clearly limited, their intentions were clear. They grabbed at Will as he tried to scramble away. He was soaked through, and covered with defrosted gore.

Outside the building, the lorry was surrounded. Driver had never been happier to be behind the wheel. He started the engine as he waited for the others to load their last armfuls of supplies and get on board. Harte was last on, after weaving his way around the sluggish corpses converging on the lorry. He squeezed into a gap in the back next to Will, then hammered on the side to let Driver know he could start moving.

As Harte looked down into the sea of decay he tried to calm himself. He'd been in situations far worse than this, with many more of the dead to contend with. The panic that he was feeling now was a gut reaction born of the nightmares he'd previously faced.

Driver accelerated and the engine whined with effort, but the lorry was overloaded and the wheels couldn't get a grip. It wasn't going anywhere. Harte could hear Jas screaming at him to get moving, but there was nothing Driver could do; he accelerated again and this time the back end of the unwieldy vehicle slipped in the slush, sliding to one side but still not moving forward. Harte stood up and looked out.

Up ahead, Kieran had started the digger and turned it around, but what did he do first – clear the snow, clear the dead, or try and help move the lorry?

'Get something under the wheels,' Jas yelled, and Jackson appeared at the back, smacking the nearest corpses around the head with his shovel, then using its blade to decapitate any that tried to get up again. Harte jumped back down to help. He'd counted as many as forty corpses coming towards them now, and now there were more, approaching from all angles, spurred on by the increasing activity and noise. He wondered if the dead were somehow picking up on the sudden panic in the air. Was the survivors' frantic, barely coordinated activity actually exciting them, increasing their desire to break free from the ice?

While Jackson was dealing with the nearest corpses and Kieran was doing what he could with the digger, Harte concentrated on trying to clear the slush away from around the lorry's wheels. Mark followed Harte's lead and began to clear around the front tyres, and Jas reluctantly jumped back down onto the street himself. It quickly became clear to Hart that Jas was panicking. For all his aggression and the authority he frequently tried to impose upon the group, it was obvious that he was losing his nerve.

'Get that fucking digger over here,' he yelled, his voice hoarse. 'We need space – there's too many of them.'

Kieran tried to do as he was told, but he hit a bollard which had been hidden by the snow and now he couldn't get through. He tried reversing, but he was wedged in, and all the digger's noise and stop-start movement was doing was attracting more and more of the dead, who were emerging from the shadows all around, dragging themselves from hitherto hidden places, the icy bonds which had previously held them captive weakening almost by the second.

As fast as Jackson was getting rid of the corpses, more

were arriving. Harte wondered if he was the only one who could see what was happening: all their panic and bluster was directly responsible for making their situation worse. Even if Driver was able to get the truck moving, and if Kieran managed to free the digger and get out of the way, there was a very real danger that the sheer mass of dead flesh now advancing towards them might be enough to block the road and stop them moving forward. All the bodies were being channelled in their direction.

He glanced up at Jas, fighting near the front of the vehicle, noting the anger and desperation in his face, the effort he was having to exert just to stay alive, and he was immediately reminded of the time they'd spent trapped in the hotel. And in that split-second he asked himself if being at the castle was really any better: different walls, a few different faces, but the same shit, and the same problems.

But it still had to be better than being stuck out here, didn't it? Harte really wasn't sure any more.

He finished digging out the near wheel, then chucked his shovel at a dripping corpse which had him locked in its sights, hitting it just above the pelvis and folding it in two. He checked the pockets of his thick winter jacket, patting himself up and down until he found what he was looking for: his lighter. He grabbed hold of Mark and spun him around, ducking as Mark went for him until he realised it was Harte and not one of the dead.

'Tell Driver to kill the engine,' Harte ordered. 'All this noise is just making things worse. Get everyone on the lorry, get out of sight and wait until it's clear. I'm going to draw them away.'

'But how—?' Mark started, but Harte was already gone, barging his way through the mass of corpses at the back of the truck until he ducked down and disappeared.

Ainsworth sighed and did as he was told, working his way through the chaos to get close to Driver.

*

Harte pounded down the road, trying to keep his balance in the slush as he dodged the outstretched arms of a corpse in a crusty, blood-soaked blue hoodie. He veered over to the right, running towards the petrol station he'd spotted when they'd turned off the seafront. 'All I need to do,' he panted to himself, 'is give them something else to focus on.'

Way behind him the two engines had been silenced, but he could still hear those fucking idiots arguing, Jas yelling pointless instructions at the others, and Jackson shouting equally pointless things back. Fucking morons.

There were two cars by the pumps on the petrol station forecourt, one facing in either direction, and a tanker parked a short distance away. Harte was distracted momentarily by the violently animated and remarkably well-preserved remains of the female passenger of a red Audi and by the wild thumping of an equally well-preserved dead man wearing a gore-soaked polo shirt bearing the logo of the petrol company who was trapped behind the thick kiosk glass. He grabbed the handle of the nearest pump – he could feel the coldness of the metal even through his thick glove – and squeezed. The dribble of fuel he managed to extract he spilled down the front of the pump, and then he waved it over the back of the Audi. He repeated his actions at the next pump, and the next, then he ran over to the tanker. On the blind side he saw with relief a wide hosepipe was still connected to an inlet valve. He had no way of telling whether the tanker was empty or full, but he could still hope. He forced the valve open and pulled the hose away, relieved at the sudden overpowering stench of fuel.

I just wish this would all stop for a while.

Moving fast and determined that he wouldn't talk himself out of it, he pulled off his right glove with his teeth, reached into his pocket and pulled out his lighter. He flicked the wheel—

*

The explosion was deafening, the heat and light it produced strong enough to make it feel as if the sun had burst through the clouds again. There was a stunned silence inside the lorry. No one moved. Jackson watched from the back of the digger as many of the dead began to turn and shuffle away, almost unbearably slowly, but moving away nonetheless.

'What the fuck did he just do?' Mark said quietly, watching from the back of the lorry with Jas and Will. 'I swear, he didn't say anything to me about blowing the place up.'

Jas stared at the fireball. As if hypnotised, virtually all of the dead were now stumbling towards the flames, the men in the lorry instantly forgotten. He scanned the street ahead, but there was no sign of Harte.

'What do we do?' Will asked. 'We can't just leave him.'

'Don't see we have any option,' Jas replied. 'No one could have survived that. What was the stupid fucker thinking?'

He was about to shout for Driver and Kieran to try moving again, to take full advantage of the distraction while it lasted, when Jackson sprinted past, hurtling towards the burning petrol station. Even from that distance he had to shield himself from the heat. The massive explosion had been devastating: debris was scattered all around, smoking chunks of matter surrounded by corresponding pools where the remaining snow had been melted away. The dead paid him little attention, even when they were close enough to attack. A few of them were burning, ignited by the intense heat even before they'd reached the flames, and continuing to move until there was nothing left of them. With a deep, stomach-churning creak, the forecourt roof collapsed, crushing everything below and fanning the flames still further. Roiling clouds of toxic black smoke billowed up into the sky and drifted away.

Jackson tried to get closer, but the heat was too intense. As the lorry pulled level with him Jas jumped down and pulled him away, keen to get started back. For the briefest of moments the two men squared off against each other.

'Leave it,' Jas said. 'Harte's had it. We need to get out of here.'

'But what if he—?'

'He's dead, and we will be too if we don't move it.' He marched back to the lorry, conversation over.

Jackson stayed there a moment longer, trying to take in everything that had just happened. His eyes swept the devastation as more of the dead, now completely unfrozen, staggered around him, focused entirely on the burning petrol station. Behind him, Driver started the lorry again.

'Let's *go*,' Jas yelled, and this time Jackson turned and ran back to the digger, which Kieran had finally managed to manoeuvre around to face the right way. He looked back over his shoulder one last time as they pulled away, long enough to be sure that Driver was finally able to follow. This time, with the road ahead clear, the heavy vehicle moved freely along the slush-covered tarmac.

PART II

ONE HUNDRED
AND ELEVEN DAYS
SINCE INFECTION

20

The helicopter skimmed over the surface of the ocean, the pilot and four passengers quiet and subdued. They were each too wrapped in their own thoughts to talk to anyone else; sharing the feelings they were each experiencing was out of the question for now. The pain they felt coming back here was still too raw, harder than they'd imagined.

This cold, empty, desolate place had been where they'd each lived and loved, where they'd been born and where they'd grown up: the place where their families and friends had been. The place where they'd lived their very best and their very worst days. The place where, somewhere, lay the dust-covered memories of the lives they used to lead and the people they used to be: a soldier, a computer consultant, an outdoor activities instructor, a student . . . What had happened to the world had stripped away everything and left them all the same. Now they were just rank-and-file survivors, nothing more and nothing less than the last of a dying breed, perhaps.

The way they'd lost everything was still impossible to even begin to try and understand. Their normal, relatively comfortable lives had been snatched from them in seconds and there hadn't been a damn thing any of them had been able to do about it, no way of retaliating or reclaiming what they'd lost. Since that first morning they'd been living through an all-consuming nightmare so intense they'd thought they'd never get through it. But they had. Against all the odds – and those odds were considerable – they'd somehow survived and come through to the other side relatively unscathed. On a small, rocky island a short distance off the coast of the mainland they'd begun to forge something resembling normal lives again – nothing like the lives they'd led previously, but still infinitely better than anything they'd thought possible in those first dark, terrifying days after the rest of the world died.

But now, for the first time since leaving, they were heading back, and it was a daunting prospect.

As the ocean below gave way to a once-familiar landscape, they slowly began to talk about what they could see. They flew relatively low, skirting over empty shops and houses, following the route of once-busy roads which were now silent and led nowhere.

'What a fucking mess,' Michael Collins said, barely able to comprehend the scale of the visible devastation below them. He didn't know what he'd expected to see here – he'd purposely tried not to think about it until now – but the reality was humbling. None of the streets were clear, all of them filled with decayed remains, litter which had been picked up and blown on the wind, and other waste which had been abandoned when the bulk of the human race had been brought to an abrupt end last September and accumulated ever since. There had been no clean up. No emergency response. No international aid. Everything was just as it had been left that first morning – a little more rotted, rusted and ruined, that was all.

Richard Lawrence too was struggling to concentrate. He made himself look up, not down, for fear of being distracted by the eerie chaos below. Today more than ever he was feeling the intense pressure of being the group's sole pilot – perhaps even the last pilot left alive anywhere. It was weighing heavily on his shoulders, making him feel as if everything was down to him and him alone, that their continued survival was his sole responsibility. That was a difficult cross to bear. A short shuttle-run from the island to the mainland didn't sound like much, and in the overall scheme of things it wasn't, but the lives of the four people flying with him were in his hands. What if something went wrong? What if something happened and they couldn't make it back to the island? The consequences didn't bear thinking about. Cormansey was so isolated, the people such a small, fragile community – they would struggle to stay alive. That was why they'd come back here today: to collect supplies and to find some alternative transport. The long-term plan had always been for the islanders to become self-sufficient, but that was still a way off. On a practical level they still had a huge amount to learn, and emotionally . . . well, emotionally they hadn't even started. Their new lives were just beginning, but the wreckage of their old lives needed to be sorted out too. A period of adjustment and acceptance was, inevitably, necessary before any of them could hope to start moving on.

Some of the people living on Cormansey had made a more successful start to island life than most, while others seemed to be there almost by default, the ones who'd hidden in the shadows of university buildings, in underground bunkers and airfield control towers, those who'd been propped up and carried along by everyone else. Right place, right time. Michael himself had taken nothing for granted, and he'd worked damn hard to stay alive. He knew he was luckier than most, because he'd already started to rebuild. He had a partner (girlfriend? wife? lover? None of those titles sounded right any more), and his relationship with Emma was the most important thing in his small and increasingly self-contained world. Some of the others had wanted him to stay on Cormansey, not risk this trip back, but he'd insisted. Emma was pregnant – the first pregnancy on the island – and Michael felt duty-bound to provide for his unborn child. He thought about Emma and the baby constantly. He and Emma said nothing to each other – because there was nothing either of them could do to affect the outcome – but they both knew the great risks involved in childbirth in this new world, not just the lack of any medical facilities, decent or otherwise, or the usual concerns. They'd been told about a baby born just after the infection had struck; the poor little thing had lived for only a matter of seconds outside its mother's womb before being killed by the same deadly germ which had wiped out everything else.

Sitting next to Michael in the back of the helicopter were Donna Yorke and Mark Cooper. Emma had often talked about those two, speculating about what a good couple she thought they'd make together. They certainly spent a lot of time in each other's company, and sometimes they even stayed over at each other's houses, but Emma thought that was as far as it had gone. Michael wondered in passing whether they were too scared to admit their feelings. Not that it was any of his business, nor was he particularly concerned. He remembered feeling what a risk he was taking when he and Emma had first become close: island life could be very restrictive if things went wrong. It would be impossible to escape if you fell out with anyone; imagine how awkward it would be for everyone if such a relationship soured. Everyone would have to try and keep their heads down in the midst of any name-calling and blame. Cormansey could feel like a huge, open space when you were alone, walking miles from one house to the next along the silent, traffic-free roads, but you still saw the same few faces every day. Necessity had forced the community to become increasingly close-knit. They all relied on each other, and it had been clear from the outset that their ongoing successful survival would require collective effort. Maybe Donna and Cooper did want to be closer, but right now any commitment was just too big a risk for them to take.

Harry Stayt, sitting next to Richard in the front of the helicopter, was scanning the ground below. 'I think we should stick to the coast,' he said. 'Things look as shitty as ever down there – it's probably not worth risking going any further inland just yet.'

Richard agreed, and as he banked right, taking them back towards the ocean, Michael looked out at the endless expanse of water, the deceptive stillness, the sunlight glinting off the gently rolling waves, and wished they were anywhere but here. He wanted to be home again.

They set down in the next decent-sized port they reached, Richard skilfully manoeuvring the helicopter to land on the roof of a multi-storey car park. He didn't fancy risking his precious machine by leaving it at ground level. Harry continued to scan the area as they descended, ticking boxes on his mental check-list: compact but decent-sized shopping area – *check*; easily accessible marina with plenty of boats still moored there – *check*; a safe, remote place to land – *check*; no vast crowds of bodies baying for their blood – *check*.

'Nice day for it,' he said as he got out of the helicopter and stretched. It was cold, though nowhere near as harsh as it had been recently, and he was thankful for the several layers of insulated winter sports clothing he was wearing underneath. The air quality wasn't too bad up here – not as good as they'd been used to on the island, of course, but bearable nonetheless. He caught the odd trace of the stench of death they were all intimately familiar with, but it was less prevalent than he remembered, and the brisk sea breeze carried it away before it outstayed its welcome.

Michael walked to the edge and peered over the restraining wall into what he presumed had been the town's main shopping street. He and Emma'd once spent a couple of days hiding out on the roof of a car park like this. That had been right at the beginning of their nightmare – one of the worst days of the worst times, just after they'd lost their farmhouse hideout and their friend Carl Henshawe. He tried not to dwell on those memories. They'd been completely lost and directionless back then, with no idea how they were going to survive – or even if they wanted to.

'Everything okay, Mike?' Cooper asked, disturbing his thoughts.

He was glad of the interruption. 'Fine,' he replied, 'just checking out the locals.'

Cooper looked down. There was some stilted movement in the streets below, but nothing in comparison to how it had been. There were just a few of the dead left here now, still restless, still animated, but moving with very little speed.

'Instead of just looking we could actually go down there and get this done,' Harry suggested sarcastically. Michael looked back over his shoulder and saw him leaning against the helicopter, casually cleaning his sword with a piece of cloth. The crazy bugger had made no secret of the fact he'd been itching for a chance to use it again. Michael had often seen him standing in the middle of a field just outside Danver's Lye – the small village at the heart of Cormansey life – practising his swordsmanship like a frustrated martial arts master without any pupils. Jack Baxter was always winding Harry up, asking him if he cut hedges as well, because his needed a trim.

'What do we reckon, then?' Richard asked, returning from the far side of the car park roof, his hands buried deep in his pockets. 'There's a decent-looking marina back there – we should find something suitable there.'

'Sounds like a plan,' Donna agreed. 'Find ourselves a couple of boats, get them loaded up, then get out of here and get back home.'

The five of them walked together down the spiralling access ramp which led to ground level, clambering over the wreck of a plum-coloured Mini with a black and white checked roof which had crashed into the side, blocking the road midway down. Michael rounded the final corner and stepped out onto the street, his pulse racing, feeling an uncomfortably familiar unease he'd not felt since he was last on the mainland. He gripped a crowbar tight, ready to fight, anticipating an attack. Nothing came at him immediately, but the tension didn't reduce. *This doesn't feel right*, he thought. The living were conditioned to expect a battle with the dead now.

'Here we go,' Harry said, quickening his pace and taking the lead, sword in hand. Up ahead, at the far end of a long, straight street otherwise devoid of all movement, a single corpse was approaching. Harry walked towards it purposefully, but he stopped when it was still a short distance away, feeling both curious and disgusted. The deterioration of the dead was remarkable.

In the months since this had all begun, everyone who'd survived had seen more than their fair share of horrific sights. Harry himself remembered the time he'd found a still-moving man who'd been virtually cut in two by a broken plate-glass window, or that child he'd found trapped under the roof of an overturned car, its legs crushed but its arms still thrashing. But those grotesque memories paled in comparison to the creature stumbling towards him now. So badly deformed and decayed was it that he had to wonder whether it had ever been human. This was the stuff of nightmares.

It beggared belief that this thing was even able to keep moving. The clothing had been stripped from the bottom half of its body, exposing spindly legs that looked like brittle tree branches, and a gaping black hole where his genitals had been eaten away by rot. What skin the dead man still had was all dark greens and browns. The bottom of his feet had been worn away where he dragged them along the road; Harry could see the bones sticking out through what was left of the flesh, almost like he could feel his own big toe poking through a hole in his sock. He wished the dead man would stop because the closer he got, the more sickening detail was revealed and the more grotesque he became. His nose had been devoured by decay and insect infestations, which had also combined to alter the shape of his drooling mouth so it now looked like an uneven zigzag rip: a ghastly caricature of a long-gone smile. One of his eyes was completely missing, but the other still moved slightly, as if it were looking around. Though it never settled on anything in particular, it was enough to leave Harry in no doubt that the corpse knew he was there. The skull was covered in gooey clumps where the hair had fallen out, but a few remaining greasy strands were glued across the pock-marked scalp.

Harry took a step forward, but then stopped again, un-nerved. He could see several more creatures in the distance now. He had to force himself to remember that as foul as they looked, the cadavers seemed to be mere shadows now of the vicious enemies he and the others had faced previously.

Without warning the dead man took another step forward and lunged at Harry, who shook off his apathy and shoved it away with his gloved hand. He was surprised by its lack of strength, and how light it was. The corpse staggered and caught its balance, then slowly came forward again. Each movement took it an age.

Harry stood his ground, counting the seconds before it was close enough to attack again. *Christ*, he thought, *we don't even have to run from these things any longer. We can walk away fast enough to escape them.*

'What's the hold-up?' Cooper shouted.

'They're completely fucked,' he yelled back.

At the sound of Harry's voice, the dead man became even more animated, and it was obvious it was desperately trying to move faster, but Harry had finally had enough. He lifted his sword and brought it around. It flashed in the sun as the head dropped from the corpse's shoulders and hit the ground with a wet thump. The rest of the diseased frame started to take a final step forward, then collapsed at Harry's feet.

Normally Harry would have immediately charged at the other corpses moving towards him, but he didn't bother. He was filled with a sudden newfound confidence.

'See that?' he asked as Cooper and the others finally caught up with him.

'Didn't put up much of a fight, did it?' Michael said.

'We can't get too cocky,' Donna warned. 'A couple of

hundred of them will still cause us problems if we let them get too close.'

'You think?' Harry asked. 'I don't reckon there's even a couple of hundred left.'

'You might be right, but I'm not taking any chances.'

Cooper agreed. 'Donna's right. Don't forget yourselves, and don't take anything for granted.'

He led them down towards the marina, stepping over what was left of the decapitated corpse. Their footsteps echoed eerily.

'My dad brought me here when I was about nine,' Richard said, looking around. He was a little older than the others; Michael guessed he was fifty, maybe fifty-five. No one talked much about their ages any more. It seemed irrelevant now. 'He'd just lost his job,' Richard continued, 'and Mum was working all the hours she could, so he brought me and my sister here for a couple of days in the summer holidays.'

'Changed much, has it?' Donna smiled.

'A little. The sea looks the same . . .'

'But everything else is fucked.'

'Pretty much.'

There were several more bodies around them now, and when Michael looked back, he saw that a small crowd was moving in the general direction of the car park where they'd left the helicopter. No doubt they were still reacting to the aircraft's noisy and unexpected arrival. As long as they didn't make too much noise themselves, Michael realised, the dead didn't even seem to notice them – and those that did could easily be avoided. All they had to do was side-step them, or increase their speed slightly.

The car park was close to the town's large, once-busy bus station, a great glass and metal construction that looked like it had been recently built. Harry had come to a stop outside a set of automatic doors – which, thankfully, were now as useless as every other set of automatic doors in the country. He was staring at the appalling sight on the other side of the glass. Inside the station, the concourses were filled with bodies; maybe hundreds more were still trapped on buses and in shelters and waiting rooms.

'It was rush-hour,' Donna said quietly. 'Remember that?'

Michael recalled the daily hell of the rush-hour grind all too well. Like the people who had died here, he'd once had to cram himself into overfull buses and trains to get to and from work each day. He remembered it with a kind of nostalgic fondness now, but another look into that desolate, horrific scene was enough to snap him out of his daze. The interior of this building was a mass grave, with many bodies lying piled on top of each other, and many more still languidly moving through the shadows. Some of them gravitated towards the glass, mouldering hands pawing the windows and doors as if they were trying to attract his attention and get help. The time for that was long gone.

Leaving the others for a moment, Michael walked further around the perimeter of the station, unwillingly captivated by the succession of horrific sights unfolding in front of him. A bus had become trapped in the station exit after hitting the wall on one side and getting wedged in. Now it completely blocked the way out. When he peered inside, he could just make out the sticky mass of putrefied waste, little more than a bone-filled soup, that was all that remained of its passengers after months of constantly grinding against each other in such a confined space. He couldn't work out how many people had died on the bus, but even now an offensive-looking yellow-brown bile was still dripping out from under the door.

As Michael continued walking he saw that this had been a railway station too, not just a bus depot. He stepped over the mouldy remains of a corpse lying at the bottom of a steep staircase, its neck apparently broken by the fall, then climbed up onto an elevated walkway, a pedestrian bridge to get people over the train tracks below. It looked like it had also been designed as a viewing area of sorts, and from the middle he had a clear view over the entire station below: the tracks, the engines, the platforms and the concourses. Jesus, he thought, this place really had been packed when the world had been brought to an abrupt end last September. The station was positively *heaving* with decay. And as for the trains themselves . . . He could only look for a few seconds before having to turn away. At every window in every carriage there were countless dead faces staring out, all still trying to escape, even after all this time.

Harry took out a few of the nearest corpses as they walked towards the marina – it didn't feel right not to – but they simply ignored many of the others. It was almost as if time had stopped and everything had frozen. It felt impossible, almost surreal, and yet, bizarrely, it also felt *good*.

It's like we're in control again, Cooper thought as they walked – *walked!* – through the kind of open spaces it would have been impossible to cover on foot last time they were on the mainland. He crossed a crazy golf course, striding over the little hills, hopping over the dried-up streams, weaving around the faded wooden windmills.

Today was such a stark contrast to the last time he'd been on the mainland. He remembered his desperate escape from the overrun airfield at Monkton. He'd been stranded with Emma, Juliet Appleby and Steve Armitage. Though he never admitted as much, he still had nightmares about that day. Maybe his time back here now would change all that? He hated the trendy expression, but perhaps being here again would bring them all some closure?

21

They kept the car park – and more importantly, the helicopter – in view as much as possible while they explored
the rest of the town. After finding a small, industrial-looking
boatyard first, they worked their way through the increasingly exclusive-looking sections of the marina, eventually
ending up in the more secluded area where a number of
fantastically expensive boats had been moored. Most were
empty. In one, a luxurious cruiser named 'The BarJerr' (obviously a grotesque amalgamation of the late owners' fore-
names, Cooper thought) Harry found a body preserved to an
unfortunate degree by the dry conditions and relatively
steady temperature inside the cabin. It was still wearing a
pair of hideous shorts and sandals, and a shirt once pastel-
pink but now stained anything but. It threw itself at him with
sudden speed – just like they used to, he thought – but it was
no match for his strength and he cut it down with a well-
aimed stroke, leaving it hacked into two uneven halves on the
deck, when they moved on to the next boat.

After identifying a number of possibilities, they eventually
decided on two boats moored next to each other which
looked like they'd do the job: the *Duchess* and the *Summer
Breeze*. They were both of a similar size, thirty feet long, and
obviously strong and seaworthy, but more importantly, they
were in relatively good condition given the fact they'd been
left in the water untended since September. They looked easy
enough to sail. Cooper and Harry both had some experience
with boats, albeit very different types of vessels and wildly
different circumstances, but it would be enough to get them
back to Cormansey.

Their twofold objectives were straightforward: transport and supplies. Harry claimed to know enough about electrics, propellers, waterproofing, outboards and the like to get the job done, so they left him to secure this part of the marina, then get the two vessels ready to sail.

Cooper, Richard and Donna addressed the supplies question. They found a nearby supermarket, broke in quickly and began looting, initially working at frantic speed and falling into old habits, grabbing whatever they could get their hands on, as corpses began to crowd the building and slam up against the windows. But after a while their nervousness faded and they began to work at a gentler pace, taking their time to gather food which would last, stuff they could easily transport and distribute. They concentrated on food which would keep the people on Cormansey healthy and strong, as well as medicines, tools and clothes. Cooper couldn't find everything he was looking for, and he made a mental note to try and find a garden centre, DIY store or farm shop before they returned to the island. *We need to start thinking ahead now*, he thought, realising just how much their situation had changed since they'd last been on the mainland. *We need to start planning for the future, now that it looks like we might actually have one. We must be able to plant and harvest crops, to grow as much of our own food as we can. We should get into a position where everything we need can be found on the island and we never have to come back here again, not unless we want to.*

A short time later he found Donna, standing in silence in the middle of a clothing department, just looking around at the dust-covered mannequins. Jack Baxter had been moaning to her recently about all the clichés in the post-apocalyptic books he used to love to read. 'I don't want to end up looking like an idiot,' he'd told her. 'I want to wear decent, comfortable clothes, not knobbly hand-knitted jumpers and coats made out of sewn-together animal skins!'

Donna hadn't moved for a while. Cooper wondered what was wrong.

'You okay?' he asked, startling her.

She caught her breath and turned around to face him. 'I'm fine,' she said, smiling briefly.

'You sure?'

'Sure.'

'What were you looking at?'

She pointed at two female dummies directly in front of her. The wig had slipped off one of them, partially covering its face and leaving half of its unflatteringly egg-like head bare. The other had a beard of cobwebs stretching from its chin to its chest, at odds with the short party dress decorated with thousands of sequins that sparkled in the afternoon light trickling in through the window. It had a handbag slung over one plastic shoulder, and it was wearing a pair of gorgeous (Donna thought) – if completely impractical – stiletto heels.

'Love those shoes,' she said.

'Have them, then.'

'Are you having a laugh? I mean, I know I *could* take them, but what's the point? When am I going to get to wear them, when I'm walking into the village? They're not all that practical for trudging across fields, are they?'

'Sorry,' Cooper said quickly, feeling unexpectedly insensitive.

'It's not your fault.' Donna sighed, looking sadly at the jeans and mud-splattered boots she was wearing. She shoved her hands into the pockets of the same winter coat she'd worn every day for as long as she could remember. 'I was just thinking, are we ever going to be able to dress like that again?'

'Well, I'm not,' he joked, immediately regretting his ill-considered jibe when he saw the expression on her face.

'I can't believe we ever used to look like this,' she said. 'I used to love getting dressed up for a night out with the girls –

getting ready was half the fun. We were usually pissed before we'd even got out the front door.'

'Bloody students,' Cooper mock-grumbled, hoping to lighten her mood, but she didn't bite. Instead she thought more about what she'd just said, and tried to picture the others on Cormansey letting their hair down. Would any of them ever bother? Even if they did, maybe all of them piling into the island's single pub, glamming up for old times' sake, perhaps even finding a way to play music, she knew it wouldn't be the same. It'd be like play-acting – it would inevitably leave them all feeling emptier than ever, highlighting the fact that all of this was gone forever now. It was time to accept that that part of her life was over.

A few doors further down the street, Michael was collecting baby stuff, working through the list Emma had drawn up with help from some of the women on the island. She wasn't even halfway through her pregnancy yet, but he didn't know when – or if – he'd get another opportunity like this. He'd not felt able to ask anyone else to get this stuff for him, not when some people had lost kids and others assumed they'd never have any, not now, but standing alone in the baby store, the handwritten shopping list gripped tightly in his hand, he wished he could feel even a fraction of the excitement he'd always imagined an expectant father should.

It was strange, he thought, of all the silent, empty places he'd been since most of the world died last September, this felt like the quietest, emptiest place of all. It was eerie. He was used to being alone – they all were – but being here took loneliness to a whole other level entirely. The walls around him were covered with paintings of fairy-tale characters, oversized alphabet blocks and black and white photographs of innocent toddlers and proud expectant mums. He didn't think the place had ever been this quiet before; every time he'd walked past somewhere like this it had always been filled with the constant wail of exasperated parents berating their bored, unhappy or cross offspring and incessant nursery rhyme music piped through the PA.

Michael had been quite looking forward to coming here, but the reality had proved to be disappointingly grim. He'd fetched himself a trolley and dutifully begun to fill it with baby clothes, nappies, bottles, all the powdered milk and food he could find which still had a decent shelf-life, but as he worked, the old familiar doubts began to reappear. Here in this place, with Emma so far away, it was impossible not to think about what sort of future his unborn child might – or might not – have. It was still possible – perhaps even *probable* – that the baby would die immediately after birth. But if it did survive, what kind of a life would it have to look forward to? He imagined the child growing up on Cormansey, outliving everyone else, and suddenly it didn't seem too fantastic to believe that his child might truly end up being the last person left alive on the face of the planet. How would he or she feel? Michael couldn't even begin to imagine the loneliness they might experience as their elders gradually passed away – think of all those years knowing you were never going to see another person's face, that no one would ever come if you screamed for help . . .

Snap out of it, he told himself. *Get a fucking grip.*

Angry with himself for allowing himself to get so defeatist, he started shoving the trolley, pushing it forcefully into the next aisle – and then stopped. Lying in front of him was a body; he assumed she'd been a young mum, and judging by the clothing hanging like tent canvas over what remained of her emaciated frame, she'd probably been pregnant when she'd died. Just ahead of her was a pushchair, which had toppled over onto its side.

And it was empty.

Michael panicked. Although he knew his fear was irrational, knowing that at any moment the ghoulish remains of a dead baby might be about to scuttle across the floor and attack him was upsetting him. He grabbed the rest of the things he needed and ran for the door, feeling like he was being watched.

When the four of them finally returned to the marina they found that it had been surrounded. Harry had built a temporary blockade to keep the dead at bay, but they'd continued to advance, moving almost too slowly to see, but still trickling forward like thick molasses.

22

They had intended to spend at least one night on the mainland, maybe two or even three, if necessary. The group planned to make the most of their situation and relax – and that actually seemed possible, now they realised how little a threat the dead posed in their pitifully weak condition. They lit bonfires in metal dustbins and positioned them in open spaces around the marina and the closest parts of the town, to draw the corpses away from the boats.

While the others had been looting Harry had managed to get both engines started. He'd even managed to rig up a basic radio in each boat. That had been unexpectedly unnerving, scanning the wavelengths and hearing nothing but unending static. For a while he'd wondered if he might find someone else transmitting, like he'd always seen happen in the movies. But he didn't. There was nothing.

It had taken a while to load up the boats, splitting the supplies equally between them, and yet there had still been plenty of space. Cooper suggested they should 'shop' again in the morning, both to make the most of this expedition, and to replace all the food and booze he intended gorging himself on tonight.

Michael found another boat moored well away from all the others, an enormous luxury craft so large it warranted a section of the marina almost to itself. It would probably have cost more than his house, maybe even the entire street. Until they were back on Cormansey, in a couple of days' time, he suggested they spent their nights here. It would probably be their last opportunity to eat, drink and relax in such comfort for a while. There were rooms enough for all of them to sleep, and a large lounge. Harry managed to get the electrics working (he was proving bloody useful to have around) and the five of them settled down to an evening which, unexpectedly, was beginning to echo the normality of their old lives.

Richard was in the galley, cooking. In times past he'd been a keen cook, even taking a couple of evening classes after work. He'd gone along at first because he'd thought it might be a good place to meet women, before realising that cooking was something he actually enjoyed. Though he'd long since tired of the bachelor life, he'd never had much luck with relationships. A helicopter pilot who loved to cook – how could women resist him? He used to joke about that with his friends, but there had been a serious side to his light-hearted moaning. He wasn't getting any younger, and he'd been actively looking for someone to settle down and share the rest of his life with. He'd joined a couple of dating websites, and even put what he called a 'last chance' lonely heart advert in the local paper – but it had all been academic, because the end of the world had come along and fucked everything up before he'd met anyone. Now, like most of the rest of the men who'd survived, he was damned to a life of enforced celibacy. It hadn't mattered at first, not until recently, after he'd been on the island for a while and had started to think about the future, and about things like love and sex and relationships again. But it was beginning to really play on his mind now – he'd found himself daydreaming about finding a camp populated exclusively by nubile young female survivors, all desperate for the company of men . . .

His idle thoughts were interrupted by a loud crash and a scream of protest from the other end of the boat and he ran quickly to the lounge. He relaxed when he saw that it was nothing more than Harry knocking a bottle of beer over the table where he and Donna had been playing cards.

'Be careful, for Christ's sake,' Richard said, though he was acutely aware that he was sounding like an overzealous parent – truth was, all he was worried about was the fact there were a finite number of bottles of beer left in the country, and he couldn't bear the thought of one drop of drink being wasted.

'Food nearly done?' Harry asked, wiping the table with his sleeve, his voice slightly slurred.

'Not quite,' Richard said, already on his way back to the kitchen. 'You can't rush perfection.' He was really enjoying working in the well-equipped galley, with stuff which actually worked. In his house back on Cormansey he used a portable gas-ring, which sat on the top of a perfectly good but completely useless electric oven. Other people cooked on open fires, if you could call it cooking. In the early days on the island there'd been a spontaneous, almost ceremonial disposal of pretty much everything electrical: telephones, computers, televisions – they'd all been thrown on a huge pile in the middle of Danver's Lye and set on fire. No one had seen any point keeping anything like that.

Richard opened the oven and sniffed the cottage pie. *Bloody hell, that smells good*, he thought, his mouth watering. The meat and vegetables were tinned, the sauce was out of a jar, and the mashed potato on top was freeze-dried – but none of that mattered. What he'd have given for some fresh ingredients, though. *Imagine that*, he thought, licking his lips, *steak . . . a bacon sandwich for breakfast . . . a mug of tea first thing in the morning, made with real milk . . .*

He was giving semi-serious consideration to the practicalities involved in finding a couple of dairy cows and winching them over the ocean to Cormansey when he heard something outside. He froze in apprehension and listened carefully: it was a definite noise, close to the galley window . . . and now there was movement too. The starboard side of the boat dipped down slightly.

Cooper was already onto it, running for the door to the deck, a fire-axe held ready to attack.

'Bodies?' Donna asked.

'Must be,' Michael said, moving to one side so Harry

could push past him. He was carrying his sword, and was completely sober. Cooper paused and listened before going outside. The boat rocked again. There was something moving around the stern. They could hear it scrambling around the hatch now, trying to get inside.

'Many of them?' Harry asked as Cooper peered out through a porthole window.

'Can't see much out there,' he said. 'We could do with some deck lights. Probably just a couple that managed to get down here.'

'It's the noise Harry's been making,' Richard suggested, semi-seriously.

'Or the smell of your cooking,' Harry shot back. 'I'm surprised, though: the temperature's dropped out there. I'd have thought they—'

He stopped mid-sentence as the door onto the deck began to rattle and stood ready with his sword. Cooper moved to open it, but it flew open before he got anywhere near. A single bedraggled figure fell into the room and immediately scrambled to its feet. It lurched towards Donna, its arms outstretched. In spite of the drink, her reactions were lightning-quick and she'd grabbed it by the collar and slammed it up against the nearest wall before anyone else had moved. She threw it to the ground and dropped down herself, holding it ready for Harry to finish it off when—

'—don't . . .' the body on the floor said.

Donna, stunned, jumped to her feet and staggered back, struggling to comprehend the fact that here was another survivor, lying on the deck in the middle of the room. His face was gaunt and unshaven, although he didn't look like he was starving.

'Food smells good,' he said as he picked himself up and brushed himself down.

'Where the fuck did you come from?' Michael asked.

'I've been here for a couple of weeks,' the man replied. 'My name's Harte. Ian Harte.'

23

Ian Harte didn't offer much information save that he'd been hiding out in an apartment block just north of Chadwick since he'd arrived in the town two weeks earlier, then he started asking questions, almost monopolising the conversation.

'You said you're from an island?' he started.

'That's right,' Michael said.

'And there's more than fifty of you?'

'Yep.'

'Jesus! That just doesn't seem possible—'

'None of what's happened since last September seems possible,' Cooper said. 'If you think about it, fifty-odd people flying over to an island is one of the more believable aspects.'

'I suppose so,' he admitted. 'It's just that until I heard your helicopter this morning, I thought I was going to be on my own for ever. You know what it's like – I thought I was imagining things. By the time I got here I couldn't hear the helicopter any more, but I decided to head for the centre of town just in case, and I saw it parked up on top of that car park. I waited up there for you to come back, but then I saw the fires you'd lit around the marina . . .'

'And you're on your own?'

'I was,' Harte replied. 'Look, this may be a stupid question, but when you first went over to this island, did you use a plane as well as a helicopter?'

'How the hell did you know that?' Richard said.

Harte grinned broadly and sank the last of the beer in his bottle before saying, 'I knew it! Couple of months back,' he explained, 'I was hiding out in a hotel with a group of others, and we saw a helicopter flying backwards and forwards, day after day. Later there was a plane – it must have been you lot. We tried everything to get your attention. We wrote messages on the ground with sheets, we started fires—'

'I didn't see any messages,' Richard said. 'I'd have investigated if I had. And as for your fires – if you'd seen what I've seen from up there since it all kicked off, well, you'd have known no one would've given fires a second glance. There's always something burning somewhere. Unless it was a bloody enormous great blaze I wouldn't have paid it any attention.'

'Bit of a long shot, though,' Harry mumbled, not yet sure what he thought of Ian Harte. 'I mean, what are the chances of you hearing us all the way back then, then finding us again today?'

'Pretty bloody astronomical,' Harte agreed.

'It's probably not as far-fetched as you might think,' Richard said. 'Think about it: how many hundreds of other people like Harte might we have missed? The skies are clear, and as far as we know, we're the only ones still flying. The chopper would have been visible for miles. It's not unreasonable to believe that—'

'Never mind all that,' Donna interrupted, cutting across him, 'whether he heard us or not isn't important.' She turned to face Harte. 'You said something about a hotel, and other people. What happened to them?'

Harte's face dropped. He helped himself to another bottle and gathered himself. 'We made a few mistakes,' he admitted, 'most of them trying to get your attention, as it happens. We ended up being completely cut off by thousands of those dead fuckers outside. We were stranded, and it took us weeks to escape—'

'So how did you get out?' she pressed. 'And was it just you, or did others get away too?'

Harte looked a bit uncomfortable. 'What is this, the fucking Spanish Inquisition?'

'We just need to know, that's all.'

He continued with his reluctant explanation. 'Before we

162

got to the hotel, we'd been based in some flats, and a couple of the girls there got sick. We didn't know what it was, or how they caught it, but it killed the pair of them – that's how we ended up on the run, and that's how we ended up at the hotel. We'd been there a while when one of our guys, Driver, started complaining that he was feeling sick too.'

'So what did you do?'

'We quarantined him.'

'Sensible.'

'That's what we thought.'

'This is all very interesting,' Michael asked, 'but what's this got to do with anything?'

'It turned out the crafty bastard was having us on – there was nothing wrong with him. As soon as the shit hit the fan and the bodies got too close, he bailed on us without anyone realising. He came back weeks later, when the dead first froze.'

Cooper stared intently at Harte. 'So what are you not telling us? There's got to be more to it than that.'

'Nothing,' he answered quickly, concentrating on up-ending the bottle, doing all he could not to make eye-contact.

'Bollocks.'

'Give the guy a break, Cooper,' Harry said.

'I mean,' Cooper continued, 'there are a lot of gaps in your story. How many of you were trapped in the hotel? What happened to the rest of them? And why're you now out here on your own?'

The silence while they waited for his answer was deafening.

'I screwed up,' he eventually admitted. He took a deep and resigned himself to the fact that he was going to have to stop beating around the bush and explain everything that had happened to him since leaving the hotel.

'While Driver was on the run, he found another group, based in a castle about fifteen miles or so from here.'

'How many?' Michael asked. They were all listening intently.

'Twenty-one, once we'd all turned up. They'd been there from the start – the place is pretty basic, but it's rock solid, and it's built on a hill, so the dead have never been able to get near enough to cause any real problems.'

'So why the hell would you leave a place like that and come out here on your own?' Donna asked. She glared at him, demanding an answer.

'Remember that cold snap just before Christmas? It was really bloody cold here, and there was loads of snow.'

'We remember,' Michael said. It had been hard going on the island back then too. They'd almost run out of firewood, so they had resorted to using just a few houses, cramming everyone in to try and conserve fuel supplies – that was one of the main reasons they'd decided to come back to the mainland so soon.

'I came out to this place with a lorryload of blokes from the castle,' Harte continued, 'and we broke into a shopping centre. We'd been collecting stuff for hours, but they kept trying to get more so they didn't have to come back again. By the time we were ready to move out, the thaw had started and we were surrounded.'

'The Minories,' Richard said.

'What?' Cooper asked.

'That's it,' Harte said.

'The Minories,' Richard repeated. 'We passed it when we were looting earlier. I thought it looked like it had been done over. All the doors were buckled and the glass was smashed. It was by the station, remember?'

'The station,' Harte said with a shudder. 'You want to stay away from that place.'

'And you didn't think to say anything about that at the time?' Cooper asked Richard, ignoring Harte.

'I didn't see much point – we were looking for food, not empty shops. And anyway, there was no way of knowing how long it had been since it was cleared out. I couldn't tell if the damage had been done three days ago or three months. I didn't bother saying anything because I assumed all the good stuff would already have been taken.'

'And you also assumed no one else was around?' Donna said, surprised by Richard's apparent belligerence.

'I assumed they'd have heard the helicopter if they were still around,' he answered quickly. 'And that's exactly what happened, isn't it?' He pointed at Harte. 'He heard the helicopter and he turned up, didn't he?'

'So why are you still here?' Cooper asked, keen to get the conversation back on track.

'Did you see the petrol station?'

'What petrol station?'

'Exactly. I torched a petrol station to distract the dead so that the lorry could get away – only I did the job a little too well. I blew the fuck out of the place.' He laughed wryly. 'The size of the explosion took me by surprise, and I got caught on the wrong side of it. By the time I'd come around and managed to get back to the mall, the rest of them were long gone.'

'Jesus,' Richard said under his breath. 'So you were stuck out here?'

'That's about it. I found a safe place in what was left of the mall, so I stayed there for a while, getting myself together. Eventually I moved on.'

'And it never crossed your mind to try and get back to the castle?' Cooper asked, sounding less than convinced.

'Of course it bloody crossed my mind,' Harte answered quickly, 'but it's not as easy as all that. There was the weather for a start, and the bodies. And it's too far – you couldn't walk it.'

'You could have taken a car – there are plenty lying around. Or you could have cycled there, come to that.'

'I didn't want to take the risk – even if I managed to make it safely back to the castle, there was no guarantee they'd see me to let me in.'

'You could have yelled at them – surely they'd have heard you with everything else so quiet.'

'Yeah, and so would the dead. You don't understand: they couldn't get right up to the castle walls, but there were thousands of them surrounding the place – tens of thousands, probably. There's no way I could fight my way through that lot on my own.'

The conversation faltered. For a moment the only sounds were the creaking vessel and the lapping of the waves against its hull. Michael had been quiet, watching the conversation from across the cabin.

'Forgive me, Ian,' he said, 'I know we've only just met, and I might be making a hell of a presumption here, but everything you've just told us is a load of bollocks, isn't it?'

'Come on, Mike,' Harry protested, 'that's a bit harsh, isn't it?'

'You think?'

'No,' Harte said, 'I swear it's the truth: we were here looting, I blew up the petrol station and—'

'Oh, I don't doubt any of that,' Michael interrupted. 'It's everything since then that I have a problem with. How long ago did all this happen?'

'About two weeks ago. Why?'

'Because if you'd really wanted to get back to the castle you would have managed to by now. I know I would. You planned to stay out here on your own, didn't you?'

Harte looked down into his beer, then up at the others again. 'So what if I did? What difference does it make? I made a choice, that's all.'

'What choice?' Donna asked.

Another hesitation, then he sighed. 'There was never a plan – I don't know if I really made a conscious decision, whether I bottled it or just made a stupid mistake. I'd been stuck with those fuckers for weeks, and I was sick of all the in-fighting, all the bitching and arguing. I don't know what you lot are like, but even though there are hardly any of us left alive, the group mentality gets a bit much, you know? It doesn't matter if you're stuck with five people or five hundred, you always end up with some cocky fucker who thinks they're in charge, and you know it's only going to be a matter of time before things turn ugly. That's why it all went pear-shaped at the hotel, and I could see that's what was happening again at the castle.'

'So there's a cocky fucker like that back there?'

'At least two, with a few more waiting in the wings. There's Jackson, the guy who was in charge of the castle group, and there's Jas.'

'Jas?'

'I'd been with him virtually since day one, and he was always a good guy, but I was starting to think the time we spent trapped in the hotel had sent him a little stir-crazy. He and Jackson, they were constantly at each other's throats, and I could just see things heading down that same old slippery slope again. So when the opportunity arose, I took a leaf out of Driver's book and did a runner.'

'So what's it actually like at this castle?' Cooper asked.

'Basic, but pretty good, all things considered,' Harte said.

'Twenty-one people, you say?'

'Twenty now.'

'Supplies?'

'They should have enough to get them through the winter, assuming the lorry got back, that is.'

'And the bodies are held at a safe distance?'

'The place is built on a rise, so they physically can't get up to it. There's an access road leading up to the main gate – some of them manage to get up that, but that's nothing that can't be handled with a couple of vehicles and a little brute force. Anyway, what about this island of yours?' he asked, keen to redirect the conversation. 'Many bodies left there?'

'None,' Richard told him, 'we cleared them all out when we first arrived.'

'You cleared them out? *All* of them? Jesus, how many was that?'

'Three or four hundred, give or take.'

'So you've got plenty of room?'

'Loads of space. Why, are you trying to hitch a lift now?'

'I wouldn't say no,' Harte immediately said, needing no time to think about his answer.

'Just one thing before you get too carried away,' Cooper said, 'and I don't want to piss on your parade or anything, but this is important: whatever your real reasons for being out here alone, we can't ignore the people back at the castle. There's no reason why you can't come back with us, but we need to make the same offer to them too.'

'That sounds reasonable,' Michael said. 'The more the merrier.'

'I'm not sure . . .' Harte started.

'Way I see it, they owe you,' Cooper said.

'And how do you work that out?'

'Well, first of all, sounds like they ran out on you – did they stick around to find you after the fire? And when you turn up there tomorrow morning in a helicopter and offer to help whisk them all away to a place where there are no bodies and where they'll be completely safe, they'll think you're the best fucking thing since sliced bread.'

'Sliced bread, remember that?' Richard said to himself, laughing sadly.

'You don't know that,' Harte protested, sounding increasingly nervous. 'You don't know how they'll react.'

'You're absolutely right,' Cooper admitted, 'I don't know for sure. But here's the deal: we'll give it a try, and if things don't work out, I promise we'll get you out of there and over to Cormansey with us. It's either that or you go back to wherever you've been hiding in the morning and crawl back under your rock. You'll end up spending the rest of your life on your own, though, picking through the bones of what's left of this place.'

Harte didn't say anything but reached for another bottle of beer, then sank further back into his seat. He knew full well that he had no choice. He would be going back to the castle tomorrow.

24

Harte's guts were churning. It could have been because he was in a helicopter, hundreds of feet above the ground, or maybe it was because he was hung-over from all the beer he'd drunk last night. And it might have been nervousness at the prospect of returning to the castle – returning from the grave – and facing Jas and the others after being away from them for weeks. Most likely it was a combination of all those factors. He kept his head bowed and focused on the floor between his feet, trying not to think about anything.

'That it?' Richard asked, shouting to make himself heard over the noise of the helicopter rotors. Harte looked through the window at the castle: a grey mound surrounded by a narrow band of green, then another dark circle of land where the remains of tens of thousands of bodies gathered ominously, still looking like they were poised to make their deadly assault. Within the castle walls he could see the off-white roofs of the six caravans and several lorries too. Smoke rose up from the fires. One or two people emerged, reacting to the noise, then more of them appeared.

'That's it,' he answered. It had only been two weeks, but he thought Cheetham Castle looked very different to how he'd left it. As Richard took the helicopter down, he saw the number of bodies waiting around the elevated settlement had increased – but it must just have appeared like that because he'd never approached the castle from this angle before. From up here it looked like they had combined to form a single, uninterrupted rotting mass – a ring of dead flesh. That was consistent with what he'd noticed in town: where there were fewer bodies, they sometimes lasted longer. When they were crammed together like this, the constant jostling for position, grinding against each other, caused their fragile flesh to deteriorate much faster. Even now more of them were still moving towards the castle. They walked alone now, not in the larger packs like before, and they were painfully slow, but still they came. It beggared belief that these creatures had probably been walking like this for weeks, maybe even months, and were only now reaching the castle. From up here they looked like stick figures, and their speed was barely visible; that they were still drawn to the living after all this time was both terrifying and remarkable.

The road leading up to the castle entrance was as full of bodies as he'd expected. There were mounds of dead flesh on either side where they'd been shovelled away, but by the looks of things no one had been outside in some time. There were several people on the top of the gatehouse, though he couldn't make out faces from up there.

'You ready for this?' Donna asked, sitting next to him.

'I guess,' he replied, sounding less than convinced. He looked at the other three travelling in the helicopter with him. They all looked much calmer and more relaxed than he felt. Cooper was watching the ground intently, surveying the scene. They'd left Harry and Michael back at the marina to look after the boats, Michael, in particular, because he had more to lose than the others. Harte would gladly have traded places with either of them now. He'd have given anything to be back in his seafront apartment in Chadwick – bored out of his brain, maybe, but without a damn care. *You're a fucking idiot*, he said to himself. *You should have stayed where you were.* Suddenly all that boredom and undeniable loneliness were vastly preferable to what he was feeling now.

Donna picked up on his obvious unease. 'You'll be all right,' she said. 'They'll understand why you didn't come back.'

'You think?'

'Stick to your story and you'll be okay,' Cooper agreed

from the front. 'You fucked up, got yourself in trouble when you torched the petrol station. You came around and they'd gone. That's true, after all. And fifteen miles is a long way these days. The snow stopped you getting back.'

'Yeah, but the snow was gone a couple of days after that—'

'Then improvise, for crying out loud. Seriously, they're not going to care what happened! Like I said last night, you turning up in a bloody helicopter will give them plenty to think about. They'll have more important things to ask than why you disappeared.'

Harte said nothing. He leaned against the glass and watched the ground below come closer and the faces come into focus as Richard lowered them towards the castle court-yard.

'Clear the ground,' Lorna ordered, trying to spur some of the others into action, enough at least to clear space for the helicopter to land. Around her, most of the others stood in dumbstruck silence, staring up into the air and watching the aircraft descend. *Christ*, she thought, *you'd think they'd never seen a bloody helicopter before.*

She kicked over the remains of last night's fire, sending clouds of smoke and still-warm ash up into the air, then dragged away the partially burnt lumps of wood. Between them, Bob and Howard pushed a broken-down car out of the way, straining with effort as the noise and downwind from the helicopter increased. They were both cursing Will Bayliss, the lazy bastard, who'd been promising to get it fixed for the last fortnight, but as usual he'd done nothing.

The ground was clear, and now the crowd which had gathered to watch the helicopter shuffled further back as it came in to land.

'It *must* be the same one that kept flying over the hotel,' Caron shouted to Lorna.

'How could it be? What are the chances of that happening?'

'I don't know, but how many other helicopters have you seen since everyone died?'

'If it is the same people,' Lorna said caustically, 'then they're a few months late.'

'But still very welcome.'

The helicopter seemed to pause slightly before gently dropping down the last few feet. Whirling dust filled the air, but no one moved. The engine stopped, and when the noise had faded away to nothing, the expectant silence which replaced it was strangely unsettling. A man disembarked, then a woman, then the pilot.

Jackson was the first to move. He strode up to the nearest of the two men, and confidently offered his hand. 'Alan Jackson,' he announced, smiling broadly.

'Cooper.'

'Good to meet you, Cooper.'

'This is Richard and Donna,' he said, introducing the others.

Harte was watching from the back of the helicopter, his heart thumping. Thankfully no one seemed to have noticed him yet. He wanted to stay in here and hide, but he knew that as the only person who knew everyone, he should be the one right in the middle of the conversation, not watching from a distance like a naughty kid sitting on the stairs, eavesdropping on his parents. *Oh, grow some bollocks*, he ordered himself, and he jumped down and landed on the gravel, directly in Jackson's line of vision.

'Hello,' was all he could say.

Jackson looked at him and grinned, but he couldn't speak either.

'Where the fuck have you been?' Jas demanded, storming over.

'You must be Jas,' Cooper said perceptively, but he was ignored.

'We thought you were dead,' Jackson said, still struggling to take everything in.

'Obviously not,' Jas said.

Harte's eyes flickered from face to face. 'I'm sorry,' he said, not quite sure why he was apologising. His mind was swimming – all the reasons and excuses were suddenly becoming confused. 'I must have been too close to the petrol station when it went up – I didn't know anything until I came around later. You'd all gone by then and—'

'Bollocks,' Jas said, 'you'd have been burnt to a crisp.'

'Give it a rest, Jas, it doesn't matter,' Jackson said. He pointed at the helicopter. 'Don't you think we have a few more important issues to discuss right now?'

25

Jackson ushered the new arrivals into the caravan he shared with Howard and Bob, and went on through into one of the bedrooms. Jas, the last one in, pulled the door closed behind him, shutting everyone else out. Jackson returned carrying bottles of water, Coke and beer and gestured for everyone to sit. They shifted stuff out of the way to find enough space to squeeze onto the cluttered U-shaped sofa at the end,

'Drink?' Jackson asked.

'Decent set-up you have here,' Richard said.

'We shouldn't complain,' Jackson replied, 'though Christ alone knows we do. We're all fortunate just to be alive, and the fact we found this spot is a real bonus.' He set about opening bottles.

'Wise move, setting yourself up in a castle,' Cooper said.

'You're not wrong,' Jackson agreed. 'Think about it logically – places like this have already been standing for hundreds of years. They've survived wars and who knows what else. A few thousand dead bodies was never going to be that much of a threat to them.'

'Well, it's thanks to Harte here that we found you,' Cooper said, deliberately involving Harte, giving him credit to try and deflect any bad feelings the others might be harbouring.

'I just did what anybody else would have done,' Harte said, sounding less than confident. Would everybody else really have faked their own death for an easy life? he wondered.

Jackson just nodded and grinned. He looked genuinely pleased to see him.

'So you're all getting by here?' Cooper asked.

'We're doing okay,' Jas said, sitting opposite. 'Things will get a lot easier when we've seen the last of the dead.'

'I don't think you'll have long to wait,' Donna said. 'From what we saw in the air just now, there's not a lot of activity out there.'

'*Any* activity is too much activity,' Jas replied, sounding surprisingly forceful. 'We've lasted here until now without any problems. Another couple of months and maybe we'll look at moving on.'

'Why wait?' Cooper asked. 'Seriously, from what we've seen since we've been back on the mainland, things aren't as bad out there as you probably think.'

'What do you mean, since you've been back on the mainland?' Jackson asked. 'Where the hell did you come from to get here?'

'They're from an island,' Harte said enthusiastically, answering for the others.

'An island?' Jackson repeated in disbelief.

'And you haven't heard the best of it,' Harte continued. 'There are no bodies there. They cleared them all out!'

'It's a lot easier to do in such a small, isolated area,' Cooper explained. 'It's nothing like the situation you've had to deal with here.'

'The dead are less of a problem than they used to be,' Jackson admitted.

'But they are still a problem,' Jas quickly added. 'I'm sure Harte's told you about the day he left us – those things were frozen solid when we set out; by the time we were ready to head back they were all over us.'

'It wasn't that bad,' Harte said. 'And you forget, Jas, I've been out there since then. They're becoming less and less of a threat each day.'

'They were *all over us*,' Jas repeated, labouring the point, 'and I for one am not going out there again until every last one of those fuckers has rolled over and given up the ghost for good.'

'So you've not been out again since that day?'

'We brought enough stuff back with us so there's been no need to go out again. And if we're sensible, we can make what we've got left last until the dead are completely finished.'

'Seriously,' Cooper said, 'you might want to reconsider your strategy. There were still bodies walking around Chadwick yesterday and today – we just walked past them. Honestly, you can outrun them now without even having to run. The threat is over.'

'Then why don't you go up to the gatehouse and watch them on the road and on the bridge? They're still coming, friend, and they won't stop until they're physically unable to move. We're still surrounded here. The threat is *far* from over.'

Richard, sensing the tension in the air, changed tack to try and diffuse it. 'Harte says you've got about twenty people here.'

'That's right,' Jackson answered, 'what about you? How many of you are on this island of yours?'

'Over fifty, including the five of us.'

'Five of you?'

'We left a couple of men back at the port – apart from the lack of seats in the helicopter, we didn't want to risk bringing Michael over here until we'd checked the place out, no offence.'

'None taken. But why? What's different about this Michael chap?'

'He's going to be a dad.'

The caravan fell silent.

Jackson, taken by surprise, wasn't sure what to say. 'How—?' he started.

'Jesus, how d'you think?' Donna muttered.

'I mean, was it before everyone died or—?'

'After,' she answered. 'Emma and Michael got together after it had happened.'

'Bloody hell.'

'It's not that incredible,' Richard said. 'Women used to have kids all the time.'

'I know that, but since the world fell apart . . . I don't know what I'm trying to say. An hour ago it felt like everything was coming to an end, then you turn up here out of the blue in your bloody helicopter, telling us about your island where there are no dead bodies, and then that you've got a woman who's pregnant and . . . and it's like you've come here from another world. Truly amazing.'

'I wouldn't go that far,' Jas said belligerently.

'Well, I would. It sounds like these folks have achieved a huge amount. There's a lot we could learn from them.'

'With the greatest respect,' Jas interrupted, turning towards Jackson, 'we don't have a damn thing to learn from *any*one. All this lot is doing is what we *used* to do, and it's what we'll do again once the bodies are gone and we're out of here.'

'No one has to learn anything from anyone,' Donna said calmly. 'You make it sound like we're from different tribes! We might be all that's left, and that's the main reason we came back here with Harte. We think it makes sense for us all to group together – we think you should all come over to the island.'

'I'm not sure—' Jas began to say before Jackson spoke over him.

'Makes sense, providing we can all get there.'

'We've got a couple of boats ready in Chadwick,' Cooper explained. 'That's one of the reasons we came back, to get some alternative transport, take the pressure off Richard here.'

'Sounds good.'

'Just damn well wait,' Jas said, his voice louder and more forceful this time. 'You can't make a blanket decision on behalf of all the people here, not without consulting them, and not without thinking it through. There might be some who don't want to go to an island – not sure I do. It sounds risky to me, a little too cut-off and exposed.'

'It's not perfect,' Cooper admitted, 'but I've yet to find a better place. As good as this castle looks to have been for you all, I think the island is better. You've still not got your freedom here.'

'Doesn't matter if we're surrounded by a sea of dead flesh or by the ocean itself, we're all still prisoners.'

'Jas is right about one thing,' Jackson said. 'I was wrong to assume. Everyone here has the right to make their own choice. We'll get everybody together and give them the options. We're talking about decisions which will affect the rest of everybody's lives, after all.'

26

'Harte? Ian Harte, is that you?'

The voice caught him by surprise – he didn't think anyone else was out here. He'd been sitting in a quiet corner where he could see the helicopter, not wanting to stray too far in case Cooper and the others upped and left without him.

'Lorna?' It was dark and he couldn't see her, but he got up and followed the noise her boots made crunching through the gravel. When he saw her he grabbed hold of her and held her tight. He hadn't realised how much he'd missed her. She led him over to the caravans and sat down on a pile of wooden pallets. In the light coming from the window of the nearest caravan, he thought she looked tired, old even. With her hair scraped back her face looked angular and stark in the gloom. She looked pensive, which was out of character for the woman he remembered. She'd always been relaxed and comfortable in herself, regardless of how bad everything else was around her.

'I looked for you earlier,' Harte said. 'You okay?'

'Fine,' she replied, sounding less than convinced. 'I was working – I'm on my break right now.'

'On your break? From what?'

'Cooking rota.'

'You on a cooking rota? Bloody hell, Lor!'

'It's not funny.'

'I didn't say it was,' he said quickly. 'Just a surprise, that's all.'

'Tell me about it.'

'So Jackson's cracking the whip around here now is he?'

'Jackson and Jas – I swear, they're like a double act some-times.'

'Good cop, bad cop?'

'Bad cop, worse cop.'

'Well, all that might be about to change. You've heard about the island?'

'I've heard rumblings. You don't hear much news in the kitchen – not that there's usually any news to hear.'

'Are things really that bad?'

'No, I'm probably making it sound worse than it is. But I can see things going downhill if we're not careful. The fewer people there are left, the more narrow-minded some of them are becoming. I swear it's like we've gone back fifty years – sexual equality and all that stuff's a thing of the past now.'

'It must be grim if they've got you cooking.'

'Cheeky bastard. You're right, though – us *ladies* are politely excused from doing anything physical or even remo-tely dangerous. Most of them are happy with that, old maids like Caron, Sue and Shirley. Zoe's a stubborn bugger; she just locks herself in her caravan and refuses to come out unless it suits her . . .'

'So most of the work is down to you.'

'Pretty much.'

'What about Melanie? She still here?'

'Oh, she's here all right, dirty bitch.'

'That's a bit harsh.'

'Is it? She's just a communal fuck-buddy. Whenever she wants anything she just flashes her tits and flutters her eyelids at one of the blokes and they cover for her.'

'You could try that.'

'You could fuck off! I've got more self-respect. Anyway, I'd destroy the piss-poor excuses for men we've got here – I'd eat you alive for starters.'

'Look, I'm not arguing; I know you would!' He paused, then asked her if she was going to go to the island.

'I'm planning to,' she answered quietly. 'I really don't like the way things are going here.'

'Why? What's happened?'

'Oh, it's just all the usual bollocks you get when there are too many dumb blokes stuck in the same place together with limited options: they stop thinking sensibly and spend all their time playing bloody stupid mind-games with each other.'

'Jas and Jackson?'

'In fairness Jackson does try to keep Jas in check, but from where I'm sitting it looks like Jas is the one with more influence these days. You've heard about Howard, haven't you?'

'I haven't heard anything – I have hardly seen him. I tried to talk to him earlier, but he was in a right fucking foul mood.'

'He lost his dog last week.'

'Shit – what happened? Did it get sick?'

'Mark Ainsworth happened. Apparently Jas had said something to him about Dog using up food meant for us, so Ainsworth threw the dog out. In the middle of the night. He just opened the gates and kicked the poor little bastard out. Howard was in bits, and they wouldn't let him out to look for her.'

'Fuck me!'

'And that's not the worst of it.'

'There's worse?'

'Hollis.'

'Yeah, where is he? I was looking for him—'

'Gone,' she said, sounding subdued.

'Gone where?'

'No idea. They kicked him out too.'

'Why?'

'Were you here when he had that accident?'

'The shit-pit? When he accidentally busted Steve More-combe's arm? That's a point – I haven't seen Steve either.'

'You wouldn't have. He's dead.'

'Dead? How?'

'How d'you think? His broken arm got infected. Sue's supposed to be a nurse, but if you need anything more than a fucking headache tablet, she's next to useless. I swear it was like when Ellie and Anita died. All we could do was watch the poor sod fade away. It happened last week, and it was fucking horrible, it was.'

'But Hollis . . . it was just an accident – it wasn't like he meant to do it.'

'I know, but you know what he's like; he takes it all so personally. The toilets hadn't been emptied, so he went back to sort them out. Jas caught him on the digger and they ended up fighting. He practically threw him out. He gave him a choice – spend all his time in his caravan, virtually under lock and key, or leave. So he walked.'

'Fuck!'

'To be honest, I think Hollis was happy to go. And have you seen the state of the shit-pit since you've been back?'

'I went to use it earlier, but I couldn't face it. The stink was terrible. I found a quiet bit of wall and took a piss over that instead.'

'Exactly. The toilets are overflowing, the pit reeks, there're flies everywhere . . . Hollis was the only one who kept on top of the waste, so to speak, and now he's gone, no one else is willing to get their hands dirty. Jas has just shot himself in the foot – well, all of us, really. I swear, Harte, it's getting to be like the Dark Ages here.'

'Everything all right?' a voice asked from behind them, startling them both. Harte spun around. He couldn't immediately see who it was, but Lorna knew straight away. It was Mark Ainsworth.

'Have you met my stalker?' she whispered before raising her voice to answer. 'We're fine, thanks. Just catching up on a little gossip.'

'You sure?'

'I'm sure.'

'Just be careful what you're gossiping about, right?'

'Will do. Thanks, Mark.'

Harte listened carefully until he was sure that Mark had gone again. 'What's his problem?' he whispered.

'Where do I start? A guilty conscience, for one thing. That and the fact he's probably jealous.'

'Jealous of what?'

'Us talking – unfortunately he's taken a bit of a shine to me – he's setting his sights a little higher than a quick fumble around the back of a caravan with Melanie.'

'Are you serious?'

'Deadly.'

'You've changed, Lor. When I first met you, you'd have eaten blokes like Mark Ainsworth for breakfast. Christ, I remember how you used to run rings around Webb and the others back at the flats.'

'I'm still the same,' she said quietly. 'It's the situation that's changed. I'm keeping the blokes sweet while I have to, that's all. I'll do their cooking and a little bit of cleaning and I might even flutter my eyelids at them when it suits, but if they fuck around with me or overstep the mark, I'll break their balls.'

'I don't doubt you – I'm certainly not going to argue.'

'I wouldn't. Anyway, it won't be for much longer. I've just been biding my time until I get out of here, and you bringing that helicopter here has just changed everything.'

27

In an ideal world, Cooper thought, which this place was most definitely not, he'd have been in and out of the castle in a matter of hours. As it was, they'd already been hanging around for most of the day and it looked like they'd probably have to stay overnight. He'd been to some hellish places during his years of service, and he'd had more than his fair share of awkward situations to try and resolve with diplomacy. This was no different than some of those war-torn hellholes.

Jackson was keen to leave the castle, but Jas most definitely was yet to be convinced. Cooper thought it better to spend a little time trying to get all of them onside, rather than going in heavy-handed and screwing everything up, but even his patience was being tested tonight. He felt like they were going around in circles – he had to keep reminding himself they were actually trying to *help* these people. Every time he made a suggestion, Jas and some of his posse would shoot it down, no thought, no consideration. He was on the verge of getting the others together and just flying back to Chadwick.

The small classroom was packed, and stiflingly hot, thanks to the paraffin heater running on high at one end. It was brightly lit, lamps running off a series of connected extension cords which were in turn connected to a small but bloody noisy petrol generator outside. Condensation was running down the windows. Harte felt increasingly uncomfortable, and not just because of the heat. He'd been shocked by the things he'd seen and heard since returning to the castle. The atmosphere was continually changing, almost from minute to minute, depending on who he was talking to.

He'd quickly discovered that the looting expedition to Chadwick had been the last time anyone had left the castle, and since then some of the direction Jackson had previously provided had been ignored. The wooden construction to investigate the well – which he himself had helped construct many weeks ago – remained in exactly the same unfinished state as when he'd last seen it. There were huge piles of waste around the edges of the courtyard, and as he'd already discovered, the cesspit and toilets were full to overflowing. There'd also been a fire in one of the caravans; he'd noticed it after talking to Lorna earlier – but it didn't look like anyone had made any attempt to do anything about the wreck.

Harte wasn't really sure where he should be sitting, so he positioned himself at the edge of the group, quite near the front. He took comfort in some of the familiar faces he could see – Lorna, Caron, Driver and Howard – though he found himself aligning more with Donna, Richard and Cooper. He hadn't ever seen it – he didn't even know if it really existed – but their island of Cormansey, despite its apparent bleakness and basic lifestyle, sounded idyllic to him, his idea of heaven. Too bad a vociferous handful didn't seem to share his opinion. He could tell that Cooper was getting annoyed.

'I don't see what the problem is,' he was saying now. 'We're offering you a place that's safe and free from walking bodies and all the complications they bring.'

'Well, why don't you just fuck off back there, then?' Jas said unhelpfully. He'd been increasingly obstructive since this 'town hall' meeting had begun, what felt like hours ago now. Unfortunately he seemed to have plenty of vocal support. 'Listen, I agree with what you're saying in principle, but this island of yours is completely the wrong place. You're cutting yourself off.'

'Cutting ourselves off from what?' Donna demanded, unable to believe what she was hearing. 'There's fuck all else left.'

Jas continued, 'I think it's better to stay here and wait a

little longer. We've got access to what's left of the entire country – better than some barren little island with nothing but half a dozen houses.'

'But the island is much more than that – it really is the best bet for all of us,' Cooper said. 'I've been honest: there's still plenty more work to be done – but with more of us there it'll be finished quicker, and then we'll be self-sufficient. It's clean and safe.'

'I've got no intention of spending the rest of my life living in some hippy-dippy new-age commune,' Kieran announced.

'Seems to me we're all going to have to become self-sufficient whether we like it or not,' Jackson interrupted, beginning to sound as frustrated as Cooper. 'There's no alternative now, is there? There's no government any more, no benefits system, no McDonald's, no utility companies, no Internet—'

'No government,' Ainsworth smirked. 'Sounds pretty good to me when you put it like that.'

Jackson sighed. 'Come on, grow up.'

'All we're trying to do is be realistic, that's all,' Donna said, exasperated. 'The supplies here on the mainland will run out eventually and—'

'—and by then we'll *all* be dead and buried,' Jas said. 'With only this many of us left, we'll be picking meat off the bones for years yet. There's nothing you've got on your island that we haven't got here, but there's plenty here that you'll go without. You're isolating yourselves unnecessarily. Cutting yourselves off like this seems bloody futile.'

'I think you're looking at this completely the wrong way,' Donna said, refusing to give up. 'You're still thinking about things in terms of your old life and all the stuff you *used* to need – but all that's gone now. Everything's changed. Here's an example – cars and roads. We don't need them any more, because you can walk the entire length of the island in a couple of hours.'

'I understand that, but why *should* I do without cars?

189

There are millions of 'em, just lying around for the taking – I can have any car I could ever dream of. It's just a question of finding it and getting it started. What you're suggesting is limiting yourselves to some kind of mediaeval lifestyle.'

'You're the one living in a castle,' Richard said under his breath.

'No, we're not limiting ourselves,' Donna protested. 'Bloody hell, Jas, what do you think's going to happen when the bodies are completely finished and you finally pluck up courage to go back outside? Are you just going to flick a few switches and turn the world back on again? You won't get the power working, or the gas. What happens when all the batteries in all the cars finally run flat, or when all the fuel's used up and you've drained every tank dry? What do you do then? You're going to end up building yourself an island of your own, and you'll be as stranded and cut-off as we are.'

'Bollocks.'

'She's right,' Jackson said, speaking to Jas at first, then turning around so that he could address everyone in the room. 'It's all about economies of scale now. The world's too far gone to pull back from the brink. We've got no choice but to go right back to basics, and no matter what you say, Jas, Donna's right: your world is going to keep getting smaller and smaller until it's just you. They've already antici-pated that on the island. And because of their location and their attitude, they're going to try and build something from the ruins instead of just "picking the meat off the bones", as you put it. I don't know about the rest of you lot, but I think our best bet is to leave here with these people and head for their island.'

'Well I don't,' Jas said, his voice loud enough for everyone to hear, but also strangely unemotional and detached. In the expectant pause before he spoke again, the only sound was the steady low thumping of the generator outside. It sounded like a headache felt. 'Leaving the mainland would be a mis-take,' he continued, 'and it's a mistake you'll find hard to put right. They're not going to operate charter helicopter flights to fly you back if things don't work out, are they? Anyone who leaves here will be risking everything. We'd be completely cut off. What happens if things go wrong? Where's the escape plan?'

'If we do it right we won't need to escape,' Lorna said.

Jas looked at her with disappointment. 'I thought you'd understand, Lorna – you should know better than most that you *always* need an escape plan. Do you remember what happened when we were at the flats? Or have you already forgotten about Ellie and Anita?'

She shook her head as a number of low, uneasy-sounding conversations sprang up. 'Of course I haven't forgotten them,' she said. 'You're just scaremongering.'

'No, I'm not,' he said. 'This is an important and valid point. For those of you who don't know, Ellie and Anita were with us a long time back, right at the beginning. They both got sick and died – we don't know what killed them, or why it didn't finish the rest of us off. We packed up and moved on, rather than hang around and find out. So tell me, if there's an outbreak of something like the disease that killed Ellie and Anita on the island, where are you going to run to?'

'What do you think the source was?' Cooper asked.

'Don't know,' Jas replied. 'We assumed it was the bodies. We were surrounded by masses of them.'

'Problem solved, then. We don't have any bodies on Cormansey, so nothing to worry about.'

'We *assumed* it was the bodies,' Jas repeated, 'but I've always wondered if that really was the case. No one else got sick after them, and we were all exposed, some of us a lot more so, in fact. It might have been something else – something they both ate, something they smoked, something naturally occurring – don't forget, we're moving into an age now where our chances of getting ill are going to increase. Smallpox, TB, the Black Death . . . who knows what might make a reappearance to bite our arses?'

'Donna's right, now you *are* just scaremongering,' Cooper said. 'The risks of getting contagious diseases are hardly going to increase when there's no one else left to catch them from. Look, I still don't understand why you're doing this: we came here to offer a solution, not to cause more problems.'

Jas stood up and pointed accusingly at him. 'Have you not listened to *anything* I've said? Your bloody "solution" might well turn out to be the cause of the problems. The bottom line is, isolating ourselves on an island is just too big a chance to take. We can't risk it. *I* won't risk it, and if anyone else here has got any sense, they won't either.'

Jackson also got to his feet. He'd had enough. 'We're not going to get anywhere like this. I suggest we all sleep on it. Make your decisions overnight. Those who want to leave can go first thing. The rest of you can stay.'

Jas nodded his agreement. Meeting over. He left the room, followed by several others – Kieran, Bayliss, Ainsworth, Paul Field and Melanie among them.

Cooper helped himself to a can of lager and downed it in one as other people began drifting away. Donna pulled up a chair next to him, a drink in her hand too. Richard waved his hand, declining the offer: as their designated driver he stayed dry, ready to take the controls of the helicopter in a hurry if they needed him to. And although it was looking increasingly likely they were going to be spending the night here, he wasn't taking any chances.

Harte spotted Caron, still sitting at the back of the classroom with Driver. He walked over and sat down next to her. 'You okay?' he asked.

'Fine,' she replied, before adding, 'all things considered. It's a little stifling in here tonight, don't you think? Bit too much testosterone for my liking.'

Harte smirked. Good old caustic Caron: hers was the wine-addled voice of reason. He'd forgotten her uncanny ability to cut through the bullshit and see things for what they were.

She dropped her voice and whispered, 'That helicopter guy, he said they've got a girl on this island of theirs that's pregnant.'

'They have. I met the father.'

'He's here?'

'Back in Chadwick. They didn't let him come here – didn't want him to risk butting heads with Jas and his crew.'

'Sensible. Shame, though.'

'What's a shame?'

'The pregnant girl. Having a kid born into all this mess.'

'And that's half the problem, I think. No one knows if it'll be born at all. Providing it doesn't come out coughing up blood, it should be okay . . . I guess.'

'Suppose. I don't fancy its chances though. Poor little thing will probably grow up wild. Doesn't bear thinking about really.'

'So what are you going to do, Caron? Stay here or leave?'

'I'm not sure yet,' she answered honestly. 'There are plenty of aspects which appeal, but you know me: all that hard work and physical graft? I'll get my hands dirty when I have to, but I'm no cleaner, and I'm certainly not a farmer. My child-bearing days are long over, so I'm not a lot of use to anyone any more, am I? Mind you, that's how I like it. I just want to retire quietly. All I need is a decent supply of food, a few bottles of wine and a library. I'm happy just reading and drinking until I drop.'

'I know you too well – you say that, but I think you want more than that.'

'Well, I do quite like the look of that helicopter pilot,' she half-joked.

'You know what I mean.'

'Nope, a little peace and quiet and some booze: that'll do me nicely, thank you very much.'

'The island sounds peaceful. Mind you, try finding somewhere that *isn't* quiet these days.'

'I know.' She sighed, then admitted, 'The truth is, I'm

really not sure what I want to do yet. I need a good night's sleep to try and help me decide. I can see plenty of reasons for staying, but I can find as many good reasons to go.'

'Well, I'm going,' Driver said. 'I'll tell you this for nothing, first chance I get I'm buggering off to this island. Always fancied retiring to the country, I did.'

28

Harte lay awake all night on his sofabed in the caravan next to Jackson's, worrying. Jas and Kieran were on the other side, with Mark and Paul Field, who'd moved in after an 'accident' with a wastepaper bin, a bottle of booze and a box of matches. Donna, Cooper and Richard had gone in to Jackson's late last night, and they hadn't yet come out. He'd spent hours watching the helicopter in the middle of the courtyard, desperate for it not to leave without him.

After tossing and turning restlessly for hours, he finally fell into slumber around four, until noises outside woke him with a start. He was out of bed so fast it made him feel nauseous, and as he pressed his face against the window he saw that there were people gathered around the helicopter. He ran outside, frantically pulling his clothes on as he went.

'Morning,' Richard said casually as Harte ran towards him, all arms and legs and panic. 'All right, are you?'

'Thought I was going to miss my flight,' he answered breathlessly.

'You are,' Cooper said from behind him, startling him. He spun around. Jackson was there too.

'What are you talking about?' he asked. He turned to look at Jackson. 'What's he on about?'

'We were talking in the caravan after the meeting,' Jackson explained. 'Some of the things Jas said last night were right: this is a big decision for people to make, and we can't rush them. Cooper here has kindly agreed to give us all a little more time to make up our minds about what we want to do.'

'We're flying back to Chadwick this morning,' Cooper began. 'We're going to—'

'I'm coming with you,' Harte interrupted. 'You *said*.'

Cooper shook his head. 'We need you here – look, we need to get back to the marina to let Harry and Michael know what's going on, and in the meantime, you and Jackson will be organising this end of things, finding out who's going and who's staying, getting things packed up.'

'But why me? You don't need me for that – anyone could do it.'

'You know the area better than most,' Cooper said, patting him on the shoulder. 'You've spent a couple of weeks scavenging around Chadwick, and you know where to find the boats we're planning to take. Your man Driver has agreed to transport everyone, but he needs your help to get there. This is important, Harte.'

Harte looked at him, feeling deflated and unexpectedly angry. 'This is *bullshit*,' he spat, turning his ire on Cooper. 'I agreed to come back here on the condition you'd get me out again.'

'And that's still going to happen,' he said calmly. 'It's just that you'll be leaving here by bus, not helicopter, that's all. What difference does it make? We're going to wait for you in Chadwick until midday tomorrow, so come the end of the week you'll be on Cormansey. These people need you, Harte – Jackson and Driver most of all.'

Harte tried to argue with Cooper but he couldn't. There was no point.

Just past midday: a clear sky and a cool breeze. Jas was standing on the top of the gatehouse with Kieran. Below them the rotor blades on top of the helicopter had just started to spin. The noise and speed increased rapidly, blowing clouds of dust across the courtyard and sending people scattering for cover. The aircraft rose majestically and Jas watched as it climbed effortlessly, and was gone in a matter of minutes. All that noise and bluster disappeared in a remarkably short period of time.

'So what do you think?' he said to Kieran. Kieran stared into the distance, looking as far as he could see in the general direction the helicopter had taken.

'I'm guessing fifty-fifty,' he answered. 'Maybe more will want to go than stay. The grass is always greener, and all that shite.'

'And that's all it is,' Jas said, 'shite. Most of the people here are just sheep, following the rest of the herd. If you told them to swim the Channel because there's no dead bodies in France, most of them probably would.'

'They're not that bad.'

'Some of them are.'

Kieran thought for a moment before asking, 'So what are we going to do?'

Jas walked to the other side of the gatehouse roof and looked out between the battlements over the dead world beyond the wall. Kieran followed him. Down below he could see what was left of the dead, still drawing ever closer, even after all this time. Of course the noise of the helicopter had piqued their unwanted interest this morning. Christ, they were pitiful-looking creatures now. He watched one of them, one leg broken, the other missing, as it lay on its belly and slowly dragged itself across the muddy grass. Another tried to move past a corpse that had expired against the trunk of a tree. In its clumsiness the two ribcages had become entangled, and now the body which was still moving was dragging the other behind it.

The dead appalled Jas. He didn't admit it to anyone else, but they still scared the hell out of him – how could anyone not be afraid of monsters like these foul and hideous, ungodly beasts which stopped at nothing to reach the living. They were detestable fuckers with no consideration for their own physical condition, let alone anyone or anything else's. Even today, months after death, when their physical bodies had deteriorated to such a repulsive extent, they were still a threat. There was nothing human about them now; they were just evil: driven to keep attacking until they could no longer function. He wondered how anything could be filled with such relentless, remorseless hate.

'We can't let anyone leave,' Jas said, finally responding to Kieran's question. 'Can't they see what they're doing? They're making a huge mistake.'

'We could try talking to them again,' Kieran suggested. 'Maybe now they've had time to think they'll see things differently.'

'I doubt it.'

The two men remained looking over the battlements for a while longer. Eventually increasing noises from around the courtyard distracted Kieran. 'I'm going to see what's going on down there, okay?'

'Okay,' Jas said.

Suddenly alone, Jas leaned against the wall, then sank down to the floor. He held his head in his hands and tried to make sense of the whirlpool of emotions he was feeling. He thought about everything he'd gone through to get to this point: that first morning when he'd lost his family, the time at the flats, and the circumstances under which they'd been forced to leave, their nightmare incarceration at the besieged hotel . . .

It was the weeks he'd spent trapped in the hotel which troubled him most. Just the thought of those dark, endless hours was enough to bring a tidal wave of horribly familiar feelings of helplessness, panic and dread crashing over him. He'd found it almost impossible to deal with the cruel finality of their imprisonment there – the fact that there wasn't a damn thing he could do to help himself – and the prospect of being backed into a corner like that again now terrified him. And despite all the assurances he'd heard again and again, that was how this island seemed to him: he'd be giving up all semblance of control if he went there; he'd be trapped, unless he could persuade the pilot to fly him back, or find someone who could sail a boat to get him back to the mainland. And travel to and from the island was inevitably going to get harder with time, not easier.

Cheetham Castle wasn't perfect: it was an ill-equipped, uncomfortable place – but that didn't matter, it was just a staging point – a stepping stone, a shelter where they could weather the final days of this tumultuous storm – and it had served its purpose adequately. It would soon be time to move on, but not yet. And definitely not to Cormansey.

Without thinking, Jas slipped his hand into his inside pocket and pulled out the wallet he'd carried with him constantly since before his nightmare had begun. In it was the last remaining photograph of his family. It had become increasingly ragged over time, and he'd been looking at it more than ever. He gazed deep into the last image of his wife's beautiful brown eyes – still sparkling and intense in spite of the wear – and then, as he always did whenever he felt his options were reducing, he asked her what she thought he should do.

Tell me, Harj: do I stay or do I go?

29

The short winter days and long nights conspired against all of them. In Chadwick, Cooper and the others spent much of the rest of the day collecting more supplies, mindful that they needed to make the most of their time on the mainland. Taking more people back might reduce the space they had available, but at the same time increasing the size of Cormansey's population also meant they needed to take as much as possible. They unpacked and repacked the boats, discarding anything they decided was unnecessary, and loading the bulk of the supplies onto the *Summer Breeze*, the slightly smaller of the two. Both boats could carry ten people each, maybe a few more at a push, so working on the assumption that Jas and his inner circle wouldn't be leaving with them, and with four spare seats in the helicopter, they worked out that they should easily be able to fit all their passengers and their belongings on board the *Duchess*.

They spent their third night on the mainland on the luxury cruiser again, as comfortable as before but strangely subdued. Maybe the people back at the castle hadn't shared their enthusiasm for island life? Donna was surprised. She thought some of them would have turned up by now, at least.

'They'll be here,' Cooper said, seeming to read her thoughts. 'You know what it's like when you're leaving somewhere,' he half-joked. 'There's always more to sort out than you expect.'

She smiled. 'I know,' she said. 'I just want to get going, that's all. I want to go home.'

*

At the castle, Driver had moved his old bus for the first time in weeks. He drove it into the centre of the courtyard, right where the helicopter had been sitting a few hours earlier, and started to check it over thoroughly, keen to satisfy himself that the vehicle would be able to get them all the fifteen miles or so into Chadwick. The distance was strangely daunting: in times past he'd have covered it in a matter of minutes, barely any time at all, but things were different now.

Moving it there would make it easier for everyone who wanted to leave to get their belongings (and any supplies they could half-hitch in the process) loaded up. As soon as he'd parked up there had been a steady stream of people getting on and off.

Jackson and Harte watched from a distance. 'First light and we'll be off, okay?'

'Okay,' Harte said, 'the sooner the better. Got any idea how many are leaving?'

'Thirteen or fourteen, I think,' he replied, 'including you and me.'

'Good. Just Jas and his mates staying behind, then?'

'Looks that way. Jas, Kieran, Melanie, Mark and Will, I think. Phil Kent's undecided.'

'It's probably for the best: there's no point them coming if they're not committed. Jas does have a point, but we're all taking risks whatever we do now, and I know where I'd rather be.'

'As long as we're all happy with our own personal decisions, that's all that matters.'

On the far side of the bus, out of sight, Mark, Kieran and Jas were shifting boxes of supplies from the café kitchen and the back of two lorries and a van, stashing them away in the gift shop and museum.

'You sure we should be doing this?' Mark asked.

'We need this stuff,' Kieran replied quickly. 'There'll be plenty more where they're going tomorrow – it's different for us. We're not leaving here, so we have to make this last. This is our share. We worked for it and we're entitled to it. We're just making sure they don't take what's ours.'

'Get as much as you can move,' Jas said. 'The more we lock away, the less there is for them to take.'

30

It was gone eight before the sun rose fully, but as soon as there was enough light to see, the castle courtyard became a hive of frantic activity as those who were leaving grabbed the last of their belongings and stashed them on the bus.

By just after ten they were ready to load up the remaining supplies. Jackson, Bob, Howard and Harte walked over to the kitchen to start, but where they'd expected to find large stocks of provisions, instead they found just an empty space.

As soon as she heard what had happened, Lorna began checking around the rest of the castle. She found the bulk of the missing supplies hidden in the gift shop behind display racks and the counter.

'Over here,' she yelled, her voice loud enough to alert everyone who was awake. 'I've found it all.'

As they ran over to the gift shop, Harte asked, 'Who has the keys for this lock?'

'There are only two keys, I think,' Howard answered.

'I didn't ask how many there were, I asked you who has them.'

'Jas has got one,' Bob said.

'And I'm pretty sure Kieran has the other,' Howard added.

'Let's get this door open. Some of that's our stuff in there, and I'm sure as hell not going to leave it all in there for Jas and his cronies to gorge themselves on when we're gone.'

'Sorry, mate but that's exactly what you're going to do,' Jas said. He'd walked, unnoticed, up behind them, flanked by Mark and Will.

'Come on, Jas, this is stupid,' Jackson protested. 'We

won't take it all, but we're entitled to some of this stuff. It's *ours*.'

'It's staying here. You're going back into Chadwick, aren't you? So you can get more. Remember, we're stopping here for a while longer yet – we need this more than you do.'

'Yes, but not all of it – Christ, there's only going to be a handful of you staying behind. And anyway, just a couple of days back you were telling us all how you were going to rape and pillage the whole country.'

'That's in the future. Until then, we need those supplies.'

'And so do *we*!' Jackson turned his back on Jas and shook the door, but it wouldn't open. He took a knife from his belt and started trying to force the lock.

'Go and find Kieran,' he said under his breath to Harte, 'try and talk some sense into him. See if you can get the other key off him.'

Before Harte could move, Jas grabbed hold of Jackson and threw him away from the gift shop entrance. Jackson, taken unawares, was sent flying. He got up, brushed himself down and ran at the door, trying to shoulder-charge it open, but it was stronger than it looked and he simply bounced back off it. He tried again, regardless.

'You'll never do it, you fucking idiot,' Jas said. 'What—'

He stopped when someone shouted behind him, 'Stop her!' and he spun around to see Lorna helping herself to supplies from the back of one of the lorries. She scooped up as much as she could carry and sprinted over to the bus, and several of the others followed her lead and did the same.

Jackson tried to force the door once more, but when Jas didn't come at him again he looked back to see him running towards the lorry, which was rapidly being emptied. Driver was standing in the middle of the courtyard, watching the chaos unfolding all around him, dumbstruck.

'Get the fucking bus started,' Jackson screamed at him as he ran past. 'Let's get out of here.'

As Lorna weaved around Jas she slipped, but without

dropping anything she managed to catch herself. She threw herself onto the bus just before Driver, who came storming up behind her. He clambered into his cab, sinking into his seat with relief, and started the engine, but when he looked behind he saw that there were only a handful of people on-board. More were running over from the caravans, terrified that they were going to be left behind. Howard stumbled up the steps, his arms overloaded.

Outside, Jas positioned himself directly between the front of the bus and the gate. Charlie Moorehouse tripped while carrying two heavy cellophane-wrapped packs of bottles of water, and while he was off-balance Mark Ainsworth shoved him right over and put a boot between his shoulder blades, preventing him from getting up. Driver could see Zoe, fighting to get past Will Bayliss, who was blocking her way back to the bus. She tried to barge him out of the way, but he stood his ground. She went to slap him but he was too fast; he caught her wrist and twisted her arm around so her position was reversed.

He shoved her up onto the bus, and spat, 'You can fuck off. I'll be glad to see the back of you.'

'Don't do this, Jas,' Jackson said, refusing to show either anger or malice as he approached the other man, arms open, but still carrying the knife he'd been using to try and force the gift shop door open. He sheathed it to show his peaceful intentions.

'Unload the supplies,' Jas said, 'and I'll let you leave.'

'You'll *let* us leave!' Jackson laughed. 'Come on, Jas, grow up. What do you think this is, a movie? We've all made our individual decisions, just like you insisted. Everyone's had their say and made their choice, and now you have to respect those choices.'

'I can't. I've got a conscience.'

'What are you talking about? You could come with us – you *should* come with us.'

'How many times do we need to have this argument?

The island is a dead end – a full stop. Going there won't do anybody any favours.'

'I think you're wrong.'

'I know I'm right.'

'Come on, Jas, it doesn't have to be like this.'

Around Jas and Jackson, the furious activity had suddenly stopped. Many of the people who wanted to leave had managed to make it onto the bus, but several more hadn't and now stood a cautious distance away, unsure what to do next. Driver inched the bus forward slightly, and that small movement was enough to start the panic again. The remaining would-be escapees ran towards the noisy vehicle, too many for Mark and Will to stop, but Paul Field rugby-tackled Bob Wilkins as he tried to run past and sat on him to keep him face-down in the gravel.

'No one's going anywhere,' Jas announced.

'He's got a gun!' Shirley Brinksford screamed as she tried to get onto the bus. Kieran had appeared, brandishing the same shotgun he'd shoved into Jackson's face when he'd first arrived at the castle.

'Get them out of here!' Jackson bellowed to Driver. Caron hauled Shirley onto the bus just as the doors closed with a hiss of hydraulics. The bus juddered forward, and as it began to pick up speed Driver could see Jackson had started running towards the gate. Jas turned around, but just as he realised what was happening, Driver managed to position the bus directly between the two of them, giving Jackson a brief advantage. Jackson reached up and lifted the heavy wooden crossbar securing the gate and threw it to one side. He grabbed one of the thick ropes hanging from either side of the gate and pulled it open, and immediately the great clot of dead flesh which had been pushed up hard against the other side of the gate by the force of the thousands more pushing from behind fell forward. A putrid dripping shadow of a man, completely unrecognisable as the remains of the teenage boy it had once been, took a few staggering steps before more of the foul things overtook it and trampled it into the mire.

Everyone, Jas and Jackson included, was transfixed momentarily by the hideous sight. How any of these things could continue to function in such a pitiful condition was beyond anyone's comprehension.

Jackson was the first to move again. He jumped the decaying body lying in front of him and ran over to the other side of the gate, but he'd only managed to half-open it when Jas came at him again, grabbing him around the waist and viciously wrestling him away. Beside them, more of the dead spilled forward, moving together like a viscous, disease-filled sludge, a slowly spreading pool of decay.

Driver tried to get through, but the gap ahead wasn't wide enough. Kieran, seeing the sudden movement of the bus, fired a warning shot, but the recoil took him by surprise – he'd only fired it a couple of times before – and he shattered the windscreen, only just missing Driver.

The air was immediately filled with panicked screams, and people who were still trying to get onto the bus hammered on the door at the same time that those inside started trying to get off. Kieran reloaded and moved around to the other side, this time firing at the massive tyres at close range, leaving the heavy vehicle listing to one side.

Jackson freed himself from Jas's grip and ran to try and stop Kieran, but Jas was too fast for him and caught hold of him again. He dragged Jackson back and slammed him down into the inches-deep foul-smelling, once-human slurry that was spreading across the courtyard like an oil slick. Jackson gagged at the overpowering stench and the feel of the ice-cold muck on his skin.

He spat out splashes of flesh and struggled to speak. 'Why, Jas?' he wheezed, his voice little more than a whisper.

Jas stood up and walked a few paces away. Jackson slowly picked himself up, slipping in the decay, every bone in his body aching. He managed only a few steps before dropping to his knees again. He clambered to his feet, stood up straight and took the knife from his belt. 'You have to let them make their own decisions, and you have to abide by what they decide. You can't decide for them.'

He ran at Jas again, and just as he lunged, Jas grabbed hold of his arm, flipped him over onto his stomach and dropped down onto his back. Jackson groaned with pain, but this time he didn't move.

'You're wrong,' Jas hissed in his ear, crouching down so no one else could hear. 'You've got this all wrong: if we want to survive, then we've got to work together, and we need to base ourselves here. There's nothing to be gained from going to this bloody island. You hear me, Jackson?'

When Jackson didn't react, Jas grabbed his shoulder, still soaked with glistening decay, and rolled him over onto his back – and he staggered away in shock. Jackson's knife had sunk hilt-deep into his belly.

Sue Preston had managed to force her way off the now-useless bus, followed by everyone else, and she ran over to help Jackson. There was nothing she could do. He was already dead. The courtyard emptied as people ran for cover. Kieran walked forward and looked down at Jackson's body. A flood of deep red blood was pulsing steadily from his wound.

On the other side of the castle grounds, another engine was started, and neither Jas or Kieran saw the black Ford Fiesta until it skidded out into the open and accelerated towards the gate, churning up gravel.

'Get the fucking gate shut!' Jas yelled, his voice hoarse with anger and shock, and Kieran and Will ran to close up the barrier. Kieran weaved around a corpse which had just enough muscle remaining to be able to walk unsteadily. It reached out for him and when he recoiled, he slipped over in the greasy decay which was inexorably spilling forward, a slow-motion flood of filth. He got up, then dived out of the way again as the Fiesta powered past, skidding through the sludge between him and Will, clipping the gate and losing the driver's wing mirror in the process, but squeezing through the gap by the barest of margins.

Kieran picked himself up again, gagging at the wave of putrefied gunk and driftwood-like bones which rippled back as he pushed his side of the gate shut. Bayliss closed the other side and between them they dropped the crossbar back into place.

'Who the fuck was that?' Jas demanded.

'That was my car,' Melanie whined.

'Never mind that, who was driving it?'

'Ian fucking Harte,' Kieran replied.

31

Eleven o'clock came and went. The waiting at the marina in Chadwick was interminable. As each minute passed by, so the likelihood that they'd be returning to Cormansey without anyone else seemed to be increasing.

'So what happens if they don't get here?' Donna asked, her anxiety mounting. 'We can't just leave them.'

'What else are we supposed to do?' Cooper replied. 'We gave them a decent timescale and plenty of opportunity. We said we'd wait until midday and we will. If none of them are here by then, we leave.'

'Anything could have happened,' Harry said. 'Absolutely anything.'

'My money's on Jas,' Richard sighed. 'He's a troubled soul, that one, scared to death of putting a foot outside the castle wall, he is. He'll have been putting pressure on all of the rest of them not to leave, you mark my words. They'll have agreed to stay there just to pacify him.'

'We've done what we said we would,' Cooper repeated. 'We've given them more than enough time. There's still the best part of an hour to go.'

'Cooper's right. They've had plenty long enough. If they were coming, you'd have thought they'd have virtually followed you back. Maybe they just decided they didn't want to go with us after all,' Michael suggested.

'Or someone suggested for them,' Richard said.

'What about Harte?' Donna said. 'You saw him yesterday. We all saw what a state he was in when Cooper wouldn't let him back on the helicopter. He'd have run here if he had to.'

'You think?' Michael said. 'I'm not so sure. You heard

how quick he was to bail out on them before. Seems to me like he's a bit of a shyster, always taking the easy option.'

'I completely disagree,' Donna countered, 'and I don't think that's fair. Maybe they're just struggling with transport or—'

'Whatever the reason, it's out of our hands now,' Cooper said firmly, ending the discussion. 'Our priority is our people on Cormansey, and we need to get back to them with these supplies. Whether the others stay at the castle or not, they'll be okay. One thing Jas was right about is the amount of stuff they're going to be able to help themselves to once the dead are finished. It's not the same back on the island. They need the stuff we've collected. *We* need it. This is about people's lives.'

'I'll be honest,' Richard said, 'whether we take anyone else back or not, I just want out of here now. This is a dead place. Too many bad memories here for my liking.'

Harte raced towards Chadwick, struggling to find his way into the town along maze-like roads which all looked the same to him. Although he'd spent more time than anyone else there, he'd been on foot. He'd never actually driven this route from the castle himself – in fact, he'd only been this way once before, on the ill-fated looting expedition from which he'd failed to return. Everywhere looked depressingly featureless: littered with debris and the remains of endless bodies. He knew he was up against the clock, especially as he'd screwed up and wasted fifteen precious minutes driving the wrong way before he'd realised. That had just added to the pressure. He'd been desperately disorientated and completely lost, until at last he'd seen the names of a couple of places he recognised. He remembered hearing Kieran and Jackson talking about them. He knew he was finally heading in the right direction.

For mile after endless mile there was nothing but trees and hedges, with the occasional building, but his speed was restricted by the appalling carnage all around, the remnants of a world left untended for almost four months. Nothing was where it should be any more. The roads themselves were becoming harder to distinguish, covered as they were in the sludge of dead corpses, now littered with exposed bones. It reminded Harte of fallen branches after a particularly violent storm.

He reached the top of a hill, and for the first time he could see the ocean in the distance. He reckoned he had twenty minutes to go, give or take, and only a few miles left to cover. The sight of the water gave him renewed hope that he'd get to the marina in time, and that he'd be able to tell them what had happened back at the castle. A bend in the road obscured his view momentarily, but within seconds he could see the ocean again, and this time he could see the town too. He accelerated, struggling to keep control on the steep hill, and then, just before it disappeared below the tree tops, he saw the helicopter, perched back on top of the multi-storey car park.

After another long, straight climb and an equally long and frantic descent he'd finally reached a part he was sure he recognised. They'd definitely driven into Chadwick this way on that ice-cold, snow-covered morning just before he'd taken leave of them all and disappeared. Part of him wished he'd stayed where he was, hiding in the flat a little further up the coast. Though the isolation had been becoming increasingly hard to handle, staying there alone would have been infinitely easier than his brief return to Cheetham Castle.

Harte couldn't help thinking he was to blame for the chaos he'd left back there. If he hadn't taken the island people there no one would have been any the wiser. Maybe the people at the castle would have been okay without him – perhaps they'd have lasted through the final days of the dead without incident, as Jas had wanted. Sure, they wouldn't have had an easy time of it, but maybe they'd have coped. They had so far – well, most of them, anyway. He thought he'd been doing the right thing, but all he'd done was put other people in danger.

The right thing for who? he asked himself as he struggled to keep the car moving at speed. *Me, or everyone else?*

He swung the car around a tight corner, a little over a mile short of the very centre of town now, maybe a mile and a half from the marina, and his wheels skidded on a greasy sheen of frost and compacted decay. For a heart-stopping moment the back end of the souped-up Fiesta threatened to slide out of control, but he recovered, and kept his foot down on the accelerator. And then, as he drove the wrong way around a roundabout and aimed for the marina, he saw something which made his heart stand still. He hit the accelerator again, praying it was just his mind playing tricks—

It wasn't.

The rotor blades on top of the helicopter were spinning.

He pressed his foot down hard, gripping onto the steering wheel as he ploughed straight through two corpses. There were more bodies around here, a sure sign he was close. When he next looked up, he could see that the helicopter had taken off and was hovering above the car park roof.

Harte looked back at the road again and instinctively slammed on his brakes – a cadaver had dragged itself into the middle of the tarmac. It was crawling along on its hands and knees, too weak now to stand up straight, and he almost didn't see it in time. He wrenched the wheel hard left and skidded around the crawling corpse.

The helicopter was definitely climbing: he could see it rising up above the rest of the buildings. A flash of light distracted him – the sun glinting off a window – and this time when he looked down again he saw another corpse in the road directly ahead, this one upright, arms outstretched, a really clichéd pose. Brown rags and saggy flaps of skin hung off what was left of its emaciated frame like sticky robes. It was too late to avoid it, so this time he just kept driving, and the body dissolved on impact, showering the car with a gutful of yellow-black gore. The foulness distracted him, and he didn't see a pedestrian crossing coming up. He reacted too late, and hit the concrete traffic island at full speed. The impact with the front driver's-side wheel was so hard that it sent the car spinning around through a complete 360-degree turn. Harte was thrown back in his seat, his feet slipped off the pedals and the engine stalled. When he tried to start it again, it wouldn't turn over, and the only engine noise he could still hear was that of the rapidly disappearing helicopter.

Frantic now, Harte scrambled out of the car. He briefly glanced at it: as well as the flat front tyre, the wing was badly damaged and a flood of liquid – oil or power steering fluid or something – was dribbling out along the road after him.

He ran through the streets as fast as he could, dividing his attention between weaving through the relentless corpses and watching the helicopter overhead, which was still hovering above the town. For a moment he allowed himself to believe that Richard and whoever else was up there with him might have seen him – maybe they were going back to the castle again, to see what had happened to the others? He glanced at his watch. It was past midday. His only option now was to try and get to the marina in time.

The roads along which he now sprinted were increasingly filled with dead flesh, drawn here over the last couple of days by the presence of the survivors and their activity in and around the marina, but Harte was moving so quickly that they were no threat to him. Some tried to grab at him as he hurtled past, but most didn't even realise he was there until he'd already gone. He darted down along the slope which led to the water, still watching the helicopter as it moved out over the ocean, flying extraordinarily low now.

He broke right to avoid another cadaver, and ran straight into one of the still-smouldering dustbin fires which had first guided him here in the darkness – was it really only a couple of nights ago? It fell over, sending sparks and ash spilling out over the cold ground, and he just managed to jump over it as it rolled in front of him. He could see the luxury cruiser up ahead, where he'd first found the others, and he pounded along the jetty and climbed on board, but it was too late – there was no one here, just the empty beer bottles and the remains of the meal he'd shared with them that night. But wait, they'd never intended to leave the mainland in this vessel, had they? He suddenly remembered that they'd loaded all their supplies onto another boat elsewhere – but where was it?

Back the other way.

It was hard to see much of anything through the mass of masts and the countless moored boats. Soaked with sweat and panting hard, he ran back towards the marina entrance, and then dragged himself out along another jetty. He ran out to the end of the wooden decking which stretched beyond the last of the boats and looked out over the water. He sank to his knees. Out there, rapidly disappearing towards the horizon, the helicopter gracefully drifted away.

Below it was a single boat.

What did he do now? He ruled out the most obvious two answers in order of impossibility: go back to the castle and try and salvage something from the chaos there, or get into a boat and try to find the island on his own. If he could find a map and compass, then remember the name of the damn island, then teach himself to navigate, then learn how to sail a bloody boat . . .

Who was he kidding? Everything was completely fucked. His best option – probably the only real option remaining – was to go back to the cruiser, or to the flat he'd previously occupied, lock the fucking door behind him, and never take a single step outside again.

'Harte, what the hell is going on?' a voice shouted from out of nowhere and he scrambled to his feet and spun around.

Michael was standing at the other end of the jetty.

32

'**Y**ou're bloody lucky. Another couple of minutes and we'd have been gone too,' Harry said as he passed Harte a bottle of water and a towel. Harte wiped his face dry and drank thirstily, then tried to ask the hundreds of questions which had flooded into his brain. He could barely speak, let alone think straight.

'Why—?' was all he could manage.

'Why what? Why are we still here?' Michael asked, and when Harte, still breathless, nodded, he admitted, 'Like Harry said, we weren't planning on hanging around much longer. Did you see Cooper and Richard? We were supposed to be following them.'

'We put the supplies on the other boat and left this one empty for all the passengers we were supposed to be taking,' Harry said, 'and when no one turned up we stayed to try and load up a few more things before we left. I swear, mate, you caught us by the skin of your teeth.'

'Anyway,' Michael said, leaning back against the cabin wall and watching Harte intently, 'more to the point, why are *you* here and no one else?'

'You're making a habit of abandoning your mates, aren't you?' Harry added unnecessarily.

Harte finished his water, wiped his face again, and tried to explain. 'It's Jas,' he said. 'The fucker's completely lost the plot. We were getting ready to clear out and he went ape-shit – we were just trying to get our share of the supplies and he flew off the handle. Before we knew what was happening there were guns going off and he was fighting with Jackson and all sorts.'

Michael looked at Harry. 'That's the guy who thought living on an island was a bad idea? Cooper said there'd probably be some trouble with him.'

'You can say that again.'

'So what exactly happened?'

'I didn't see it all. Jas reckons the island is too isolated – he thinks it's too cut off.'

'Doesn't make any difference these days,' Michael said quickly. 'Where you are is far less important than—'

'Listen, you don't have to convince me,' Harte interrupted, 'I've already had this argument. I was always planning to go with you, remember? Look, no one really knows what the best long-term option is any more – no one can – but most of the castle folks had decided that going with you guys was the safer option.'

'And this Jas wouldn't let them?'

'That's about it.'

'So what do we do now?' Harry asked. 'Just head back home like we agreed?'

'You can't,' Harte said, an uncharacteristic urgency in his voice. 'The only reason people aren't here is because they *couldn't* get away, not because they didn't want to.'

'And what about you?'

Harte looked at the other two and said, 'I came back because I need your help,' he said. 'Yes, I ran away before and yes, I did it because I was a coward and I didn't want to go back to the castle. But you've got to believe me, this is different. My friends are trapped back there, and I want to get them out.'

33

The castle was a hive of frightened activity. The beaten-up bus sat in the middle of the courtyard, as useless as a beached whale. The other tyres had been slashed, just to make certain it wouldn't be going anywhere, and all the supplies had been unloaded and removed. All around, people carried out Jas' orders, passed to them by Kieran, Will, Mark Ainsworth and Paul Field. Paul himself stood guard in front of the gate, the shotgun held where everyone could see it. His glowering presence alone was enough to deter anyone from trying to get out. From time to time he barked instructions at Howard and Bob, who were shovelling the remains of the dead into wheelbarrows, then dumping them into the already overfull cesspit. They were both exhausted, and far too tired to even think about rebelling. Jackson's body had been taken over to the cesspit area too, wrapped in a tarpaulin and dumped next to where Steve Morecombe had been buried a week and a half earlier. No one would notice the stink over there, Paul had said.

Jas watched the proceedings alone from the top of the gatehouse, keen to put as much distance as possible between himself and everyone else. It had taken him more than an hour and two cans of lager to stop shaking after Jackson's death. He was overwhelmed by a raft of unexpected emotions: guilt, fear, anger, remorse . . . but there was nothing he could do, he told himself. *It wasn't my fault. What's done is done*, he kept repeating. *I need to get this lot back on track now. Let them forget about the helicopter and that bloody island and all that bullshit. Another few weeks and we can move out of here.*

But he kept coming back to one dark thought: *I've killed a man*.

He tried to focus on something – *anything* – else, but it was impossible. He hadn't actually sunk the knife into the other man's chest, but he might as well have. Over the months he'd destroyed untold hundreds of those wretched cadavers which walked the dead world outside, dispatching even the least decayed, most human of them without a second's thought, but this was different. Completely different.

Fewer than a hundred people left alive that I know of, and I killed one of them . . .

'What do you want me to do with them?'

Jas, startled by the unexpected voice, quickly turned around. It was Kieran. 'What?'

'I asked you what you want me to do with them. Do we just keep them locked up in the caravans for now?'

Jas thought for a moment. 'Might as well,' he replied, trying not to sound as distracted and nervous as he felt. 'Use the vans nearest the gatehouse – let them calm down. We need to get everything back to how it was before those fuckers turned up here and screwed everything up.'

Kieran paused before answering, 'Okay. You're the boss.' He turned to go back downstairs, but Jas called to him before he disappeared.

'We're doing the right thing, you know,' he said, and Kieran nodded. 'Look, no one meant for any of this to happen. Fact is, they'll have fucked off back to their island again by now, so what's done is done.' He walked over. 'Get some food going – get a couple of the girls working in the kitchen, crack open a few bottles of booze, the best stuff you can find. Keep the people safe and warm and give them what they want, within reason. Let's not give them any excuses to try anything we might all end up regretting.'

34

The basic communications Harry had rigged up between the two boats and the helicopter only worked intermittently, their efficiency fading away as they got out of range, but between the frequent bursts of static and the increasingly long radio silences, Harry managed to get sufficient information to Richard, Donna and Cooper so that everyone knew what was happening.

With the *Summer Breeze* full of supplies, Donna and Cooper had little option but to continue back to Cormansey. There was nothing to be gained from them turning back. Richard stayed with them for a while, flying close and remaining in contact until he was sure they could reach the small port close to Danver's Lye. Then he flew back to the mainland, cursing the fact that yet again everything seemed to be down to him.

Harry, Harte and Michael watched the helicopter land on top of the car park, and twenty minutes later Richard arrived at the marina, breathless.

'Bloody hell, I hate being out there on my own,' he admitted. 'It's a ghost town – you turn any corner and there they are, those bloody things, waiting for you. Good job they're so slow – but they still scare the shit out of me.' He stopped talking and looked at the others. 'What?'

'You finished?' Harry asked.

'Sorry,' he mumbled, 'bit nervous, that's all.' He followed them onto the *Duchess*.

'Donna and Cooper get back to Cormansey okay?' Harry asked.

'I left them a few miles short. They'll be there by now.'

'Did you stop and land?' Michael asked.

Richard shook his head. 'Wasn't any point. I turned around and came straight back. They'll explain what's happened to the others as soon as they've moored. So what's the plan? I'm assuming that we do have a plan?'

'Get back to the castle and get those who want out, out,' Harry flippantly replied.

'Simple,' Richard said, equally flippantly. 'I'll just land in the middle of the castle and ship them out in threes and fours. No one will mind.'

'How the hell *are* we going to do it?' Harte asked, nervously chewing his nails. 'Because you're right, we're not going to be able to just fly in. Jas is going to be seriously pissed off; he's not going to let anyone in or out without a fight.'

'Then we'll have to find another way,' Michael said, stating the obvious.

'Whoa – *you're* not going anywhere,' Richard interrupted. 'You can't. You've got Emma and the baby to think about.'

'I think about them all the time,' he said, suddenly sounding subdued, 'but the thing is, I'm here now and it doesn't look like I'm going anywhere until we've got Harte's people out of this castle. There's no way I *can't* get involved, is there?'

'But you should stay out of trouble. Wait here for the rest of us to get back—'

Michael was shaking his head. 'There's no point. I told you, I've been doing a lot of thinking. Things are different now. Believe me, there's nowhere I'd rather be than back on the island with Emma. I fall asleep at night thinking about her and the baby, and I wake up every morning still thinking about them. But at the end of the day, me not being there isn't going to make a massive amount of difference. It wouldn't be the end of the world.'

'You've missed that,' Harry mumbled. 'That's already been and gone.'

Michael ignored him. This was serious. 'What I'm saying is, there's nothing I can do to help the baby be born, is there? I mean, I can do all the practical stuff, run errands and all that, but me being around won't make a huge difference to Emma giving birth, will it?'

'I think you're doing yourself a huge disservice,' Richard said. 'Your missus and your kid will need you. There's another fifty bods back on Cormansey who can do chores and run errands, but you're the only one Emma actually *needs*. You shouldn't take any risks you don't need to, that's all I'm saying.'

'But these are risks we *do* need to take,' Michael said. 'Imagine the difference another ten or so will make on Cormansey.'

'I understand what you're saying, but I still don't agree.'

'Well, that's how it is. I've made my decision. You'd all probably do the same thing if you were in my shoes.'

'This is all very lovely,' Harte said cynically, 'but it's all academic anyway. How the hell are we going to get them out of the castle? Are we just going to stroll up to the front door and knock and ask if Jas will let them out?'

'He's right,' Richard agreed. 'This is a fool's errand.'

'No, it isn't,' Harry said from the corner. 'I know exactly how we'll do it.'

35

Caron and Lorna had been locked in the café kitchen and ordered to prepare the food, as Jas had commanded.

'I'd piss in this if I wasn't going to have to eat it myself,' Lorna said, seething with anger, barely able to keep calm. 'Who the fuck does Jas think he is?' She stirred a vast pot of soup they'd bulked up with tinned vegetables. Caron was busy steaming a job lot of chocolate puddings they'd found in the stores. She hunted through various crates and trays, looking for a box of catering-size packets of custard powder she was sure she'd seen recently.

'Have you seen the custard powder?' she asked.

'No, I haven't seen any fucking custard powder,' Lorna yelled at her. 'Fucking hell, Caron, there are more important things to think about right now than pudding.'

Unfazed by Lorna's outburst, Caron found what she'd been looking for. She dropped the box onto the table next to the gas burner she was using.

'This should be nice,' she said.

'Nice! For fuck's sake, who gives a damn if the food tastes nice?' Lorna shouted. 'Are you completely fucking stupid? Haven't you seen what's been happening around here? Jackson's dead, in case you hadn't noticed.'

'Of course I've noticed,' Caron snapped, finally showing a little emotion. 'Stupid thing to say.'

'Then why are you talking about custard and things tasting nice? Our last decent chance to get out of this place disappeared this afternoon.'

'I'm well aware of that, thank you very much.'

'You don't act like you are.'

Caron stopped and stared at Lorna. 'Getting shitty with me isn't going to make any difference,' she said, instantly slipping back into 'mother mode' and talking to Lorna exactly the same way she used to try to reason with Matthew, her son. 'I know exactly what's going on. We are where we are, Lorna, and there's absolutely nothing you or I can do about it for the moment. We need to make the most of what we've still got, because the way things are going, we might lose that tomorrow. Now, have you seen any clean bowls?'

'No,' Lorna grunted.

'I don't know what's wrong with these people,' Caron continued, ignoring the blatantly obvious fact that what was *wrong* with these people was that their lives had been destroyed through no fault of their own, and even now, several months down the line, many of them were still completely fucking traumatised. Trivialising everything seemed to be helping Caron cope tonight. 'I don't know,' she wittered to herself, 'people help themselves, leave their dirty cups and plates all over the place, then moan at us when there's none left.'

'Am I supposed to care, Caron? Fuck 'em all. I'll ladle this shit into their bare fucking hands if they complain.'

'I'm going to see what I can find outside, okay?'

'Whatever.'

Caron picked up an empty washing-up bowl to load with whatever dirty crockery she could find. She knocked on the door between the kitchen and the café to get the attention of Mark Ainsworth, who was standing guard outside. He was leaning up against a wall, his head drooping, half-asleep. Caron's knocking woke him up.

'Got to go and collect up some dishes, okay?' she shouted at him through a window. He didn't say anything, just yawned and let her out.

The door slammed shut and Lorna tried to concentrate on the food and block out everything else. It was all a real effort. Her arm ached, her back ached, her head ached . . . She cursed herself, wishing she'd been as selfish as Harte – if she'd been more with it, then she'd have been out of here by now as well, and maybe even some of the others would have got away with her too. As it was, she was stuck, and Jackson was dead. Had Jas meant to kill him? It was hard to believe he was the same man she'd spent the last few months with . . .

This was like something out of a bad dream, and yet it was frighteningly real. Caron's words rattled around her head: make the most of what you've got today, because you might lose it all tomorrow. Christ, how right she was. The fact that Jas had just committed an act so foul and out of character just served to confirm something she'd suspected for a long time now: the further they got from their old lives, the less they resembled the people they used to be. What would be the end result? Would they manage to stop the rot and salvage some semblance of normality, or this time next year would they all be running around like savages? She continued to stir the soup as she thought about the empty world beyond the castle walls, without all the previously enforced restrictions about where you could and couldn't go, and what you could or couldn't do. All those rules had been removed, so theoretically she was free to roam wherever she wanted, provided she could get out of this fucking place and—

Lorna froze when a hand touched her shoulder. She spun around, her heart pounding, the ladle she'd been using to stir the soup clenched in her hand.

When she saw it was Mark Ainsworth she relaxed slightly – only slightly.

'Sorry, love,' he said. 'I didn't mean to startle you.'

'Then why did you creep up on me like that, you idiot?' she yelled back at him. 'And I'm not your "love", okay? I'm not anybody's love.'

He backed away, hands held up in submission. 'Sorry,' he said again.

'So what do you want?'

'Cup of tea would be nice, if you're offering.'

'I'm not. You know where everything is, make it yourself.'

'No need to be like that . . .'

'Piss off.'

'You want one?'

'No.'

Mark fetched himself a mug and made his drink with hot water from the steamer Caron had been using, all the time watching Lorna. She sensed him staring at her, but she refused to make eye-contact. *Just ignore him and he'll go away.*

But Mark wasn't going anywhere. 'Look,' he started, 'I think we both got off on the wrong foot. I don't want any trouble. I just want us to get along.'

'We'll get along fine if you fuck off and stay out of my face, understand?'

'That's not going to be so easy now we're all stuck here.'

'You've got your mate Jas to thank for that.'

'I thought he was *your* mate?'

'He's no friend of mine. Not after today.'

'Don't let him hear you talking like that, eh?'

'Why, what's he going to do? Kill me?'

'I won't let him hurt you, Lorna. I'll look out for you.'

'You come anywhere near me and I'll have your balls.'

'You can have my balls anytime, lover,' he said, slipping into sleaze mode with uncomfortable ease and immediately regretting it.

'Come anywhere near me and I swear I'll cut them off and shove them down your bloody throat.'

He was about to make some stupid, insensitive quip about Lorna's kinks when he stopped himself. She really did look angry enough to carry out her threats. He paused, knowing he should probably leave but still wanting to say more. 'Look, Lorna, I'm sorry,' he said, 'it's just my humour. I don't mean anything by it; it's just the way I deal with all of this.' He watched her for a moment longer. When she didn't react, he decided to risk talking again. 'You're right, we are all stuck here. I don't want to fight with you.'

'Then like I said, stay away.'

'Things are going to get difficult around here, I'm sure they are. I'll watch out for you.'

'Don't bother.'

'I want to. I like you, Lorna. I think we could—'

He immediately shut up when the door behind him flew open and Caron barged in, carrying a rattling bowl full of dirty washing-up. She looked at Lorna, concerned. 'Everything all right?'

'Everything's fine,' Lorna said, not looking up.

'I was just leaving,' said Mark.

'Good,' Lorna mumbled. She watched him leave.

'I'll catch you later, ladies.'

'Hope not,' Caron said, just loud enough for him to hear.

36

Cooper wasn't a natural skipper, and Donna freely admitted she didn't have a clue. Richard had guided them close enough so that they could see Cormansey in the near distance – and what a beautiful, inspiring sight, with a few fires burning through the endless darkness of absolutely everything else – but it had taken several hours longer for them to navigate their way to the small port near Danver's Lye. By the time they were finally ready to disembark, a large crowd of villagers was already waiting on the jetty.

Jackie Soames and Jack Baxter were near the front of the group, and Jack caught the landing rope Cooper threw to him and tied up the boat.

'Good to see you back,' Jackie said, helping Donna onto dry land, then hugging her affectionately. 'We were starting to get worried. What's with the helicopter turning back again?'

'There's nothing to worry about,' Cooper said, sounding subdued.

'Nothing to worry about?' Donna yelled at him.

'What's wrong?' Jack asked. 'Where're Michael and Harry?'

'We need to get the boat emptied so we can head back,' Donna said, ignoring his question.

'We're not going back,' Cooper told her. It was clear from the tone of his voice there would be no negotiation.

'I am, and I'll take someone else if you won't go.'

Donna and Cooper stood on the jetty yards apart, barely able to maintain eye-contact with each other.

Jackie pushed her way between them. 'Look, will one of you please tell us what the hell is going on?'

'Michael, Harry and Richard are fine,' Cooper explained, 'but we found more survivors. We were hoping to bring them back with us, but there was a complication.'

'A complication?'

'A couple of egos facing off against each other. Nothing too serious.'

'Nothing serious?' Donna protested. 'Fuck, were you listening to the same radio message as me? Harry said someone had been killed.'

A ripple of low noise spread through the crowd gathered on the jetty.

'So where exactly are the others?' Jackie asked.

'They've gone to try and get them out,' Cooper replied, 'but there's no point us going back to help – there's nothing we can do. They've got enough room, and by the time we get there they'll be on their way over.'

'Jesus,' Jackie said. 'And Michael's gone too? Bloody hell, what will poor Emma say?'

'Do we have to tell her? I mean, they should be back sometime tomorrow and—'

'Of course we have to tell her,' Donna yelled at him, barely able to believe what she was hearing. 'Michael's the father of her child. She's got a right to know.'

'Did you bring me back any fags, Cooper?' Jackie asked.

'Plenty, why?'

'And booze?'

'Loads, as ordered.'

'Good, because I think I need a drink. Anybody care to join me?'

'Not for me,' Cooper said. 'You're right, Donna, I'll go and see Emma and let her know what—'

'You stay away from her,' Donna interrupted, pushing past Cooper and moving through the crowd on the jetty. 'Leave her alone. *I'll* go.'

37

It was dark and cold. A full moon illuminated far too much of Chadwick and its dead population for Michael's liking. He was standing on the car park roof, looking out towards the ocean and doing his best to ignore everything that lay between him and the edge of the water.

'We ready?' Richard asked, hanging out of the helicopter door.

'Go for it,' Harry said, and he climbed into the navigator's seat next to the pilot's. Harte was already in the back. Michael got in, sat down next to him and buckled up.

'You're all completely sure about this?' Richard said as he ran through his pre-flight checks and started the powerful machine. 'Hell of a risk, this.'

'I don't see we have much choice,' Michael said as the noise and vibration increased. 'We have to try.'

'Fair enough.' He pulled back on the controls and took off. The helicopter rapidly climbed up into the night.

The helicopter was over the castle in no time at all and Richard banked around and peered down into the courtyard. He could already see people down there, looking up, following the aircraft as it circled. He switched on his searchlight, both to help him and make it more difficult for those on the ground to track his movements. There weren't as many people out in the open as he'd expected to see. Where were the rest of them? They'd already ruled out trying to touch down within the castle wall, but that was academic now because much of the courtyard below was filled with rubbish, and the bus occupied the area where he'd set down before. He couldn't land there even if he wanted to.

He completed another circuit, a little lower this time, sweeping around the castle and trying to distract and confuse the people down below. He could see figures up on the top of the gatehouse, and when he saw one of them lift a shotgun and fire it, he knew it was time to leave. He broke away and climbed rapidly before he flew back towards Chadwick. He was not about to risk being hit.

In an overgrown field a mile further north, Michael, Harte and Harry stood and watched the lights of the helicopter disappear. Between them they carried a mass of mountaineering equipment which they'd looted from Chadwick. Harry had much of it already prepared. While most of the survivors had cast off virtually all the remnants of the lives they used to lead, a few had found new outlets for the skills they'd previously employed. Harry had been an outdoor activities instructor, teaching schoolkids and corporate employees on team-building weekends useful skills like sailing, mountaincraft and rock-climbing.

They clambered over the low drystone wall which ran around the field where Richard had set them down. The moon illuminated everything with its ice-white light, but Michael wished it would just disappear as they approached the outermost edge of part of the vast crowd of bodies encircling the castle. Although the immediate threat the dead once posed had now been substantially reduced, and the plummeting temperature had restricted them further tonight, crossing this immense sea of decay was still a daunting prospect. The three men stood together on the last patch of clear grass they could find, each of them looking for reasons to delay the next step forward.

Harry hoisted a long coil of heavy climbing rope up onto his shoulder and looked towards the castle up ahead.

'There's nothing much in the way of cover out here,' he

said, 'but I really don't think anyone's going to be expecting us to walk through this lot.'

'I don't think they're expecting anything,' Michael said, sounding more confident than he felt. 'I think they'll have fallen for Richard's little bluff. They'll think we're all still in the helicopter.'

'Is this going to work?' Harte mumbled, far less confident than the others. Everything had made sense back at the port, but the nearer they got to the castle, the more uncertain he was beginning to feel.

'If we're careful it should,' Michael replied. 'Jas won't be expecting this – and if you're right and more of them want to leave than want to stay, then he's going to be well out-numbered too.'

'Suppose,' he said, still not convinced.

'Come on, ladies,' Harry said, tired of dawdling, 'let's just get this done, shall we? Opposite end to the gatehouse, you reckon?'

'That's our best bet,' Harte replied. 'There are no caravans or anything else around there, just the cesspit, that's all. The bloody stink keeps most folk away.'

'That'll do, then.'

Harry took his hesitant first step into the remains of the dead. His boot cracked a thin sheen of ice and sank into a layer of mud and decay that was several inches thick. The ground was unexpectedly uneven, and the mulch they had to walk through was filled with buried bones and other less obvious obstacles. He stopped walking suddenly and tried to work out the physics of the crowd: there were shapes that were more recognisable as human up ahead, but out here on the fringes everything had been reduced to a featureless sludge. That made sense: the later arrivals to the massive gathering would have been less restricted, and they would have crushed their weaker brethren under their feet as they'd advanced towards the castle, creating a compacted layer of dirt and gore. The situation would no doubt change as they got deeper into the decay.

They walked in single file. Harry attempted to lead them in a relatively straight line through the unending muck, but what they were trying to walk through made it next to impossible. Michael brought up the rear. The gruesome mire was making his stomach churn. It was ankle-deep now, and there were more recognisable remains around them: a half-buried corpse there, still – astonishingly – trying to crawl; there, another stood upright with its foot stuck, unable to get free; that there, that was another one, lying flat on its back, its spindly arms thrashing like a drowning swimmer. Their boots snapped bones like twigs, and whenever Michael lifted a foot and looked down, he could see teeming movement where his boot had just been, for the viscous sludge was alive with all manner of creatures, worms, maggots and insects, gorging themselves on this proliferation of putrefying flesh. He was thankful it had hardly rained over the last few days; a couple of heavy downpours was all it would have taken to turn this place into an impassable quagmire.

Progress was slow, their footing constantly unsteady. Obstructions – walls, fences, even streams – were hidden by the blanket of decay, invisible until they were virtually on top of them. Up ahead now was a dark, featureless mound which looked like a glistening heap of rot, and it took them some time to work out what it was, and why it was there.

At last Harte said, 'It's a car—' He took another sliding step closer, then added, 'Fuck me, look at that.' He gingerly grabbed a cadaver's shoulder with one gloved hand and tried to pull the corpse away, but its legs were stuck and when he pulled it harder still it snapped, folding back on itself so its head was now upside-down, its skull almost touching the back of its heels. As he stared into its disease-ravaged face, he thought he saw its mouth move. He shuddered, but he kept going, peeling away another cadaver, trying to uncover more. He was right, it was definitely a car, and he pushed several bodies away to reveal almost the full width of its windshield. The make, model, even the colour of the vehicle were impossible to make out with so much rot piled up all over it, but he could see that the dead driver was still behind the wheel, held in position by his safety belt. The dry air inside the car had preserved the corpse, so it was less decayed, and as they watched, it lifted its head to look at them, then raised a single bony hand and slapped it against the window. Harte jumped back with surprise. To Michael's right, another body tried to lift itself up and separate itself from the rest of the mass. Even now, after months of decay and all that it had been through, the creature still immediately identified Michael and the others as a threat and tried to attack them.

'Keep moving,' Harte said, his voice shaking. 'Try not to look and just keep moving.'

The gruesome sea through which they were wading was constantly changing in texture and depth, every single footstep unpredictable. They'd been walking for what felt like an eternity. Harry estimated they'd crossed almost a mile of dead-packed land, but it was virtually impossible, even in the bright moonlight, to see how far they still had to go. More bodies remained upright the deeper the three men went, but the constant shifting and grinding of so many of them in such close proximity for so long meant there was little left than bone. Occasionally one still had enough muscle remaining to manage a clumsy swipe at the men as they trudged past, but such attacks were easily avoided.

'Cut right,' Harry said suddenly, but Harte mis-stepped and crunched through the exposed ribcage of a corpse lying on the ground with its back arched.

Michael steadied him as he shook himself free. 'Fucking things,' he complained pointlessly as he shook off the disgusting gunk.

Harry was still walking forward when he suddenly found himself beginning to sink. For a moment he panicked, terrified that he was about to be sucked down into a quagmire, but he fought against his instinct to panic, doing all he could to remain calm, not to thrash about wildly, and heaved a huge sigh of relief as his feet at last made contact with solid ground again. 'It's okay,' he said, feeling his way forward, 'it's some kind of furrow, I think. Maybe what's left of the moat.'

Michael and Harte followed cautiously, following in his footsteps as best they could, but Michael continued to sink, first up to his thighs, then almost up to his belt, and he found himself gripping onto the remains of corpses stranded upright to keep his balance. Harte started gagging when he slipped and found his face just inches away from the slurry, and his retching started Michael off too. *Christ*, he thought as the bile rose in his throat too, *I hope this is going to work*. He didn't think he could face the prospect of having to walk back the same way if they couldn't get into the castle.

He glanced down when he almost lost his footing, but when he saw an ear floating on top of the slop, then the fingers of a hand, then half a face, he made himself look up. He was breathing hard, each time taking in a lungful of foul-smelling germ-filled air, but it was either that or he'd vomit, and he really didn't want to lose control. His head was spinning and his entire body drenched in a cold, sticky sweat. He made himself look dead ahead, focusing on Harry's back, and then, finally, he saw Harry was climbing again.

Harry changed direction slightly to avoid another corpse – he couldn't see its face, but he could swear it had started turning towards him – and then led the three of them towards clearer ground. Before long they'd made it through the slurry and away from the last of the animated dead.

Even though they were now climbing a steep rise up towards the base of the castle walls, Harry didn't let his pace drop until he'd reached the very top and could stand leaning against the ancient masonry, safe in the knowledge no one inside the castle could see him from here.

Michael reached the top about thirty seconds later, and Harte another minute after that.

'You both okay?' Harry asked.

'Think so,' Michael said. Harte just nodded, too tired to answer. Michael took his rucksack off his shoulders and emptied it. There were three bags of clean clothing inside, and each took one and began peeling off their sodden, stinking gear. They dumped it in a pile, then Harte passed around the towels and they cleaned themselves up as best they could. It was bitterly cold, but they all preferred to freeze than to keep wearing soiled clothes. The rot had even seeped through to their underwear, and they discarded inner trousers, long johns and boxers all.

It felt like it took an age to change, but eventually they stood together in the shadows of the castle wall, numb with cold, but clean.

'What do you think then,' Harry asked, 'is this the right spot?'

Harte looked up and down the length of the massive, gently curving wall. 'It'll do, I think,' he said. 'Should be fine here . . .'

Harry looked at him. Did he have more to say? He didn't look sure. 'But?' he pressed.

'Nothing . . . it's just that the wall looks fucking huge now we're standing next to it. Are we really going to get over it?'

'We're going to have to,' Michael said. 'Desperate times call for desperate actions.'

'Where'd you get that little gem from?' Harry grinned.

'Can't remember – some film or other, I expect. It's true, though.'

'Bloody hell,' Harte continued nervously, 'climbing over castle walls in the middle of the night: it's all a bit James Bondie, isn't it?'

'Give us an alternative and we'll listen,' Harry said.

'We gave up on the idea of a helicopter rescue, remember?' Michael said. 'Now *that* was more like James Bond.'

Harte was too anxious to see the funny side.

'It's fine,' Harry said, trying to reassure him. 'I used to do a lot of climbing. I've been up rock faces far worse than this in my time.' He started to unload various bits of kit from the bag Harte had been carrying – karabiners, harnesses and the like – and issued them to Harte and Michael.

'What am I supposed to do with this?' Harte asked.

'Nothing, just leave it to Michael. You remember what to do, don't you, Mike?'

Michael nodded, and hoped that he really did. Harry had given him instructions before they'd started out, but after all they'd been through to get here, he thought he'd probably forgotten most of it. But he grinned and said, 'I remember,' hoping he sounded more convincing than he felt.

Harry laid out the climbing rope, unspooling it carefully along the ground, then attached one end to his belt. 'I'll get up and over,' he explained, 'get the rope fastened to something on the other side, then you two follow when you hear my signal, okay?'

'Okay,' Harte said. 'What's the signal again?'

'It's the middle of the fucking night,' Harry said. 'If you hear anything out of the ordinary, take that as your cue to start climbing.'

'Got it,' Michael said. 'Off you go.'

Harry stood at the foot of the wall and scanned it, looking for his first handholds. He reached up, dug his fingers into the narrow gaps between the huge, ancient stones, and lifted himself off the ground. Michael watched as he hauled himself up, impressed by his dexterity and speed. He'd climbed several feet in no time at all.

'I'll never be able to do that,' Harte complained.

'You don't have to – you'll have the rope, remember?'

He looked up at Harry, way above them now, scrambling up the sheer face of the wall at lizard-like speed, as if he didn't have a damn care in the word. It had sounded deceptively simple when they'd been back in Chadwick making plans – get across the dead by foot, scale the wall and get into the castle, round up everyone who wants to leave, find a vehicle big enough for them all, then get the fuck out of the castle before anyone notices. *But plans like this always sound okay until you're there*, he said to himself. Crossing the dead had been a nightmare in itself, and as for climbing the wall . . . he honestly didn't know if he could make it. If Harry slipped and fell – well, that didn't bear thinking about. There'd be no way he could survive, and no way they could help him. He remembered Steve Morecombe, who'd died as a result of an accident he should have been able to make a full recovery from.

Bloody hell, and this was the *easy* part of the plan . . . he was beginning to seriously doubt if they were going to make this work.

Harry was more than two-thirds of the way up now. His arms ached – he hadn't done anything like this for a while – but he ignored the pain. It wouldn't be much longer now. He felt for the next handhold, a narrow gap between two huge chunks of stone which had been dressed and dropped into position hundreds – maybe even a thousand – years ago. *Now's not the time to get distracted*, he told himself as he started to think about how many years these massive blocks had remained in place, and all that had happened to the world around them in that time. Even if he made it through tonight and lasted another fifty years, his entire life would be little more than the blink of an eye in comparison to the centuries this place had been here.

It wasn't long before he'd reached the top. He peered over first, then pulled his legs over and lay flat on his stomach along the top of the wall, keeping his head down to avoid being spotted from inside. He looked down into the castle grounds. There was the cesspit Harte had told them about – he could smell it from up here – and nearby was an unmistakable shape wrapped in a tarpaulin, a body, no question about it. He glanced down and gave Michael and Harte a quick thumbs-up to let them know he was okay and he hadn't been seen. Bloody hell, all that talk of James Bond – he was actually starting to feel like a spy, except that spying was yet another redundant profession now there were so few people left alive.

Harry looked along the inside of the wall in both directions. He could see several lorries, parked up a short distance behind him. They'd make this immeasurably easier for them: as well as giving him something at a convenient height to lower himself onto, one of the lorries would also be a perfect anchor for him to tie the rope to. And if he could get hold of the keys, any of the vehicles he could see would be perfect for getting people out of the castle compound. He looked back at Michael and Harte again, still standing in the same place, still waiting for his signal, then gestured in the direction in which he planned to move.

38

Harry and Michael helped Harte down onto the roof of the lorry and the three of them lay flat and checked the place over. It was past eight, but the long, tumultuous day made it feel more like the middle of the night. The moon was still out, but most of the camp inside the castle was hidden in shadow, the tall encircling walls blocking out the light. The only other illumination came from the windows of a couple of the caravans at the far end by the gatehouse, and from the glowing remains of a small, untended fire. It looked like the bitter cold had kept everyone inside their shelters tonight, hiding away like hibernating animals.

'Do you know who wants out, and can you make them known to us somehow?' Michael whispered. 'We don't know who's who.'

'I've got a good idea.'

'So where are they likely to be, in those caravans?'

'I guess so,' he replied. 'There's a classroom, a café and a few other rooms over by the gatehouse, but I don't see much activity up there. They must be in the vans. We need to be careful, though – we don't want to find ourselves knocking on Jas' door by mistake, do we?' He grimaced at the thought.

'We should split up,' Harry suggested. 'Do a recce, then meet back up over here and decide on a plan of action once we know where everyone is. Just stay out of sight and don't get caught.'

'Wasn't planning on it,' Harte mumbled. Did they think he was stupid?

The three men climbed down off the lorry, lowering themselves as far as they could then dropping the last few feet onto the gravel. They were all dressed in dark clothes, with hats and scarves obscuring their faces, and they quickly disappeared into the shadows as they moved off in different directions. Michael took the long way around to the pre-fabricated rooms near the gatehouse, but just as Harte had suspected, he found no one there. He thought the place looked surprisingly well organised – if it hadn't been for the wrecked bus in the middle of the courtyard and the signs of fire damage to one of the caravans, all would have seemed well.

Harry went in the opposite direction, checking out the area around the cesspit. He noticed there were two bodies – the one wrapped in cloth he'd seen from the top of the wall, and another, already buried in a shallow grave with a rudimentary wooden cross hammered into the ground at one end. *So despite everything I've heard*, Harry thought, *these people aren't total savages*. He thought he heard someone coming and ducked out of sight, crouching behind a wall. He discovered he'd chosen to hide next to a trench urinal, the smell so strong it made his eyes water. Once he was satisfied no one was there, he crept back out into the open and worked his way back around to the lorries where he'd first come in.

Harte made a quick dash across a patch of open space and slipped between two of the caravans. Inside one he could hear voices. He thought he could make out Kieran, but he couldn't be sure. He turned his attention to the van next door and stood up on tiptoes. Through a crack in the curtains he could see Lorna, curled up on a narrow bed, which surprised him, as this wasn't the van she usually slept in. And there was Zoe, sitting in a corner with her back against the wall. There was Sue, and Driver too. Bingo. This was what he was after. He turned and ran back to find the others.

He found Harry hiding in the back of one of the lorries. Michael returned seconds later. 'They're in the caravans like we thought,' he said.

'Easy to get to?'

'Don't know yet.'

'So once we've got them,' Michael said, 'how do we get them out of here.'

Harry tapped the side of the lorry and dangled a set of keys in front of him. 'They were left in the ignition,' he said. 'Very convenient.'

'So what's the plan? Just get everyone we can loaded into this lorry and drive out of here?'

'It'll work as long as they don't start shooting this time.'

'Shooting?' Harry said. 'What kind of weapons have they got?'

'A couple of shotguns,' Harte said, then added, 'Nothing too serious.'

'Nothing too serious? Jesus.'

'All right,' Michael said, 'there's nothing we can do about it, just be on the lookout. So assuming we get everyone together, how do we get out of this place? I didn't want to get too close to the gate. I thought they'd have guards there.'

'There probably is someone watching,' Harte agreed. 'They'll be up in the gatehouse, I expect. We should leave it 'til the last minute. There's no lock on the gate, just a wooden crossbeam, so once you get rid of that, then you just pull the two sides of the gate open.'

'Sounds straightforward enough,' said Harry. 'Are we ready then?'

'What, now?' Harte said, suddenly feeling horribly nervous.

'Yes, now.' Michael sighed. 'What did you think we were going to do? Wait for the sun to come up so we can see what we're doing? Bloody hell, Harte.'

'Okay, okay . . .'

'So you and I will go and see if we can get these people out. Harry, you get in the front of the lorry and wait for us.'

Harry nodded, and Michael pushed Harte out of the lorry, then followed him along the castle wall until they were level with the back of the caravan where he'd seen Lorna.

'In here,' Harte said. He gestured for Michael to stay back

in the shadows, then crept across and lightly tapped on the window next to where Lorna was lying. When she didn't respond he rapped on the glass a little harder, cringing at the noise. This time she sat up and looked around, moving with a lot more urgency when she saw his face at the window.

'Wait there,' she mouthed, and she disappeared. Harte could hear her talking to someone inside, and after a short delay the caravan door opened. He could hear her voice clearly now, telling someone she needed to go for a piss. The other person – it sounded like Mark Ainsworth – gave her permission, but told her to be quick. If he was supposed to be acting as a guard, he was a pretty ineffectual one, Harte thought, relieved. Lorna shut the door behind her and ran to Harte. She dragged him into the shadows of the castle wall. Michael followed.

'Bloody hell,' she said, 'did you parachute back in here? I thought you'd run out on us again.'

'Just taking a leaf out of Driver's book: I thought it best to slip away and wait until it was safe to come back.'

'It's hardly safe now.'

'I know that, but this was the right time to do this.'

'That's not what you said earlier,' Michael interrupted. 'He's been whinging like an old woman. I'm Michael, by the way.'

'Lorna,' she said. 'Hey, are you the one with the baby?'

'Hopefully.'

'Save the small talk,' Harte said, his stomach still churning with nerves. 'We need to get everybody out of here.'

'And how exactly are we going to do that?'

'Our man Harry's waiting in a lorry over the way,' Michael explained. 'We'll get everyone who wants to leave loaded into the back of it, then get the gates open and get the hell out of here, hopefully before anyone else has realised what's going on.'

'Simple as that?'

'Hopefully.'

'Are you all in this caravan?' Harte asked.

'Mostly,' Lorna replied, 'and there are a few more next door. But there's a problem: guard dogs. There's at least one in each caravan.'

Harte looked at Michael anxiously. 'Do we take them out?'

Michael looked equally unsure. Dealing with dead bodies was one thing, but fighting a fellow survivor was a different matter altogether.

'Stay back here and give me a couple of minutes,' Lorna said. 'I've got an idea.'

39

'**Y**ou took your time,' Mark said as Lorna returned to the caravan. He sounded half-asleep. Maybe if she'd waited a little longer he'd have drifted off completely, then they might have all been able to walk out unchallenged. Her heart was pounding and the palms of her hands were clammy. She didn't know if she could go through with this. But the alternative didn't bear thinking about.

'Sorry,' she said, 'I didn't mean to take so long. I was just thinking . . .'

'What about?'

'About you, actually. I was thinking about how horrible I've been to you recently – how rude I was in the kitchen earlier. I'm sorry.'

'You've got nothing to apologise for,' he said, sounding shocked, and surprisingly honest. 'It was me, not you – I can be a real dick at times. I kind of forget myself sometimes, you know? Especially with all this shit going on around us.'

'I know.'

'So you don't need to apologise, okay?'

'Okay. Thanks.'

She watched him watching her. Poor dumb bugger didn't have a clue what to say next. He could bore everyone sense- less with stories about his irrelevant fifteen minutes (more like fifteen seconds) of fame on telly last year, but he really wasn't the sharpest tool in the box. She knew that Ainsworth wanted her – she'd known it for ages. And she also knew that he'd never expected to be having a conversation like this with her, not in a hundred years.

'Look,' she said, 'I really do feel bad about this – I want to make it up to you, but there are too many people in here. Do you think we could go somewhere else and talk?'

He was beginning to look like all his birthdays had come at once. 'Sure.'

'I think I got the wrong impression earlier,' she went on. 'It's just that it's hard to know what to do for the best these days, isn't it? And like you say, with everything that's happened here today, everyone's on a knife-edge. The stakes are so much higher now, you know? You put a foot out of place or say the wrong thing to the wrong person at the wrong time and—'

'I know,' he said, 'I feel the same, especially with Jas. It's like I'm treading on eggshells all the time. Don't say anything, but I'm starting to think he's losing the plot.'

'He's struggling, just like the rest of us,' Lorna agreed. 'Hey, I kept a bottle of wine hidden away in the kitchen. It won't help against the cold, but if you fancy a glass . . . ?'

'Or two?'

'Or three?' She started back down the steps and led him quickly across the courtyard. They both kept looking from side to side, checking no one else was around, like a pair of kids sneaking out after being grounded. They stopped outside the café door.

'Have you still got the keys?' she asked.

He rummaged in his trouser pockets, pulled out a bunch of keys and started looking through them, holding each one up one at a time until he found the one which fitted the lock. His hands were trembling with nervous excitement, but at last he managed to unlock the door. He pushed it open, then started looking for the key to the kitchen.

They'd barely got inside before she was on him, wrapping her arms around him and kissing him, hard. Mark, completely dumbstruck, forgot for a moment how he was supposed to react. It had been so long since he'd had any physical contact like this. The kiss took Lorna by surprise too, and for a few seconds she forgot herself. The warmth of holding another person close, the softness of his lips, the heat which passed between them . . . Almost everyone had neglected basic pleasures since the day everyone had died. How long had it been since either of them had felt anything like this?

'Bloody hell, Lorna,' he said in a momentary gap between her frantic kisses. He felt like he was barely able to control himself.

'Put something up at the window,' she told him. 'We don't want anyone looking in on us, do we?'

He kissed her again, then reluctantly pulled away and did as she asked. He was so hard, his belly burning with desire, that he was struggling to think straight. He adjusted himself, then started to block the narrow strip-windows with anything that came to hand – chopping boards, empty boxes, covering up the gaps as quickly as possible.

'I wasn't expecting this,' he said as he worked, feeling incredibly emotional, but trying not to show it. 'I didn't think you felt this way . . .'

'Funny how things work out,' she replied, leaning up against a stainless steel unit and watching him. He looked back over his shoulder as she started to undo the zip on the heavy winter coat she wore all the time. There was no heating anywhere in the castle but the classroom, so everyone wore as many layers of clothing as they could. She took off her coat and pulled her sweatshirt over her head, shivering with cold, then slowly started to undo the buttons on her shirt. Ainsworth couldn't take his eyes off her.

She stopped for a moment and looked at him coyly. 'Are you ready for that drink now?' she asked.

'Sure . . . thanks . . .'

Lorna moved forward and kissed him again, a gentle peck on his unshaven cheek this time, and as he felt her breasts brush against him he thought he might be about to pass out from the sudden strength of the previously suppressed emotions which washed over him. As she turned her back on him and bent over he wondered if she was being deliberately provocative . . . He studied the curves of her body, previously buried under all those layers.

Lorna reached into the narrow gap between two work units where she and Caron had stashed several bottles earlier in the week. 'Hope you like red,' she said.

'I'm not bothered,' Mark replied quickly, an unexpected vulnerability evident in his voice.

Lorna wrapped her fingers around the neck of the closest bottle and gripped it tight. Moving with sudden, unexpected speed, she stood up straight, swung around and smacked the bottle across Mark's head. He fell at her feet and she looked down at him, sprawled over like a rag-doll. She nudged him with her foot, but he didn't move. She didn't know whether she'd knocked him out or killed him, and she didn't have time to care. She took his keys, locked him in the kitchen, and disappeared back out into the shadows.

40

Harte had been waiting in the shadows near the caravan for Lorna to return. As soon as he saw her running back towards him he immediately opened the door and began to usher the people over to the lorry. There were seven of them crammed in there; Bob, Zoe, Phil Kent, Charlie Moorehouse and Driver, quickly followed by young Aiden, holding on to Sue's hand, all ran together across the gravel courtyard.

'There's room for a couple of you up front with me,' Harry hissed at them as they reached the lorry.

'Are they going to be all right in there?' Harte asked, watching as the last of them disappeared into the back.

'They're going to have to be.'

'There are more people up in one of the other caravans,' Lorna said quickly. 'I'm going to get them out.'

'I'll go with her,' Harte told him. 'Michael's waiting up by the gate. He'll open it as soon as you start the engine.'

Michael stood by the gate, squinting into the gloom, trying to make sense of everything he couldn't see. He pressed himself up against the wall, doing all he could to melt into the shadows, until he was satisfied the coast was clear. He reached up and ran his hands over the heavy wooden gate until he found the wooden crossbar Harte had told him about. It didn't seem to be secured at all, just resting in a pair of metal brackets, one at either end, just as Harte had said. After checking again that he wasn't being watched, he lifted the crossbar up and pulled it away. Then he grabbed one of the ropes that hung on either side of the gate and pulled it gently, just to make sure it would open. As he did, the bottom of the gate moved slightly, scraping along the gravel. Michael cringed at the noise it made and froze again, until he was sure he hadn't been heard, but there was nothing, no sign of any movement. He looked back across the courtyard at the caravans, which were clearly visible in the moonlight. Squinting, he thought he could just about make out a couple of figures, moving between them.

Then the fragile silence of the night was shattered by a sudden burst of noise, coming from one of the buildings near where he was standing: someone was screaming with anger and hammering on the door to be let out. The door of one of the caravans flew open almost instantly and several men sprinted out into the open, illuminated by the light flooding out from behind them. They ran towards the source of the noise.

Michael stood his ground, remaining perfectly still, watching as Lorna and Harte slipped into the open van.

'What's going on?' Caron demanded as Harte shook her shoulder. 'Harte, is that you? I thought you'd gone again—'

He tried to drag her to her feet, but she lolled back onto the sofa where she'd been sleeping – or crashed out, judging by the empty wine bottles rolling around on the floor below her.

Howard, by contrast, leapt to his feet immediately. 'What's happening?' he asked.

'We're going.'

'Where?'

'On a day-trip to Blackpool,' Harte answered sarcastically. 'Where d'you think we're going? This bloody island we've been hearing about, I hope.' He leaned out of the door, hoping to see either Michael or the headlights of the lorry, but he quickly pulled his head back in again as Will Bayliss ran across the courtyard from the direction of the gift shop. He had Kieran's shotgun in one hand and was trying to pull on his clothes with the other. Melanie followed close behind, trying to do up her jeans.

Lorna had been checking the rest of the caravan. She'd found Shirley cowering in one of the bedrooms, but no one else.

'This it?' she asked.

'Just me, Shirley and Caron,' Howard replied. 'Are you surprised? Don't forget, Jas, Kieran and Paul were in here – funny how most folks preferred to be crammed into the van next door.'

The racket from whoever was locked into that room and the excitement it was generating was enough to make Michael decide on a quick change of plan. He'd managed to get both sides of the gate open without being noticed. Though a handful of corpses had tried to stagger in, the cold was gripping and they were so badly decayed that they lasted just a couple of paces before collapsing – in fact, he suspected their forward movement was due more to the fact the gate they'd been leaning up against had moved than anything else.

Michael had started to run towards the caravan, but he turned back and tucked himself in against the wall just in time as an armed, half-dressed man he didn't recognise thundered past.

Over in the furthest corner of the castle grounds, Harry had worked out that something was wrong. He could see people crisscrossing the courtyard in the moonlight, but he couldn't tell if Michael or Harte were among them.

'Anyone you recognise?' he asked Bob Wilkins who was sitting next to him in the front of the lorry.

'No idea what's going on,' Bob whispered, 'but that looks like Kieran. He's one of Jas' lot.'

Harry waited a few seconds longer before deciding he had to move. He started the engine and accelerated out into the open, trying to get close enough to the caravans so that Harte and the others could make the quick short dash to safety. He could already see that the gates were open.

Shirley barged closer to the caravan door. 'Is that for us?' she asked, pushing past Howard and Harte when she saw the lorry's headlights approaching. Harte tried to grab her, but she was too fast, slipping between them and running outside before stopping in front of the lorry and waving her arms. Harry slammed on the brakes and gestured wildly and she ran around to the back, where Sue was calling out to her. Lorna ran out, intending to follow her, but she dived for cover, falling back into the caravan when a gunshot rang out. In the emptiness of the night it sounded unnervingly close.

'We've got to run for it,' Harte said, helping her up. 'We've got to get on that lorry.' He could see Will now, trying to head off the lorry, reloading the shotgun as he marched towards it.

'Go!' Howard yelled, trying to push them all forward. 'Just get out of here!'

Another gunshot echoed around the castle courtyard and this time the front of the lorry was hit, one of the headlamps smashed. Just as Howard tried to lead them out of the caravan Kieran appeared and blocked him, pushing them all back inside. He was armed too.

'Stay here,' he warned, making sure they all saw his gun. 'Don't any of you move a fucking muscle.'

He was under fire, and had to make a split-second decision: get some of them out, or none. Harry accelerated towards the open gate, churning up plumes of gravel and dust behind him, swerving around Will Bayliss, who was struggling to reload again. As he headed out of the gate, he ploughed into the sea of semi-liquid flesh outside the entrance to the castle. He was fighting to keep control and struggling to see clearly with only one headlamp as he drove out into the dark.

*

Lorna pressed her face against the caravan window and watched the lorry's taillights disappear from view. Behind her, Kieran blocked the door.

That's it now, she thought sadly. *We're truly fucked.*

41

'One of you get the fucking gates closed,' Jas ordered as he tried to force the kitchen door open, 'and put a fucking van in front of it to stop any other fucker getting out.'

Paul Field immediately jumped into action, keen to get away from Jas more than anything else. Melanie watched from a cautious distance as Jas shoulder-charged the door again, and then again. Inside the kitchen, Mark Ainsworth was trying to kick his way out in the gaps between Jas' attempts to batter his way in. Eventually, between them, they did enough damage to the door to be able to get it open. Mark staggered out into the café, as unsteady on his legs as any of the dead. Melanie shone a torch in his face and grimaced. He was badly bruised, one eye swollen shut. He dropped to his knees in front of Jas and spat out blood.

'What the hell happened to you?' Jas demanded. 'Who did this?'

'Lorna,' he replied, barely able to speak her name.

Jas turned and glared at Melanie. 'Find her.'

'But she's probably gone—' Melanie started to say.

'They can't have all got out. Get the rest of them rounded up.'

'So that all went well,' Kieran said. 'Nice rescue attempt.'

'Fuck you,' Harte spat at him. 'We got most people away.'

'But not all.'

'There's still time,' Lorna said. 'Jas can't keep us locked up in here.'

'Seems to me like he's going to try,' Kieran replied, looking through the window over Lorna's shoulder. 'See that? He's got someone blocking the gate with a van.'

'Well, that's us screwed then, isn't it,' Howard moaned.

'Not quite,' Kieran said. 'There's another way out.'

'Bullshit,' Harte said quickly. Forgetting himself, he squared up to Kieran, who didn't react.

'How do we know you're not pulling a fast one on us?' asked Howard.

'You don't. Now shut up and get out of sight. Someone's coming.'

There was a sudden scramble as people disappeared into other rooms in the caravan and hid under beds. Lorna crouched under a melamine table in the cluttered dining area and listened as Kieran went outside. She could hear him talking to Melanie.

'Nah, I've checked in here,' he said, 'it's empty. They must have got away in that lorry.'

'Jas is going mental – he's really scaring me, Kieran.'

'He's been scaring me since it all kicked off this morning. Stick with Paul and Will and you should be okay.'

'You sure they're not in there?'

'I'm telling you, Mel, this caravan's empty. I was going to try around the cesspit next. I thought I heard people around there just now.'

Lorna heard footsteps moving away, then Kieran returned to the caravan. She poked her head above the table and he beckoned her out. She hissed for the others to come out from their hiding places too.

'So where's this other exit?' Lorna whispered. 'I've never seen it.'

'How did you get in?' Howard asked Harte.

'We came in over the wall. Harry, the guy who just took off in the lorry, was into rock climbing and all that stuff. The rope's probably still there if you fancy it.'

'No need for that,' Kieran said. 'There is another way.'

262

'Why should we believe you?' Lorna said. 'You've been up Jas' backside for days. You're just bluffing . . .'

'I know how it must look, but I've been covering my back, that's all. It seemed to make sense to stick close to the guy who was making most noise.'

'We can argue about this later,' Harte said. 'Where's this way out?'

'I've been here since the beginning,' Kieran started. 'I found this place on the morning everyone died and I decided to stay here – I didn't think you could get anywhere much safer than a bloody castle. Anyway, there were only a few of us here to begin with, and we thought we'd got the place completely sealed off – but there we were, just sitting around minding our own business, and Jackson appeared from out of nowhere.'

'How?' Harte said, beginning to be intrigued.

'That's what I'm trying to tell you: he found another way in. He got in through the bloody dungeons.'

'Okay, so how do we get out?'

'The exit's at the back of the gift shop. Follow me and I'll show you.'

42

Kieran led the others across the dark courtyard, but Harte had barely taken two steps out of the caravan when someone grabbed him by the shoulder and spun him around. It was Michael.

'Thought you might have been on that lorry,' Harte whispered.

'No such luck,' Michael murmured, 'though I did manage to get the gate open for them. So what's going on?'

'The guy up front is Kieran,' Harte explained. 'He says he knows another way out of here.'

'And can we trust him?'

'Don't see we've got much choice right now, do you?'

The small group, four men and two women, walked across the courtyard, taking a wide, indirect route to avoid Jas and the others, who looked to be congregating around the van now blocking the gate. They were relieved to find the door to the gift shop had been left open by Will Bayliss and Melanie when the sudden movement of the lorry had abruptly inter-rupted their lovemaking.

'Who the fuck's this?' Kieran asked as they crowded into the gift shop and he caught sight of Michael, bringing up the rear.

He closed the door behind him and said, 'I'm Michael. Pleasure to meet you too.'

'Michael's the dad-to-be from the island,' Harte explained.

'Then what are you doing here, you muppet?'

'I've been asking myself the same question,' he replied. 'Now, where's this exit?'

'In here, somewhere,' Kieran said unhelpfully as he began

searching through the few boxes of supplies left in the gift shop. He quickly found what he was looking for: torches. It didn't matter that they were novelty kid's torches made in the shape of castle turrets as long as they worked. He handed them around, then distributed packs of batteries from the wall display behind the long-unused till. Lorna was the first to get hers working. She shone it around the various faces.

'Michael, this is Howard, Caron and Kieran.'

'And you're all that's left here now? Harry got the rest of you away?'

'As far as we can tell. I think everyone's accounted for.'

'Too late now if they're not,' he mumbled as he went deeper into the shop. 'Now, what exactly are we looking for?'

'Some kind of door, I guess,' Kieran explained. 'All I know is that Jackson got in this way.'

'And you never bothered to look for it before?'

'There wasn't any need: no one was trying to get out of the castle until your lot turned up in your bloody helicopter.'

'Fair point.'

They split up and scoured the walls of the cluttered room. In the months since the survivors had taken over the castle the gift shop had had a variety of uses, from Melanie's love-nest to general rubbish dump – and, judging from the smell, someone had used this place in favour of the chemical toilets too.

'There are catacombs and dungeons here, you know,' Caron said suddenly.

'What?' Michael asked.

'Ignore her,' Howard said, 'she's half-pissed.'

'I might well be,' she continued, 'but I'm not stupid. There are dungeons and all sorts under this place.'

'How would you know?'

'Because I've spent hours and hours pretending to clean, remember? I saw some displays in the museum.'

'And you didn't think to mention this?' Lorna said in disbelief.

'I didn't think it mattered. Like Kieran said, we weren't planning on leaving until a couple of days ago.'

'Wait,' Michael said, 'this guy who came *into* the castle – he came through here?'

'Jackson,' Kieran replied, 'yes – why?'

'Because if that's the case he probably got in this way.' And Michael flashed his torch at the door he was standing next to. It had a large NO EXIT sign in the middle of it, and was partially obscured by a display unit someone had clearly moved. 'We've been looking for a way *out*,' he said, 'not a way in. Jackson had been coming the other way, hadn't he? So his entrance must be our "no exit".'

'It must be,' Kieran said, shoving the display out of the way, then reaching for the emergency access bar across the middle of the door. He pushed it down and when the latches opened Michael slipped his fingers around the edges and between them they pulled the door open. A blast of cold, musty air hit them. Michael shone his torch into a small room which looked like it had been carved out of rock.

'We really need to get moving,' Howard said nervously. 'I think they're coming this way.'

'Go for it,' Michael suggested. 'Even if we just end up hiding in here for a couple of hours, it'll do.'

He led them down into the confined space, Harte and Kieran close behind and Howard, Lorna and Caron bringing up the rear. The air was ice-cold.

'Fuck me!' Harte cursed, and Michael turned around quickly to see what it was that Harte had seen. The sight of the painfully thin, ghostly-white body shackled to the wall made him gasp too.

Lorna sighed. 'Harte, you're bloody useless,' she said. 'It's a bloody dummy.'

'How was I supposed to know?' he muttered. 'Christ, what kind of place has fake dead bodies chained to the walls?'

'Castles with dungeons,' Caron said smugly. 'I told you I

saw displays. It's part of a "be a smuggler" attraction, I think.'

'Shush!' Michael said, 'keep quiet and keep moving.' He led them towards another door.

'Go through?' Kieran asked, pointlessly.

'Unless you've got a better idea?'

Kieran tried the door and it opened onto a narrow passageway which sloped downwards and curved away to the left. He reluctantly found himself leading the way, shuffling his feet along the ground to feel for obstacles. It looked like the tunnel had been carved out of the rock, with occasional brick supports. The miserable light from their torches illuminated only small patches of the walls and the low ceiling, and it began to feel almost unbearably claustrophobic. Even sound felt restricted and trapped here, any small noise they made echoing around as if unable to escape. Kieran's already slow pace slowed further as nerves set in, but he gritted his teeth and held his torch in one hand as he groped his way forward with the other.

'Shhh,' Harte said suddenly, grabbing Michael's shoulder. 'Stop!'

They immediately froze, their collective breathing the only sound.

'What is it?' Lorna asked anxiously.

'I thought I heard something,' he whispered.

'You think Jas is following us?'

'I thought I heard it too,' Kieran said, 'but I don't think it was behind us; it was up ahead.'

'Just keep moving,' Michael said, squeezing through and taking the lead. 'The sooner we get out of here, the better.'

Kieran was about to follow when he heard it again: a definite noise.

'Wait,' he said.

'He's trying it on,' Howard angrily. 'The fucker's brought us down here and told Jas to follow. I'm betting it's a bloody dead end up ahead.'

'And do you think I'd want to get myself trapped too? Get real, Howard. No, I swear, there's something down here.'

Caron started to moan, 'I'm going back,' she said, trying to push past Howard and get back up the slope. 'We never should have come here.'

'You're not going anywhere,' Michael told her, the tone of his voice immediately silencing her. 'Whatever's down here can't be any worse than your friends back in the castle.'

'You reckon?' Harte mumbled.

'It's probably just rats, or something like that,' Howard said, doing his best to find a rational explanation for the noise, but at the mention of rats Caron began to wail with fear. Lorna felt her starting to move again and she grabbed hold of her.

'Get off me!' she screamed, trying to beat her off.

'Leave it out, you silly cow,' Lorna muttered. She grabbed Caron and pushed her against the damp, cold wall, preventing her from getting out.

'Will you two keep it down,' Michael ordered from the front and started moving again, following the curve of the passage around until it opened out into another, much larger space. He paused in the entrance to the chamber. The light of his torch was enough to reveal colourful displays hanging on the walls, and another dummy that had been chained to the rock for its sins. Harte and Kieran moved up to stand on either side of him.

Harte took a couple of steps forward, then froze again. 'Fucking hell!' he yelled, 'bodies!'

'It's all right,' Michael said quickly, loud enough for those behind to hear him, 'it's just another dummy.'

'No, it isn't,' Kieran said, grabbing his arm and turning him around. 'Look.'

Harte's torch had picked out a single corpse, and as it began lurching towards him he desperately searched his pockets for anything he could use as a weapon.

'There are more of them,' Kieran said, then, 'Oh fuck, there are *loads* of them.'

Michael watched in abject terror as more and more bodies emerged. Drawn like moths to the torchlight, they staggered ever closer.

'What do we do?' Caron asked anxiously, sandwiched between Michael, Kieran and Harte on one side, Howard and Lorna on the other.

'We go back,' Harte said, already trying to move away. 'We need to get ourselves back behind one of those doors we came through.'

'But they're just going to keep coming,' Lorna said, voicing what they were all thinking. 'Fuck this, we might as well head all the way back out and take our chances with Jas and the others.'

There were at least five cadavers that Michael could see, and probably more behind. He didn't want to look at them, but at the same time he wished their torches were brighter. The thought of what he couldn't see in the shadows beyond this chamber was even more frightening than what he could. How many more were there?

The nearest of the corpses seemed to have locked onto him now, and he felt the hairs on the back of his neck stand on end as it raised its haggard face to look directly at him with mournful, sunken eyes. Someone knocked into him from behind and he grabbed at the walls in panic, desperate to find something to hold on to. And still the corpse came . . .

'Use this,' Howard said from close behind him, and shoved a screwdriver into his hand. 'I found it in the gift shop, thought I'd bring it along just in case. Now kill the damn thing!'

Still Michael didn't attack. It had been a long time since he'd seen one of the dead in this kind of condition, still capable of moving with relative strength and speed . . . This was like those bodies they'd cleared off the island when they'd first arrived there. But that was months ago . . .

Michael had no option, he knew that. None of those pathetic shysters behind him were going to be any help. Despite his still considerable bulk, Howard had managed to push past and was now cowering in the passageway with Lorna and Caron. Lorna was hanging onto Caron's arm, trying to stop her from running back to the castle. If he wanted out of here, he'd have to take control. He gripped the screwdriver like a dagger, held the torch up so he could see what he was doing, and ran towards the approaching corpse, screaming with rage.

The creature stopped, and Michael stopped in mid-attack, shocked by its unexpected and very definite response. It staggered back unsteadily and raised its arm like it was trying to defend itself. The bloody thing seemed to be cowering from him.

'What the hell's going on?' he said as he moved forward. The corpse moved further away, clumsily backing into the others hovering behind it now. 'Look at this thing – this isn't right—'

'Who cares?' Howard yelled from a safe distance away. 'Finish them! Just get rid of them—'

Harte found his nerve and moved towards the dead himself, determined to do what Michael wouldn't, but Michael shot out his arm and held him back.

'We don't have time for this,' Lorna said. 'What the hell are you waiting for?'

Michael wasn't listening. He moved closer again, and this time the corpse had nowhere left to go.

'Look at it,' he said, studying its decayed face. He ran the torchlight over it, revealing the full extent of its horrific deterioration. The little remaining skin which hadn't been eaten or rotted away had slipped down like an ill-fitting mask, leaving heavy, sagging bags beneath its clouded eyes. He could see burrowing things moving in the holes. Its drooping mouth was moving slightly, almost as if it was trying to talk.

'What about it?' Harte asked.

'Compare it to the bodies you've seen outside recently. How does it match up?'

'It's still solid,' Harte said, calmer now, creeping a little closer. 'It's still got some meat on its bones. Most of those things outside are little more than liquid now.'

'Exactly. It's like the one we saw trapped in that car.'

'What are you talking about?' Kieran asked, hovering just behind him.

'On the way to get in here tonight,' Harte explained, 'we walked across the dead outside. We found a great mound of them all stacked up, and we dug down to find out why. There was a car buried underneath them, and the driver was like this one. It had been preserved, I guess.'

'Can't you just get rid of them?' Caron asked. Michael ignored her.

'It looks like they all died about a month ago,' Lorna said. 'Kieran, how long's it been since anyone came through here?'

'We'd been here a few weeks when Jackson first got in,' he replied, 'and as far as I know no one's been down here since. Why?'

'Because these bodies have probably been down here since then, haven't they?'

'So?'

'So Harte's right. These things managed to get themselves trapped down here and they've been preserved – think about it, there's probably a pretty constant temperature, and no wind or rain . . . They used to keep food and stuff in cellars like this, didn't they? Remarkable.'

'Just bloody well kill them,' Caron demanded again from the passageway.

Much as she'd rather they battered this particularly foul aberration into oblivion, Lorna was beginning to appreciate the significance of Michael's comments. She watched as he moved towards the group of bodies again, and once again they all tried to get out of the way, as if they knew he was going to attack. But when he stopped, the creature at the front visibly relaxed, slouching its shoulders and rocking back slightly on what was left of its heels. Michael remained a cautious couple of feet away as he shone his torch directly into its wizened face once again. It didn't move, but its dark, emotionless eyes slowly moved around Michael's face.

'Poor thing,' Lorna said, surprising everyone.

'What do you mean, poor thing?' Howard said, unable to believe what he was hearing. 'You sound like you pity it – you know what these bastards have done, how much pain and grief they've caused us—'

'Yes, but none of it was their fault, was it?' she said. 'They had no control over what was happening to them, same as we didn't.'

'We should just get rid of them,' Howard suggested. 'Finish them off and put them out of our misery.'

It looked like the corpse was reacting to his words – it immediately became more animated, and reached out towards Michael, who stepped backwards, out of the way, concerned it was about to lash out at him. But it didn't, it made a second clumsy grab, and this time Michael realised it was going for the torch, not him. Not entirely sure what he was doing, he handed it over, and the body tried to grip it, but it couldn't, its bony hands just slipping off the handle. The torch dropped to the ground and Michael picked it up. In the light of the other torches they could all see the corpse's shoulders slump forward and its head drop in what looked remarkably like a bizarre approximation of frustration.

'What's it doing now?' Howard asked.

'Giving up, I think,' Michael said. 'Bloody hell, it's like they've come full circle.'

'Full circle? What are you talking about?'

'Just look at it: it's helpless. It hasn't attacked me, and I don't even think it wants to. What I mean is, I think it's got more self-control than any of the others I've seen before. It doesn't want to fight any more.'

The creature moved, correcting its balance, and it reached for the torch again, but yet again it couldn't get a strong enough grip. Perhaps sensing the futility of its actions and the limitations of its physical shell, it instead raised its hand up to its head. It seemed to be pointing at its own skull.

'What's it doing now?' Lorna asked, transfixed, all thoughts of what was happening elsewhere in the castle temporarily forgotten.

Michael couldn't believe what he was seeing. He gave them his interpretation of the dead man's behaviour, even though he knew how stupid it sounded. 'I think it wants me to kill it.'

'You're out of your bloody mind,' Harte said, trying to get past so that he could finish the damn thing off himself.

Michael blocked him again. 'I'm serious.'

He looked at the other decaying faces crowding behind the first corpse. They were all just as passive, though he remained cautious.

'How many are here?' Howard asked nervously.

'There could be hundreds,' Kieran said. 'I don't expect Jackson stopped to shut the door behind him when he was trying to get in here – that's if there even *is* a door.'

'Well, there must be something,' Lorna said, tracking the irregular movement of another corpse with her torch, 'otherwise they'd have filled this place, wouldn't they?'

'Only one way to find out,' Michael said. He began to move again, edging around the first body, doing all he could not to actually make direct contact with it. It watched him as well as it was able, having lost its fine motor skills, following his movements with its entire head, not just its eyes.

He walked towards the far end of this chamber, and the bodies there dropped back, almost as if they were trying to get out of his way. Beyond this room was another narrow, steeply sloping passageway, and a corpse was crawling towards him on its hands and knees. The pitifully slow and awkward progress went some way to explaining why so few of the dead had made it this far up into the dungeons. Michael continued down the slope, the rest of the group following, and entered another sudden swell of space, a chamber similar to the one they'd just left. This area was also filled with the dead. They lined the edges of the large space, doing all they could to keep their distance from the living. One of them, Michael noticed, looked like it was sitting in a corner, and several more were lying down – were these intentional movements, or were the bodies now so weak, so emaciated, that they were no longer physically able to support what was left of their own weight?

'I don't like this,' Howard moaned from close behind his shoulder. Michael too felt increasingly uneasy: they were now surrounded by the dead, and the stench in here was appalling.

'But if they were going to attack us, wouldn't they have done it by now?' he said, trying to reassure himself as much as anyone else. 'As long as they don't think we're threatening them, there's no reason why they should go for us.'

'It's never stopped them before – or maybe you've spent too long on your bloody island and you've forgotten what they're like.'

The mention of the island made Michael stop and check himself momentarily. What the hell was he doing wasting time here? He should be back home on Cormansey with Emma, not buried underground with a handful of idiots and several dungeons full of corpses for company.

'This is different,' he said. '*They're* different. I don't know what your experience has been, Howard, but I've watched the dead steadily changing – *constantly changing* – since the very beginning of all of this. Their self-control has improved as their bodies have decayed. It doesn't make a lot of sense and I can't explain it, but that's definitely what's happened. You must have seen it too.'

'Of course we've seen it,' Harte said, 'but why should the ones down here be any different?'

One of the corpses lining the wall nearest to him twitched involuntarily and Harte flinched. His sudden movement caused another reaction, which in turn caused another, then another, and in a matter of moments an entire wall of rotting flesh had become uncomfortably animated.

Michael positioned himself in front of Harte and held his arms out at either side, as if forming a barrier between the living and the dead. He could hardly believe it himself, but after a few seconds the bodies in front of him became calmer again.

'You see,' he said, 'they don't want a fight any more than you do. They're long past that stage now.'

'I don't understand,' Caron said, worming her way right into the centre of the group of six so that she was surrounded on all sides. She didn't want her back to any of the dead without someone else there to cover her. 'This doesn't make any sense at all.'

'It makes perfect sense,' Michael explained. 'Like I said, when your man Jackson forced his way in through here, he must have allowed this lot to get in too. The conditions here are different from those outside: the air's drier, the temperature's steady, there's barely any moisture, no light . . . so they're being preserved. What's going on in their brains has continued at the same rate it has done since they all died, but down here their physical decay has been much, much slower.'

'Bollocks,' Howard said, but Michael ignored him. He knew he was right.

'Watch,' he said. He'd seen more than enough corpses up close over the last few months and he knew beyond any shadow of a doubt that there was something very different about these. He shone his torch at the nearest few, working his way along as if he was inspecting an identity parade, moving slowly and shining the light at their chests rather than directly into their faces to avoid provoking another spontaneous reaction like Harte had inadvertently started a few moments earlier. One of the creatures over to his right was wearing the remains of a nurse's uniform, though he had to look twice to be sure that was what it was. Much of the heavily stained material had dried hard like cardboard.

He carefully moved a flap of clothing out of the way, the remains of a cardigan or maybe a light jacket, he couldn't tell which. As he'd hoped, there was an identity badge clipped to the breast pocket. He looked into its wizened face for a moment, almost as if he was asking permission, then he unclipped the badge and wiped away a layer of grime to reveal an inch-square picture of a woman's face beneath. He squinted in the poor light, trying to make her out. She looked beautiful – the first pre-apocalypse face he'd seen in some time – and her smile took him by surprise. Her face here was unspoilt by disease, and also free from the strain of having to endure the living hell they had all been trying to survive through since this happened. Her short, dark hair was cut into a neat bob, her fringe tucked out of the way behind her ear. She wore a pair of heavy-rimmed glasses which perfectly suited the shape of her soft, delicately square-jawed face. But it was her lips he couldn't stop looking at: gorgeous full, dark red lips. The fact she was wearing make-up took him by surprise, even though it shouldn't have, and her vivid, painted smile immediately took him back to a time now long gone, when appearances felt like they really mattered. Emma, like all the women on Cormansey, never wore make-up. There didn't seem to be any point any more. There was no longer any desire, let alone any need, to spend time trying to conform to society's idea of beauty when that society lay in tatters, thirty miles or so over the ocean. Michael couldn't take his eyes off those lips. It saddened him to think he'd probably never see Emma dressed up to the nines for a night out. If he ever saw Emma again. He had a long way to go before he'd be back anywhere near the woman he—

'You okay?' Harte asked, nudging him gently.

'What? Oh, sorry,' he said, feeling both sad and embar-rassed, and also annoyed with himself for getting so easily distracted. Regardless of his assumptions, just because he hadn't been attacked so far, it didn't mean he was completely safe. He wiped the rest of the identity badge clear and then looked up into the dead face it belonged to. After seeing what she used to look like, he almost couldn't bear to look at what was left of this woman now. Her dry, discoloured skin, patchy hair, misshapen face and unnaturally prominent bones left her looking like a grotesque caricature of the person she'd once been. A large circle of skin around her top lip had been eaten away. Despite the obvious individuality of each corpse's decay, in some ways they all looked the same as each other now, strangely featureless. 'This is Michelle Bright,' he announced.

Someone started to say something flippant and unnecessary, but no one paid any attention, because their sole focus was now the dead woman standing in front of Michael. At the mention of her name she'd reacted, moving forward slightly, then lifting an arm up closer to her face. She was barely able to control her awkward movements, but she managed to lightly place what was left of one of her hands against her hollow chest. *Me*, she seemed to be saying.

'Fuck me,' Howard said.

'I'd rather fuck her,' Harte mumbled, almost by rote.

Michael turned around and scowled at them both.

'This is all well and good,' Caron said, completely sober again now, 'but it's not actually getting us anywhere, is it?'

'Depends on your perspective,' Michael said.

She was about to ask him what he meant when Lorna distracted her. 'Look at that,' she said. 'Where the hell are they going?'

They watched as a slowly moving queue of corpses traipsed away in the direction from which the living had entered the dungeons, back towards the centre of the castle.

'They're trying to get out, aren't they?' Kieran said. 'They're trying to get into the castle.'

'I think that's exactly what they're trying to do,' Michael

agreed. 'They know they can't go the other way because it must be blocked, so they're trying to get out the way we came in.'

'Then we should let them,' Lorna suggested. 'It'll get them out of our way . . .'

'. . . and give the fuckers up there something else to worry about. Good thinking.'

'But when Jas and the others see them, they'll go crazy,' Harte said. 'They'll probably batter the hell out of them.'

'Look at the state they're in,' Michael said quietly, almost as if he didn't want the dead to hear him. 'It'd probably be for the best.'

He was about to talk to Lorna again, but it was too late, she was already gone. He watched her disappear back in the direction from which they'd just come. He guessed she was opening both of the doors they'd come through too, clearing the way to the gift shop. She quickly returned to the chamber where the others were waiting and took Caron's torch from her. She took the corpse of Michelle Bright by the arm and gently led it up the slope into the other chamber. The dead girl walked slowly forward, then stopped. Lorna let go and pushed her forward again. She began to walk towards a dull patch of light in the distance – Lorna's torch – following an unsteady queue of other corpses which had already started to move. Lorna placed Caron's torch on the ground too, hoping to help guide the dead along.

Following Lorna's lead, Howard, Harte and Kieran began to do the same, pushing the slow-moving bodies up towards the lights. They followed each other out of the caverns in a bizarre, completely surreal parade: a horrendously overdue funeral procession.

'Okay, let's get moving,' Michael said, pushing still more of the creatures away, ready to go deeper into the darkness.

'Wait,' Caron said, holding on to his arm, 'what did you mean about perspective just now?'

'All those thousands of bodies outside this place,' he

explained, continuing to watch the dead march, 'we assumed all they wanted to do was attack.'

'That's because they did. We all saw more than enough of that. Nasty, vicious things.'

'All I'm saying is, that might well be what they did do, but the real question is, *why* did they do it? Why did they constantly herd around us in massive numbers? We assumed it was because they saw us as a threat and they wanted us dead, but really, it's all about perspective. Having seen what I've seen in here today, I think we might have been misreading the situation. They wanted our *help* – that's why they wouldn't leave us alone.'

'That's preposterous,' she scoffed.

'Is it? I'm not sure. They wanted our help, but they couldn't control themselves sufficiently to make that clear. We misread their actions as being all about anger and hate. Maybe they were just scared? I think they knew a lot more about who they were and what they'd become than we gave them credit for. I think they wanted our help, they just didn't have any way of showing it.'

43

'**W**hat do you mean, you can't find them?' Jas demanded. Mark was standing in front of him, his face aching, his mouth dry with nerves, not knowing what else he was supposed to say.

'We've checked everywhere . . . all the caravans, all the rooms. We've been twice around the ruins. They've disappeared.'

'They can't have. Look again.'

'But Jas, it's pitch-black, mate. We've blocked the gates. Let's wait until morning. They're probably hiding around that well Jackson was working on, or somewhere near the toilets. If we wait until the sun's up we'll have a better chance of—'

'Keep looking,' Jas ordered.

Ainsworth just stared at him. *What the fuck is wrong with you?* He wanted to ask the question out loud, but couldn't. To his relief, Will Bayliss and Paul Field came running over. Hopefully they'd found something.

'Mel found a climbing rope,' Will said, breathless.

'Where?'

'Hanging over the wall, over by the shit-pit.'

'So is that how they got out?'

'I doubt it. It's too high.'

'Where the hell did they get a climbing rope from?'

'There was other stuff as well,' Paul continued, 'harnesses, belts, stuff like that.'

'So what are you saying?'

Paul shrugged, but it was starting to make sense to Mark.

'That's not how they got out,' he said, 'it's how they got *in*.

Someone must have come in over the wall, then got them all together in one lorry to get them out.'

'Those fuckers from the island? I thought they'd have long gone.'

'The helicopter was back earlier, don't forget,' Will said. 'It must have been them.'

'With a little help,' Mark agreed.

'Who, your girlfriend Lorna?' Jas sneered.

Mark didn't bite. 'I was thinking more about your friend Harte.'

'Well, at least we know where they'll be heading,' Jas continued. 'They'll be on their way to Chadwick. We can cut them off.'

'What's the point?' Will said.

'What?'

'Why bother?'

'Because they've got our fucking supplies.'

'Then we'll get more.'

'Are you fucking stupid? I thought he was the dumb one,' Jas said, pointing at Mark, who stared back at him, doing all he could to stop his bottom lip from quivering. All he could think about was Lorna, and how foolish he felt, having let her take advantage of him like that.

But the worst part of all, he thought sadly, *is that I'd let it happen again in a heartbeat. I'd give anything to be close to her like that again. All the pain and the grief I've had since from Jas was worth it for that one kiss . . .*

Melanie jogged over. 'Can't find any of them,' she said. 'They've all cleared out – and it looks like Kieran's gone too.'

'*Bastard!*' Jas yelled, kicking the ground with frustration. 'That little shit has sold me out.'

'But if they didn't get out over the wall,' Will said, 'and we know they didn't all get out in the lorry, then they must still be here.'

'Check the caravans again,' Jas ordered.

'What for? We've checked them already.'

'Just fucking do it!'

Grudgingly, though happy to put some distance between themselves and Jas, they headed over to the caravans and split up. Mark checked the caravan he'd been guarding once more, staring at the bed where Lorna had been lying and wishing he could turn the clock back so that none of this had happened – and not just tonight, either. He wanted to go further back . . . back to when he'd first arrived here. Maybe he'd have chosen his friends differently if he had his time again.

'Anything?' Jas said, standing in the doorway behind him.

'Nothing,' he replied dejectedly. He couldn't get back out because Jas was blocking the door; he was relieved when Jas finally moved on to the next caravan. He sat down on the step, held his head in his hands and listened to Jas yelling at the others when they also reported back that they'd found nothing.

44

Michael led the others deeper into the cavernous spaces underground. After several minutes of slow, shuffling movement, all of those corpses which still had any degree of mobility had been herded back towards the gift shop and the interior of the castle, leaving just those which could no longer move.

The increasing level of decay was making the small group's progress painfully slow. This far from the gift shop it was getting like the compacted putrefaction he'd had to walk through with Harry and Harte, although this was somehow worse, because of the close confines and the complete absence of fresh air. The air was filled with the foetid stink of the gases produced by the deterioration of the bodies, and Caron hadn't been able to stop herself vomiting a few minutes ago – like them all, she'd seen more than her fair share of gore over the last few months, but this inescapable stench had proved too much for her. Howard and Kieran were helping her along between them, one on either arm, or one in front and one behind if the way narrowed too much.

Just don't anyone dare light a match, Michael thought. *The whole fucking place could go up*. 'Dead end,' he announced as his outstretched hands made contact with another cold wall of rock.

'Maybe we should just turn back,' Howard suggested for about the hundredth time.

'Bit late for that now,' Michael replied. 'Besides, if Jackson got in this way, then we must be able to get out.'

He looked around, his feet slipping in the decay. He felt completely disorientated. The problem was, everything looked the same down here, particularly with such limited light from so few torches. Kieran had switched his off now, conserving his batteries. Michael understood that: he didn't want to be stuck down here without any light. Actually, he didn't want to be stuck down here at all. There *had* to be a way out.

He shuffled back towards the others, scraping his feet along the floor, trying to feel his way, moving inch by slow inch through the slurry. And then it occurred to him that he might be able to use the depth of the mire as a kind of primitive gauge.

'What are you thinking?' Lorna asked, concerned that he'd stopped.

'Just trying to work out how the dead would have moved through here.'

'Me too,' she said. 'Those bodies back there . . .'

'. . . must have been some of the first to get through. They must have followed Jackson in – presumably he would have had quite a crowd behind him.'

'If they were following in large enough numbers,' Harte said, 'then there's a chance some of them would have been trampled, like we saw outside.'

'That's exactly what I was thinking,' Michael agreed.

'So the deeper the shite,' Lorna said, 'the better?'

'Precisely.'

Caron was still green, and her stomach roiled at the thought of more dead flesh. 'You want to go *deeper*?'

Michael didn't say anything, but he shone his torch down and began feeling around with his boots. He was trying to picture Jackson's arrival, how his bluster and noise would inevitably have caused a huge swell of the dead to try and follow him into the castle. He worked his way around the edge of the room, torch in one hand, feeling the wall with the other. The rest of the group watched him as he kept moving, prodding the ground, taking one tentative step at a time. He knew he was onto something, because the depth of the muck was definitely increasing now. He'd barely been splashing in it initially, but it had passed the toes of his boots and was almost up to his ankles. He moved again, and now it was halfway up his shin.

And then the rock wall he was holding onto for support disappeared. He stopped and felt his way around the edges of the entrance to another passageway, initially obscured by shadow. He shuffled closer, feeling the unimaginably foul gloop around his feet rising with virtually every step.

'This is it,' he announced, 'it has to be.'

'Can you see anything?' Lorna asked from close behind. He shone the torch deeper into the passage.

'Not a damn thing, but we have to be close now.'

'I can't keep going,' Caron whined from the back.

'Shut her up, would you,' Michael said wearily. 'She's doing my bloody head in.'

'Give it a rest, Caron,' Lorna yelled at her before lowering her voice and adding, 'you don't have any choice.'

'Everybody ready?' Michael asked.

Absolute silence, and then, 'Just do it,' Kieran said.

'Single file. Hold onto the back of the person in front, okay?' This time he didn't wait for anyone to reply. As soon as he felt Harte grab his shoulder he began to move along the new passageway he'd found, his boots crunching and slipping through the rapidly deepening mess, trying not to lose his footing when he trod on submerged bones, doing his best to sweep them to the side so they wouldn't trip up those behind.

'Shit,' Howard cursed when he tripped and almost dragged half the group over. His frightened voice was amplified by the narrowness of the corridor they now followed. 'This is madness. We should turn back.'

'So you turn back if you want,' Michael said, getting bored with the constant whining; bad enough the appalling stench was making it increasingly hard for him to concentrate as he waded through the mire. 'But I'm getting out of here.'

Lorna gagged at the all-consuming excrescence, which felt

like it was coating the insides of her nostrils and throat. It was almost up to her waist now.

'We don't even know if this is the way Jackson came,' Howard said, still complaining. 'There might have been another way – we might have missed a turning somewhere . . .'

'He's right,' Harte reluctantly admitted, almost losing his balance again. 'Maybe we should think about going back? Those bodies will cause a distraction up there and we can—'

'As long as I can keep moving forward,' Michael said through gritted teeth, 'then I'm going to. There's still a chance we're going the right way.' Then he came to a sudden stop. The rest of the group bunched up behind him.

'What is it?' Lorna nervously asked, but he didn't answer. His legs felt weak. Was it a dead end? 'Michael? What is it? What's the problem?'

'Wait a second,' he said. In front of him he could feel another huge mound of decay. He turned around and passed his torch to Harte. 'Do me a favour, try and give me some light, will you?'

Everyone who still had a torch obliged, but by the time they'd all got their lights aimed towards him, Michael had disappeared. He ducked down, his chin almost scraping the surface of the mire, and stretched out his arms. Moments later he stood up again, dripping with decay.

'Did you slip?' Lorna asked. She held out her hand to him. 'Come on, let's go back . . .'

Michael was grinning through the filth. 'I think this is it. I think I can feel a way through. Has anybody got anything I can dig with?' As soon as he'd said it he realised it was a stupid question – none of them had anything with them other than the plastic castle torches and Howard's screwdriver. There was nothing for it. He sank both hands into the decay and pulled out a limb, a leg. He snapped off what was left of a flapping foot and used the bones to try and dig a way through. After a few minutes of frantic activity he discarded the leg and shoved his arm into the gap he'd made in the offensive gloop. He was working blind now, grabbing at whatever he could get hold of, dragging it all back towards him. Sucking, squelching noises echoed around the tunnel as more and more of the mess came away in large chunks. Then he turned around and pushed backwards with all his strength against the blockage, and felt more of the viscous remains topple away. He turned back and dug again – and then he felt cold air on his face.

He felt around, and then announced, 'I don't think there's a door, just a hole. Everyone ready?'

No one answered, but he didn't care. He took a deep breath, dropped his shoulder and charged forward, throwing himself at the clog of remains which was still blocking their way out, and to his surprise it gave way with surprisingly little effort—

—and then, suddenly, he was outside. A huge mass of death came spilling out after him, almost as if he'd burst an enormous spot on the side of the castle. The rest of the group staggered out, glistening with decay in the faint light of the moon, and stood together, soaked and stinking and not giving a damn, just relieved to be outside the castle walls again.

45

How the hell had he missed that? Will looked across the castle courtyard. It was pitch-black, still, the middle of the night – but he was sure he'd seen something moving over by the prefabricated buildings. Jas, Melanie, Paul and Mark were in one of the caravans, trying to keep warm as they argued about what they were going to do next. Jas, who seemed to rapidly be losing touch with reality, was trying to lay down the law and tell them exactly how things were going to be: they'd leave the castle before morning to track Kieran and the rest of those fuckers down.

But Will had had enough – who the hell did Jas think he was? He'd used the excuse of needing a piss to get out of the caravan for a while, and he'd have stayed out longer if it hadn't been so bloody cold, but he needed to get back inside. But that glimpse of movement over the way had stopped him in his tracks: that was them, it had to be. The dumb bastards hadn't seen him yet, he was sure of it. He slipped back into the caravan.

'Where've you been?' Mel asked.

Will ignored her. 'I've found them, Jas,' he said, grinning. 'They're in the gift shop.'

The five of them crept slowly around the perimeter wall, two coming from one side, three from the other.

'Stupid fuckers,' Jas said. 'What the fuck were they think-ing? Why go to all that effort, then just hide in the bloody gift shop? Fucking morons.'

Mark crept along behind him. He desperately wanted to see her again – there were just a handful of people left alive now, and all he wanted was to see just one of them. He wanted to tell Lorna how sorry he was, how he'd understood why she'd done what she had. He wanted to start again.

Jas stopped just short of the gift shop door and gestured for Will, Paul and Melanie to stop on the other side. He had one of the shotguns with him, and by God, this time he might actually use it. He rushed forward, pumped full of adrenalin, and kicked the door open.

—and corpses immediately began lurching towards him.

He backed away in horror as they spilled out of the open door and flooded into the courtyard. Even in the darkness the full extent of their danger was immediately apparent: these creatures were stronger than the ones they'd seen on the other side of the castle wall – they were far less decayed, their movements more controlled. Had they been hiding? Waiting for him?

'The dead!' he screamed, 'the dead are inside!'

Mark tried to drag him away. 'Come on, Jas, let's get out of here.'

But Jas remained rooted to the spot as the corpses drew ever closer.

Mark saw the other three were running for cover – were they heading back to the caravans? No, it looked like they had other plans. They were heading for the van which had been parked across the gate to block the entrance. And now someone was opening the gate . . .

'Wait!' he yelled, but they ignored him. He started to run, but then he looked back at Jas, who hadn't moved. The nearest of the dead had raised their arms, ready to attack, and were almost upon him now. Mark looked back again when he heard the engine starting, and watched the van moving with sudden speed as it skidded around in a tight circle then straight out through the open gate and into the muck outside. It was impossible to see what was happening from here, but Mark had no doubt the dead would be pouring in through the gate too. After standing strong for so long, the castle was about to be overthrown.

He grabbed Jas by the arm and pulled him away. Jas looked absolutely terrified – Mark couldn't ever remember seeing anyone look so scared, not even at the beginning. 'Come on, Jas,' he urged, 'we have to get out of here.'

46

After the euphoria of getting out of the castle, Michael, Lorna, Harte, Kieran, Howard and Caron were struggling to keep moving. They were freezing cold, and disorientated.

'Where do we go?' Howard asked, teeth chattering.

'We need to find somewhere to shelter and get some fresh clothes. We're going to get hypothermia if we don't,' Kieran said.

'You know the area better than the rest of us,' Harte said. 'Where do you suggest?'

'I'm not sure,' he said unhelpfully. 'I need to work out where we've come out – I know there are a couple of villages nearby, but we don't want to be walking all night in the wrong direction . . .' His voice trailed away.

Michael was immediately concerned. 'Problem?'

'Shhh,' he said, 'listen.'

As everyone fell silent they could hear an engine in the near distance.

'More of your lot coming back for us?' Lorna suggested hopefully.

'I doubt it,' Michael replied, wishing he could be more positive. 'Even if it is, fat lot of good it's going to do us: they'll check out the castle, but they won't bother searching the area around it, will they? It' d like looking for a needle in a haystack. If I know Harry, he'll be doing exactly what he said he'd do, and that's getting those people over to Cormansey.'

'What if it's Jas?' Caron asked anxiously.

'Do you really think he'll still be interested in us?'

'I don't know – but what if he is?'

'Then we'll deal with it. Right now we've got a more pressing problem: getting back across a mile or so of dead bodies.'

47

When Harry arrived back in Chadwick, he was deeply relieved to see the silhouette of the helicopter perched on top of the multi-storey car park. He drove the lorry along increasingly familiar roads towards the marina. His passengers remained almost completely silent.

Zoe, sitting up front between Harry and Bob, stared in disbelief at the dead world they were travelling through, a continuous stream of tears rolling down her cheeks. She hadn't left the castle since they'd rescued Driver's lot from the hotel near Bromwell. This was the first time she'd been back, and the first time she was truly able to appreciate the full extent of its remarkable deterioration. Being back in Chadwick *hurt*.

What was left of the population of the town was causing Harry little concern this morning. They were too badly decayed to pose any real threat any more. Beyond a low hillock of body parts – the remains of the crowd which had been drawn by their noise – he could see the road which would take them down to the sea. He swerved around what was left of the corpses and drove as close as he could get to where the *Duchess* was moored.

At the sound of the approaching engine, Richard appeared on the jetty.

Harry stopped and his frightened, silent passengers piled out.

'Well done, mate,' Richard said, shaking Harry's hand, but he realised immediately that all was not well. 'Problem?'

'This isn't everyone,' he said. 'We got in okay, got this lot loaded into the lorry, then it all went shit-shaped. There was nothing I could do – they were firing at us. I had to get out.'

Richard looked anxiously along the expectant faces gathered on the jetty. 'Michael?'

Harry shook his head. 'Don't know what happened to him. Or Harte – I lost the pair of them.'

The two men stood and stared at each other in silence for a moment longer, both thinking the same thing.

'We talked about this,' Richard said at length. 'We knew there was a chance something like this might happen.'

'I know that, but it doesn't make it any easier, does it?'

'What do we do now?' Zoe asked.

Harry took her arm and pointed out their boat. 'Get everything and everybody loaded up onto the *Duchess*,' he said gently.

'What about—?' she started to ask, but stopped, not bothering to finish her obvious question.

'What do you think?' Harry asked Richard. 'We can't just give up on them and ship out.'

'I don't like it any more than you do,' Richard said, 'but we both know that's exactly what we have to do. It's what we agreed last night. It's what we *all* agreed.'

'I know, but—'

'But nothing. *We agreed.*'

Harry knew he was right. 'Will you do me a favour before we ship out?' he asked hopefully. 'One last flyover – just a quick look. It's the least we owe Emma.'

Richard thought carefully before saying, 'Okay. It'll be dawn in a few more hours. We'll wait until the light breaks.'

48

Over the months the castle had been completely encircled with dead flesh. The thought of having to hike back across it had filled both Michael and Harte with dread, but the reality had proved to be less of an ordeal than they'd expected – certainly no worse than what they'd just been through underneath the castle, which had turned out to be good preparation for trudging through the ankle-deep, half-frozen once-human slime outside. It was somehow easier the second time around.

They felt strangely invisible – a good thing if Jas did decide to come looking for them. In the low light of early morning, the living were hard to distinguish from the decayed remains they were walking through, especially as they were all soaked in gore. If Jas or any of his cronies appeared all they'd need to do would be to stand still and wait until they disappeared again.

Michael looked back over his shoulder at the castle they'd somehow managed to escape from, then at the ragtag group of people who were picking their way through the carnage behind him. He could tell a lot about each of them by the way they were dealing with tonight's events. Harte and Kieran were stomping through the slime, just desperate to get across to the other side in the shortest time possible. Howard was constantly grumbling. He was seriously unfit, and he seemed to be spending more time looking for his dog than trying to get away from the remains of the dead, but they'd emerged from the other side of the castle grounds and he understood that he didn't have the luxury of time to try and find the devoted animal. Howard had never wanted to own a dog – now he found he missed her as much as he missed everyone else he'd lost.

The two women were complete opposites: Caron was infuriating; the slowest of all of them, and continually moaning about the dirt under her nails and asking how long they had left to go, like an irritating kid in the back seat of the family car. Lorna, on the other hand, was strong and unflappable, and she was doing her best to keep Caron in check. She was clearly tough – he wasn't sure he'd fancy his chances against her in a fist-fight.

Michael caught her eye when he realised she'd stopped. Something had obviously caught her attention: her head was raised and she remained perfectly still, like an animal sniffing the air for a scent.

'Problem?' he asked.

'Don't think so,' she said. 'Do you see that house over there?'

Michael squinted into the dark. It took him a few seconds to spot the building she had seen. In the pre-dawn gloom it was just another dark shape among many, but after a moment he was able to make it out.

Harte did too. 'I see it,' he said. 'What's the problem?'

'Oh, there's no problem,' she casually replied. 'There's a light on in one of the windows, that's all.'

Suddenly revitalised, the group moved at speed towards the house in the distance. The nearer they got, the clearer the light in the downstairs window became.

Caron was still complaining as they approached it. 'These bloody bodies,' she whined, 'are we ever going to get away from them? You said we only had to walk a mile or so and we'd be through them.'

Michael stopped and looked down at his feet, thinking about what she'd just said. 'We are through them.'

'But how can we be? There are still loads of them around, look.'

She was right, there were still a lot of corpses nearby – more to the point, most of them were on their feet, and some were still moving, which suggested these creatures had never made it as far as the crowd around the castle. They'd long since made it through most of the gory sea which had surrounded the castle.

'This is something else, isn't it?' Lorna said, clearly coming to the same conclusion as Michael. 'These bodies are here because of whatever's in that house.'

She started running towards the building. Harte called for her to be careful, but she wasn't listening. Before she'd made it even halfway down the garden path, the front door opened.

'Hello, you,' said Hollis.

49

It hadn't taken long for the *Duchess'* new passengers to empty the supplies from the back of the lorry and get ready to leave. They were loading the last few scraps and searching around the jetty for extra lifejackets when the noise of another lorry approaching distracted them.

'Michael and the others?' Harry wondered.

'Must be,' Richard said.

'I'm not so sure,' Zoe said. They both looked at her and she said, 'I assume he knows his way around here?'

'Yes, why—?'

'Because whoever that is,' she continued, 'they don't have a fucking clue. Listen. They're driving up and down the main roads. They're probably trying to find this place.'

'Shit,' Harry cursed. He knew she was probably right. 'We need to get going.'

'You get the boat moving; I'll get back to the helicopter,' Richard said. 'I'll take a couple with me, just in case.'

With that he turned and started to run. As Harry watched him go, Zoe began marshalling the others.

'One last flyover,' he shouted, 'remember?'

Richard stopped and turned back. 'There's no point while it's still dark.'

Harry knew he was right; there was no chance of seeing anything yet. 'But you *will* come back.' It wasn't a question.

'Once I've got you lot safely on your way.' And he ran on, closely followed by Driver and Phil Kent.

Zoe and Charlie Moorehouse remained on the jetty as the others boarded the *Duchess*. They were both armed with batons, although neither knew if they'd be able to fight.

Harry wished he had his sword – bloody hell, he couldn't even remember where he'd left it. He was about to do a final headcount and check everyone was accounted for when a van sped down the sloping road which led into the marina. It skidded to a halt just short of the *Duchess*.

'Let's go,' Harry said, pushing Charlie onto the boat. 'Get out of here before they start shooting at us.'

'Wait!' It was a woman, shouting from over by the lorry, not Jas. Zoe took a few steps forward. Melanie, Will Bayliss and Paul Field ran towards them.

'Let us on, Zoe,' she cried, '*please.*'

'Where's Jas?'

'He's coming – he's probably not far behind us. Please!'

Paul and Will approached, their arms loaded with more stuff from the back of their lorry.

'There's a few more boxes in there,' Will said. 'We should take as much as we can.'

Harry looked up. He could hear another engine approaching now. Was this another trick? An attempt to delay them so Jas could get his precious supplies back?

'Fuck the food,' he said, 'we've got enough.'

'Please let us on,' Melanie said, tears streaking her face.

'Don't trust them,' Zoe said. 'They're with Jas.'

'Not any more,' she sobbed. 'We just want to get away from here, same as you do. Please, Zoe . . .'

What choice do we have? Harry asked himself. *I don't know any of these people. But I do know one thing: if any of them tries anything, I'll kick the fuckers overboard.*

'Get on,' he said, and all three of them pushed past, clearly desperate to get away. Harry undid the mooring rope and jumped onto the boat. The *Duchess* felt uncomfortably low in the water. He pushed his way through to the cabin and took the controls. He fired up the engine, reassured by the noise and sudden movement.

'He's coming!' someone shouted from the stern of the boat. Harry looked back and through the sea of heads filling almost every available square inch of deck space behind him, he could see another vehicle driving down towards the jetty.

Jas jumped out of the beaten-up old Renault which had once belonged to Shirley Brinksford's husband and screamed with frustration and anger as the boat sailed away from the jetty. Mark Ainsworth stood a short distance behind him, too scared to run.

They looked up as the helicopter flew overhead, guiding the *Duchess* away from the mainland and out towards Cormansey.

50

'**F**uck me, it's cold,' Michael said, wrapping his arms around himself before heading upstairs to check the bedrooms for some clean clothes. Caron was in the kitchen looking for food, while Howard and Kieran were busy exploring the rest of the building. They were all finding the situation unexpectedly strange, the sudden return to something almost resembling normality almost jarring.

Lorna was in the living room with Hollis, where he'd obviously been basing himself. He'd barely used the rest of the house.

'I didn't want to go far,' he explained. 'I knew I wasn't welcome in the castle, but I still didn't want to cut myself off completely, so I decided to stay close. You can see the castle gate from upstairs. I thought you'd all leave at some point, and I thought I might be able to tag on with some of you.'

'We *are* leaving,' she said. 'You heard the helicopter, didn't you?'

'I thought I was imagining it at first,' he said, sounding close to tears. 'What with all the grief I've been having with my ears, I didn't think it was real. I thought I'd got tinnitus or something like that.'

'Did you see the lorry leave?'

'What lorry?'

'A few hours after the helicopter, some of them got away in a lorry.'

'No, I didn't see – I guess I fell asleep. I kept watch for a while after the helicopter had gone, but I figured that was probably it.'

'You daft bugger.'

He shrugged. 'If I'm honest, I felt so bad about what happened to Steve that getting away was the important part – that's all I was really bothered about.'

'What happened to Steve wasn't your fault.'

'I didn't help matters, though.'

'Don't beat yourself up about it. Anyway, like I said, we *are* getting away. We're going to an island.'

Harte stood in the doorway, watching the two of them talking. It saddened him to see Hollis like this: a shell of the man he used to be. The expression on his face was hard to read. He didn't show any emotion when Lorna told him about the island – either he hadn't heard properly, or he didn't believe her – or maybe he just didn't care any more. Feeling like he was intruding, Harte walked away to look around the rest of the house again.

The only body he'd seen since they'd arrived was a single motionless corpse curled around the bottom of a rotary washing line in the garden. Whoever it was, it looked like hanging out the laundry had been the very last thing she'd done before her life had been brutally truncated. She'd managed to peg out a few items of clothing, and there they'd remained hanging for months: a couple of towels, a floral summer dress, a few items of children's underwear . . . The clothes were weather-beaten and faded now. Before he'd even realised what he was doing, Harte found himself trying to fit together the pieces of the family which had lived here: a little girl, seven or eight years old, living with her mum (lying dead in the garden). On one of the kitchen counters he found an opened letter addressed to Mr John Prentice. He wondered what John used to do for a living, where he might have been when he'd died. Had he been one of the tens of thousands of corpses outside the castle wall? Then Harte found himself wondering what had happened to the little girl. The thought of turning a corner and running into a waist-high three-months-dead corpse of a child unsettled him more than it should have.

It had been a long time since he'd been in a house like this. The last house he'd visited was the semi-detached he and Jas had torched to provide a distraction so that Webb, Hollis and the others could massacre some of the endless hordes of bodies which had gathered around the flats. Fat lot of good that had done them. Christ, that was so long ago now. Almost as long ago as the days when he'd taught in a school and lived in a place not too dissimilar to this one . . .

He passed Kieran, who was in a small study, sitting in front of a computer, shining his torch around the room. He was holding the mouse in his hand, and the way he was leaning back in the chair made him look as if he was about to browse the Web or send an email. He looked up and saw Harte watching him.

'Funny how things work out, eh?' he said.

'What do you mean?'

'My life used to revolve around these bloody things. Now there's not even power to turn them on.' He threw down the mouse and shoved the keyboard away, then got up and walked out.

Caron had taken off her dirty clothes and thrown them outside; now she was sitting on a sofa at one end of a long, narrow conservatory running across the back of the house. It was cold, but she was appreciating the view through the glass walls and ceiling: close to being outside, but still safe and protected. All around her were dead potted plants sitting in tubs of bone-dry dirt. The dressing gown and pyjamas she wore had probably belonged to the woman lying dead in the middle of the back garden, but that didn't seem to matter now.

'So how long have we got?' Caron shouted, addressing her question to no one in particular.

'Long enough to catch our breath and get cleaned up,' Lorna shouted back.

'I think we should wait until it's lighter before moving on,'

Harte suggested. 'Give us a couple of hours to get our heads together.'

'Doesn't seem much point racing anywhere, really,' Michael said, sounding hopelessly dejected.

'I thought you'd be desperate to get back to your island.'

'I am.'

'So what's the problem?'

'There's no problem getting back to Chadwick,' he explained, 'but that's probably as far as we're going to get. Unless any of us can sail, that is.'

'Harry will have waited, won't he?'

'For as long as he could, but I expect he'll have long gone by now.'

'So what are you saying?'

'That I don't know how to sail a boat,' he admitted, 'so I don't know how I'm going to get home.'

'It can't be that difficult,' Howard said.

'You might be right: sailing might be a piece of piss. But can you navigate? Can any of us read a bloody map?'

'Won't the helicopter come back?' Lorna wondered.

'He might.'

'But we can't just give up,' she said, 'you especially.'

Michael held his head in his hands, suddenly close to tears. The futility of his situation was beginning to sink in. Being away from Emma like this was tearing him in two. Until now he'd been distracted, and before tonight he'd been confident that he'd either be flying back to the island or sailing there alongside Cooper or Harry. Now those options had disappeared and he was stranded. The narrow strip of water which separated Cormansey from the mainland might as well have been a thousand nautical miles wide.

'So when do we leave?' Howard asked, feeling guilty at having given Michael's situation such little consideration.

'Harte's right,' Michael said. 'Let's give it a few hours We should head out just before dawn, I reckon. Things might look better in the morning.'

Caron went to bed in a little girl's room. Thankfully she must have been on her way to school when she'd died because there were no bodies here. The room was just as it had been left: untidy. Lived in. The bed was unmade and a pile of clothes had been dumped on the floor outside the wardrobe door. *Perfect.*

Unlike most of the others, Caron had been sheltered from much of the devastation since everything had fallen apart. At first she'd been content to play homemaker, taking comfort in the mundane familiarity of chores, only going out into the open when she had absolutely no choice. Since the beginning she'd been little more than a passenger, ferried about and protected from the madness by whoever else she'd been around at the time. She found it surprising – and quite reassuring – just how easy it was to slip back into the routine of all she'd lost. Little things she'd forgotten about suddenly began to feel like they mattered again, although she knew it was only temporary. On a dressing table in another bedroom she found some moisturiser and make-up, and she sat in front of a mirror and did her face – and that small act filled her with a whole raft of bittersweet memories. The coldness of the cream in her hand, working it into her skin with the tips of her fingers, the smell . . . in a world overfilled with cesspits, rotting flesh and germs, the delicate floral scent seemed unnaturally strong now, almost overpowering.

She went into an en-suite bathroom off the main bedroom, which none of the others seemed to have used, and there she allowed herself the luxury of using the toilet. It was so sad that she had been reduced to this: that having a real wooden lavatory seat on a real porcelain loo should feel like such a blessing. There was enough water left in the cistern for a single flush, and she pressed down the handle and listened to every second of that beautiful crashing, running, swirling noise which she hadn't heard in months.

Caron wondered what life on this island would actually be

like, if they ever got there. Would it be any better than this strange, backward world she'd almost begun to get used to? Or might it be like some strange hybrid of what she knew now and what she remembered? Steampunk, she'd heard someone jokingly call it, not that she knew what that meant. She imagined things wouldn't be quite as rough and ready as the early days at the flats, then the hotel, then the castle, but it wasn't going to be anywhere near as refined as the life she used to lead. The possibilities were endless, and all her questions were unanswerable.

She climbed into the little girl's bed and covered herself with the dressing gown she'd been wearing. The mattress was so comfortable – *so normal*. She stretched out in the darkness and listened to the familiar sounds which surrounded her: someone talking downstairs; the house groaning as the temperature changed and pipes expanded and contracted. Floorboards creaking as someone moved about. She could even hear snoring from the room next door.

It was just like it used to be.

51

'What do you mean, he's not here?' Emma demanded, cradling her belly. She was standing in the lounge of The Fox – Cormansey's only pub – surrounded by the other folks who'd spent the night there with her, waiting. The hours between the arrival of Donna and Cooper on the first boat and the second boat captained by Harry had felt endless. Harry was exhausted, barely able to stand, and he could do little to defend himself as she assailed him.

'I'm sorry,' he said, 'I don't know what happened. It was chaotic back there. It was pitch-black, and there were people running everywhere. Some of them were shooting at us, for Christ's sake. We had to get away.'

Donna tried to pull Emma away from him, but she was having none of it. 'But you just *abandoned* him?'

'You tell me what else I was supposed to do, Emma. Michael would have done exactly the same thing: it was what we both agreed before we set out. Getting as many people away and over to the island was what mattered most.'

'I don't believe this,' Emma sobbed, finally relenting and almost falling onto a chair. She looked around the room, illuminated by oil-lamps and candles which had almost burned down to stumps, desperately staring at each of the new faces, hoping she'd just made a mistake and missed him, and knowing full well that she hadn't. He wasn't there.

The new arrivals were all watching her, keeping their distance, looking at her as if she was some kind of freak with her distended belly and swollen ankles. Donna crouched down beside her, holding her hand.

Richard Lawrence waited in the doorway. He cleared his

throat, feeling he ought to say something, but Emma spoke first. 'Are you going to go back, Richard?'

'In the morning.'

'Why not now?'

'Because I'm bloody exhausted, Emma, that's why. I need to rest first, otherwise I'll end up pitching in the sea. I'll go back tomorrow.'

'Please, Richard, go tonight. Go now—'

'Emma, I can't – there's no point. I'll never be able to see them in the dark. We have to wait for daylight. Anything else would be stupid.'

52

Lorna was the first one awake, and she turfed everyone else out of their beds. There was the usual early morning reluctance to take that first step of the day, but then the memory of what had happened last night quickly returned, acting like smelling salts and forcing them all into action. Michael moved with more determination than any of them. To the rest of them, getting to the island would be an unexpected bonus. To him, it was the only thing that mattered.

They heard the wind and rain before they had taken even a single step outside. Yesterday's calm weather had given way to atrocious conditions. Dense grey clouds filled the sky, low enough to hide the tops of trees and the castle turret in the distance.

After stripping the house of anything worthwhile (mostly clean clothes and coats – Hollis had already used virtually everything else), they walked out onto the street. The wind was fierce, seeming to want to push them back inside the house. Michael took the lead and walked to the edge of the small front garden, and then he stopped. All around the house were the remains of more bodies, far more than there had been when they'd arrived. Some were just about able to walk; most weren't even whole, just broken pieces of things which had once been people.

Lorna turned around when she saw that Hollis had retreated and went back to him.

'They're always here,' he said, 'but never this many. It's like they knew where I was.'

'It's not what you think,' she told him, 'they're not a threat any more. They won't attack – look.'

She led him forward and they watched as Kieran approached the nearest of the dead. On the ground near his feet lay a head and torso, which repeatedly stretched out its arms and attempted to pull itself along, though it moved only inches at a time. Across the road, another rain-soaked creature crawled forward on all fours, though its limbs frequently buckled under its negligible weight.

'But they're *still* coming,' Hollis said.

Kieran watched them with a heavy heart. He'd barely slept, thinking about the corpses they'd found under the castle. He knew why they were here now, probably better than they knew themselves: they wanted help. They wanted release from the endless torment of feeling themselves decaying and being unable to do anything about it. The kindest thing, he decided, was to put them out of their misery. He crouched down closer to the one at his feet. He looked at it, and remembered the hundreds he'd killed before today, picturing all the violent battles he'd been involved in. Could it be that they'd been wrong about the dead all along? Had they always wanted help, but just not been able to show it?

Using the crowbar he'd taken from the garage, he worked his way around the small group of cadavers, finishing each one off in turn. It didn't feel like when he'd killed them before . . . today there was no flourish, no satisfaction, no relief, just a strange sadness as each of the corpses slumped and finally became still. The last one, he thought, had moved its head to watch him as he approached. For a split-second it was almost as if it was trying to make eye-contact. It had been standing directly in front of him, rainwater running over its broken skin and dripping off the last few wisps of hair still clinging to its damaged scalp. It didn't flinch when he raised the crowbar. He put a hand on its shoulder to steady it, then plunged the weapon deep into its left temple. Instinctively, he caught the body as it fell and lowered it gently to the ground.

*

Howard had found a map in the house. He'd folded it to the right area before they left, but even so the squally wind made it difficult to handle. Distracted, he tripped up a kerbstone and growled with frustration. Kieran, following close behind, caught up and looked over his shoulder.

'That's north,' he said, pointing over to their left, 'so we're west of Chadwick, I think.'

'South-west,' Howard corrected him, finally making sense of the map. 'We can either follow this road or try heading cross-country.'

'Whichever's shortest,' Michael said, 'but we need to stay visible in case Richard comes back.'

'You think he will?' Lorna shouted, fighting to make herself heard over the wind.

'If this weather ever lets up he might.'

Kieran and Howard had already stopped again to re-check the map. 'Short-cut,' Howard announced, pointing towards a small park before marching off, head down into the rain. The others followed him into a sad, lifeless place. Winter had bleached the colour from everything, leaving everything grey and brown.

The group of seven walked in silent single-file along the edge of a school playground. They did all they could to avoid looking too closely, but it was hard not to see the remains of small bodies lying about the place, almost as if they were chicks which had all fallen from the same nest. Further ahead, one little corpse had become entangled with the barbed-wire fence bounding a field. Rags of school uniform flapped around what was left of its skeletal frame. Its unexpectedly white skull had been pecked clean of flesh – the dead child had obviously been unable to protect itself from the birds, insects and other scavengers which had found it. Kieran tried not to, but he couldn't help imagining what the poor little thing might have been thinking as it had stood there, trapped, feeling itself being steadily eaten away. In light of what he now believed, had this one been scared? Had it spent the last months of its time waiting here for its parents to come and take it home, wondering why it had been abandoned? He felt deeply depressed.

After following the road between the school and the field to its end and walking for a mile or so down a steep, narrow lane they reached a farm. The place was deserted, save for a handful of chickens clucking around the muddy yard as if nothing had ever happened. A number of untended animals had died in sheds; they found what was left of six cows dead from starvation in their caged milking stalls. Michael could see wisps of sheep fleeces in the surrounding fields, but he couldn't tell from this distance whether they were healthy animals or carcasses. It didn't matter. This place was as dead as everywhere else.

53

'River coming up ahead,' Howard announced, 'and we need to be on the other side of it.'

'Just keep walking 'til we find a bridge, then,' Lorna said.

'No shit, Lorna,' Howard sighed. 'Why didn't I think of that?'

There had been no let-up in the atrocious conditions since they'd first set out. It was late morning now, and the sky was just as black, and it was still pouring with rain. They were all soaked through. As they trudged across a muddy field of ruined crops which should have been harvested months ago, Harte wondered how many millions of pounds worth of food like this had gone to ruin, then corrected himself. It wasn't right to think about the financial value of things any more: pounds, dollars, euros – none of those counted for anything today. *Anyway*, he decided, trying to be more optimistic, *crops can be regrown.* There was no reason this couldn't be turned around in the future – on a much smaller scale, of course. *After all*, he thought, remembering his parents with fond sadness, *Mum and Dad grew their own vegetables for years.* He cursed himself for having constantly mocked his parents' attempts to be self-sufficient. *There's no point doing all this*, he used to regularly tell his dad as he watched him struggling to tend the hard soil in the vegetable patch at the bottom of his garden. *Food's so cheap these days, and you can get pretty much everything you want from any supermarket. There's no need to work yourself into the ground like this.*

You were right, Dad, Harte silently admitted as he marched on through the cloying mud, skirting around a scarecrow-like corpse which had sunk to its knees in the mire. He wished his old man was here to witness him eating humble pie. He would have loved that. 'You bloody teachers,' Dad always used to say, 'you think you know everything about everything. But all you do is tell kids about life when you haven't even lived it yourself. You go to school, go to university, then go straight back to school again. Where's the sense in that? There's a whole world out there you're missing out on.'

Fair point, Dad, he thought, *but would anything have equipped any of us for this?*

Before they reached the river, they came across a collection of buildings at the roadside, the smallest of villages, and hidden by the hissing rain until they were almost right upon it. Howard gazed around him at the tired-looking cottages and shops. What was this place, and how long had it been here? Who even cared? He used to be interested in local history, but not any more. The story of this place was probably still accessible, in some book in a dust-filled, permanently silent library somewhere, but it was irrelevant now. Standing as they were on the cusp of what increasingly felt like mankind's last days, what had gone before them now mattered not one iota. Who'd lived in the house they were now passing, who'd built it, who'd designed it, who'd owned the land, who'd sold it to them . . . all those were now pointless, forgotten details, never to be recalled. *And it was worse than that*, he realised, continuing along a train of thought he was beginning to wish he'd never started, *hardly anything that ever happened matters any more*. Every war that had been fought, every deal that had been brokered, every discovery made . . . they were all completely irrelevant. From the flat-screen television in the window of the shop opposite to the Large Hadron Collider – none of it counted for anything today.

In spite of the appalling conditions and all the pressures and uncertainties they were feeling, being out in the open like this was surprisingly liberating. It was, Lorna realised, the first time they'd been beyond the walls of their various hideouts since 'the death of the dead' as she'd heard one of the others call it. It was by no means a comfortable experience, but it was definitely better than how they'd been forced to spend the previous three months or so.

'It's like a bloody ghost town,' Kieran said as they walked together through the village. Without realising, they'd bunched up closer to each other.

'It *is* a ghost town,' Caron said, holding onto Hollis' arm. 'They all are.'

She looked from side to side, squinting through the rain to make out the shapes which surrounded them. There were few bodies left here. She saw one couple in a parked car, sitting bolt upright together. Their mutual decay had rendered them bizarrely ageless and sexless, and a host of ferociously active spiders had woven a grey connective bridge of webs between their heads. She imagined that if she opened the car and touched either one of them they'd both crumble to dust.

'Aye aye,' Harte said, quickening his pace slightly and crossing over towards a small general store. 'I don't think we're the first ones here.'

'How can you tell?' Caron asked, trying to look over his shoulder into the shop but at the same time not wanting to get too close.

'Some of the shelves have been stripped,' he explained. 'And look, they've cleared out the fags too.'

She took another couple of steps nearer. He was right: behind the counter, a wall display had been stripped of every last packet of cigarettes.

'Was it recent?' Lorna wondered.

'Don't think so,' Harte replied from just inside the store. 'There's plenty of dust in here. I can't see footprints or anything like that. I guess they just took what they needed and moved on.'

'Makes you wonder, though, doesn't it?' she said to him as they carried on down the road again.

'What does?'

'That place – it makes you wonder how many other people there were like us.'

'They might still be alive – there might be hundreds of them. In the major cities, maybe? You never know, things might be better elsewhere.'

'Yeah, right. I don't think that's really likely, do you?'

'You never know,' he said again, though the tone of his voice suggested that even he was struggling to believe what he was saying. 'Some folks might have fared better on their own.'

'They might,' Lorna said, 'but I don't think I'd have wanted to be on my own through all of this, would you?'

'No way.'

She walked a little further before speaking again. 'You know, that's what makes what Jas did even harder to accept. There're hardly any of us left alive now, and yet we're still busy trying to score points and fuck each other over. It's fucking heart-breaking.'

They found the person they presumed to have been the cigarette-looter a short while later. Michael made the grim discovery at a detached house half a mile outside the village. There were obvious signs of huge amounts of corpse activity all around the building – vegetation crushed underfoot, collapsed fencing, a gummy brown residue coating everything, bones everywhere – and right at the bottom of the back garden, hanging by its neck from the bough of a gnarled old oak tree, was another corpse. And they could tell this person had died only a few weeks ago. This poor soul had probably cracked under the strain of trying to stay alive while being under siege from the dead. And the cruellest irony of all was that you could see the castle. If that poor bastard had had the courage to look out and look up, he might have seen that he wasn't alone.

54

While Michael and Kieran were trying to get a dark blue Volkswagen van started, the rest of them sought shelter under a tree. There was little protection, though, but they were past caring now. They were all numb with cold, and every layer of clothing was drenched.

The van's engine refused to turn over.

'This is bloody stupid,' Howard moaned. 'Give it up and try another car – or let's just keep walking, anything but just standing around out here like this.'

Michael kicked the wheel of the Volkswagen with frustration.

'Howard's right,' Lorna said, 'we should keep moving. This isn't helping anyone.'

Michael kicked the car again. 'How am I supposed to get back home when I can't even get a bloody car started?' he growled.

Howard emerged from under the tree and pointed down the road. 'Look, there are some buildings up ahead. We could stop there for a while, warm up, get some food inside us . . .'

Michael reluctantly accepted he was right; this wasn't doing them any good. At least getting under cover for a while would allow them to take stock, build up a little much-needed energy for the next push towards Chadwick. They were not even halfway there yet. As desperate as Michael was to reach the port, the thought of walking as far again made his heart sink – and that was before they'd even thought about what they were going to do when they got there. The boat had gone, so they had no means of getting back to the island. What was the fucking point?

Michael was too tired and dejected to discuss the situation any further. He looked down at the ground, feeling irrationally angry, both with himself and everybody else and doing all he could to avoid making eye-contact with anyone. In the undergrowth just ahead of him was a yellowing skull, every trace of flesh worn away. As he watched, a large, well-gorged, glistening worm crawled out of one eye socket and slithered down until it disappeared into its gaping mouth, like something off the cover of the cheap horror novels he used to keep hidden under his bed when he was a kid. His mum hated him reading them, worried that he was too young, they were a bad influence. If only she could see him now. In comparison to the world he'd been living in since last September, nothing he'd ever read or seen in any horror film felt even remotely frightening any more. Just behind the skull was another one, lying on its side. And ahead of that, an arm or a leg, he couldn't immediately tell which. And there was the distinctive curved shape of a spine and butterfly-like pelvis, then the upright parallel bones of a ribcage . . . the closer he looked, the more it seemed the entire world had become one vast, never-ending graveyard. Did he and the others even have any place here any more?

'Come on, mate,' Howard said, gripping his shoulder, trying to sound enthusiastic. 'Not far now.'

The factory had produced car parts back in the day. There were some cars parked outside the grey, warehouse-like building, but none of them had enough energy left to even think about trying to get any of them started. For now all they wanted was a little shelter and warmth. Getting inside was easy; everyone here had died towards the end of the early shift, and the main doors were closed but unlocked.

They stood together, dripping-wet, in a small reception area. To their left a dead receptionist still sat at her desk, her skeletal face resting peacefully on her keyboard. Hollis pushed the door shut behind them, and as it closed it shut out the noise of the howling gale and driving rain outside. The silence was welcome, but short-lived.

'What's that?' Caron asked, although she already knew what it was: the noises coming from elsewhere in the building had to be the sounds of the dead. What remained of the early shift had been stirred up by the unexpected arrival of the living.

'What do we do?'

Michael looked at her. *Stupid bloody question*, he thought. 'We get rid of them, I guess.' He dumped his stuff by the reception desk, taking off his sodden overcoat and piling it next to the small bag of supplies he'd looted along the way, then walked deeper into the factory. Kieran and Harte followed close behind.

Before going through the main door to the factory floor, they came upon a small empty office. Harte beckoned the other two to follow him. It must have belonged to the fore-man or shift manager, and it had a wide safety-glass window which afforded them a full view over the entire shop floor. The office itself was dark, but the rest of the factory was illuminated by the light from the dirty Perspex panes in the corrugated roof above.

'Fuck,' Kieran said under his breath.

In amongst the mass of workbenches and machines – lathes and presses and other less immediately recognisable things – were dozens of bodies, trapped in the factory since the very beginning and now withered away. And from all sides, those which could still move had started to drag them-selves towards the faces watching them from the office window. Michael felt like he was looking at some kind of bizarre zoo, as if the dead been held in captivity here. The three men found themselves transfixed, unable to look away, even as the dead drew closer and closer. They behaved in much the same way as every other corpse they'd come across, staggering awkwardly on legs powered by wasted muscles, lurching into the path of others and being pushed back. The nearest of them slammed up against the glass and began clawing it with numb, slow-moving fingers. And yet for all the familiarity, there was something undeniably different about this encounter.

'Look at them, poor fuckers,' Harte said quietly. 'I know we've had it bad, but they must have been going through hell, stuck here all this time.'

Harte was right. 'All they want is for it to be over,' Kieran said. 'They've changed – they just want us to end it for them, don't they?'

'I don't think it's that they've changed,' Michael said. 'There's nothing to say they haven't been like this all along; they just couldn't control themselves enough to show it. If anyone's changed, it's us.'

'What are you on about?' Harte sneered.

'It's our attitude to them that's different now. I've hated these things since day one, and I've done all I could to get rid of as many of them as possible. And it makes me feel bad that all this time, all they wanted was to die.'

'So you helped them – nothing to feel bad about there. We had no way of knowing.'

'Suppose. Doesn't make me feel any better, though.'

'Get a grip. You're talking crap.'

'Maybe I am,' he said, looking at the mass of constantly shifting, horrifically disfigured creatures crowding in front of the office window now, blocking out the light. They slid from side to side, covering the glass with stains of their decay. They all wore overalls, originally dark blue, and marked with patches of grease and oil, now also covered in the remains of themselves. 'They just came to work one day and never went home again,' he said under his breath. 'They're just people – just people like us. We've *all* lost everything.'

Kieran left the office and went out onto the shop floor. The bodies around the window reacted immediately, trying to move closer towards him. Michael watched as he walked into a central area of relatively clear space and waited, and one by one, those corpses which could still move gradually made their way towards him. And, one by one, Kieran destroyed them.

Howard found a van in a dry shelter around the back of the building, half-loaded with car parts, ready for a delivery run which had never happened. He carefully removed the driver – who had died half-in and half-out of his vehicle – then turned the key in the ignition, expecting nothing. When the engine burst into life he yelled out with delight, surprising even himself with the uninhibited volume of his voice after so many weeks of enforced silence. The beautiful mechanical sound had an immediate revitalising effect on the others.

'There's still a few hours before dark,' Lorna said as they grouped around the van. 'We could be at the port and away before long.'

No one replied – no one needed to. Within minutes they were ready to leave.

55

Still the constant wind and rain refused to let up, buffeting the sides of the van as Harte drove them towards the centre of Chadwick.

'Head straight for the marina,' Michael said, nervously stating the obvious.

'What else was I going to do?' Harte quickly replied, 'stop for a pizza?'

He was struggling to see out of the windscreen, though the wipers were on full speed. Michael sat next to him, his stomach churning with nerves. Had the others got away safely before the weather had broken? Had they got away at all? If they'd delayed leaving for any reason, then there was a strong possibility they'd still be here, under cover somewhere, waiting out the storm. But what if the storm had hit during their crossing? That didn't bear thinking about.

Harte drove down roads he'd followed many times before, past landmarks he recognised, sparking strong memories: the burned-out petrol station he'd used as cover to make his escape from Jas and the others, and The Minories, the shopping mall they'd been looting that day. And as they approached the town, he looked towards the blocks of flats where he'd spent a couple of weeks alone in the midst of all this chaos. Strange now, he almost felt a kind of fondness for those days. Things had been easier while he'd been on his own, much less complicated, but it hadn't been an easy ride. The solitude had been alternately stimulating and soul-destroying. It was by no means perfect, but there was a lot to be said for the isolation.

He could also see that the helicopter had gone. That had to be a good sign, didn't it?

He tried to follow his usual route to the marina, but he couldn't get through; the roads were blocked with many more slow-moving corpses than had been here last time.

'We might as well leave the van,' Michael suggested. 'It's not far now – we'll get there quicker on foot.'

Harte stopped the van, but before anyone else had a chance to move or say anything, Michael was out and running towards the marina. He sprinted down the road, skidding in gore, occasionally changing direction to avoid the odd corpse which reached out desperately for him. The others followed as best they could, their line becoming spaced out as gaps appeared between the fittest and slowest. Caron and Hollis brought up the rear with Lorna, who refused to leave the other two behind. When they finally reached the water's edge they found the others. Howard, Kieran and Harte had stopped short of Michael, who stood alone at the end of the jetty, hands on his knees, doubled-over with effort and breathing hard. Even from a distance they could sense his pain.

The marina had been destroyed.

Every boat – every single boat, no matter how large or small – had been damaged beyond repair. And this wasn't storm damage: everywhere they looked they saw ruptured hulls, broken masts, slashed sails . . . several smaller vessels had been burnt-out and were now just floating wrecks. Others had sunk, parts of them still jutting out of the water, reminiscent of the way the bones of the dead now littered the land.

Michael slowly stood up straight, turned around and walked back towards the others. He looked completely beaten.

'Who did this?' Caron asked as he pushed past her.

'Who do you think?' he replied. 'Your bloody friend Jas and his lackeys.'

'Are you sure? It might have been—'

'I'm sure,' he said angrily, turning back to face her. 'No one else would have done anything like this. Such a fucking pointless waste. No one from the island would have done this.'

'But why?'

'To stop us getting away,' Howard suggested.

'Either that, or it's to stop the others getting back,' Kieran said. He looked around the boatyard, trying to take it all in. In spite of everything he'd witnessed since last September, this was unexpectedly shocking: the sheer senseless, wanton destruction was eating at him. He felt ashamed to have ever had any allegiance to Jas. He'd always thought he was better than this.

'So what do we do now?' Lorna asked. 'There's no way we're getting off the mainland now.'

'And there's no way Richard will be able to bring the helicopter back in this weather either,' Michael said.

'We should wait until the storm passes,' Howard said. 'Maybe there's another boat somewhere . . .'

'We've already been through this: even if there is, who's going to navigate?'

'Okay, but we can't just sit here feeling sorry for ourselves.'

'You give me an alternative and I'll listen.'

'What about the castle?'

'What, go back there? No thanks,' Harte said quickly.

'What, then? Stay here? This place is a ruin.'

'Isn't everywhere?' said Caron.

'So what exactly are you saying?' Lorna demanded, looking directly at Michael for an answer. 'After surviving everything we've been through, are we just supposed to roll over now and play dead?' Her outburst was met with silence from the others, but she continued, 'I'm not going to give up now, and neither should any of you.' She pointed at Michael. 'For fuck's sake, you've got a baby coming. You can't stay here. Your missus is going to need you.'

'You think I don't already know that?'

'I think you're missing the point, Lor,' Caron said, holding her arm against the wind. 'It's not that he doesn't want to go back, he can't. *We* can't.'

'Not now, perhaps, but there's always tomorrow. We can

find another port, find a boat that's still seaworthy, *learn* to navigate if we have to. But I don't think it's going to come to that.'

'Why not?' Kieran asked.

'Because surely the helicopter will come back at some point?'

Everyone looked at Michael.

'Richard might come back, I guess. I hope he will, but I can't assume that he'll—'

'I don't think we can do anything *but* assume. We've got to hope he flies back over.'

'So what if he does,' Harte said. 'Don't tell me, we'll try and attract his attention from the ground.'

'Haven't we been through this before?' Hollis said, an increasingly rare interjection from the exhausted, beaten man.

'Bloody hell,' Howard sighed. 'How many times have we tried that?'

'Yes, but things are different now,' Lorna said.

'Are they?'

'The stakes are higher, for a start. This is absolutely our last chance. And the bodies are different too. We don't have to worry about them like we used to.'

'So?'

'So all we have to do now is concentrate on doing something big enough that he can't miss from the air.'

'It won't work,' Harte said, sounding dejected. 'Richard told me: he said there's always something burning somewhere, those were his exact words. We'd have to burn the whole bloody town for him to see us.'

'Then let's do that,' she quickly replied. 'Let's torch the whole place if we have to. Because there's another thing you're not considering here.'

'And what's that?' Michael asked.

'This time Richard knows we're here. If he does come back, he'll actually be looking for us.'

56

'This one,' Kieran said, stopping outside a modern-looking block. The building was on the edge of a fairly new development not far from the marina, probably thrown up in the last property boom and left half-empty as a result of the property bust which had followed almost immediately. 'Look at it: it's perfect. Beachfront location, not far from the centre of town, and it's fucking huge.'

He was right: if they were going to set fire to any building, Michael thought, realising how weird that sounded, then this was definitely the right one.

'When do we do it, then?' Howard asked.

'We're too late now,' Michael said, 'it's almost dark. And like I said, Richard's not going to come out while the weather's this bad.'

'We should wait until morning,' Lorna suggested. 'Do it as soon as the storm passes.'

The building they'd earmarked for destruction seemed the logical place to stay and sit out the night. They took over a well-appointed ground-floor flat, glad to have a chance to finally shut the door on the foul conditions outside and rest a while. They found enough food and drink in the nearby shops to last the evening, more dry clothes, and some brighter torches. It felt strange sitting in a place they were planning to destroy, surreal, almost. Kieran thought it felt like their last night on Earth.

They found the owner of the flat in the bathroom, spread-eagled in the tray at the bottom of the shower cubicle, naked and still moving, but unable to get out. The temptation had been to just leave her there, but that didn't feel right. Lorna picked her up and draped a soft towelling wrap over what was left of her body. The shower tray was filled with disgusting sludge: strands of hair, teeth, fingernails and other less recognisable items in an inch-deep, semi-dry gunk of putrefied flesh.

The girl was virtually mummified now, but they could see from the pictures around the dusty, open-plan living space that she'd been a very beautiful young woman before she'd died last September. Her name was Jenna Walker, according to the credit cards Lorna found in her purse. Bizarrely, she felt uneasy looking through the dead girl's things while she was still in the house, but now, it felt equally wrong to think of her as an *it*, to ignore the person she'd once been.

She'd been only a couple of years older than Lorna herself was now. She'd worked in the research department of a large petrochemical company a little further down the coast. She'd lived alone, but the calendar hanging in the kitchen suggested an active social life. Lorna wondered if she'd had a boyfriend; had she been close to her parents? Had she read all of the hundreds of paperback books piled up in her bedroom and on shelves around the living room? Had she enjoyed the DVD she'd left next to the TV?

Getting to know Jenna felt like a necessity, but it also made what she had to do that much harder. The more she knew, the harder it was to think of Jenna as just another corpse. Giving her back her name and her history, finishing her time with a little care and dignity, all combined to give the whole experience a melancholic, funereal feel which Lorna hadn't expected. She took the corpse by the arm and slowly pulled it along the corridor into another apartment. She could feel the girl's bones under her fingers as she shuffled along, much of the meat now rotted away.

She looked down into Jenna's decayed face, her features still just about recognisable from certain angles and in a certain light, and remembered the girl in the pictures as she finished her time with a bread knife through the temple. Shame it had to be so brutal, she thought, but there was no other way. She couldn't asphyxiate her or give her an overdose of pills, couldn't strangle or drown her, the easy ways.

When she'd finished Jenna she felt like she'd just carried out a gangland killing.

Lorna returned to the flat and sat down with the others, tired and subdued, but more determined than ever to get away from this hellish place at the earliest opportunity. Even if they ended up drifting out to sea on a boat loaded up with food, destined never to find Cormansey, that would surely be preferable to spending what was left of her life in this desolate tomb of a country.

She slept intermittently, but never relaxed fully. It felt like only minutes had passed when Michael woke them all.

'It's time,' he said, pulling back the blinds and letting bright daylight flood into the room. 'Storm's passed.'

57

The air outside was unexpectedly clear and fresh. A strong wind blew in off the sea, temporarily dispersing the tang of decomposition which was usually so prominent. The ground was still wet, but yesterday's storm had completely cleared, the angry grey clouds which had clogged the skies all day had disappeared.

There were a handful of bodies outside when they left the apartment. Maybe they had followed the survivors, or perhaps they had been drawn here by their noise; as the small group worked to get things ready they continued to converge on the building. No one bothered to do anything about them; they just worked around them, knowing the fire would bring an end to them all soon enough.

Each person worked individually and without complaint, finding it infinitely easier to be outside now that the dead were no longer a threat. Several cars had been left in the car park outside the block of flats, and Harte rolled some of them closer to the building. His plan was simple: crowd the base of the apartments with enough vehicles so that when the heat from the fire they intended starting indoors was fierce enough, the fuel in the cars would explode and fan the flames.

While Harte worked, Michael, Kieran and Hollis went to hunt down more cars, siphoned fuel into the petrol cans and buckets they'd amassed, then carried them back to the flats. Lorna and Howard drenched the ground floor of the building with the petrol and opened all the windows and interior doors. After working for a while, Caron sat herself down on a low stone wall on the other side of the road and watched.

Once most of the fuel had been used up, they were ready to start the fire. While Kieran splashed petrol around the entrance, Harte stood watching, holding the Molotov cocktail he'd constructed.

'You done?' he asked as Kieran jogged back over to where the others were waiting. They'd all taken cover on the other side of the stone wall now, leaving him on his own.

'We're done,' Kieran shouted.

Harte nervously held a lighter in one hand, the petrol bomb in the other. The fumes were stinging his eyes and nose; he wasn't sure if they were coming from the bottle or the apartments. The stench reminded him of when he'd burned down the petrol station, and the memory of that blast increased his nervousness tenfold.

'Get on with it,' Hollis yelled at him, and spurred on, he flicked the lighter before he could talk himself out of it. The petrol-soaked rag caught immediately and he threw the bottle and turned and sprinted back towards the others as fast as he could run.

Kieran grinned at him. 'Crap shot!' he laughed as Harte dived over the wall, then scrambled back up again. He was right, it had been a bad shot: the bottle had smashed against the side of the front entrance, missing the door completely – but it didn't matter. They'd drenched the place, and the fumes caught light almost instantly. Flames filled the air like a scorching mist, billowing left and right, then racing inside and tearing up through the block. It wasn't quite as dramatic as he'd been expecting, but it was enough. He stood back, arms folded, and watched with satisfaction as the fire began to take grip.

'Quite therapeutic, actually,' Howard said, and Harte remembered back to those days at the flats when Webb used to spend his time beating the shit out of random corpses and calling that therapy. He thought he knew how Webb had felt now: a little wanton destruction of property wasn't doing anyone any harm, but Christ, it made him feel a lot better.

Even if they didn't make it off the mainland, maybe he could fill his time smashing things up as a way to vent his frustrations.

Less than a minute had passed, but the fire had already begun to take a substantial hold. Dancing orange light was visible through many of the first-floor windows, illuminating the insides of the individual flats. He watched one particular window, directly ahead of him, as the fire snaked in through the open doorway. The furniture caught, looking almost as if it had burst alight spontaneously. The fire moved quickly: a couple of seconds later and the curtains were burning, then flames began to lick up against the window as if they were trying to escape. Somewhere else another window shattered, exploding outwards, the flying glass followed by a belch of white-hot flame. And then another went, then another, and now a couple of the cars had caught too. It wouldn't be long before the fuel tanks caught, then the raging firestorm they'd started would be burning out of control.

Several bodies were already moving towards the growing inferno. Lorna thought she must be imagining it, but it really looked as if they were speeding up, as much as they were able. As she watched, one walked right up to the apartment building, apparently oblivious to the flames which now surrounded it. A loose rag of clothing caught light, and in an instant the whole body was consumed. It staggered on for a few more seconds, completely enveloped by fire now, before collapsing. The same thing happened again; then again. Another one walked towards a part of the building where the flames were particularly ferocious, and so intense was the heat that it spontaneously combusted.

'So what do we do now? Just sit here and wait?' Caron asked. She looked at the others, their faces bathed in the strangely soothing flickering orange glow.

'It's going to get too dangerous here,' Michael said, as, almost on cue, there came a series of quick, successive explosions like gunshots; aerosols or something equally flammable detonating inside. The noises spurred on the approaching dead.

'So where do we go?'

'There's only one place to go, isn't there?' he said. 'If Richard does come back for us, he's going to head straight for the car park.'

'The car park?' Caron said, confused, but before anyone could explain a fuel tank exploded and sent the vehicle up onto its nose, then crashing back down against the side of the burning block of flats.

When the noise had subsided, Michael pointed out across town. 'See that multi-storey car park over there? That's where he lands, so that's where we need to be.'

Without waiting for any of them to respond, he started walking.

58

The noise coming from the burning building was astonishing. Frequent explosions continued to ring out, making the otherwise silent town sound like a battlefield. Although it was dry today, there was still a fierce wind blowing, whipping off the sea and gusting along the streets, fanning the flames into ever-greater frenzy.

More bodies were coming towards them, and despite all they'd seen over the last day, there was still that moment of instinctive, nervous hesitation whenever they got this close to any of the dead – that split-second fear of attack – but it was immediately clear that these corpses was now completely focused elsewhere. They weren't interested in the living any longer; probably weren't even aware they were there. The fire in the near distance was acting like a call to the faithful. *The longer it burns*, Harte thought to himself, *the more of them will be drawn away from the rest of the town*. In a bizarre way, it felt like they'd begun cleansing Chadwick.

'Look at that,' Hollis said, pointing at a modern-looking office block. The frontage was made up of huge panes of glass, most of which were now filled with bodies: a huge mass of dead workers who'd been trapped in the building since September, now crowding against the glass, unable to go anywhere but still desperately trying to get closer to the distant flames. Even from here the blaze was clearly visible, burning bright against the muted colours of everything else.

Harte stopped and watched them watching the fire. When another explosion echoed around the town, the dead became even more animated and began hammering against the window to get out. Like the bodies beneath the castle, these people had been sheltered from the worst of the elements. Harte caught his breath when a corpse stumbled forward and clattered against the other side of a glass door right next to where he was standing. Even now his instinctive reaction was to run or to fight, and it took great effort for him to maintain control and not do either. The corpse flinched again, reacting to another flash of flame. Harte saw it still had a name badge clipped to the pocket of its gore-streaked shirt: Ryan Fleming, Head of Research. And like Michelle Bright, the dead nurse under the castle, and Jenna Walker, the young chemist whose home they'd just torched, Ryan Fleming suddenly mattered.

Apart from Kieran, the others had all continued walking. The street was filling with drifting smoke, making it increasingly difficult to differentiate between the movements of the living and the dead.

'What the hell are you doing?' Kieran asked.

'Letting them out,' Harte shouted back at him, and without stopping to consider the consequences, he forced the door to the building open and guided Ryan Fleming's dishevelled shell out onto the street, still half-expecting it to turn on him and attack, but it didn't – *he* didn't. He lifted his tired, diseased head to look up at the light in the distance, then slowly walked away towards the fire.

Harte watched it go, and was gently pushed to the side as more corpses followed him, spilling out of the office building.

'It made me feel better,' he said to Kieran with a nonchalant shrug of his shoulders.

In the next property along – a coffee shop – he could see more of them now, tripping over the tables and chairs where they'd drunk their last, and he released them all. And in the building next to the coffee shop there were even more corpses pawing to get out, and in the gym a short distance further down the street. Even though he'd seen thousands upon thousands of them before, Harte continued to be distracted by their grotesque appearance. Several of the gym members were still dressed in figure-hugging outfits which still clung to their figures, but their shapes had altered dramatically since they'd first put their gym kit on months earlier, and now the Lycra was bulging with decomposition. Some of them were imprisoned by the fitness machines they'd been using at the moment of death; he could see at least two of them who'd died mid-press and who were now pinned down by bars and weights.

The others had now disappeared out of sight around a corner, so Harte wedged the door open, then hurried after them. There were three steps down onto the street and he looked back briefly as the dead began to stumble out after him, some of them losing their footing and falling, then being trampled by others before picking themselves up again and carrying on.

Kieran had waited for him. 'Do you think they know what they're doing?' he asked.

'I have no idea,' Harte admitted, 'but like I said, it makes me feel better.'

The two men ran on, Kieran stepping to one side to let another rancid corpse crawl past. Behind them now the street was full of the dead, disappearing into the ever-increasing clouds of smoke.

Michael glanced over his shoulder but he couldn't see Kieran or Harte. No matter; they all knew where they were supposed to be heading. He recognised the street they were walking along now. On his right was the road which led to the baby shop, and up ahead was the supermarket Donna, Richard and Cooper had looted on their first day back on the mainland. That felt like weeks ago now. He looked up into the narrow strip of sky visible between the roofs of the buildings on either side of the road as he walked, wishing he could see the helicopter, willing it to be there. The sky was a beautiful deep blue this morning, but it was increasingly hard to see through the clouds of smoke which were being blown in their direction.

'Where the hell did you come from?' he heard Howard say as he walked into Lorna's back. Michael waved the smoke out of his eyes to see better.

'Same place as you, you fucking idiot,' a voice he didn't know replied.

'Then why don't you fuck off back there again, Jas,' Lorna shouted angrily.

Michael could see more clearly now: there were two men he didn't recognise standing in the street directly ahead of them. One of them, Jas he presumed, was carrying a shotgun, and he was striding forward menacingly. The other man held back.

Caron, Howard and Hollis moved away.

'Why did you do it?' the man was demanding. 'You idiots, you fucked everything up.'

'*We* fucked everything up?' Lorna said, pushing her way to the front of the group again. 'Last time I checked, *you* were the one causing all the grief. You were the one who tried to keep us locked up. You're the one who killed Jackson.'

There was a hint of emotion in his face, just a momentary flicker. 'I didn't kill him,' he said, sounding marginally less aggressive. 'He fell on his knife.'

'And you expect us to believe that?'

'I don't really care what you believe. I'm not interested.'

'Then why are you here?'

'Would somebody tell me what the hell is going on?' Michael said. 'Who are these jokers?'

'*This* is Jas,' Lorna replied, spitting out his name and confirming Michael's suspicions. 'And this other useless strip of piss is Mark Ainsworth.'

Another explosion came from the direction of the burning apartment block, this time so loud and violent that Michael felt the ground shake beneath his feet.

'So where are your other playmates, Jas?' Caron asked,

being deliberately antagonistic. 'Are you two all on your own now? Have they all abandoned you?'

She didn't realise how close to the truth she was.

'They've gone, useless bastards,' Jas admitted before adding, 'and it looks like they've taken your places on the last boat out to your precious bloody island.'

Michael reeled, feeling like he'd been punched in the gut. It was bad enough that he was left stranded here, but the thought that this callous, murdering wanker's associates – probably the same fuckers who were responsible for all the grief back at the castle earlier, putting everyone's lives in danger – had made it back to Cormansey when he hadn't was unbearable. He pushed his way through and lunged at Jas, taking him by surprise. He grabbed him by the collar and smacked him up against the window of a health food shop. Inside, a corpse immediately began hammering at the glass to be set free. For a moment Jas seemed more concerned by the dead body behind him than by Michael.

'Was that your doing down at the marina?' Michael demanded. 'Did you wreck all the boats?'

'So what if I did?' Jas was powerfully built and fired-up, and now he forced Michael back, shoved him to the ground, and aimed the shotgun into his face.

'Don't be stupid, Jas,' Lorna yelled, trying to pull him away. Michael scrambled back up onto his feet, but Jas came at him again and kicked his legs out from under him. Michael hit the ground hard, landing flat on his back, all the air knocked out of him. Lorna forced herself between the two men as Jas went for him a third time.

'Jas, stop – *Jas!*' Mark tried, but his words had no effect.

'Leave him alone,' Lorna ordered. 'You stupid bastard, Jas – he's got a child waiting to be born on that island and you've taken away his last chance of getting back there.'

'He's better off here,' Jas replied as Mark tried to pull him away. 'Anyway, that kid's as good as dead.'

Michael groaned with anger and pain and stood back up, but Lorna blocked him, stopping him getting any closer.

A corpse brushed past Jas. He fired twice into its chest, sending it flying across the street.

'You all think I'm some kind of villain,' he said, struggling to reload. He looked around at the frightened faces staring back at him – people he'd once called friends at one time or other. 'I'm not – I didn't want for any of this to happen. Contrary to what you might think, I didn't kill Jackson either, I swear . . .'

He stopped talking as the air filled with another thunderous noise. For a second several of them thought it might be the helicopter returning, but it was quickly clear that this was something else entirely. Howard took a few steps back, neatly side-stepping several more cadavers, and saw that a billowing cloud of dust and smoke was rolling steadily towards them. The air here felt hot and dry – had part of the apartment building collapsed? It was impossible to tell, but the flames were spreading fast, and through the haze he could see the furthest advanced of the dead were now catching fire long before they reached the burning apartments.

Harte and Kieran came running out of the chaos towards him. 'We need to get out of here,' Harte shouted, wiping tears from his stinging eyes. 'The whole bloody town's going to go up in flames.'

He stopped speaking when he saw the expression on Howard's face.

'Harte . . .' Howard started to say.

'What is it?' Harte demanded, still running, then turned the corner and saw Jas. Jas saw him too, and immediately raised the shotgun and aimed it at him – and then Kieran appeared, and Harte was immediately forgotten.

Jas directed the full force of his anger at Kieran, screaming, 'You sold me out, you fucker!' He charged into Kieran, sending him flying, then caught his balance and aimed the shotgun at him. Kieran had tripped up the kerb and landed on his backside.

'You were *wrong*, Jas,' he said, barely able to get the words out.

'Jesus, Jas,' Lorna shouted, 'is there *anyone* you're not pissed off with? Doesn't that tell you something? Like, that *you* might be the one who's got this wrong?'

Jas glared at her, but he was momentarily distracted as another random body collided with him. He recoiled, shoving the foul thing away, but it continued to move towards him. It was trying to get to the fire in the distance, but Jas, misinterpreting its actions as an attack, forced the shotgun up into the creature's gaping mouth and fired, splattering what was left of its brains over the pavement in a firework-shower of dark-brown gore. He spun around and saw another cadaver walking listlessly towards him, and he fired again, hitting the cadaver in the right shoulder. It collapsed, but immediately tried to drag itself forward with its one remaining good arm.

'Jas, for Christ's sake, stop!' Harte shouted, but his words had no effect; Jas was feverishly reloading the weapon.

'They're coming!' Jas screamed, the panic in his voice now clearly evident as he gazed around at what he saw as an oncoming army of the dead. The collapsing building had attracted the attention of many more of the creatures, who were surging towards the inferno.

'They might be coming,' Harte said, still trying to stop him, 'but they're not coming for you, you idiot – haven't you worked it out yet? The dead aren't our *enemy* – they're as scared and as lost as we are.'

Jas spun around again: another corpse, and another shot to the face.

This time Mark tried to stop him, grabbing him by the shoulder to try and talk some sense into him, but in Jas' all-consuming panic, his finger tightened on the trigger and he fired. Mark was blown backwards, colliding with a corpse, then dropping to the ground, a bloody gaping hole in his chest.

'What the hell have you done?' Lorna screamed. She ran to Mark and stood over his twitching body, barely able to comprehend what had just happened. She didn't need to get any closer to know he was dead. She looked up to see Jas, pulling yet more cartridges from his pocket and reloading the shotgun. 'What *happened* to you, Jas?'

'The last three months happened,' he replied looking for his next target, shrugging off Harte as he tried to restrain him. Harte dropped fast when Jas took aim and fired at another cadaver, then another . . .

The rest of the living scattered as he reloaded again, regrouping around the back of a garbage truck, and Harte tried to call to Lorna over but she wasn't listening. She was still crouched next to Mark's lifeless body.

Jas fired at yet another cadaver.

'The last three months have fucked us all up,' she said, 'but I thought you were better than this. It didn't have to be this way, Jas – you, me, the dead . . . we're all victims, you know. It's not about us versus them or you versus me, it's just about us all trying to survive.'

'I *know* that,' he said, lowering the shotgun momentarily. 'I know that better than *anyone*! That's what I've been trying to tell you: you won't survive on that island, none of you will. It's a dead end. You should stay here. You should stay here with me.'

Lorna stood up and walked over. Though she was terrified he was going to lift his weapon and start firing again at any moment, still she felt a need to try and talk him down. She could see how desperate her was. She glanced down the street. In the distance she could see the glow of the flames, and she could feel the heat of the burning building as the stiff wind continued to gust the smoke towards them and fanned the fire even further.

'We have to go,' she said, gently putting her hand on his arm. 'It's not safe here.'

His voice cracked. 'It's not safe anywhere. Don't go to the island, Lorna, please don't.' Then he suddenly pushed her away and fired another shot into the smoke.

She saw another body go down, and behind it, the dead approaching in ever-greater numbers. 'I know you're scared,' she said, moving behind him, 'and I don't pretend to understand why you did what you did, but your best chance is to come with us now, and try to get to Cormansey. There's no future for any of us here, but there might still be on the island.'

'You think?' he said, taking aim again. 'You all think I killed Jackson. You *know* I killed Ainsworth. But I didn't mean for any of it to happen . . .'

'I know that, and we can put it behind us. It might be a struggle on the island, but—'

'I'm not going,' he said abruptly. He fired once more.

'But this is *madness*. Come on, Jas, you're just confused. Think about Michael – he's going to be a dad. What would you be doing if your kids were still alive? Would you have wanted them to stay here, or would you have wanted them to go to the island?'

Jas instinctively pressed his palm to his chest, feeling for the outline of his precious wallet, then another group of bodies stumbled into view and he went to fire at them, but the shotgun was empty. Lorna tried again to pull him away, but he shrugged her off and marched towards the nearest corpse and clubbed it to the ground. Then another, then another – and now he was surrounded. The slow trickle of cadavers had become an unsteady flood, with more of them approaching all the time, attracted both by the distant flames and by Jas' blustering noise.

Lorna ran over and tried once more to pull him back, but he pushed her again, desperate to destroy every last one of the disease-ridden carcases which now seemed to be converging on him. There were scores of them, everywhere he looked: some limping, some crawling, some barely moving at all but still somehow coming forward. Some were still just about recognisable as people, others were little more than animated gelatinous heaps of decay.

Jas felt his legs weaken. He really was surrounded now, with more of them approaching every minute – more than he could deal with alone. He glanced back over his shoulder, looking for help, but he was sealed off, and he couldn't even catch a glimpse of Lorna any more.

Lorna could still see Jas, just, and she was poised to push her way into the crowd to try and forcibly drag him away when Harte grabbed her from behind and pulled her to safety behind the garbage truck.

'Leave him,' he said.

'We can't—' she started, but they were all shaking their heads.

'We can,' Harte said. 'We've got more important things to worry about.'

He stood back, and now she saw Hollis, slumped on the ground, his back leaning against a grubby shop window. His clothes were soaked with blood. Lorna couldn't process what she was seeing. She tried to talk, but no words came out.

Caron was sitting by Hollis' side, gently stroking his arm. She turned to Lorna. 'He got caught in the shooting,' she explained. 'We didn't even realise he'd been hit . . .'

Lorna crouched down next to Hollis. He looked up at her, his filthy face streaked with tears. There was blood on his lips.

'I know I don't look so good these days,' he murmured, his voice hard to hear, 'but I didn't think Jas would mistake me for one of them.'

'Oh, Greg . . .' she said.

'You lot go on,' he mumbled, blood bubbling from his mouth. 'I'll never make it.'

'He's right,' Harte said, 'we need to go.'

'What's the point?' Lorna demanded, sobbing. The tears carved clean lines through the dirt and soot on her cheeks. 'Let's face it, we're fucked.'

'Bloody hell,' Hollis said, forcing a grin, 'things must be bad if *you* reckon we're fucked.'

'I'm just being realistic, that's all,' she sobbed.

'Realistic!' Harte protested. 'Christ, Lor, we've spent three months trying to avoid the walking dead, hiding in castles and hotels and the like, and you decide today's the day to start talking about being *realistic*!'

'He's got a point,' Kieran agreed.

'But we can't just leave Hollis . . .'

'Yes, you can,' Hollis said. 'Go on, Lorna. Get them all out of here.'

'No!'

Hollis managed to lift his head slightly and looked up at Harte, who acknowledged his friend.

'Come on,' he said, gently picking Lorna up. She shook him off and turned back to Hollis, but she realised it was too late. She'd seen enough death to know there was no life left in his tired, glassy eyes.

Harte peered out around the front of the garbage truck. There were an incalculable number of dead bodies now, trudging inexorably down the street towards the fire in the distance: an unstoppable thick brown river of decay. There was no sign of Jas; he'd long since been swallowed up. The bulk of the corpses seemed to be coming from the direction of the station, and the road to the car park was still relatively clear.

'What do you reckon?' Howard asked.

'Sprint for the car park,' Harte replied. 'It's our only option: We've got to get up there and hope Richard turns up before the whole bloody town burns down.'

They grouped together, ready to move.

'Wait,' Caron said, looking around. 'Where's Michael?'

59

Michael was waiting for them at the entrance to the car park.

'Where the hell have you been?' Kieran asked.

Michael answered with his own question. 'Who's missing?'

'Hollis is dead,' Lorna replied. 'Shot. And Mark.'

'And Jas?'

'He's dead too, presumably. We lost him amongst all the bodies.'

Michael nodded.

'Did you have something to do with that?' Howard asked, looking at his face. 'What did you do?'

'It wasn't just about sorting Jas out, you know,' he said, holding his hands up. 'All I did was open up the station – I saw hundreds of them trapped in there when I first came to this place, and I figured I should let them out before we leave.'

'*If* we leave,' Kieran said.

'I wanted your friend Jas to get an idea of what he would really be up against if he stayed here.'

Lorna shook her head and started to climb. She wasn't sure whether she believed Michael or not, but what did it matter? She took Caron's hand and led her up the spiral access road. She had no idea what they were going to do when they reached the roof.

They climbed over a plum-coloured Mini which had crashed into the barrier, then stopped on the third floor of five and peered down into the streets below. The town was steadily filling with fire, building after building disappearing into the smoke- and heat-haze, and flickering light weirdly illuminating the clouds of smoke that now filled the sky. But somehow things didn't look as bad from up here as they had at ground level: the fire hadn't made as much progress as they'd feared.

Michael joined them, and he too looked around. He was relieved; they'd have a good few hours before they'd need to move again.

Howard peered over the edge and looked directly down. He could see the station which Michael had opened up; even now there was a massive column of bodies still trying to escape. It looked like they were playing a bizarre game of 'follow-my-leader' as they spilled out onto the street and walked towards the red-hot devastation in the distance.

And then, just for a second, he thought he caught a glimpse of Jas, still fighting in the midst of the chaos. It was impossible to be sure from up here – was it really him, or had he just seen more corpses, reacting to each other's presence? Whoever it was had gone again in just a few seconds.

Kieran looked into the distance, where the bodies nearest the conflagration were burning up. He watched them with an unexpected mix of emotions: relief, first and foremost, that the time of the dead was finally coming to an end. These were undoubtedly their final days, their final hours, perhaps. And he also felt an undeniable sense of achievement, that he'd made it through to see this moment – that he'd survived, when so many millions of others hadn't. And, strangely, he realised he felt pleased: one way or another, everyone's suffering would soon be over, living and dead alike. And now he understood why Michael had done what he'd done.

He looked around to find the others had left him behind. He started to run again, half the climb still to complete. His lungs felt as if they were full of smoke, and now every step was an effort. His thighs burned, but he kept on moving, refusing to stop until he made it to the roof.

He crossed the tarmac to stand with the others who were

looking out over the burning town. A heavy pall of black smoke continued to rise up from the area along the seafront which was on fire. The dark, billowing clouds were blowing towards them, almost blocking out the sun. From up here the world looked decidedly apocalyptic – like Judgement Day. *What am I thinking?* he asked himself wryly. *This can't be Armageddon. The world ended months ago.*

'You lot took your time,' a voice said. Kieran spun around, his heart thumping, and found himself face to face with a familiar, scruffy-looking figure with a duffle bag over one shoulder and a newspaper tucked under his arm.

'Fuck me,' he gasped. 'Hello, Driver.'

'What the hell are you doing here?' Lorna demanded, hugging him hard.

'What do you think I'm doing here? I heard there might still be people around who needed a lift.'

'You old bugger!' Howard laughed, grabbing his hand and shaking it vigorously.

'You're a wily old sod, Driver,' Harte added.

'But what about the others? Didn't they get to the island?' Michael asked, adding, 'I'm Michael.'

'I presumed. I'm sure they did. I volunteered to stay back here.'

'You *volunteered*?' Caron said. 'Why?'

'Because I knew there'd be more of you to come. There've been times recently when you've been almost as slippery as me,' he said, pointing at Harte. 'I thought if anyone could get away from that castle again, it'd be you. Harry suggested here – thought it'd be the safest bet. He said you'd probably end up back up here looking for the helicopter. Looks like he was right.'

'So where is it?' Michael asked, looking around, wondering how he could have missed it.

'What, the helicopter?'

'Yes, the helicopter! What did you think I meant?'

'Oh, it's still on the island, as far as I'm aware.'

'So what are we going to do?' Kieran was looking bemused. 'Are you planning to bus us all over there?'

'Something like that,' Driver said smugly. 'I've got another way out.'

Caron looked at Driver, her mind a whirlpool of conflicting emotions. 'I could kiss you,' she said.

'Maybe later,' he said, quietly pleased, as he led them back to ground level.

60

The descent took less than half the time it had taken them to reach the top of the car park, but once they'd reached ground level the mayhem out on the streets immediately refocused Michael. 'So what's the plan?' he asked, gesturing around.

'We head for the boats,' Driver replied.

'No use going down there,' Kieran said, 'Jas totalled the place.'

'I know, I watched him. Can't abide vandalism like that – yes, I know you lot have just torched half the town, but I'm guessing you did that for a reason. What he did was just plain stupid.'

'So where are we going?'

'I had a word with your mates Richard and Harry before they left,' Driver said to Michael. 'There's another option – providing we can get past this lot.' He was watching the nearest of the corpses with the same nervous distrust they'd seen Jas display.

'They won't hurt you,' Caron said.

'And you expect me to believe that after everything we've been through?'

'We wouldn't be here if it wasn't true,' Michael said.

'Fair point,' Driver agreed. He'd no choice now anyway. 'Right, this way,' he announced, and led them back towards the marina, carefully skirting around the edge of the vast crowd of corpses which were still swarming out of the station and heading for the fire. They paid no attention to the living, the fire their only focus.

The air was horribly dry, the smoke increasingly dense, but

it took them only ten minutes to get to the marina and Driver marched them quickly past the ruined yachts where Jas had vented his maddened anger and frustration.

Michael was beginning to think he knew where they were going. Driver led them past the gaps where the *Summer Breeze* and the *Duchess* had been moored and into the more exclusive area where he'd spent his first night here. *Surely he can't have got that huge boat started?* he thought as he ran towards it.

'Not that one,' Driver said, gesturing a little further along the jetty; 'that one.'

He pointed at a boat a fraction of the size of the luxury cruiser. It was beautifully appointed, but looked barely big enough to take the seven of them.

'Lovely,' Harte said sarcastically. He turned to look at Michael. 'Think we can get it going?'

'We can give it a go,' Michael replied, sounding less than confident. He didn't see they had any alternative.

'Your friend Harry's already sorted out the engine,' Driver told them. 'He said you lot left him here on his own for a day – this boat was in pretty good working order, but he didn't think it wasn't big enough. Because he didn't think he'd need it he didn't say anything, but he decided to get it ready as a back-up.'

'Good man, Harry,' Michael said under his breath.

'This is all well and good,' Caron said, eyeing the small vessel with some unease, 'but we've still got the little problem of trying to sail it.'

'And then we've got to find the island,' Kieran added. 'Are there any maps . . . ?' His voice trailed off and he looked at Driver, who had his back to them, watching the burning town they were so desperate to leave.

He turned back to them. 'Have any of you lot ever heard of a bloke called Tony Kent?' he asked.

Six blank faces returned six blank expressions.

'Was he someone you used to know who sailed boats?' Howard suggested.

'Something like that,' he replied. He tried another question. 'Do any of you know what I used to do?'

'You drove buses,' Harte said quickly.

'Correct. And before that?' Silence. 'Before I drove buses, I was a tour guide. Before that, I studied.'

'Well done you,' Lorna mumbled.

'And before that,' he continued, ignoring her, 'I did fifteen years' service in the Royal Navy.'

'You *what*—?' Harte breathed.

It took a few seconds for the importance of what he was telling them to fully sink in. Michael was the first to understand. 'So you think you can—?' he started to say, then stopped, too afraid to finish his question.

'What? Get you to the island? I'm a little rusty, but I think we'll be okay.' Driver grinned.

Harte grinned back at him. 'Bloody hell – I always said you were a dark horse!'

'When?' Michael asked. 'Now?'

'Well, I've no reason to be hanging around here. Don't know about you lot.'

The fact that Caron, Kieran, Howard and Michael were already rushing to board the little boat had already answered Driver's rhetorical question.

Lorna and Harte remained where they were for a moment longer. 'So who is Tony Kent?' Lorna remembered to ask just before she stepped off dry land.

'Who do you think?' Driver replied, thumping his chest. 'It's me, you daft bugger.'

She wrapped her arms around him and squeezed.

Taken aback by the sudden show of affection, he wiped a tear away from the corner of his eye and hoped she hadn't noticed.

'So what are we supposed to call you now?' Harte asked,

determined not to let his emotions get the better of him. 'Is it Tony now, or still Driver?'

'I think it's time for Tony to reappear,' he said with a smile. 'I think I've done all the driving I'm going to.'

'What about Sailor?' he laughed, and Driver – *Tony* – mock-glared at him, then ushered him on board. It was as tight a squeeze as he'd predicted, but they were all on.

Driver shoved his well-read newspaper into his bag, then left it on the jetty.

61

This little cruiser had never been designed for making sea crossings. It would have been more at home drifting along the Norfolk Broads and similar, gentler waterways, and being overloaded was making the little vessel struggle even more. The euphoria at having finally made it off the mainland quickly disappeared, to be replaced with an undeniable unease. They felt uncomfortably low in the water, and despite the clear sky overhead, the vicious wind continued to whip up the waves, repeatedly knocking them off course. The seven survivors crammed onto the boat were cold, wet and afraid.

But it could have been worse.

They could have died last September along with everyone else, Lorna thought. They could have got sick like Ellie and Anita and ended their time alone, desperately frightened, wallowing in their own waste. They could have cracked under the pressure of everything that had happened like Webb and Martin Priest and Jas, or died senselessly like Ainsworth, Hollis or Jackson. They could have fallen apart in any one of a hundred thousand different ways, but they hadn't, not yet. They could have been trapped in the burning chaos of Chadwick, or buried under the castle, or they might still be trapped on the first floor of the besieged hotel, but they weren't. Unlike most people she'd come across since the end of the world, the seven of them still had a chance, however small.

But no matter how positive she tried to make herself feel, the endless grey water surrounding them was making her feel their situation was increasingly hopeless once again.

Driver was using a compass and a map to navigate, and

doing his best to hide any sign that he was struggling from the others. Although he was shielded from the worst of the spray which had already soaked everyone – and everything – else, the rolling waves were making it increasingly difficult to concentrate. And they'd just reached a psychologically important point, he realised as he looked up and around for inspiration: his last visual reference had disappeared. Far behind them, the only trace of Chadwick was the pall of smoke, now just a smudge on the horizon. Other than that, there was absolutely nothing to see except water and sky.

He turned back to the bow again, wanting to avoid catching anyone's eye and starting another uncomfortable, slightly panic-tinged conversation which wouldn't do anyone any good. Instead, he just looked into the churning waves. Port, starboard, aft, bow . . . all he could see in every direction was water.

Another hour, maybe slightly longer, and the silent nervousness in the boat had reached new levels. Conditions were definitely deteriorating. The already strong wind had picked up markedly, and although the sea wasn't particularly wild, it certainly felt that way to the seven people in the inappropriately small boat.

Caron was beginning to panic, so Lorna, despite feeling increasingly anxious herself, did what she could to calm her. Michael squeezed through the others to reach Driver, and Harte joined him.

'How much longer?' Harte demanded as the boat swayed to one side, lurching sickeningly.

'How am I supposed to know?' Driver grumbled.

'You must have some idea,' Harte replied.

'Sorry, mate: forgot my sat nav.'

'Don't take the piss.'

'Well, don't talk bollocks, then. You can get out and walk if you like.'

'Do we have any life jackets?' Caron wailed from behind.

'Do we look like we have life jackets?' Harte protested angrily. 'Wouldn't we be wearing them if we had them?'

'Would you all just shut up and let me concentrate,' Driver shouted. 'All this noise is doing my bloody head in.'

'You mean you haven't been concentrating so far?' Howard asked, semi-seriously.

But the pointless bickering continued.

Michael clung to the side of the boat as the biggest wave they'd yet seen crashed against the starboard side, soaking everyone and filling the bottom of the boat with an inch of water – and cranking Caron's nervousness up to another level.

'Do you have any idea?' he asked quietly.

Driver looked at him. 'I'm not going to lie to you,' he said, 'I'm not completely sure. I mean, yes, I have my bearing, and I've been sticking to it as best I can, but it's difficult. This boat's not ideal, you know, and the weather's getting worse.'

'So what's the plan?' He was desperately hoping Driver did have a plan.

'Keep heading in this direction for another hour, if we can, then start with the flares.'

'Flares?'

Driver looked down and kicked the door of a waterproof cupboard with the toe of his boot.

'That was the plan we sorted,' he explained. 'Richard said to sail as close as I could to where I think the island is, then set off a flare, and put one up every hour.'

'And then?'

'And then hopefully he'll see us at some point and come out and guide us in.'

Michael nodded thoughtfully. It sounded like a pretty piss-poor plan, but it was still slightly better than he'd expected. At worst they would be setting off flares all night, until

62

The rising panic of Driver's passengers had been muted slightly by a number of factors. Her continual wailing and complaining seemed to have worn Caron out and she was quieter now – numb, almost. She leaned against the side of the boat, as drenched as the rest of them, shivering with cold. The release of the first flare had also helped temporarily, but the increasingly ominous silence which followed did not. Firing the second flare had again eased the tension, but there was still no sign of the helicopter.

'Show me again where you think we are,' Michael said, looking at the wet map over Driver's shoulder. He peeled it off the instrument panel and managed to tear it in the process.

'Careful! Anyway, what's the point?' Driver said, rolling with the swell. 'It won't make any difference.'

'Please.'

Driver reluctantly showed him, drawing a line with his finger between Chadwick and Cormansey. 'That's the bearing I've been following, but like I've already told you, I don't have any way of accurately measuring how far we've travelled. We could be a couple of miles from the island, we might not even be halfway.'

'I know, I know,' Michael mumbled, staring hopefully at the map as if he hoped to somehow find a missing clue, pick out something he hadn't noticed before. Any kind of marker would help – *anything*.

'Rocks,' Lorna yelled from the stern of the boat, and the entire group forced themselves around in the enclosed space, feet splashing through several inches of water. *Christ*,

Michael thought, *she's right*. There, out on the horizon was a small rocky outcrop. He turned back to Driver, who was already poring over what was left of the map, trying to match up what he could see. He circled an area south of Cormansey.

'Look at this: lots of little islands – it's got to be one of them, hasn't it?'

In the complete absence of anything else on the map, Michael thought he had to be right.

'Head for them?'

'Safest option. At least we can use them to navigate by, maybe even moor up for a while if it looks like we're going to run dry.'

Suddenly revitalised, the others held on to anything they could as Driver turned the boat and began to sail for the rocks, praying that more of them would come into view as they got closer. Michael said nothing, but he glanced around at the other faces here with him, and then at the ocean, which seemed to stretch away for ever. The vastness of the water had brought home his individual insignificance: it didn't matter a damn how smart or how lucky he'd been to get this far, how brave or how strong he was. His fate – and everyone else's – now rested on this increasingly unsteady boat and the rolling waves through which they sailed. Even Driver was of little use now, though he remained at the controls, valiantly doing all he could to keep the boat on course, but his actions seemed to be having little effect.

Jagged spears of rock were appearing all around them, and the icy water swirled around the boat around with renewed vigour, dragging the hull down, then forcing it back up again, then sweeping them around, then back the other way. The bottom of the boat scraped along a rock.

'Is this the part where the boat gets smashed to pieces and we all drift off in different directions, hanging on to bits of wood?' Caron said unhelpfully.

'Shut up!' Lorna snapped at her, increasingly afraid she might be right. The hull scraped again, a loud, sickening noise, then the boat lurched as a massive wave crashed against the nearest rock and broke over them.

'There!' Michael yelled before ducking down as another wall of ice-cold water crashed down over them. He'd been pointing at something, but the violent rolling motion made it impossible to see what it was he'd seen. More as a result of the movement of the water than anything Driver was doing, the little boat was pushed away slightly, then sucked in towards the rocks again, but that brief moment was enough and Driver saw it too: a small outcrop with a narrow strip of shingle beach.

'Just aim for that,' Michael said, holding onto Driver's shoulder and trying desperately to keep them both standing upright as the boat rolled. 'Just get us ashore.'

The water level inside the boat was increasing, and Harte saw that they'd sprung a slight leak. He kept his mouth shut and covered it with his foot – no point adding to the panic now. Kieran leaned over the side and looked down into the swirling waters, trying to gauge how deep it was and how strong the currents were. He was so desperate to feel his feet on dry land again that for just a second he seriously considered jumping.

'Don't do it,' Howard yelled, grabbing his arm and pulling him back. 'If the waves don't smash you against the rocks, the cold will kill you.'

'Recognise anything?' Driver asked Michael as he fought with the controls. The boat's small, stuttering engine was having next to no effect now; it was just going wherever the sea pushed it.

'Not a damn thing,' he shouted back over the wind, 'but just get us onto land and we'll take it from there. Keep the last flare with you, whatever you do – we can set it off once we've landed.'

Finally Driver managed to circumnavigate the rocks, and started getting them closer to the little shingle beach. And with unimaginable relief, they all felt the direction of the boat change too as the waves and the engine combined to push them into the small cove.

'What was that?' Kieran asked, and he leaned down over the side of the boat again to make sure. And then they all heard and felt it: the bottom of the boat scraping along the sea bed.

Michael didn't stop to think, but jumped over the side of the boat – and immediately lost his footing, going under the fierce surf. The ice-cold temperature stunned him, and stole the air from his lungs. He managed to get his head out of the water, but cracked the back of his skull against the hull of the boat. Though he was barely able to coordinate his movements, he forced himself to his feet and started ploughing through the waves towards the shingle beach. Harte followed his lead, landing with a little more success, and between them they managed to catch the mooring rope and pull the boat to shore, the waves at last helping their progress.

And then, finally, they were there. The boat was hauled up the beach, out of reach of the crashing sea. The others disembarked and immediately went to Michael and Harte's aid, wrapping them in layers of their own slightly less wet clothes.

'We need to find some shelter, fast,' Howard said, scouting around the small beach, looking for somewhere they might be protected from the biting wind.

'Use the boat,' Driver suggested. 'We can drag it further up the shore.'

'Do we have any food?' Caron asked. 'Anything we can give to these two?'

'A few scraps,' Kieran replied.

'Harry left a few odds and ends, just in case,' Driver added.

'Anything we can start a fire with?'

'The boat,' Howard said unhelpfully.

Harte dug a trembling hand into his pocket and threw Caron his lighter. He was shaking violently, blue with cold.

'We need to do something,' Lorna said. 'If we're out here much longer we'll all end up with hypothermia, never mind these two.'

'I'll go and look around,' Kieran said. 'If I can get up onto the rocks I can get a better view.'

He was gone before anyone could say anything. Lorna and Caron helped get Michael and Harte to the rocks and nestled up with them beneath a slight overhang. Howard and Driver were close behind, Driver carrying the last flare from the boat. *Though Christ knows what good it's going to be*, he thought despondently.

Kieran returned a few minutes later, clambering down the rocks, then running back down the beach towards them.

'Anything?' Howard asked

He nodded as he struggled to catch his breath. 'There's a wreck over there – looks like a fishing boat or something. It's not much, but it'll get us out of the wind for a while, at least.'

As the seven of them struggled up the rocks Lorna had images of huge trawlers in her mind. She was horribly disappointed when she saw it was just a small vessel – and it appeared to have been there for some time. At first glance it appeared to be little more than a pile of corroded metal and wood.

'Is this it?' Caron asked.

'It's better than nothing,' Kieran said. 'It'll have to do.'

Gingerly, Caron moved closer to the wreck, recoiling when she saw that what was left of a crewmember was still on board. His skeleton – stripped of all flesh and bleached white by months of beating from the saltwater waves – had been trapped by what looked like a rusting winch.

'Wait . . .' Michael started, but his throat was dry and his body was shaking, and he couldn't finish his sentence. They looked at him and he looked back, but still he couldn't speak.

'What is it?' Lorna asked.

He looked from her face, to the wreck then back again. He

summoned his very last reserves of energy to say, 'I know this . . . I've seen this before . . .'

Kieran was the first person to understand what Michael was trying to say, but he didn't waste time explaining. While the others were still trying to work out the importance of Michael's words Kieran raced up the rocks in front of them and stopped when he reached the top. He gestured wildly for the others to follow, and they did, painfully slowly, pushing and pulling each other towards the top.

Finally they reached Kieran, who was sitting on a low stone wall. 'Well we're either back on the mainland,' he began to say, 'or—'

Michael stared up ahead, almost unable to believe it. He looked around, trying to get his bearings, and then he broke free of the others and started to walk. His legs were numb and he struggled to keep moving, but he knew this was it. *No more running. No more fighting. One last push.*

It seemed to take for ever, but less than ten minutes later he had reached the door of the small cottage. It was shut, and his hands were too cold to turn the handle. He hammered on the door. After a few seconds, it opened.

'You took your time,' Emma said.

'Sorry,' he replied.

'Are you going to stay here now?'

'For ever.'

TWO YEARS, SEVENTEEN DAYS SINCE INFECTION

63

THE LAST FLIGHT: DONNA YORKE

Have we done the right thing? Our first night on the mainland in an age, and it feels strange . . . almost like we're trespassing. The first night of the rest of our lives, Cooper said.

Two years, two deaths, three births. We lost Howard to illness and Jim Harper in an accident, but we gained one more than we lost. After Emma, Juliet Appleby and Melanie Hopper both got pregnant and had boys.

Life on the island has been hard, but successful. We've done well – better than any of us ever thought possible, I think – but things have steadily changed there and I don't feel the same about the place as I used to. Neither of us do. The birth of Maggie, Michael and Emma's first child, was a turning point for all of us. When that little girl was born last year, we all knew we had a better chance of surviving long-term than we'd originally thought. We sat in the pub and held our collective breath on the night she was born, waiting for the germ to kill her, none of us expecting her to survive. When she lasted a minute, I began to believe the impossible might have happened. Days later and we were still expecting the infection to get her, but it didn't.

And now she's over a year old and Emma's pregnant again, and I couldn't be happier for them. Lorna is pregnant too. I feel a weight of expectation, but that's not for me – not yet, anyway.

The babies have taken the edge off the air of finality we've all felt since the day the world died. For a while things started feeling less hopeless than they had been. But while most people on Cormansey seem to think that everything's changed and we're back in control now, I don't. As it happens, I still think our days are numbered. It's just that we might have a few more days left than we expected, that's all.

So we're going to make the most of them.

I came back to the mainland once before, with Jack and Clare, but it was too soon: we weren't ready. We thought we could live here again, but we were wrong. We lasted a while, then got ourselves picked up again the next time Richard and Harry came back for supplies.

But things feel different this time. Coop and I hitched a lift over, and now I don't think we're ever going back – I don't know if we even can. The flight that brought us over here had been planned for some time. Richard said he thought it might be the very last flight, depending on how hard the winter is on Cormansey.

Jack used to love to read. When we were over here before he was always telling me how he used to like a good end-of-the-world story more than anything else. He talked a lot about them, and on his recommendation I read a few last year, but the endings pissed me off. They'd often finish with some smug little community of do-gooders rising up from the ashes against all the odds: a merry little band of farmers and cooks and teachers and you know . . .

Well, call me selfish if you like, but I've never really gone for all of that. It's taken me all this time to realise I don't want to just jump straight back on the horse again. I don't want to build up a carbon-copy, small-scale imitation of what we used to have. I want to *do* something with what's left of my life – and that's not tending sheep, boiling water over log fires and wearing home-made clothes. Why should I? Why should any of us? I tried it, but it didn't work out. There are too few of us left to make a difference any more. Too much damage has been done. They tried to stop us – they said we'd be back like last time, but Coop and I made up our minds.

We left just after ten this morning and we were back on

the mainland by eleven. Everything has changed beyond all recognition here. Buildings have started to disappear – swallowed up by moss and weeds, a crawling layer of green slowly overtaking everything. There are huge cracks in some of the roads, crater-like potholes in others, and some buildings have already collapsed. And when you look closer, hidden among all the greenery and rubble, there are bones everywhere – all that's left of everyone else. Jack said it was going to be like this, but until you see it for yourself you can't begin to appreciate the scale of it all. It makes you realise how insignificant you actually are.

Before we left the island I went to see Jack one last time. He had his face buried in a book, as usual. He said he'd come across a word in the dictionary that summed everything up, and he told me to look it up once I got here.

Coop and I walked through a town this afternoon. We took tins of food from a supermarket and strolled down the overgrown high street like we owned the place, drinking wine, shouting out, generally doing what the hell we wanted. It felt good, like a lot of ghosts had been laid to rest. Later we found this house, empty and structurally sound, and set up camp for the night. Coop was asleep in minutes, but I can't switch off like he does. Maybe I will in the future, but not yet.

There's a small office on the ground floor of the house and I found a dictionary and looked up Jack's word, just like I promised him I would.

Aftermath. I didn't know it had two meanings. The first was obvious, the one that everybody knows: something that follows after a disastrous or unfortunate event, like the aftermath of a war. But it was the second definition that struck me: a new growth of grass following mowing or ploughing. Jack was a deeper man than he'd ever admit. I thought our little community was the aftermath, but he doesn't. He sees the greenery which is slowly covering everything as the aftermath of the human race.

Acknowledgements

In the previous AUTUMN books I've already thanked a lot of people: the editors and teams at the various publishers involved with the series around the world, the artists I've worked with on cover designs, websites and marketing, and my friends, family and fellow authors who've all been tirelessly supportive.

But there are plenty more people I've yet to acknowledge. There are far too many of you to list here individually, and I'm sure to miss someone out and cause offence if I try. So this impersonal, blanket 'thank-you' will have to do.

As I write it's almost ten years to the week since the first AUTUMN novel appeared online, and this book marks the very end of the series. My sincere and heartfelt thanks to everyone who has helped me in any way, shape or form over the last decade. From those who've read the books and provided feedback, to the thousands who downloaded the first book back in the day, to those who've helped promote each new novel along the way, I appreciate your support more than you can imagine. Thank you.

And as I first said back in 2001, please keep spreading the infection!

DAVID MOODY
U.K.
2012